Antithesis

B.A. Cochrane

First Edition

PAGE PUBLISHING
Conneaut Lake, PA

First originally published by Page Publishing 2024

ISBN 979-8-89315-263-0 (pbk)
ISBN 979-8-89315-297-5 (digital)

Printed in the United States of America

antithesis (noun)
an·tith·e·sis (an-ˈti-thə-səs)
"a person or thing that is the direct opposite
of someone or something else"

CHAPTER 1

Breakthrough

It was about twelve thirty in the afternoon on August 29. I-Corp was set to make an announcement regarding their most recent breakthroughs in artificial intelligence. I-Corp was usually veiled in secrecy, and the people did not want to miss the opportunity to catch a whisper or two about their latest achievements. The president of the company, Peter Jensen, hadn't arrived yet, but this didn't stop the people from their gathering.

The news media arrived early and was out in full force. Their vans lined both sides of the street and were easily visible with their towering satellite dishes and other broadcasting equipment reaching out toward the sky. There were other vehicles present, but they weren't visible due to the sea of people moving up and down the street. They all seemed to be moving at the same speed and in tandem with one another like waves in the ocean toward the shore at high tide. The number of people continued to increase, and they flowed toward the cordoned-off area in front of I-Corp. The area directly in front of the office building was somewhat cleared. The security detail cordoned off the area just enough that Peter Jensen could arrive by car, get out, and immediately address the crowd. The steps up to the doors had news reporters standing on both the right and left side. The only thing in place to hold them back was a long yellow caution tape that stretched to the road, where his vehicle would stop.

The anticipation was building for weeks. As the day drew closer, the media ramped up their reports on I-Corp, and the rumors went from I-Corp announcing bankruptcy to I-Corp announcing it had cured cancer. Small bits of information had been leaked out to the press over the past couple of months, and it almost seemed like another Republican presidency with all the leaking. Keeping the project data secure had always been a priority as leaks could lead to issues in funding or other problems that could otherwise derail the project.

Phoenix hadn't changed much over the past twenty to thirty years. It was still a busy metropolis, centered in the midportion of the southern half of the state and nestled in a large canyon in the middle of the Sonoran Desert. Being in the desert, it could get unbearably hot there, as compared to most states, but the mantra of the folks who lived there was that since it was a *dry heat*, it wasn't really as bad as it sounded. A typical day in August could get as high as 124 degrees Fahrenheit. To the person who is not from the area, it feels every bit of the number showing on a thermometer on any given day.

As Peter walked out of his house to get into his vehicle, he was met with a rush of hot air. The blast of heat hit as hard as a gust in a thunderstorm and felt like the inside of an oven.

If I could only bottle this up and send it to Alaska, I'd be able to retire in a month, he thought.

His longtime assistant, Leah, arrived to pick him up in a company car. He didn't like the thought of being driven around, when he was more than capable of driving himself, so he spent little time in those vehicles. The company vehicles were usually reserved for important dignitaries and government officials, so he felt a little more special than usual. Normally, he would drive to work in his own vehicle, but he knew that parking would be difficult, and he had some last-minute preparations that he figured he could work on in the car.

The drive from his home in Scottsdale to his office in downtown Phoenix usually took him about a half hour, on a good day. It was a Monday morning, and the streets were busy with people going about their daily commute, so he planned for an hour. He felt that the full hour would give him enough time to make it to the office without having to fight the morning traffic, and he could practice his speech. Leah was known to be a careful driver, so he factored that in as well.

As he got into the vehicle, Leah turned her head around to greet him. "Good morning, Peter!"

"Good morning, Leah."

"Are we making any stops before the office?" she asked.

"No," he replied, "we don't have a lot of time this morning. I'll have to get my morning coffee when we get to the office."

Leah smiled as she reached over the front seat and handed him a cup of coffee. "Here you go!" she exclaimed.

Peter smiled back as he scanned the cup, taking off the lid to inspect its contents. "You are too good to me, Leah," he said with a huge grin.

Leah started to laugh. "You can make it up to me with a huge raise."

Peter started to laugh with her. "If things go well in the next few months, you'll get that raise and likely some additional responsibilities."

"Fine by me."

"If you don't mind, take the Black Canyon Expressway," said Peter.

Being the strategic thinker that he had always been, he planned a press conference at an offsite location. He purposely didn't give the full details to the press or the public. He was no stranger to public-speaking events, so he knew that technology rollouts could cause quite a stir and cause people to come from all over.

With technology, most people feel an air of excitement and wonder, but there is always that fringe few that resist even the slightest advances in technology, and they can often be a challenge for the security at technology events. Knowing this, Peter arranged a large security detail at his office, and many of his guards would be in plain clothes.

He was a cautious man, and he was no coward, but he always had a lingering fear that someone with violent motives would get through his security measures and do something stupid, such as shooting up the place. Historically speaking, mass shootings were commonplace in the United States. They were especially bad at events with largest number of people present. Large events were ripe picking for crazy people who wanted to unleash a barrage of insanity and violence. While Peter never witnessed anything like that as one of his own events, he wasn't going to give anyone the opportunity.

Leah worked for Peter as his executive assistant. She was a sprite young woman of thirty-seven, with flowing red hair and a smile that could light up a room. She was an educated woman who dedicated her life to technology and was a jack of all trades for I-Corp. Anyone who knew Leah would say that she was the heart and soul of the corporation and that she was the one who really built the company. While Peter was the lead scientist at the company, he didn't like doing paperwork or filing reports. Leah worked well with Peter, and she didn't mind doing different jobs because it kept her days from becoming stagnant or routine. She also enjoyed Peter's company.

Peter was a single man and in his mid to late forties. He wasn't seen as a very personable man to outsiders, but for those who knew him, he was as gentle as a lamb and as intelligent as a dolphin. Peter worked so hard that he rarely found time to date and get to know people of the opposite sex. Leah being his assistant and around him all day was about as close to a real relationship that Peter has had. Even back in his college years, he wasn't into relationships. Most of the people who have known him have always secretly thought that his ultimate goal was to create a perfect wife for himself, but that was just a rumor. Peter hated it when people would joke around about his lack of female companionship. He especially hated it when people would joke about him having a relationship with one of his machines. He had a normal sense of humor, but for him, having a relationship with a machine was akin to a tomato having a relationship with a frankfurter.

"Mr. Jensen, we are about a mile out from the office, would you like a tranquilizer?" said Leah.

Leah was also Peter's part-time pharmacist. She took good care of him because she felt that if she didn't, then he would crawl into his office, lock the doors, and become a hermit, only coming out for short bathroom and coffee breaks and to have Leah order the occasional lunch from the local burger shop.

"No, I think I'll be able to manage it this time," replied Peter. "Just pull up to the front and make sure you get right to the door, past that rope. I can only imagine how many people are going to be out there trying to get to me."

"Why is it that we didn't tell all these people that we are having the press brief at the stadium this evening?" she said.

"Leah, you know as well as I do that, we can't just have a meeting in front of the office, nor can we have it inside the office. Where would we fit all the people?" he replied.

"I just think that you should have made arrangements with the press so that they would at least know that we are having it this evening rather than this afternoon. I mean, what are you going to tell this crowd when they get angry at you for standing in this heat for nothing. Thank goodness I'm the driver, and I'm not your security detail." She chuckled.

Peter looked up toward Leah and sarcastically said, "Have I ever told you how important you are to me?"

Leah let out a muffled grunt. "Well, not that I can recall. It's nice of you to say that."

"You misunderstood. It was a question, not a statement," he replied while rolling his eyes.

"Mr. Jensen, Peter, I know you love me. You would be lost without me," she said with a huge grin.

Peter glanced at his watch and looked out the window. "I am beginning to think that we are lost, as long as this ride is taking. Did you forget where to go?"

"You are a regular comedian, aren't you? You should book out the Apollo Theater sometime and make a new career for yourself." She laughed.

Peter wasn't exhibiting his normal nervousness. Public-speaking events usually made him so nervous that he would speak extraordinarily little. He usually had some foreign object that he would fumble around with as he passed the time. For a man who normally had the energy level of a teenager, he looked exhausted. His excitement level was high since waking this morning, and he raced around his house getting ready. Now he looked like a kid who was coming down from a sugar binge. Leah could see that he was more tired than usual and figured that he was just exhausted because he had been working sixteen-hour days for the past month.

"Oh my goodness, look at all those people!" Leah said. "It's like we are pulling up to some huge movie premiere in LA. Would you ever have thought that you'd see so many people in downtown Phoenix?"

Peter jumped up in the back seat and peered out the window. He was jolted back to life when Leah yelled out about the crowd. "I guess they want to know about the launch. Do you think?" said Peter.

"Well, you may not have wanted that tranquilizer, but I'm starting to think I want it," Leah replied. "Maybe I should have worn that blue dress after all!"

"Just wait until they find out that the release is later this evening. I know you aren't a fan of it, but I don't want to chance some negative event that is going to put a wrench in our rollout or future funding. You know how those army folks get when you start asking for more money," he said sarcastically.

As they started trolling closer to the building, the crowd noticed the vehicle and, as if it were scripted, turned toward them. The crowd turned in unison like they were a group of zombies looking for a meal after a long drought. About a hundred people turned around and started running toward the vehicle. They pounced on the vehicle as if it were filled with a band of musicians on their way to a concert.

The car crawled slowly through the crowd. Some escalators moving as fast would have been considered broken. Their movement toward the office was so slow that Peter worried that they wouldn't make it to the door in time to let the people know that the event would actually be at another location, later in the evening.

Peter and Leah could hear the muffled but raucous noise of the crowd and the media going crazy. It was almost a gurgling sound.

None of the words could be made out, and several different voices were swimming around in the air, all mixed together as some kind of strange voice soup that could not be explained. For Peter, this wasn't a comfortable sound. He knew he was about to let down a crowd of at least two hundred, if not more.

"Well, here we go," exclaimed Peter. "How is my hair?"

His nervousness was ticking upward the closer that the car got to the office. He was running his fingers through his hair like he was trying to straighten a cowlick on the back of his head. There was no cowlick, so all he really was doing was running his fingers through his hair as if it were some nervous tick left over from a bad high school experience.

The car crawled its way up to the curb, just past the cordoning rope, and then came to a soft stop. Peter was now fumbling along with his notebook, checking to make sure that he had his notes for the press release.

"Have you ever had that sinking feeling?" he asked.

Leah now stopped, turned around, and looked straight at Peter. Her nervousness was apparent. She had a determined look on her face. It was as if she was standing in the front of the line, waiting for the doors to open at the electronics store after consuming large quantities of turkey and stuffing. Peter knew this look. He was feeling the same as she looked.

"Well, I'm sure I have, but it's not me that has to go out there now, is it?" she said with an unconvincing smile.

"I suppose not," he said. "Maybe, you would like—"

Leah cut him off. "There is no way that you are turning this over to me. It's your party, and you are the birthday boy. Now get out there and knock them dead."

The sun was noticeably absent due to the shadows cast by the towering buildings. It was nearing the mid part of the day, and it looked as if it were nearly dusk. The sun may have been blocked, but one wouldn't know it based on how hot it was in the shade. It was already nearing 120 degrees in the Phoenix area, and the shaded areas only provided a small amount of relief from the blistering heat.

Peter was no stranger to the heat. He had a lesson in heat exposure the first week that he lived in Arizona. Since he was from the East Coast, he had never really had to deal with desert conditions, and the heat that came along with it, but the lesson he got was priceless. He had only been in town for three days when it happened to him. He was out getting lunch and bought himself a can of lemon-lime soda while he was out. Not thinking about the time, he realized that he was almost late for his early afternoon meeting, forgot the can of soda when he rushed back from lunch to make the meeting on time. Sodas and closed vehicles sealed up tightly in the hot Arizona sun do not go well together. Peter learned this lesson the hard way. After he was finished working that evening, he returned to his vehicle to find a soda can sitting in the cup holder, absent a top and all its contents. Frantically, he scanned the vehicle for the top of the can and the lemon-lime soda that was within the can. It was nowhere to be found.

Isn't that something? Where the —— did that soda go? he mused.

He started to drive away from his office building, and on the dash was a blinding light in the right-hand corner of the windshield. It was the sun reflecting off the top of the soda can. He was relieved to find the top of the can but still had no clue on the contents of the can. Since the hole in the top of the can was sealed and unopened, he knew he hadn't consumed the soda. It was a big mystery. About three days later, Peter got into his vehicle and set out for work. It was at this time that he learned the fate of the contents of that can.

"Oh my god, how am I going to clean up this crap?" he asked himself vociferously.

When he got into his vehicle, he immediately noticed millions upon millions of tiny dots everywhere. The top of the vehicle looked as if it had been redecorated in extreme leopard! There were literally hundreds of thousands of tiny black dots all over the vehicle. Being a scientist, he was smart enough to figure out that what he missed a few days before was that heat turns liquids into a gas. While he was in that meeting, the can overheated and turned that can into a sugar vapor bomb.

His soda bomb left a pattern that any armchair forensics expert could decipher. The dots were tiny droplets of lemon-lime soda with all of its sugary, high-fructose-corn syrupiness. The heat caused the can to explode, and out came a mist of sweetness. It eluded Peter for days, but the caramelized color and odor now was unmistakable. The smell of burned marshmallow was not in his imagination after all. Now it all made sense!

As Peter reminisced about his soda can misfortune, he realized that there were a lot of people in that crowd. A quick and shocking mental picture crossed his mind. He suddenly had a shuddering feeling that moved like lighting up his spinal column. His whole body twitched. He wondered to himself if something like that could happen to a person. He hoped that the heat would not do that to a person, but he wasn't quite sure. He wouldn't want to be in the headlines for creating a pink mist around Phoenix.

"You're nuts!" he said under his breath. "That couldn't happen!" he whispered. "Could it?" He shuddered again at the thought.

"Are you all right, Mr. Jensen?" Leah asked nervously. "I didn't quite catch that."

"What?" he asked with a concerned look on his face. "Um, it's nothing. I was just thinking out loud."

"Break a leg." Leah beamed.

The crowd surrounded the vehicle on every side except the driver's side where the rope was placed. On each side of the sidewalk, there were people lined up and standing behind the rope. They were lined up all the way up the sidewalk and up to the front door. One would think they were at a major red-carpet event if the desert motif of Phoenix were not present all around them.

Peter slowly opened the door to the vehicle, and immediately, the hot air blasted into the cold vehicle. Peter shuddered a second time. The outside temperature seemed to be rising by the minute and was so hot that one could fry an egg on the sidewalk. The temperature the day before reached a whopping 124 degrees, which is rare for Phoenix, but it happens. The temperature today already looked to be heading toward that number, and it was still early in the morning. The global warming fanatics on both sides of the issue have always loved Phoenix because the temperature fluctuates daily and were probably on the news at that very moment arguing that the current temperature proves that global warming is a fact or that it is a myth.

Peter moved out of the vehicle, onto the sidewalk, and immediately into such a raucous crowd that he could barely hear himself thinking. Reporters on every side of him were screaming out questions while the sound of camera clicks abounded. To his left, he saw a tiny hand, poking out from the crowd and waving a small notepad furiously. He knew right away who it was. It was Laura Stroud. He knew Laura better than any other reporter because he attended Washington State with her when he was doing his undergraduate work many years ago. He knew that she would be at the event, and he knew to look for her because he talked to her about it a week prior, telling her that he would give her the first question if he could find her. Laura didn't know that she wouldn't be getting any questions in immediately. Peter hadn't told anyone that didn't have a reason to know.

Peter walked up to the center of the stairwell and stopped suddenly. He turned around to face the crowd, and the sound of the crowd diminished to a slow roar. He looked directly toward the street where he was dropped off. Leah was able to get the car out of the crowd, and the spot where the car was parked was now filled in. The people moved in, like the water on a high tide, coming to shore. The sea of people now was enclosing all around him.

"Good afternoon!" he said. "I would like to thank you all for coming out today. This has been a long time coming, and I'm sure that you are just as excited to hear about our breakthrough as I am to tell you about it."

Peter clasped his hands together and stood still like an oak tree on a calm day. The crowd was growing more anxious by the moment. "Thank you for coming out. It's great to see such excitement. I know." Peter was interrupted by a disturbance in the crowd.

The disturbance was coming from out of the mid center of the crowd, located directly in front of Peter and the building. At first, the screaming was unintelligible, but as the ripples in the crowd grew close to the front, it became quite clear and easy to make out.

"Repent now!" screamed a man holding a small New Testament Bible.

"This is not exciting news! This is an abomination. Turn from your evil now while there is still time," the man exclaimed.

The man crawled out of the mass of people and stood directly facing Peter. He had a look of purpose in his eyes. His face was flushed from the heat, and sweat could be seen rolling down the left side of his face. The mas was wearing a white T-shirt adorned with a tiny fish over the left breast area of the shirt. He had dark-blue jeans and brown leather sandals.

As suddenly as he began speaking, a two-man security detail hurried toward him on their way to remove him and prevent him from making a scene. The guards moved swiftly over to him through the sea of people and grabbed him by the arm.

"Well, isn't this a surprise?" one of the guards exclaimed.

"You can't do this," the man screamed. "I have rights."

"If we see you again, you'll have the right to remain silent. You know that one, don't you, Charles?" the first guard stated.

"Better check that fruitcake for weapons," said the other as they escorted the man away from the crowd and out of sight.

Almost as suddenly as it began, the shouting was over. The man was no longer in sight, and the crowd didn't seem to react in the least to the screams from the one lonely figure who decided that he wanted to be there in protest. Meanwhile, Peter, looking aghast, stood there silent. He was shaking his head as if saying no, and then he began to speak again. "Listen, folks, everywhere that there is progress and throughout history, we have had those who feel that they, alone, are the moral majority. Now I am for the rights of free speech, but it has its time and place." Peter began talking a bit softer as the crowd was now interested again and silent.

"The history of humankind has been plagued with zealots since the dawn of mankind. I can picture the first group of men, back in the Stone Age. One of the men creates a wheel and is excited for the future. The other is flabbergasted and thinks only of his internal fears."

Peter paused for a moment, scanned the crowd, and then he continued. "It is fear that has created all of the problems in this world of ours. It is fear that has started every war. It is fear that has stopped progress, time and time again."

He started talking louder. "What has fear gotten us? I commit to you today that it is the men and women who stand in the face of fear and in the face of religious zealotry that are the true thinkers," he exclaimed.

Laura finally made it to the front of the line. While the commotion was occurring, she took advantage of the situation and moved directly to the front. She was so small that nearly no one noticed. She held out her hand toward Peter and shouted, "Is it true that the Mechas are now more intelligent than humans?"

The crowd went silent. It was if someone shouted out something so profane that no one could believe it. The looks of disbelief on the faces of the crowd said it all. They too wanted to know the answer to the question.

Peter looked directly at his friend, Laura, who was considerably loud, given her size. "Mechas? Is that what people are calling androids these days?" Peter paused for a moment. "Well, to not put so fine of a point on it, yes!" he roared. Peter looked down at the ground, averting his eyes from the crowd. He knew that what he was about to tell the crowd was going to upset them. This was the moment that he feared during the drive to the office. He lifted his head back up toward the crowd and then told them what he dreaded to tell them.

"We will be making our official announcement this evening. We have booked Diamondback Stadium for the big reveal. As you can clearly see, there isn't a lot of room out here, and it's considerably less spacious inside the office building. We want you to see for yourselves what a real breakthrough looks like, and it's just not possible to do that out here on the street. We appreciate that you have all come out to learn of our accomplishments, but I am going to have to ask you to wait just a little while longer," he said.

The crowd grumbled and was noticeably upset. Their cheers turned to moans. They waited for hours for the news release by

I-Corp, and some waited even longer. The press was noticeably upset because they couldn't ask any questions, and they spent hours setting up in front of the office building. Laura got the only question, and had she not interrupted Peter's speech, she likely wouldn't have gotten that.

Peter moved toward the door and then turned back to the crowd. "I almost forgot. Tonight, you will be meeting the best and the brightest in the technology world. The event starts at 7:00 PM sharp, so you will want to get there at least an hour early so that you can get the best seats possible. We chose this venue because we want the people to have the opportunity to see our accomplishments for themselves and in person. I apologize for the late notice, but security is of the utmost importance, and we had to wait until the last minute to inform everyone. We didn't inform the media in advance for security reasons and the sake of everyone involved."

Peter turned again and began to walk up the steps. Leah finally made it back from the parking garage and raced up the steps to meet Peter at the top. Out of breath, she reached out and opened the door for Peter. Grudgingly, the crowds disbursed outside of the building, and within a matter of minutes, the streets went back to usual, and traffic again clogged the streets.

*****

Peter, now in his office, walked over to his desk.

"That could've gone better," he said. "Why is it every time that we have a breakthrough that some moralistic idiot gets up on his soapbox and has to try to ruin things?"

Sitting on the couch in the room was a well-dressed man. He was wearing a bluish-gray suit and a red tie. He sat as if he had the world's best posture and with his hands clasped together in his lap. He was a handsome man and looked to be in his mid to late thirties. The man's name was Jared Hadad. He was an associate of Peter for the past nine years. He was a stout man of about six feet in height with brown hair and dazzling green eyes.

Jared grew up in Britain after his family emigrated there from Turkey around the end of World War I. He attended Harvard for a short time and set a record for completion of his master's degree and doctoral work, having completed both in under three years. Jared was about as bright as they came in the tech business and even more skillful in the art of negotiations and business deals. He was a soft-spoken fellow, and his mannerisms were as soft as the tone in his voice. He exuded eloquence class with every word spoken and gesture expressed. He no longer worked directly with I-Corp. He left the company about two years prior and went into the world of politics. His natural charm and ability to think on his feet and speak without use of a teleprompter made him a natural politician and statesman.

Jared looked at Peter and spoke softly. "Things like this are normal human behavior. People are not going to automatically trust something as great as artificial intelligence. Think about it, these people have heard horror stories for years from the most wealthy and elite people in the United States. People fear the unknown, and right now, they have few details on the project we have worked on over the past decade."

Peter looked back at Jared, who walked over to the bar and poured himself a drink. "I suppose you are right. The last breakthrough that we announced didn't go all that well, did it?"

"I believe that every endeavor has its problems. That's why we started this work. The whole existence of this project has always been to eliminate the problems and the downside of artificial intelligence," said Jared.

Peter, still standing by the bar, looked down at his drink and began to swirl the concoction of whiskey, mango, and pineapple juices around. After he was satisfied that he mixed it well enough, he glanced over at Jared who was still seated on the couch.

"Jared, you and I both know that we have to be incredibly careful about breaking this. Most folks don't understand the difference between artificial intelligence and superintelligence. To them, it's all about making machines that walk, talk, smile and play chess really well."

"I certainly understand their concerns," said Jared. "If it were myself, I would share their concerns. The difference between those people and people like us is that we understand the benefits of superintelligence. We are on the cusp of creating greatness. When the world sees the applications of superintelligence, any fear or apprehension will melt away."

Peter walked over to Jared and placed his hand on his left shoulder. "Well, Jared, you are right, as is usually the case. How is the campaign trail treating you?"

Jared looked up at Peter, who withdrew his hand. "You know, campaigns. It's a lot of flying around, talking to people, and kissing babies. The great thing about being who I am is that I can pretty much go anywhere and not feel that sense of awkwardness when meeting people for the first time. My plane has circled this club so many times that I don't think that there is anyone left to meet. Keep in mind that elections in Great Britain aren't the same as they are here in the states. The term for prime minister lasts five years instead of the four that it does here."

"Don't go overboard on me, Jared," Peter replied. "We really need this election. Just think of where we could go if we had someone on the inside, both here and in the UK, providing a rallying cry for the next big leap forward. You are just going to have to give people something that they can't ignore to show them that you are the right guy for the job. Just make sure that you leave the people with a bit of a wow factor, but also something that will soften even the hardest critic."

Peter returned to his desk. He sat down and began twirling his straw in his drink again. He must have been feeling a bit anxious again as his drink was as mixed as it could possibly be at this point.

Jared looked at Peter and stood up. He walked over to Peter and placed his hand onto Peter's shoulder. "Pete, don't worry. I am certain that this election will be a landslide. I live in a country where it's all about the popular vote. Any critics that are out there are so few and far between that they won't even make a dent in my numbers. Have you seen my competition? That woman is laughable. Her whole campaign is built on empty rhetoric and promises that no person could ever keep. There is absolutely no need to worry. You take care of the media tonight, and I will guarantee that you will get the results that we want."

"Don't get overconfident, Jared. You seem to forget that you haven't been elected yet. Why you ever claimed to be of Jewish descent in a political contest is beyond me. What the hell were you even thinking? I know you're smart, but whatever made you think that people are looking for a religious person to be running that country?"

"Peter, I hate to break this to you, but there is a certain part of the population that is still Christian. There's still a large population of Jewish folks. Most folks may not believe in anything other than their own self-serving interests, but there is still a sizable group of Catholics, evangelicals, Muslims, and who can forget the largest group, the spiritualists. I'd say that all those groups together make up at least a quarter of the voting population."

Peter looked puzzled. "Just how does that benefit you? You are claiming a religion that isn't even British. That religion is from halfway around the globe. How are you going to convince anyone that being Jewish is the right type of religion for a prime minister? Don't you know that John F. Kennedy himself almost lost his election here in the US because he was considered to be too Catholic?"

Jared smiled at Peter. "Have you ever known me to be wrong about my instincts?"

"Well, to be truthful, no, but that doesn't mean squat, and you know it. All that tells me is that you are due to make a mistake or muck up something. You might just be the most arrogant person alive," Peter said jokingly.

"Peter, please don't mistake me for that television personality who became president here in the States a few years back. I am not referring to Ronald Reagan. I'm talking about that guy in 2016. Besides, his arrogance got him elected. There is a certain part of population that wants a man who is sure of himself. Would you like a president who can't make up his or her mind on every serious issue, or would you rather have a president who is firm in his beliefs and confident to the point that he can show the people that they should also be confident? That same logic applies across the ocean as it does here," Jared rebutted.

Jared walked over toward the door. As he reached the door, he stopped and shot a glance over to Peter. In a soft voice, he said, "Great things will happen. You will see. This is just the beginning."

Jared proceeded out the door. Peter, still seated at his desk, glanced at the phone and went to pick it up but, halfway through putting the receiver to his ear, had a change of mind. He set the phone back down into its cradle, got up from his chair, and walked over to his window. He stood at the window, staring at the city below. He had a great view from the thirty-eighth floor and could see half the city from his office. The view was spectacular. The whole city was surrounded by mountains, and the dark-brown of the rocky faces contrasted beautifully with the blue sky on the horizon. This was one of the things Peter loved best about the city. Even more beautiful was when the sun would go down, and he would retreat to his favorite restaurant, located atop one of the smaller mountains and overlooking the entire city in its splendor. Looking down toward the city itself, he could see that the downtown area was unusually quiet, considering that it wasn't even rush hour yet. The cars that were bumper to bumper earlier in the day dissipated and left the city looking like it was a holiday.

Peter's favorite views came at night. The lights of the city at night were so brilliant that it made the star lit sky look empty. There was every manner of color in the lighting, and some of the lights would move, quickly from east to west and in varying patterns. It surely was a sight to behold, and Peter treasured every moment. He would sit outside along the railing on the back porch of his house, which was set on a cliff. Looking down, one could see the desert grasses and a rocky surface mixed with a saguaro cactus or two until those fell out of sight and into darkness the further down and away from the light one looked.

At night, the temperatures would plummet, and it would feel much colder than during the day, but all one needed to do was stand next to a giant sunbaked rock if he or she were cold. It was as if the world knew that people would need a place to warm themselves at night and intentionally placed large natural heaters out and about the landscape as to warm the souls of those who were lucky enough as to reside in such a picturesque place.

Peter stood at the window, and he pondered the achievements that led him to this beautiful place. *Did I do the right thing?* he asked himself. *Can one really improve anything, or is it all just a fantastic deception? How can one improve what seems already to be perfect?* He believed that his work was important and that what he created was an answer to everything that ever plagued the world. He genuinely believed that it was the answer to all the world's problems. He dreamed of creating a completely sentient machine since he was a child. Now that he had done it, he wondered if he had gone too far. He remembered an adage he once heard, "Just because we can do something does not always mean that we should."

Peter had breakthroughs before, and his last was considered to be the largest technological advancement in human history. Back around the time that the US was still a democratic republic, he came out with Sonia. She was the world's first artificial intelligence that actually looked and moved like a human being.

Sonia was an incredible feat. She was autonomous and highly intelligent. She was not a superintelligent being, but she was a beginning to what I-Corp recently accomplished. She was a "stepping stone to greatness," according to Jared, who worked heavily with her and on Peter's new project as well. After the initial breakthrough with Sonia, Peter knew that he would have a tough road ahead. He knew that there would be those who would adore his new technology and that there would be others who would not be so willing to warm up to a machine.

Peter thought about the man who caused the scene earlier in the day. He knew Charles well. Charles made quite a name for himself as a police officer several years ago. Peter didn't meet him until after he retired from law enforcement and only met him as an adversary. Charles was a true thorn in Peter's side because he attended every rollout event that he held. Charles seemed to Peter to be deeply religious, but so much so that it made him look as if he was fanatic. Peter was not a religious man, so he could not empathize with him to understand where he was coming from and why he seemed to be opposed to every new technological advance that was announced.

Peter walked back over to his desk and sat down. He picked up the phone, and he dialed for his assistant. "Leah, get me Jack Rogers over at Newsline. I need to talk to him as soon as possible." Peter then paused for a moment. He was lost in his own thoughts.

"Is everything all right, Mr. Jensen?" asked Leah.

"Everything is fine. Could you please get Rogers for me?" he replied.

Peter hung up the phone and sat back in his chair. He placed his hands on his desk and stared at a tiny replica of Sonia that he had sitting on his desk. He took a deep breath and let out a huge sigh.

"You can do this," he said.

CHAPTER 2

Zealots

Charles Duncan was a portly man. He was a short guy with a bit of a taste for the finer foods. This was if he wasn't putting away his normal cuisine. That usually consisted of every comfort food known to man. You could say that he was overweight, but that was an understatement. After leaving the police department, he had a healthy weight of 170, but that number quickly grew to a hefty 250. While he was actively working as a police officer, he would work out frequently. When he became a civilian, he stopped working out as frequently and his eating habits caught up to him like a police officer on a high-speed pursuit of a bike thief.

Charles lived about fifteen minutes from Phoenix and closer to the northeastern part of Scottsdale. He was a few minutes from Black Canyon Highway and was set in between quite a few restaurants. Anyone who knew him would say that it wasn't a coincidence that he found a home surrounded by fast-food joints and other restaurants. Interestingly enough, he was in between some fancier restaurants in the Scottsdale area and the more middle-class fare of the northern Phoenix area. He didn't quite fit into the upscale community of Scottsdale as he had always been more of a blue-collar fellow. He also didn't fit into the lower levels of society. Having a home that was as middle of the road as he was seemed fitting.

Charles was now retired from the Phoenix Sheriff's Department. He spent twenty years on the force and worked the barrio neighborhoods just south of Tempe. He grew up just northwest of Phoenix in a small town called Glendale. When he was growing up, Glendale consisted of very few homes and a dive bar or two. Aside from a handful of fights that would take place at the local bars, the only entertainment was watching the occasional tumbleweed rolling around town. Every now and again, a sandstorm would rear its ugly head and coat the whole town with a thick layer of dust. One who loves to clean would consider a place like this as a virtual heaven as the place was so dusty that the number 1 activity was cleaning the dust-off things.

Charles was shot in the line of duty twice, and in one event at the Metro Mall, he came across a knife wielding man and had to take lethal action. He was no stranger to firearms and was as accurate as one could be. Living in a desert has its advantages and one of those advantages is that there are miles of nothingness, with which to line up a few targets at a local dumping area and fire away.

Charles was a fairly normal fellow. He saw himself as a patriot and a law-abiding citizen. He was usually coolheaded, which was a great temperament for someone in the law enforcement realm. When he got into his last deadly confrontation, some folks saw his use of force as overkill. They said this because he fired six to seven rounds at the man, who was killed in the altercation. His critics were convinced that he wanted to kill the man rather than to wound him. They argued that anything over two rounds fired into a person was excessive and that it was more like rage than trying to arrest someone.

When that incident happened, in the early part of the twenty-first century, Charles was in his midtwenties and only a couple years out of the academy. Like many other young law enforcement officers, he was gung ho and by the book. He graduated above average in his class but not at the top of his class. He was a middle-of-the-road student at best. He was used to being middle of the road in almost everything, so his efforts to achieve were not an overwhelming force.

After the shooting, Charles was interviewed by his department's internal affairs office. He was also forced to see a psychologist in order to determine if he was mentally capable of going back into the rigorous work of law enforcement. The internal affairs investigation completed, and it was their determination that he used a lack of judgment in his actions with the man at the mall. Witnesses to the event said that the man was fleeing the scene and that he had dropped the knife, but Charles strongly stood by his argument that he believed the perpetrator was lunging at another patron of the mall and that the use of force was necessary after the man failed to respond to verbal commands. There was no good video at the time to confirm Charles's story, so the witness testimony was relied upon heavily.

Charles was terminated from his role with the sheriff's department shortly after the investigation was concluded. There wasn't enough evidence to support charges for murder and rather than giving the department a black eye by having an officer convicted of manslaughter or negligent homicide, they quietly dismissed him without charge and with the understanding that it was really a resignation. Charles didn't want to fight the dismissal, so he accepted the consequences of his actions and left the department.

Putting his law enforcement career behind was easy for him. He knew it was time for other pursuits, and he transitioned out of that role easily. Easy is one way to see it, but most folks would call a termination by forced resignation difficult. He didn't have much of a skill set aside from his law enforcement work. He also didn't have the best references in seeking a new job because he was dismissed for shooting someone, and the public was very aware of it. *Easy* meant that he didn't really have a problem leaving and that was because he narrowly escaped a murder charge.

For the first few years, he struggled with alcohol addiction. He started drinking as a way to mask the pain and embarrassment that he felt, and this led him to get involved with drugs as well. He hit rock bottom after his termination. His failed attempts at coping with the loss of his job and subsequent drug and alcohol abuse led him to financial ruin. If it weren't for Chris Watson, he would probably still be on the street or dead. He met Chris by accident, and that one chance meeting changed his entire life.

Charles saw that his life had taken a downward spiral and that he was as low as he could go. He saw it as fate. He believed that he was being punished for killing a man, and he even started believing that he killed the guy intentionally. He realized that he had become that thing that he spent years putting behind bars. For him, it was the most humbling situation he could find himself in.

He met Chris a couple years previous when he was out one evening, enjoying a local coffeehouse in Glendale. This was no ordinary coffeehouse. This coffeehouse was an actual house that was transformed into a beatnik hangout. It was complete with couches and chairs in every room, and small pockets of books scattered about the place. The walls were adorned with the artwork of many local artists from the Phoenix area. It was a rather large house, and the architecture suggested that it was built around the turn of the twentieth century. While it looked old, it was well-kept. The wood floors showed significant wear to the surface, and some spots on the floor had a nice shine while the areas that took the most foot traffic were grayish with no shine at all. The ceilings were quite rustic and had tin panels adorning them in a few of the rooms; whereas, the remaining rooms were plaster. The walls were a hodgepodge of different finishes with some rooms having wallpaper that was adorned with little flowers that were velvety to the touch and burgundy in color. Other rooms were painted in array of different colors, with each room having its own unique style that somewhat matched the artwork in the rooms.

As Charles walked through the rooms in the immense home, the floors would squeak. Noticing the sound, he slowed down his pace because he didn't want to disturb the many people spread out in the home. He knew that the people who were reading wouldn't want to be disturbed from their fantasy worlds.

The people were quietly nestled into just about every nook and cranny in the place. Charles was looking for a place to sip his coffee and read a small book that he found while in the front room of the home. After walking into nearly every room, Charles came upon a smaller room with a couch on one wall with a small chair set next to it, and across the room was a second couch with a small table and a cute little rug under the table. The room wasn't empty. It had two people inside, and the young male in the room was reading poetry, softly to his young female companion. The young man in the room was Chris, who didn't know it at the time but would play an integral role in Charles's life in only a matter of two short years.

Charles sat down on the vacant couch across from the young man and the young woman. He sat there, fascinated that someone would read to another adult. Love was definitely lost on him. He hadn't experienced true love before and seeing a display of affection such as he witnessed made him curious. He sat there quietly as the man continued to read to his companion. He seemed not to notice that Charles had walked in the room and seated himself directly across from him and his girlfriend.

Charles knew that they had to have heard him squeaking himself into the room. He didn't want to seem creepy by sneaking in and gazing at them from across the room, so he spoke to the pair.

"I'm truly sorry to disturb you, but would it be okay if I sat over here?" he asked, pointing at the general area where he was already seated.

"By all means, sit. We were just about to go up front and reload on the coffee." The young man chuckled.

"You can sit here," said the young woman.

"I appreciate it, but I would hate to impose on you like that. I am not staying long, and I was really just looking for a place to park for a minute or two and read this funny little book I found in the last room," he snorted.

"What book did you find?" she asked.

"Well, it's not so much a book as it is pamphlet," he replied. "The other books were rather large, and I was just hoping to have a little bit to read as I finish this coffee."

Chris looked directly at Charles, and he glanced down to see what he was reading. As soon as he looked down, he smiled as if he just got the punch line of a very subtle joke.

He stood up and walked over to Charles. "You, sir, are correct. That is a pamphlet. To be a bit more accurate, it's called a track."

"A what?" said Charles.

Glenda, who was Chris's companion, responded, "A track!"

"You mean like a racetrack?" said Charles.

"Ha! It does sound funny, doesn't it?" Chris retorted. "It's a message about salvation. Well, actually, the one that you have may not get you salvation, but it will get you some strange looks around here!" he said boisterously. "You see, the track that you have is from the church of Satan. You know, those guys who dress up in capes and a lot of red. I didn't realize that they were making those and passing them out. The world sure has gone and gotten itself a wee bit crazy, since 9/11, now, hasn't it?"

Chris, still standing, reached into his back pocket and pulled out another track and handed it to Charles.

"Does every religious group have their own brochures?" Charles laughed.

"I don't know. I never really thought about it until just now. After seeing that thing you were reading, I would have to say yes," he replied.

"Well, I didn't realize it was religious literature. I just picked it up because it looked like a comic book. I'm not overly religious, but I'm also not some devil worshipper. I guess I would actually prefer to read the one that you had in your pocket," said Charles.

Glenda stood up and took the few steps necessary to stand next to both Chris and Charles. Seeing this, Charles stood up as well.

"You will have to forgive Chris. He hasn't learned how to be civil yet. He would talk to you for a year and still wouldn't remember to introduce anyone. I'm still waiting on him to tell me his name myself," she said, laughing out loud.

"Well, as I always say, Glenda, I'm no angel!" Chris said softly. "My name is Chris, and this beautifully charming young lady is my girlfriend, Glenda. It's nice to meet you."

"Chris and Glenda? Well, that shouldn't be that hard to remember. Glenda from Glendale," he joked. "Wasn't there a witch named Glenda?"

"Yes!" Glenda shrieked. "My parents named me after that movie! I guess that their hypocrisy has no bounds. They named me after their favorite witch."

"How does that make them hypocrites exactly?" asked Chris.

"I don't know. I lost my train of thought," she replied.

All three began laughing.

Chris gained his composure and looked back at Charles, who was still laughing quietly. "Look, Charles, is it? We actually need to get going, I forgot that Glenda and I have dinner reservations at eight. It was nice meeting you. When you are done reading that brochure"—he chuckled—"pass it on to the next person that you meet. Before you do, write down my number that is on the back. I put it on there for whoever reads this particular brochure and has questions."

"Oh, okay, uh, great! I can do that," he replied. "It was nice meeting you two. Hey, thanks again."

Chris and Glenda walked out of the room.

*****

Charles hadn't seen Chris in several years. Since he wasn't overly interested in a new religion, he put the track in his wallet and left the coffeehouse without giving it a second thought. He never took the track out, and it remained in his wallet, next to his sub-club card.

Charles kept that card inside his wallet for years. It wasn't until he finally hit rock bottom, many years later that he accidentally stumbled upon it again. He pulled out his last dollar bill one night as he was paying his drug dealer for some methamphetamine, and out of his wallet came the track. The track fell silently to the floor, and Charles picked it up. He realized at that very moment that the track had a purpose. It hit him like a ton of bricks.

Charles read the track, and sure enough, on the back was the telephone number for Chris. He was so struck by the thought that fate brought him that track that he called Chris that very night. The two talked for a while, and before he knew it, he was in rehab and back into the real world. The two maintained a friendship over the next couple of years, and Charles became the portly man that he is today. He traded his drug addiction for a food addiction but figured that food was a hundred times better than drugs. Charles was a changed man. You wouldn't know it by looking at him, but he was completely transformed.

Charles was so moved by that little piece of paper folded up in his wallet for all those years that he turned his life around and was now the pastor of a local church. The track that Chris gave to him was from a local Baptist church. Within the four tiny pages was a cartoonlike drawing of Jesus and a snapshot of the gospel. There were so few words in the track that it really was only a sentence or two. The verses that were written were John 3:16 and Romans 3:23. Just enough to let Charles know that he was not alone in his sinful condition and that Jesus was born in order to be his savior and the savior for all mankind.

Charles studied those verses for weeks, trying to understand the meaning. He read the entire Bible in a matter of months and then again, taking pause to study each verse for meaning. He knew that if God would save a man that was in such a poor condition as he had been that he would do the same for anyone. He made it his new life's work to spread the good news. He had no problem getting up in front of people and giving his testimony. He knew that even though he had a sordid past, full of sin, that he was saved through the grace of an all-loving God. For this reason, sharing was easy for him. As a police officer, he used to lecture people about the law on a daily basis. Those folks rarely listened, and they destroyed their lives. He now gave testimony on God's law, and still there were those who would not listen. Armed with his testimony about a broken man who received God's grace, he managed to get many to listen.

CHAPTER 3

Technological Advances

Diamondback Stadium was filled with people, even though there was no game on that evening. The sun was running away to the opposite side of the earth, and the temperature dropped significantly. The lights at the stadium came on all at once as if someone took a picture with a giant camera. The brightness of the lights was an awesome sight. Everything in the vicinity of the stadium was lit. It was so bright that it was nearly impossible to tell that the sun had set. The heat that the sun provided was now gone. The locals were huddled up against the giant rocks that now acted as a heat source.

The people shuffled into the stadium in a massive line about ten people wide. The line seemed to go on for a mile or more. Everyone wanted a glimpse at the new technology, even though they weren't quite sure what the technology was. Technology releases became commonplace after the invention of the personal computer. New releases were now as commonplace as paying taxes at the checkout line in the local grocery store. It seemed as if there was some new technology every other day or two.

Technology has a way of changing things. In the past, technology was simple. When some inventor made a machine that would slice bread, it appeared as if everything that could be invented now was. What could be better than sliced bread? The basis of every new technology and whether it was good was based on one simple factor. What could the technology do to make life easier? Another way of saying the same thing would be that technology is considered good if it can make one lazier. Technology has always been considered as good for society.

With the invention of the automobile, people were suddenly able to travel long distances in short periods. Prior to that, people had to ride horses to get from point A to point B. When one has the experience of riding a horse day in and day out and then is suddenly introduced to the convenience of an automobile, it is like the heavens opened and started raining manna. Unlike the automobile, horses got tired after only a few miles. One may have gotten fifty miles in a day on a good horse if he or she maintained a slow pace and stopped frequently. Horses need to rest whereas automobiles do not.

The automobile was deemed to be one of the greatest technologies of the nineteenth and twentieth centuries. The drawback was that production was limited, and the cost was more than the average Joe could afford. This led to new technologies in manufacturing, and suddenly there was a boom in technology.

Other technological advances came throughout the twentieth century. There was the air conditioner, the atom bomb, and eventually the first computer. The first computers were as large or larger than cars. The size was a limiting factor at first, but as technological advances kept coming, the size of the computer dropped dramatically, and the price did as well. Within a few short decades, the computer became a regular part of everyday life. No longer was a computer just something that people used in order to run their business or to calculate large math equations.

The personal computer was the new next best thing to sliced bread. The computer allowed people to literally slice bread via a simulator. Yes, some chucklehead thought that it would be funny to create an app for cell phones that allowed people to slice bread. The game was simple and consisted of a samurai sword and a loaf of bread. It was a success because of the novelty of it. It was born out of the old saying about sliced bread's greatness as an invention. As these things go, people love to play games that are nostalgic.

The first computers were really used for the defense of the United States as are most technological advances. It wasn't until the early 1990s that computers became mainstream in society. By the end of the nineties, the internet was in full swing, thanks to a man who was vice president at the time. That man's name was Al Greer. While he didn't really invent the internet, he was simply crazy enough as to try to claim the technological feat. The world loved Mr. Greer until the fuel crisis of 2027 and believed in his rants about global warming up until he died in a freak accident that involved wine corks and cattle. He had some crazy idea about reducing carbon dioxide by reducing cow flatulence. He ironically got the idea off the internet.

If there had ever been a man that truly lived up to his last name, it was Al Greer. Anytime a projectile is involved and proper safety precautions are not met, one is just asking for disaster to strike. Little did he know that the psi of a cow rectum with a cork inserted is rather high. At first, it was like a New Year's celebration; a cork or two popped with that familiar sound and fanfare. The excitement soon ended when the barrage came. Had he only been wearing protective goggles; he might still be with the world today. He has been missed.

The computer was just the beginning in a long line of technological advances. As things tended to go, the devices got smaller, then a little larger again, and eventually, so small that they became difficult to use in normal applications. Eventually, every computer, no matter its size, found a use in everyday life. People started with a computer that they used from behind a desk. They moved to computers that they could hold in one hand. They switched to computers that were just about the size of a standard envelope and eventually settled on computers that could be worn around the wrist. Those computers were called watches and the name fit perfectly. All that people did was stare at their wrists all day. It wasn't until some scientists invented a holographic heads-up display that people started looking normal again.

The crowd that was headed into the stadium was filled with people wearing computer wristwatches. Finding a person without a wristwatch computer usually meant that the person was deeply religious. The religious people tended to not wear them out of a fear of being overly worldly or a fear of being tracked by the government. One needed only to look at the person's wrists to tell if a person was religious or not.

Charles had a wristwatch computer on both wrists. He wasn't afraid of the technology and often told his congregation that they need not worry about wrist watches. Most of his church members wore the watches. They found that they were useful for communicating among one another. Some folks saw it as taking the mark of the beast and feared it, and others simply were afraid that it would somehow be used against them. Charles reassured people that it couldn't be the mark of the beast because it could be worn on either wrist, and the mark was supposed to be on the left hand.

Being the unrelenting man that he was, Charles waited outside the stadium for hours. He got there early so that he could relay his message against technology. It wasn't necessarily technology that he railed against, but the last decades' attempts at creating superintelligent machines. He feared this because he, like others like him, knew that if something could go wrong, it probably would.

He stood at gate 1, and as the people filed in past him, he yelled out to them, "Don't let these people deceive you! They are trying to play God. Only God can create intelligent beings!"

A young boy and his father stopped next to Charles for a moment. The boy couldn't have been more than twelve. Charles looked at the boy.

"Young man, the future belongs to people like yourself. Don't embrace something that is going to take your future job from you."

The boy's father looked a bit puzzled. He had a smirk on his face. "My son knows that technology has its risks. He has had computers around him since the day he was born. In the twelve years that he has been around, computers have saved his life twice and allowed him to do things that I never could as a child."

Charles engaged the man. "Not all technology is bad. See, I wear a computer on my wrist too. It's not small computers that are the problem. Don't you see it?"

"See what?" The man interrupted.

"Don't you see that the technology has long surpassed us humans? What started as a way to make life easier hasn't done that? Life is much harder now," Charles shouted.

"It may be harder for you, but what about the other eight billion people on earth? People aren't dying from diseases thanks to computers. People aren't suffering from hunger thanks to computers. From what I can see, the only one here with a problem is you," the man retorted.

The boy chimed in, "I don't need some freak telling me how computers are bad. Look at you. You are just some short fat jerk who hates computers because you couldn't swallow the last one. Come on, Dad!"

Flabbergasted, Charles replied, "Son, don't talk like that, you—"

The man interrupted. "Don't tell my kid what he can and can't do. He may be in the wrong, but I'll be damned if I let some fat slob try to tell me how to discipline my kid."

"Look, I'm sure he is a nice kid, but had you let me finish—" Charles started.

The man interrupted again. "I'm done with you. Go find some other people to try to convince. You're wasting your breath. This is the twenty-first century. Start acting like you are a part of it!"

Charles was about to say more, but the man grabbed his son by the arm and pulled him away. Charles stood there silently. He felt so bad for this young boy. The boy had a mouth like a sailor, and his father could've cared less about it.

Meanwhile, inside the stadium, the people were quickly filling up the seats. The whole place was alive and loud. There were chants of "USA! USA!" reverberating across the place. It was a strange chant indeed. The last time that chants of "USA! USA!" were heard was when the last conservative president lived on Maryland Avenue in Washington, DC. It was only a handful of years ago, but that presidency was the last for the United States as a democratic republic. The people were so thrilled about the United States being the leader in technology that they couldn't help themselves.

The politics of the day became quite liberal when the last Congress took over and changed the US Constitution. What once was a republic had turned into a socialist democracy. The politicians assured the people time and time again that it was all in the name of fairness, but the people never got their fairness and are still looking for the "democratic" part of the new government.

With the country now a bastion of liberalism, disguised as progress, technology has risen sevenfold. The environment changed from one of conservative values to one where pretty much anything goes. The politicians who came into power after the last Republican president decided that morality was relative to the individual. The old days had laws to prevent things like cloning and euthanasia. Those laws were quickly repealed in the name of "morality and common sense." "Cloning for the purpose of saving lives" is what they called it when the laws were repealed. The laws of the land were all changed to "meet the needs of all humans."

The stadium was now at a dull roar. There were still a few stragglers, who hadn't reached their seats, but most were now settled in and waiting for the show to begin. The lines outside were much smaller, and it wouldn't be long before the show would begin. With the sun moved out of sight for the evening, the air was cool, so most folks were wearing light sweaters or suit jackets. The crowd was a virtual melting pot of people. There was no one type of person in attendance. From rich to poor and educated to noneducated, the seats were filled with a diverse crowd.

Rich people still existed in America, but those who were fortunate to call themselves rich were usually former politicians. The people of the day learned that fairness has its limits. Fairness is relative to who the judge is. Most folks were equal now, and the great redistribution of 2028 saw to that. Equal meant that they could live where the government allowed them to live and to work where the government wanted them to work. Fairness and equality also meant that the government was the law giver and, as the law giver, could set any law deemed necessary to prevent any one person from attaining more wealth than the next person. Of course, exceptions had to be made in order to keep the economy running, so the political class allowed for certain former politicians to own businesses or "manage" them for the government.

The stage was set right around where the pitcher's mound was normally located. There was a huge backdrop of screens that displayed the words *I-Corp*, *progress*, and *change*, flashing in rapid succession across the screens. Just in front of the screens sat a United Nations flag, and to the right of it, a US flag. There was a row of chairs set to the right and left of the flags. Those seats were reserved for any dignitaries and the other important people. Since there were twelve seats. One could only assume that there would be at least twelve people on the stage. A small podium was set in the center at the front. The setting was familiar as people have seen similar stage sets as this for years as politicians rounded the earth campaigning on change and hope.

The stage was empty except for one young lady who was setting a pitcher of water on a small table next to the podium. There were two glasses, so one could assume that there would be at least two speakers at this event. As soon as the young woman walked off the stage, the lights in the stadium flashed off and on again. This was a signal to the crowd that the conference was ready to begin.

Just in front of the stage was a large press area. There were twelve rows of chairs set that went six rows deep. The chairs for the press were all taken by different types of media personnel. About a third of them were writers for internet news sites. The remaining two-thirds were from the various television networks.

Sitting in the front row, center stage, was Laura Stroud, Peter's former classmate and friend. Laura was dressed in a lovely blue dress that resembled the dress worn by Betty Bubble in the old Flintlock cartoons. The dress was rather short in length and had a large bell-like base that extended down to just above her knees. Her arms were highly visible since the dress had no sleeves. Her dark-brown hair was straight and down to the middle of her back. She had already taken her seat. She knew that she would get the first question at tonight's event, so she sat calmly, waiting for the event to begin. To her right was a television personality out of Seattle, who had recently taken a position with America's National News Network, which was now the number 1 news network in the country.

The news business has had its share of unethical behavior in the past. After the election of 2024, the new Congress enacted new fairness laws to combat bias in reporting. The laws established a new government watchdog group that was responsible for fact-checking all news that was to be reported. Media outlets were suddenly required to submit their stories to the Federal Information Bureau, to have the stories fact-checked prior to being reported. The goal was to eliminate any inaccuracies and bias in the news being reported. By submitting the news to a central agency and creating laws against the free flow of information, the questionable news of the past has been replaced by "news you can trust."

The life span of a news career became short after the change in reporting laws took place. Any reporter that reported anything negative about a politician or the government was released from the news organization immediately and replaced with someone who would report what they were given. This worked well for the politicians but not for any reporters that had ethics. Anyone wanting to report news that fell out of the mainstream was relegated to the internet. The government controlled the internet and would allow people to report on news, but even these sites were monitored and would have blackouts or server issues quite frequently. If anyone reported something that the government did not approve of, they would be censored and then fined.

The lights flickered one last time, and as the lights came back on, music began to play over the loudspeakers. The person who selected the music must have been a teenager in the 1980s and a fan of techno music because an oldie from the band the Information Society began to blare across the stadium. The words *pure energy* were heard with the sounds of techno dance music energizing the crowd.

The crowd jumped to their feet. Some began dancing where they stood, while others just clapped and their hands. Everyone in the stadium was now standing, and the music continued to blare away. The images on the screen changed slightly, and now the words *I-Corp*, *progress*, and *change* were flashing across the screen. There was also an image of a naked human with his arms extended out above his head in a V shape. His legs were also extended outward in a V shape. The image was bluish and looked like a human-anatomy diagram. Visible inside the head was a brain, but it was different from the human brain. It had the same shape as a human brain, but it was silver, and flashes of light were dancing around within it. It was a spectacular sight, and the image rotated around in a complete circle in three dimensions as if it were a hologram.

The music continued to play on with that familiar voice of Leonard Nimoy, saying "pure energy." As the song played and the guests continued to dance, a line of people started walking across the stage from the left side to the right side. The line of people must have been prearranged because there was an order to the precession. The first person on stage was a female followed by a man and then the pattern continued until the twelfth person was on the stage. That last person was a man.

The people walked in a single-file line at a slow pace until the woman on the end reached the first chair on the right side. At this point, the woman stopped and turned toward the audience. Each person reached his or her chair, stopped and then turned toward the audience. This continued until the last man was standing directly in front of the last chair on the left. The music continued to play as the twelve people stood, silently looking at the audience.

Suddenly, Peter emerged and climbed up the steps on the right side of the stage. He walked briskly to the center and turned toward the audience when he reached the podium. From the left side of the stage, a female emerged. She also walked briskly to the center of the stage and stopped next to the podium, turned toward the audience, and stood next to Peter. The female was followed shortly thereafter by a young man with a thirteenth chair. He set the chair just to the left side of the podium and just behind the small table that was sitting next to the podium. The woman sat down in the chair, and Peter remained standing at the podium.

Peter grabbed the microphone and adjusted it slightly. It was a little too low for his liking. He then opened his notebook and began to shuffle through the papers that he had inside. He was still a little nervous. His mind started racing. His hands started to perspire and felt cold. A cold shudder went up the back of his spine. He was no stranger to public speaking. He had been in front of large crowds before, but he never really enjoyed this part of his job. The last time that he gave a speech was the introduction of Sonia, the world's first artificially intelligent humanoid.

Sonia was an older model, constructed around 2023. At the time, her creation and debut to the world was quite the sensation. She could speak, move her arms and fingers, and even smile. At the time, she was the hottest news topic in the world. She made headlines for months as she toured the country. She appeared on talk shows and even had a cameo role or two in some of the sitcoms of the day.

The public was excited about Sonia because she was a new technology, but really, people saw so little of her after the first few months of her debut that she quickly became yesterday's news. She was supposed to be the machine that ended the world's problems. She was as intelligent as they came and slightly less intelligent than a human. Her promise was not in the intelligence that she had at the time but the intelligence she would gain over the next decade. She was a part of a project that combined I-Corp and several governments think tanks. Since she was a part of a larger project with mass funding and government support, she was one of five models. The other models were similar, but it was thought that the people would be more receptive to a female artificial person, so she was the only model that was shown to the public. The male models were used primarily for the law-and-order projects and defense projects. The project was a first of its kind. Computer technologies were just at the point where artificial intelligence was possible, so she was really a first-generation model.

The five machines were based on cloud-based computing, which made learning exponential. They shared every bit of knowledge that they acquired. When one unit would learn a specific subject, all the knowledge was uploaded to the cloud, where the remaining units would then have access to the knowledge. The amount of knowledge learned over a six-month period was the equivalent of a bus full of students learning through a college level, but in only six months. Since Sonia and the other machines started their learning around 2022, they had almost ten years of knowledge stored. More extraordinary was that they learned so much that they eventually surpassed the knowledge of any one human being. It was the ability to share and store information that made this possible. If the machines did come across a problem that was difficult to solve, they were instantly able to collaborate on a solution to the problem, which further increased their learning capabilities.

Peter was heavily involved with the project as it was his brainchild. He spent years working on artificial intelligence, and it was pretty much his life's work. When he was in graduate school, he had the opportunity to become a fellow, working with higher-level projects for the university and funded by the US Department of Defense. The idea at the time was to create a machine that was capable of fighting and potentially policing the public. The project was chosen for major funding since both jobs were considerably dangerous and very costly to the government. Having machines fight a war meant fewer disabled veterans and veterans who were killed in action. It also meant having a fighting force that didn't need logistics such as food and water. The other added benefit of a machine fighting or policing force was that machines didn't tire easily. Combat can be both emotionally taxing and physically demanding, causing fatigue that takes down time in order to recuperate. It was thought that a machine as a soldier would be easier to control and to maintain.

Previous attempts with the Department of Defense at creating robotic soldiers got into the first stages, with a handful of prototypes, but the machines were just too stiff and slow from a maneuvering standpoint. The first-generation prototypes didn't have any thinking capabilities and had to be used as avatars, which was extremely labor intensive. Aside from that, the radical change in leadership of the US government caused dollars for defense to fall to levels never heard of. The new breed of politicians in the United States wasn't interested in much of a fighting force, so they scrapped the old robotics programs and used the funding for other projects. The politicians figured that since they had nuclear warheads, they could defend through the threat of retaliation. Wars with US involvement have "ended." According to the people running the country at present, the strategy appeared to work as the US has been involved in no conflicts since the last Republicans were in office.

Peter knew that there was a lot at stake with this speech. He was already on the media's blacklist for the stunt that he pulled earlier in the day. They were upset with him because he only gave them two days' notice, and he never informed them of the change in venue until this morning. He knew that it was risky to not inform the press of the full details, but for him, it was a risk worth taking, simply for the security aspects. The entire event was kept secret from the public. It wasn't until two days prior, that the media was made aware of any kind of information release, and the information that they received was limited. They were told that there would be an announcement today, but the time wasn't given. Peter knew that the media would show up in full force at his office complex, and he knew that it would be all over the news for the entire day. Fortunately for him, the gamble worked, and people came out by the thousands.

Two days was short notice for any event, but with something this big, short notice was made for a more secure rollout. Anyone who would want to try something violent wouldn't have much time to prepare, and protesters would have little time to organize. As he scanned the crowd, he thought that the risk paid off because the stadium was filled with excitement and people of all walks of life. More importantly, he felt secure.

Peter started to speak. "Thank you for coming out this evening! Could everyone please be seated?"

The crowd grew silent, and the people in the audience started sitting down. Some people on the left side of the stadium started clapping, and soon, the entire stadium was in an uproar, and people were back on their feet.

"Thank you," said Peter. "If you would kindly take your seats, we will begin."

Peter's voice was a little shaky, and he became very aware of the nervousness coming out as he spoke. He reached to the podium, grabbed a glass, and began to pour himself a glass of water. "I think this is just water, but right now, I am kind of hoping that I'm wrong, and that it's just vodka and tonic," he said jokingly. "Thank you for coming out this evening. I know that it has been a long day, and some of you, I recognize from earlier."

His comfort level increased. "We have come a long way, haven't we?"

The crowd stood up and applauded loudly. They jumped up so quickly that it was if he told them that they all just won the lottery. Seeing this, Peter smiled like the Cheshire Cat for a moment and then regained his composure.

"Thank you," he said. "Today marks a day in history like none other. We have done it!" he exclaimed.

Again, the crowd jumped to their feet. The roar of the crowd could be felt all the way up on the podium. It was so raucous in the stadium that the feet stomping, and applause caused the entire arena to shake. It felt like a minor earth tremor. Peter's glass had ripples bouncing back and forth across the glass, and the condensation on the glass ran quickly down the sides of the glass as the shaking continued.

"Thank you!" he said. "You guys are literally rocking this house!"

Peter again picked up his glass and took a sip of water. He scanned the audience and had a beaming smile. He could feel the energy of the crowd, and this put him at ease.

"For nearly twenty years, we have worked diligently to create an intelligent machine that could think through some of the world's greatest problems but also remain within our control. We set out to design a machine that could care for our sick, teach our children, fight our wars, and potentially even cure cancer!"

The crowd jumped to their feet yet again, and the sound emanating from them was deafening. Peter glanced over to the woman seated to his right and then turned around toward the people seated behind him. He started clapping and was cheering along with the crowd. After a few moments of cheering on the crowd, he gestured to them to quiet down.

"Thank you!" he said.

"In just a few moments, we will be showing a short video up on these screens. The video will explain the brief history of our work and our recent successes. Now before we do that, I'm sure that you are all wondering who this lovely young woman is that is seated next to me."

The woman next to Peter remained seated and smiled back at Peter and to the crowd. She waved to the crowd, acknowledging them. She had a beaming smile on her face, and it was easy to see that she was excited to be a part of the event. She reached for an empty glass and filled it with water. She then took a sip of the water and returned the glass to its place on the table.

Peter began to speak. "Years ago, when we made our first breakthroughs in artificial intelligence, you met our first-generation artificial person, named Sonia."

The crowd cheered.

"Tonight, I would like to reintroduce you to Sonia 2.0," he exclaimed.

The crowd was ecstatic and jumped to their feet. They had no idea that it was Sonia who was seated next to Peter at the podium. Some had their suspicions, but she only looked vaguely familiar. No one could be sure that it was her, as they knew that the real Sonia didn't have the capability to walk. The original Sonia looked like an artificial person and not a real woman. She didn't have any hair, and the back of her head was made of clear plastic and computer components were visible within her artificial skull. This new Sonia was almost an exact replica of a human being. Her skin appeared normal but radiant. Her hair was long, straight, and blond. More noticeable was that she walked and moved just like a normal person.

"Before Sonia speaks to you tonight, we would like to tell you a little story about discovery. If you will kindly pay attention to the screen above, we will begin," said Peter.

The stadium lights went off in a flash, and darkness encompassed the stadium. The only lights visible were for safety, and the light being projected onto the screen. The screen was dark except for a series of numbers being counted down from ten. The countdown got to five, and the crowd got into it and started to count down to zero along with the video. "Five, four, three, two, one, zero," gasped the crowd in unison.

A familiar voice was heard through the speakers as the movie began. The voice was of none other than the gentleman from Hollywood who was well-known for playing God in several recent Hollywood movies, James Richardson. He had a deep, raspy voice, probably because of chain-smoking for years.

"The dawn of man"—the voice began—"since the dawn of man, people have looked to technology to make life easier. The invention of the wheel brought people commerce and the ease of transporting goods and services. The discovery of fossil fuels led to an explosion in invention. Humanity has always been on the search of new technologies in order to improve life. The first men came to us from space dust, and they crawled out of the world's oceans. Technology took people from a primitive being and turned them into superior beings that have leaped for the stars and landed on the moon. Computers changed the way we communicate with one another, long gone are the days when people rode horses to deliver news or sent pigeons to notify of urgent situations. Computers have allowed for the missions to the moon and the most recent trip to mars. Without technology, man would still be stuck in the age of stone tools and famine," he exclaimed.

Peter sat quietly in his seat with his hands folded neatly in his lap. His nervousness had long faded, and he was content with the progression of the evening. He worried, in the back of his mind, that some hecklers could still get in, but he made sure that anyone who appeared to be a part of the religious right would not be allowed into the building. His security was on the lookout for anyone with religious paraphernalia or dressed in clothing with religious symbols on it. Identifying people of faith was generally easy. They usually were dressed in a more conservative style and were noticeably absent of the wristwatch computers. Anyone not wearing the watch was automatically a suspect.

Peter knew that there were few in the fringes of the right that would wear the watches, but he also knew who those few were. Charles and his congregants were rather easy to spot on a good day, because their identities were captured in previous events. Facial recognition cameras made it easy to identify just about anyone, so Peter was relatively sure that he would be able to prevent these few individuals from entering the arena.

Peter was so afraid of religious people attempting to ruin his event that he advised his security to ask anyone who was not wearing the wristwatch computers a simple question. The question was simple and would easily weed out the overly religious people from those who were not. The question was "How do you feel about evolution?" Anyone answering that evolution was a myth or that it wasn't true would be kept from entering the arena. Most religious people don't believe in evolution, so anyone having a problem with the theory of evolution would immediately be suspect for being overly religious and would be kept out. Those few who identified as religious and believed evolution generally were not the type that have a problem with artificial intelligence, so asking this question would simply ensure that no overly religious people entered. Peter knew that it wasn't a perfect way to keep the religious people out, but between his facial recognition and list of repeat offenders and his questioning; he knew that his chances of having a fanatic-free evening were greatly increased.

The video continued. "The progress of tomorrow is no longer limited by the computing power of the human mind." The speaker concluded.

The crowd went crazy. The people leaped to their feet. Loud whistles and boisterous cheering abounded. The stadium was shaking from the thunderous cheers. The people were excited to say the least.

The lights in the stadium returned in a blinding flash. The cheering in the crowd grew louder. The cheers were sustained without a break for what seemed like an hour, even though it had only been a couple of minutes. Sonia slowly raised from her seat and moved over to the podium.

"Thank you," Peter exclaimed loudly. "I would like to introduce our latest breakthrough—Sonia, 2.0!"

The crowd, still on their feet, grew loud again with their cheers and feet stomping rattling the stadium. It was like a miniature earthquake.

"Please, please take your seats!" he exclaimed.

Sonia began to speak. "Thank you! I am Sonia."

The crowd jumped up yet again and cheered again and then sat back down. The precession of standing and sitting again, repeatedly, was like a Saturday morning at mass in a Catholic church. Sonia scanned the crowd and remained silent. She waited for the crowd to quiet down before speaking again.

"Today is a great day for humanity. I am the first in a line of superintelligent machines, created for the sole purpose of assisting people like you. I was created for the purpose of assisting the human race and for no other purpose. When people are in need, I will be here. When people are sad, I will be here. The applications for the entire human race are immeasurable. I am a caregiver. I am a companion. I am a communicator. I am the product of twenty-first-century technology. I am the answer to many problems plaguing the human race," she concluded.

Peter returned to the podium. "Now that we have the formalities out of the way, we will begin to take questions. In fairness, we will be limiting people to one question each, and we will be holding people to this. I'm sure that in the days to follow that there will be more questions, and we will be happy to answer them as they come."

Peter paused for a moment and then resumed. We will be releasing information to the news media over the next few weeks, so if you follow the news releases, you may find the answers that you seek in those news releases. With that, we will take our first question of the evening."

Peter looked directly at the center of the first row. "You, miss, excuse me, but I don't remember your name."

He knew Laura very well, but he didn't want the world to know that he was picking his friend for the first question.

"Thank you," she said. "I'm Laura Stroud, and I'm with action news *Phoenix*," she exclaimed. "I am sure that most people want to know, but what would you say that the benefit is to the average person? Why would people want a machine that can outperform the human intellect or the other AI machines before it?"

Peter sunk back a bit. He wasn't expecting to have to answer such a deliberate question right out of the gate. He assumed that the questions he would receive would be about how useful that they expected the new AIs to be or if there was a potential cure for a disease on the horizon. This question was more along the lines of ethics and really was more suited to people like Charles and his group of fanatics. He was aghast that his friend would betray him in such a manner as to go beyond protocol and ask a deep and ethical question.

He regained his composure for a moment. "I'm sorry, Laura, was it? Well, frankly, we expect several great things from Sonia and every synthetic that we have created. We expect that there will be research on everything from apples to xylophones and everything in between. While we don't have any absolute goals for the machines, we do have some that we are considering. For example, we are looking into a model for home health care. We are also considering a model for childcare. The potential is unlimited."

Peter was beginning to get nervous, and he took his left index finger and placed it between his shirt collar and his neck. His tie suddenly felt constraining, and he placed his finger there in an attempt to loosen it a bit. He scanned the crowd to find another reporter and, over on the left side in the second row, saw a familiar *National News* reporter named John Eubanks. "John, I believe that you were next," said Peter.

John stood up and looked at his notes. "Thank you. I think that what most Americans really want to know is, how we can sleep at night knowing that we have these machines running around autonomously. How can you assure the public that the proper fail-safes have been put into place to prevent malfunctions and people from being harmed?"

Once again, Peter was taken aback. He was not liking the line of questioning he was receiving. With all the fanfare and other pomp, he expected more excitement and questions that emphasized the good that could come from a breakthrough such as this.

"John, that is a great question, and I think that it is a question that I will let Sonia answer. We knew from the beginning that safety was of the utmost concern, and we have made every precaution possible to prevent a negative event. Sonia, would you be so kind?"

"Thank you, Dr. Jensen. I would be more than happy to respond to this question," said Sonia.

Sonia rose up from her seat and took a spot next to Peter at the podium. She scanned the audience for a moment and then looked down at John, who asked the question.

"In the early days of artificial intelligence, people worried about fail-safes and safety measures to prevent errors from occurring. The fail-safes that were in place at the time consisted of programming that would ensure a safe outcome. One of the biggest concerns always has been that a machine would not serve the same interests as a human when asked to perform a certain task. For example, if a human were to ask an artificial person to take him to the airport "as fast as possible," would the artificial person or other intelligent machine do this literally, or would the machine know enough as to do it quickly and in a safe manner? I am sure that we can agree that absent the knowledge of figures of speech, the machine could just go as fast as possible without thinking of the repercussions and accomplish the task and cause accidents and injury along the way. This would not be safe, so when we designed our programming, we included algorithms to understand all figures of speech as well as what humans call sarcasm. This is one of thousands of such algorithms that have been created in order to create a machine that cannot cause harm to a human or other living being. Does this answer your question, John?"

John looked contented with the response. Knowing that he could not ask a follow-up question, he quietly took his seat.

The remaining questions took another hour to be asked and answered. The overwhelming majority of the questions were regarding safety and the ability to shut down the machines if needed. The questions were all answered in a way that left the news media and the people in attendance without worry. If there was any worry, it didn't show in any of the audience members.

The presentation ended with no major hiccups and no protests. This was something that Peter worked hard to avoid. The excitement died down more and more as the people left the building and the area became quieter. For Peter, the event could not have been more of a success.

CHAPTER 4

Rumors of War

The fanfare of the artificial intelligence conference died down over the next few weeks. The news folks never really liked to dwell on one thing for too long and was always looking for that next big news story. Since artificial intelligence had been out for quite some time, a rollout of a new and smarter AI may have been a huge breakthrough but wasn't something that would last in the normal news cycle.

The latest news that Charles was hearing was all about politics and financial woes for the country. The country had been in a recession for several years because of climate change and food shortages from crop failures. There was little news on anything outside the normal format. That's the way the news was in this era. The format was always the same. It was a mix of the woes of the world and how the government would save the people from those woes. There was the occasional break from this, but by the time the actual news made it through the government censorship machine, it didn't really classify as news any longer.

The news on the new advances in artificial intelligence just didn't have any staying power. That was more than likely because the political figures of the day hadn't found a way to exploit it yet. As far as the public was aware, the technology wasn't really all that big of a deal. They really didn't know enough about the project as to form an opinion in favor or against it. Only the true hardliners stayed on top of this kind of stuff, and they would get their news from the black-market internet news outlets that reported on niche items such as this.

When artificial intelligence was first made public to people, the media made it out to be the next best thing. Artificial intelligence was touted as the answer to the world's problems. The government was heavily invested in the AI business, and in order to have the public on board, they talked about it daily and for months. Now that the conference was over and the money already spent, the government didn't really see a need to report on it as much.

Charles was extremely interested in artificial intelligence. He researched every bit of news that he could find on the subject and was known to frequent every internet news site that he could. He was especially interested in the new superintelligence that was developed. He didn't trust AI, and he didn't trust the government. He was not in favor of any machine that could potentially cause harm to others and certainly was fearful of a machine that could do more than the old AI standard of answering basic questions and moving a couple arms, followed by an eerily fake smile. He feared the potential of a machine that somehow was able to liberate itself and not have the interests of people at heart.

Charles was home resting after a long day that consisted of two funerals, a wedding, and four hospital visits. A minister had several different hats to wear, and it wasn't all about standing behind a podium preaching. A minister became a part of a larger family when he took on a leadership role. When one had a hundred families that he was a part of, he tended to stay busy. With the food shortages throughout the world, it seemed as if the funerals and hospital visits were without end.

Charles was no slacker, and when he would rest, he would rest hard. His choice of relaxation technique was working in his garden. While the average person would view this as more work, Charles found it to clear his mind and help him relax.

Maintaining a garden in Phoenix could be quite the challenge. Charles's garden was filled with tomatoes, cucumbers, and lettuce.

He loved to eat bacon, lettuce, and tomato sandwiches, so he would grow these vegetables because of it. He seemed to like the bacon more than the other two ingredients, but no one created a technology for growing bacon without raising a pig. This would be a technological advance that Charles would be on board with, but he knew that it would never happen.

The great thing about gardens in Phoenix is that they aren't prone to the vast array of insects and other pests that one would find in other states, such as Florida or New York. Since it is a desert climate, insects are far and few between.

The drawback of maintaining a garden in the desert was that the climate was excessively hot during the day and cooler than preferable during the night. Keeping the temperatures exactly right and maintaining a good humidity was a challenge. This was the main reason that Charles built the greenhouse out of glass rather than just some corrugated plastic panels. The garden required a lot of water because of the arid climate, so he used a combination of a drip irrigation system and a misting system.

The greenhouse was cooled with a small window air conditioner set in the back wall. He put the air conditioner in it to prevent the temperature from becoming unbearably hot for the plants. When he first started gardening, he didn't have the air conditioner, and the temperatures inside the greenhouse got so hot that all his plants died. Putting the air conditioner inside allowed the place to be cooled and keep it at a range that was good for the plants and for him. It had to be comfortable for him because he liked to be able to spend long periods inside.

Charles loved to spend time out in his garden, but another thing that he loved just as much was arguing with people. It didn't matter what the topic was, he would argue just for the sake of arguing. When it came to things that he was passionate about, he would make it look like a sport.

A common argument for him was about how gardening in Arizona was spectacular. He personally thought that it was a great state for growing gardens and would brag about it often. Others that he would meet didn't always agree and would often tell him that gardening was best suited for states that had a lot of greenery. What those unsuspecting people didn't know was that Charles could spend hours debating them on the topic and love every second of it.

On other occasions, he would argue with strangers that he would meet while he was out and about. He could somehow spot someone from outside of the area, and whenever he did, he made it a mission to bump into them and mention how Arizona is the true sunshine state. Since most of the travelers he has met were from the eastern part of the US, they would disagree and tout Florida as the sunshine capital of the US. He would gleefully begin his arguing and cite the occurrence of rainstorms in Florida as his basis of fact on why Florida really isn't as sunny. He would argue that it was generally sunny in Florida, but that Phoenix historically has more sun-filled days than Florida because it rarely rains in Arizona.

When Charles was a police officer, he spent a lot of time arguing with people. The people would argue about the speed that they were traveling, how they really didn't notice the street signs and just about every other reason that they could think of in order to keep from getting a citation. When he left that line of work, he kept the habit of arguing with people.

Charles kept a small radio in his greenhouse, as well as a police scanner. He kept the scanner inside his greenhouse because it was where he tended to spend much of his free time. He was no longer a police officer, but he still had that police-officer air about him and was always interested in knowing what was going on around him.

Charles was usually busy with his church obligations, so getting some time in his garden was a treat for him. Oftentimes, he would take a book along with him and would just sit in the small padded chair he had set in the back corner and read. Plants aren't generally conversational, so it tended to be a great place to read a book or listen to the radio. The misters only sprayed over the plants, so the greenhouse would be somewhat like the state of Florida, after an afternoon rain shower. It was warm but not hot, and it was humid but not wet.

"Oh, my!" said Charles, as he held up a bright-red tomato.

Charles would often talk to himself when he was alone. He would also talk to his plants.

"This has got to be the biggest tomato that I have ever seen," he said with a huge grin.

He stared at the tomato, admiring it. The tomato was still attached to the vine, and he turned it back and forth, looking for any kind of defect. He had a slight grin on his face and a look of pride.

"Boy, oh boy, that is a nice one!" he said as he reached for his garden shears. He brought the shears close to the vine and gently clipped the tomato from the vine. The tomato was the size of a softball and as brilliant red as he had ever seen.

"You, sir, are coming with me," he said to the tomato.

Charles was comforted because he knew that he would be eating another bacon-lettuce-and-tomato sandwich for his dinner. He couldn't resist after seeing such a fine specimen of tomato. He gently set the tomato into a small basket that he kept under his workbench.

He was trying to lose weight, and he figured that the BLT was a surefire way to eat somewhat healthy and to also enjoy what he was eating. He figured that a little bit of bacon wasn't going to worsen his condition and that the slight amount of mayonnaise was a far cry from the sauces that he would normally enjoy.

"So, gals and guys, let's see what we can see on the radio. How about that?" he said cheerfully while looking at his plants.

Charles moved over to the back of the greenhouse and sat down in his chair. He kicked his feet up onto a small round footstool that he had sitting next to the chair. The footstool had a dingy floral pattern on it and a few tears in the cloth.

"Oh, there we go," he said in approval as he nestled into his seat. He leaned over slightly and gave out a slight grunt as he was reaching for the lamp's On switch. "Unhfff," he grunted. He had the chair set just a little too far from the lampstand.

"There we go," he said after finally turning on the switch.

Turning on the radio didn't present the same challenge as the lamp. He had been in this very situation previously and fixed the problem. He had one end of remote tied to a small length of twine, and the other end of the twine was connected to bamboo-like arm of the chair, by way of some gray duct tape. He used the remote for turning the radio on and off and adjusting the volume. He wasn't awfully familiar with the functions on the remote, so for tuning, he just turned the knob on the front of the radio.

He pressed the On button, and sounds of music mixed with static suddenly filled the room. The radio was somehow on an AM channel and was picking it up very faintly. The music was hard to make out, and there was just enough of a melodic sound flashing in and out to tell that it was a song that was playing and not just some random noise.

"That's not going to work," he said to the tomato as the noise screeched out of the radio. He looked at the tomato plants with a concerned look. It was if he was checking to see if the annoying sounds had in some way affected them.

"I don't think that's the kind of stuff you are all wanting to hear, is it?" he said as he sat back down into his chair. "Did one of you somehow change it to this peach of a channel?" he asked the tomato plant on the end of the bench. After realizing that he was talking to a tomato plant, he looked back toward the radio and swiftly pointed the remote at it. "I suppose not," he said with a disappointed tone.

Rather than selecting the channel number directly, he turned the dial repeatedly to the right. The radio whirled, past the various stations, and all that could be heard was a mixture of garbled chatter with the occasional melodic tone or two. He flew through the channels as he turned the dial, and when he reached the end of the dial, he slowed down and began twisting the knob back and forth.

"Whoever developed this dial was a moron!" he exclaimed. "Why couldn't they just give radios channels like a television?"

He continued to turn the knob to the left and right, and finally, the radio sounded off with clear-sounding channel. Had he read the manual on the remote, he may have been able to save time by going directly to his channel of choice, but he didn't. Charles wasn't the type to read an operating manual, and when he got this radio, he threw the operating manual into the trash, just after pulling it out of the box.

After he reached his normal radio news station, he was interrupted by a sharp and stinging pain in his leg.

"Ouch!" he proclaimed while jumping up out of the chair.

The remote fell from his hand and fell to the floor as he investigated the reason for the pinching feeling that he had on his right upper thigh.

"Stupid radio!" he shouted.

The radio started blaring out a plethora of words in the background. "Breaking news…Israeli forces…sirens."

Charles was a bit confused because he was only half listening to the broadcast as he hunted down the perpetrator of his leg pain. He heard enough to know that the there was some kind of attack in Israel or possibly Damascus.

Charles looked at the chair and, sitting right next to the armrest support, in the seat cushion, laid a small tack. The tack must have somehow fell off the tiny corkboard that he had set up on the wall.

"How in the world did you get there?" he asked. "If I didn't know any better, I would think that you were planted there by those roughhousing tomatoes or that I was suddenly growing roses with a bad attitude." He looked up at the corkboard and knew immediately where it came from. "I may have to find a new home for you," he said grudgingly as he looked angrily at the corkboard.

The corkboard wasn't exceptionally large and was sitting to the right side of the air-conditioning unit. He used the bulletin board for posting notes on his planting and watering schedule and other things that were important enough to reference.

As he returned to his seat, he began to listen to the news still coming out of his little one-speaker radio. The tack, penetrating his leg, caused him to be quite distracted from the news that had just been reported. The reporters were now talking about a collision that had traffic jammed up near the airport. Charles was intensely curious as to the earlier story and hoped that by turning the radio to his second favorite station that he would be able to hear the entire news report.

"I think we had better turn it to that other station," he said as he glanced back at his tomato plants.

He sat back down in his chair and leaned over to the radio. He began turning the dial repeatedly to the left, and the familiar collage of sounds flowed out of the radio. Once he reached his normal station, he twisted the knob back and forth until he got a somewhat clear signal. He immediately heard the reporters talking in a hurried and serious tone. The reporters on this station usually spoke in a laid-back manner, so the change in their normal pattern of speech piqued his interest on the news story.

"This can't be good," he said as he sat back into his chair.

"Early this morning, Israeli forces were awoken by the sounds of air-raid sirens and explosions. Missiles, thought to have originated from Damascus and from Iranian ships located near the Port of Sudan, struck near the West Bank areas of Ramallah and Jericho. The Gog Golshiri regime of Iran has claimed responsibility for the attack. The missiles were reportedly fired in retaliation to an earlier air strike carried out by the Israeli Air Force within the past forty-eight hours. That strike was centered on a target at Khmeimim Air Base in Syria," the reporter bellowed.

"Jericho? Port of Sudan? Why would they be? That's impossible," he said with a puzzled expression on his face, questioning what he heard. "Why in the world would Iran be firing missiles from the Port of Sudan?"

Charles leaped from his chair a second time. It almost appeared as if he had been pricked by the same thumbtack twice, but he hadn't. This time, it was because the news startled him. He had to get inside the house. He had to talk to Chris.

He ran to the door as quickly as he could muster. He fumbled to open the door and was in such a hurry that he fell forward when the door opened. He moved so fast that he couldn't keep up with his own momentum. He picked himself up from the ground and resumed running toward the rear door of his house. He reached the door and turned the knob, but the door was locked.

"Not now! Of all the times to forget my keys!" he yelled in frustration.

He rushed back to the greenhouse, but this trip wasn't quite as fast as the first. He sprinted so hard on his first race to the house that he tired himself out. He hadn't exercised like that in years, and his body just couldn't maintain a quick sprint.

He reached the greenhouse door and went inside. The radio was still playing, and he could hear that they were still talking about the attack on Israel. The voices on the radio were now different because it was now 6:00 PM, and the hosts of the radio program changed, and a new news program was now playing.

Tired from his recent relay race, he sat back down in his chair. His breathing was rapid as if he were still running at a full pace. He leaned in toward the radio and turned the volume knob up slightly. He could hardly make out the words over his heavy breathing.

The reporter that was speaking was a woman named Jill Royce. Charles recognized her voice almost immediately. She interviewed Charles during the first AI announcement in the early 2020's and wasn't exceedingly kind in her interview. She referred to Charles as a fanatic and mocked him throughout the interview.

"I see that she got promoted from her last job," muttered Charles with a bit of disgust.

Charles sat in the chair with his arms resting on both armrests, and his feet flexed outward from the chair in a V shape. His breathing started to slow, and he could hear the radio a little better.

*****

"Yes, James, they did do that, but it was in self-defense. That air base was used as a staffing point for air attacks for the past four years."

James responded, "All I am saying is that if Israel expects no response for a blatant attack on Russian and Syrian forces, then they need to have a reality check. They didn't respond in any kind of equal fashion. When Russian forces fired those missiles last month, it was due to a failure in their aircraft's targeting computer. It was an accident, and those who investigated it with the UN Security Council have said themselves that it was purely accidental."

"Jim, you are so much like your father that it's scary sometimes. Everyone knows that it was no accident. The UN is being governed by a known patsy of the Russians. They lost the last bit of credibility that they had when they allowed—"

"Here we go again!" James interrupted.

"If you would let me finish," Jill replied. "What I was trying to say was that, a leader from a Muslim nation is always going to side with another Muslim nation."

There was a slight pause for a moment. James then responded in a slow and calm voice, "Russia is hardly a Muslim nation. They may have a sizable population of Muslims, but they still have a large Christian population."

"Okay, James, I see how you want to play it," she replied sarcastically.

"What do you mean?" James questioned.

"If a nation elects a Muslim president and every other political office holder is Muslim, then that pretty much makes it a Muslim nation," Jill said in a condescending tone. "They may have a Christian minority, but that means nothing in a state where sharia, its law, is king. The whole nation is backward now. Besides, they aligned themselves with almost every Muslim nation in the Middle East, less than a year after Golshiri took power in 2029. If that doesn't make them a Muslim nation in your eyes, then you need a reality check."

There was a slight pause as James thought of a rebuttal to Jill's argument.

*****

Meanwhile, Charles looked perplexed as he sat in his chair. He was still exhausted from his sprint and needed to rest for a few more moments, but the arguing back and forth on the radio was not making his mood any better.

Frustrated by the arguing, he yelled out to his plants, "Is this a news report or a debate?"

*****

"We will just have to agree to disagree," said James. "President Golshiri is a good man and has done a lot of good for Syria and Iran. They could have just flat out taken over those two countries a few years ago. They didn't. After the Assad regime fell, then President Putin could have just annexed Syria like they did the Crimean Peninsula," James said forcefully.

Jill continued to argue with James, and the elevation in her voice revealed her anger toward him.

"They may as well have annexed it. When a country parks half its military in a foreign land, that's more of a conquest than it is anything else," she argued. "What do you call it?"

James let out a gasp as he responded. The frustration was noticeable. "Well, the US has had a military presence around the globe for years. Now you know what nations like Iraq and Korea felt for years. They were told by countless politicians that they were there to keep the peace, but how in the world can you call fifteen-plus years of war peace? It wasn't until three years ago that the people finally were liberated," said James.

"Liberated?" Jill chuckled. "Pulling out the troops from the Middle East and Korea was the dumbest thing anyone could have ever done."

The arguing back and forth was like watching a ball in a tennis match. They volleyed their responses back with a ferocious speed and a fervent desire to win. Charles didn't know that this was a news report any longer. The news had been replaced with a history lesson on the military strategies of countries in the Middle East.

The arguing continued as Charles regained his composure.

"And look at what it has done for the whole world!" James retorted. "There hasn't been a full-fledged war in the Middle East since those troops were pulled. Aside from a rogue missile here and there, it has been relatively peaceful," he explained.

*****

Charles sat there in his chair, hoping he would hear more about the details of the air strike, but all he kept hearing was commentary and the back-and-forth ranting of two opposing idealists. He felt like he was back in the era of bipartisan politics, where there was generally a healthy debate between the two major parties. With the government reforms of the day, the debating was still there, but it lacked a fiery passion and usually centered on whose brand of liberal policies were better. This discussion was more like the debates of old, where one side would be hawkish and the other side leaning more toward making peace.

Charles was glad to hear what sounded like conservatism being argued, even if it was only for a few minutes on the radio. Conservatism wasn't a popular ideal any longer, and anyone who sounded like a conservative was usually branded as a fanatic, like him.

Charles leaned into his radio and turned off the power. He sat quietly for a few seconds and just stared out into the room, with a blank expression on his face. He knew that any news out of Jerusalem was important news, but he also knew that if he wanted any real news, he would have to get it from a credible source. He would have to get his news on Israel from someone who had ties to Israel. The news coming out of Israel was too important to just ignore. The whole world seemed to revolve around the happenings in Israel since the beginning of human existence.

He got up from his chair and walked calmly to the door. He now had the keys to the back door of his house. He approached the door slowly, unlocked it, and went inside. Now that he was inside, he was feeling a bit tired and a bit run-down. His excitement died down a bit after listening to the talking heads bantering back and forth about the politics of the day. He realized that it wasn't as big of a deal as it sounded. Sure, Israel fired some missiles. Sure, Russian forces fired back. This wasn't anything earth-shattering. Those two nations were always known for such back and forth. The only thing that was new about it was that they were now lobbing missiles at each other rather than at others.

Charles walked to his kitchen and stopped by the wall, next to his refrigerator. On the wall was an old-school rotary phone with a cord that was so long that it could strangle half of Maricopa County. He looked at it as if it were quite the prized possession. *Am I the only person in the world who still has a rotary phone?* he wondered. There couldn't be many in existence if there were any at all. His was canary yellow with a little bit of fading.

The cord was skin-toned-peach and about twenty feet long. The cord dangled next to his refrigerator like the pendulum on a grandfather clock, every time that he walked past it. It was almost as if the cord was taunting him. As he walked up to the cord, it began its typical dance and moved back and forth. Charles got a shuddering feeling and had a flashback of the last time he attempted to untangle it. He learned the hard way that phone cords like his could get twisted around a person and strangle them like a python. It was after that debacle that he decided that he would just let the cord be and take on any shape that it desired. Even twisted into a ball, it was enough to reach his recliner in the next room, and if he could get there without incident, he would be satisfied.

Cords like his would be next to impossible to find if he needed to replace it. If he did need one, he could probably find one online at one of those online antique shops or the "Gotta Have It" app, but it would probably cost an arm and a leg. He thought, jokingly, that the cost of an arm or a leg was likely due to previous python-like events that others have also suffered.

He pulled the numbers on the phone, one by one. The first number, a six, seemed like it took an hour to return to its starting position. Frustratingly, he assumed that a spring in the phone must be caught in its own cord-like event, because it was painfully slow and the normal clicking sounds were replaced by Morse code sounds. It was almost as if the phone was sending out an SOS, asking for mercy and to be finally tossed out. If the six wasn't bad enough, the zero that followed took almost twice as long as the previous number. The Morse code that emanated in Charles's imagination, this time, was "Can you hear me? I said 'SOS.'"

The zero always puzzled Charles. One would think that the zero would snap right back, without even a click. After all, it was a zero. Logic dictated that a one would have one click, and a nine would have nine. It only made sense to Charles that the zero would follow suit, but it didn't. It was a painful joke that the manufacturers must have intentionally played on every unsuspecting buyer. It was as if some disgruntled engineer or designer had just been told that he was going to have to work the weekend or that he was getting laid off soon. He could picture a frustrated worker, intentionally tampering with the design, in retaliation for the extra helping of work that he received. That angry engineer played the whole world by giving them ten long and painful clicks, when they would clearly expect one.

It was probably the straw that broke the camel's back from a phone improvement perspective. The push-button phone came out relatively quickly after the rotary phone. Charles naturally assumed that it was because the slow clicking drove the entire rotary dialing world nuts. He surmised that new designers were hired to stop the bleeding at the phone company and were ordered to work in a furious fervor to get a new phone design out as quickly as possible.

Well, that's one way to sell a lot of replacement phones, Charles thought humorously.

Charles trudged forward, regretting his previous decision to keep the old rotary phone. Surely this would be the one antique that people would remember solely for the feelings of great joy that they experienced when they were finally able to afford a new model.

The phone started ringing on the opposite end of the line. After the fourth ring, Charles thought that all his dialing was in vain, but he wasn't about to let go that easy. He knew that he easily had three rings left before the answering party would assume that it was a determined telemarketer or a disgruntled friend or family member and ignore the call.

"Come on, come on," Charles muttered into the receiver.

Just as Charles was just about to give up, he heard a clicking sound and then the voice of his friend.

"Uh, hello?" Chris asked in a cynical and curious manner.

"Chris, is that you?" Charles asked. "Where are you at right now?"

"Well, considering that you just called my home number, I would have to say that I am at home. Who is this?" he asked.

"It's me," Charles responded. "It's Charles."

"Oh, thanks for making me think that I was being phone-stalked again. That's the drawback on putting my number on brochures," he said jokingly. "What's up?"

"I was just wondering if you caught that news report," he said emphatically.

"Actually, I did and believe it or not, I was going to call you to see if you had heard it," Chris responded. "What do you make of it?"

Charles calmed down a bit and responded, "I think that we may want to reconsider that trip to Jerusalem. If they are lobbing missiles at each other, then that's the last place that we should be. Do you think?"

"Let's take a wait-and-see approach," Chris responded calmly. "We have a lot of nonrefundable tickets that we don't want to lose out on. Besides, our trip isn't for months from now. Let's see what happens in the next few weeks, and if it's the same old business as usual, then I think it will be fine. Sound good?"

"Yeah, that is what I was thinking too. I'll give you a call when we get closer to our trip date, and we can go from there," Chris replied.

"Sounds great. I'll talk to you later," Chris responded.

After exchanging pleasantries, they both hung up their phones. Charles was hungry now, and the excitement and trailing exercise got his appetite ready for a bacon-lettuce-and-tomato sandwich.

CHAPTER 5

Brinksmanship

The missile attack on Israel by the Golshiri regime was the first missile strike in Israel in a few years. The last missile strike in Israel occurred in 2027 and was carried out by Syrian forces, in retaliation for an earlier strike by Israeli forces.

Tensions in the region were high for a number of years prior to 2027. The Syrian civil war went on for years, and over this period, the Russians kept increasing their military presence. The tensions reached their breaking point when Russian, Syrian, and Turkish forces amassed on the border in fall of that year. Russia moved several mobile rocket launchers toward the border, and Israel called it an act of aggression.

In response to the buildup, Israeli forces moved closer to the border in an attempt to stave off the aggressions. Russian officials stated at the time that the placing of the equipment along the border was for strategic purposes and pertained to the civil war, but Israeli officials called it a ruse to invade. Israel took an offensive stance and fired at the mobile launchers, destroying six in total. After the shots were fired, Russia moved their equipment further north in an attempt to prevent further escalation.

The border between northern Israel and Syria has been known as "the purple line, or also known as the cease-fire line" since the

1973 Yom Kippur War. The border has been one of contention between Israel and Syria since the end of that conflict. It has operated somewhat similarly to the demilitarized zone in the Koreas, prior to reconciliation between those two countries in 2026. The line was set up as a kind of border between Syria and Israel after the 1973 war after a cease-fire was reached.

The civil war was all but over by the end of 2029, just months after the new Golshiri regime took control on the ground and brokered a peace deal within Syria. When they came to power, a new world power was born. The regime was able to unite a number of nations and, in the process, end the civil war in Syria.

The primary nations in the Golshiri regime included Russia, Iran, Syria, Turkey, Ethiopia, Sudan, and Libya. The media was responsible for the name Gog Golshiri regime. It came about after the treaty was signed in 2029 between Russia, Iran, and Syria, at the end of the civil war in Syria. Russia didn't keep its promises to the leaders of Syria in their support of the Assad regime, and when the civil war ended, they took control of Syria as a territory of Russia. They sought to annex it into Russia but decided to set up their own puppet government instead. They did just that and established their own military bases in the region "to control the peace."

Gog Golshiri was elected president after Putin ended his last term in the late summer of 2029. At that time, the Russian economy was in turmoil. Natural gas prices plummeted across the globe, causing the Russian economy to fall into a major recession. The recession caused high unemployment, which meant that the people couldn't feed their families. Food shortages in Europe, caused by climate change, only made the problems worse. Putin was blamed for the ills and lost the election in favor of Golshiri, who promised to bring a new prosperity to the country.

The Muslim population in Russia grew at a rapid pace at the end of the twentieth century, and by 2029, was just large enough to get Golshiri elected. He made promises that specifically pandered to the Muslim population. He promised to eliminate unemployment. He promised to end the food shortages. He also promised to change the laws of the country to reflect the values of the Muslim population by enacting sharia throughout the region. When he made these promises, the Muslim population in the country stood together and voted as a block and sealed a narrow victory for him.

Golshiri's popularity rose quickly after he took power because he kept his promises to his Muslim constituents, and in his first one hundred days, he and his party worked feverishly to change the country into a quasi-Muslim state. They changed parts of their constitution to enact a series of laws that modeled sharia laws. They didn't openly call it sharia, but that is what it was.

After Golshiri transformed Russia, he set his sights on Syria and ended the civil war that raged for years. Other leaders in the Middle East quickly took notice of his achievements and warmed up to him rather quickly. They signed a treaty with the Golshiri regime that was similar to the European Union. This brought them together as the world's first Muslim super alliance. The leadership of the treaty nations agreed that they would be much more powerful, economically, and militarily if they had a solid alliance with other nations and a standing army to defend their alliance nations.

Israel had been enjoying years of peace, even though there were no formal peace deals in place. Iran was not as threatening to them for several years because the Iranians were busy keeping their military assets ready for a potential war with Russia. Russia looked as if they were going to begin conquering everyone in the Middle East at one point. They had their military assets spread around in Syria in such a way that it looked as if they were about to invade every nation that surrounded Syria. The Iranians were also busy fighting continued famine and daily protests, aimed at the government because of skyrocketing inflation and high unemployment. With these distractions, Israel became more of an afterthought and the focus was primarily on protecting themselves.

When the Golshiri regime took over in Syria, the civil war ended rapidly. The economy turned around and the country went from being a battered and war-torn cesspool to one that flourished. The Iranians saw the transformation and seized upon the opportunity to align with the new "Muslim Russia." With Golshiri in place, they had no need to defend against Russian aggression and turned their hatred back to Israel and the United States.

With the relative peace in Israel, the US pulled out of the Middle East and Asia after decades of being planted there. The liberal socialist government that came to power saw no need to be the guardians of the planet any longer, and they felt that having troops all over the planet was just causing unnecessary aggression between the US and the rest of the world. The removal of the troops did have a net effect of calming tensions in the Middle East, but Israel was not incredibly happy about the move.

Israel may have had a handful of years of peace, but that didn't comfort the Israeli's much. They still considered their neighbors as potential adversaries and kept themselves prepared to deal with any threat. They really had no choice but to expand their military assets and the overall size of their military. They did this primarily by increasing the number of missiles and warheads capable of long-range missiles that they owned as well as increasing their naval forces and armored divisions. They knew that if they had to defend against an attack, then they would need more armor, so about 50 percent of their budget increases were dedicated to the expansion of their armored divisions.

The most recent missile attack had Israeli forces on high alert. Aggression from such a large multinational alliance was a bit different from the norm. In the past, it had always been threats of destruction by Iran or some other nation, but there was no real alliance to speak of. The Muslim world of old was too busy squabbling among themselves. The inner rivalries between the different sects of Islam kept them from being able to align and a disorganized group of Muslim nations was never a real threat to anyone. The rise of ISIS in the past showed that Muslims could align and that there was power in numbers. They somehow settled their differences, and when the Golshiri regime came to power, they made an alignment that rattled the core of the earth.

A few days after the latest retaliatory strikes, the Golshiri forces started to amass along the northern border with Syria. Historically, any time there was a force gathered somewhere in the Middle East, it was a surefire sign that trouble was brewing.

Israel saw the threat and immediately mobilized their Thirty-Sixth Armored Division in the Golan Heights region. They left the bulk of their forces in place around Israel and figured that they would be able to hold any aggression from Syria with this part of their forces, along with their air force. They were used to playing the back-and-forth game among various nations, and even though the numbers were growing into the thousands of troops, they didn't see this as anything more than another attempt at threats of attack. They were relatively certain about this and decided that the one division and the Air Force would be more than capable at holding this small force at bay, if they were to attack.

As the days ticked on, the number of troops near the Syrian border grew. The numbers went from about two thousand troops in a few days to about ten thousand. Israeli leaders still believed that this was nothing more than a show of force and remained at their current threat level.

The United States took a wait-and-see approach with everything because leaders of the day were war-weary and didn't really want to get involved in another Middle Eastern war. The current president was no war hawk, and the Senate was filled with liberal socialists that cringed at the thought of war. Media outlets reported day and night about the buildup in troops and politicians argued that they were not about to get involved in another two decades of war. Their primary argument was that there was simply no funding. The costs of all the social programs in America had the US economy hanging on by a thread and any unexpected expense like this could send the US economy into a downward spiral that would be worse than every recession the US has ever had, combined. This may have been the first time that a liberal Democrat ever argued for policy on not spending and adding to the national debt.

The US sent envoys to Israel, Russia, and Syria. The envoy to Russia was summarily dismissed and not allowed to enter the country. The envoy to Syria was also dismissed, and no word was given as to why. The normal diplomatic cables between the two countries went silent.

The US envoy to Israel assured the Israelis that they would be there if needed. Knowing the current political atmosphere, the Israelis knew this meant that they would be on their own unless things got out of control. The Israelis had known for several years that the US had all but lost all its love for their nation and that, with the current political climate, the alliance between the two was strained more than ever.

The European Union was having struggles of its own and sided with the United States, saying that they too could not afford the costs associated with another Middle East war. They promised support if Israel was attacked, but they were sure to highlight the *if*.

The troop and logistical buildup from the Golshiri regime continued for weeks. Three weeks passed from the time of the missile strike, and envoys from Israel were in constant communication with envoys from the Golshiri regime. By this time, the troop numbers were getting more difficult to count.

The world sat by and watched with bated breath as the rumors of war mounted. The media was primarily focused on the rumors of the day, and they opined that there would be other wars that would start if there was an actual invasion into Israel. Whether the world liked it or not, every nation seemed to be involved in some kind of war—that is, if one listened to the rumor mills that were churning out the rumors 24/7. The media didn't care if there was any truth to it. They saw dollar signs, and during times of economic uncertainty, profits become doubly important.

Meanwhile, the stance of the Golshiri regime was that they were building up troops in defense of their southern border in Syria. They alleged that Israeli aggression in the past few weeks was a sign of a potential invasion and that they were preparing, only in defense of their borders. The world had not seen such brinkmanship on earth since the Cuban missile crisis.

Each side was set and waiting for action. They were set along a line created by the United Nations in 1949, commonly known as the Green Line. It was like a gunfight in the Old West. It was as if two gunslingers were waiting for the other to flinch, before unloading their fury upon each other in a cloud of smoke and a barrage of bullets. The only difference between an Old West gunfight, and this one was really the sheer number of gunslingers and the types of guns. Men in the Old West were known to ride horses, not tanks. Cowboys fired their six shooters, not howitzers. It was as if this was the largest game of chicken known to modern man.

Weeks turned to months. The troop buildup climbed rapidly at first and then, at about a month, started to slow a bit. After about three months, the troop movement stopped completely, and the chessboard was set. Armor units were set in rows on the Syria side of the border, and Israel didn't even flinch. They waited patiently as it all played out. Without so much as a whisper, the two sides sat opposed to each other, each side waiting to see who would fire first.

The media-driven rumor mills were running out of scenarios on what could happen. They still crafted their webs, but the stories were growing old, and a lot of people lost interest. The stalemate seemed as if it would never end. It was eerily similar to the buildups at the demilitarized zone with North Korea after the end of the Korean War. Some of the news pundits joked that the world has missed the Korean epic that wrote itself into history and that the world was just seeing a shift in the geographical location of that tale. They mused that the end of the Korean stalemate was a way to return to a sense of normalcy around the globe, as if the world needed a good stalemate. They said that when the Koreas finally reconciled, then it triggered an "aggression deficit" in the world and that the Israeli and Golshiri aggression filled the void.

In Europe, Jared won his election to become prime minister of the European Union. He kept a close eye on the Israeli and Golshiri situation. He knew that with tensions high in the region that he may have to act. Being a new face for the European Union meant more scrutiny, and Jared wanted as little of that as possible.

He was the first male prime minister in years, and the fact that he was male and won the election made a lot of people question the validity of the election. There were many that called the election a scam. Some claimed that it was rigged in his favor, while others said that there must have been a technical glitch in the voting machines. It was hard to locate any large group of people that favored him as the new leader, but he did win in what was ultimately penned "a fair election" throughout the media circuits.

People knew that Jared had a background working with I-Corp and that I-Corp was a company that worked with the world's first superintelligence. His critics pointed to that fact and accused him of stealing the election by using his superintelligent machines. They couldn't point to anything real or concrete, so the people ultimately accepted the win.

The other leadership in the European Union continued to follow the news out of the Middle East as well, but their stance remained static, in that they wanted nothing to do with a new world conflict. They preferred to keep their true focus on strengthening their economy and controlling the hyperinflation that plagued them for the past several years.

*****

Meanwhile, in the United States, Charles and Chris were in their last-minute preparations for their trip to Jerusalem. They carefully monitored the situation for months and ultimately decided that they could potentially wait for years to go if they wanted to wait out the aggression in the region. They figured that it would be safer to go sooner rather than later, and by the looks of things, it could be months before anything happened, if at all. One of the main reasons that they didn't cancel the trip was that they had a total of five people who were traveling there for a mission trip, and the other people in the group were dead set on going. No matter what was happening in the region, they were going to Israel.

Another reason that they needed to get there as quickly as possible was that they had plans to meet with David Sumpter, who was an old friend and former colleague of Chris. David was an archaeologist and worked on several dig sites in Jerusalem over a number of years. His current and largest dig site was near the Gihon Springs. He began working the site two years previous and was funded by the Temple Group of Jerusalem. David was fascinated with biblical history and was determined to learn as much about ancient Israel as possible.

David's current dig began after a couple of rare coins were located in the area by a couple teenage boys and their dog. The coins were brought to the Temple Group in order to date them, and when they were confirmed to be from the Herodic period, the Temple Group hired David to do a dig in the area. David was chosen because of his background in theology and because he wasn't as well-known as other archaeologists in the area. The Temple Group wanted the dig to remain as low key as possible, so they chose an archaeologist who was less well-known in order to prevent rumors in the media.

The Temple Group, being the group in charge of rebuilding the Jewish Temple, was constantly under the microscope when it came to archaeological finds related to the First and Second Temples. The region had such a history of violence related to the location of the temples that any time the word *temple* was mentioned, news reporters would pop up like moles in a whack-a-mole game any time the word was mentioned. The media wasn't kind either. Any time that the temples were mentioned, they would inject the words *myth* and *epic story* into their verbiage in an attempt to mock religion. The media was filled with religious skeptics who loved to stir up trouble in the name of ratings. Any time that they could start a fight between Muslims and Jews, they were quick to pounce on the opportunity.

Chris stayed in constant communication with David over the past few weeks. He was a nervous Nancy when it came to putting his group into harm's way and was itching for any opportunity to back out at the last minute. To his and Charles's dismay, David always spoke with a nonchalant attitude regarding the situation in the north. It was if he had some sixth sense about the area and knew that everything would be fine. Every time that Chris and he spoke, he would reassure him and calm him down just enough to keep him from changing his travel plans. Whenever Chris would bring up the words *violence* or *provocation*, David would smooth it over by reminding him that the locals were not worried about the north, and if they weren't worried, then he need not be worried.

After Davis smoothed things out with Chris and reassured him that everything would be fine, Charles and Chris made plans to leave for Tel Aviv. They planned to leave from Phoenix, change to a connecting flight in New York, and eventually arrive in Tel Aviv, where David would pick them up at the airport upon their arrival.

Charles, being his normal, indecisive, and worried self, tried his best to dissuade Chris from leaving before the tensions were resolved in Israel. He went back and forth with Chris for the entirety of the previous week, giving him constant doomsday scenarios to scare him into changing his mind and then would quickly change his tune and try to talk him back into going. He would plant a seed of doubt in his mind very slyly and then, only hours later, recant and tell him how everything would be fine and that God would be looking over them, providing for their safety. One of the things that he told him was that he heard that there was a plan by anti-Israel terrorists to hijack a plane out of New York, headed for Israel, and upon arrival to Israel, fly it into the US embassy in Jerusalem. He let Chris think about the scene he planted and then, an hour later, told him that the security on planes was so good now that hijacking was nearly impossible. It was only at the end of the week that he revealed to Chris that he was just nervous about the trip and that he was conflicted about it. Chris reassured him that everything would be fine and that they needed to have faith that things would proceed as God wanted them to proceed. This made him feel much better, and he eventually relented and agreed that he would stop trying to scare him out of going.

The trip to Israel was a first for Charles. It would be the first time that he ever flew across the ocean, and it would be the furthest trip that he had ever taken. The longest trip that he ever took was to Nogales, Mexico, from Phoenix. He went to Nogales on several different occasions in his younger years. He wasn't as averse to travel when he was younger because he had a rather large group of friends, with whom he would travel, and they always ended up having a great time.

*****

Meanwhile, Peter and I-Corp were silent over the past few months. They had nothing new to report to the general public. They were doing as well as ever and still working with the Department of Defense on their contract to provide a workable AI soldier. That project was huge for I-Corp but slow going because there were several political groups that were opposed to the use of artificial intelligence in a combat role. The deal that they were able to sign was to provide a workable prototype only and nothing more. I-Corp was determined to have the prototype available within two years from their last press release because they didn't want too much time passing in between media announcements. They wanted to slightly remain in the public mind, and timing was everything. If they waited longer than two years between each major news announcement, the people may forget, and forgetting would mean starting a completely new ad campaign. Two years would not look overly aggressive, nor would it be so long that the people forgot who I-Corp was.

CHAPTER 6

The Dig

It was nearing the mid part of February when Charles, Chris, and their four fellow congregants landed in Tel Aviv. It was colder outside than he expected. He walked to the doors of the airport and poked his head outside for a moment and then returned back to the group with a huge perplexed look upon his face.

"What's wrong?" asked Chris.

Charles was sure that it was going to be sunny and warm in Israel. As he stood there looking perplexed, he was sure that he was right about Israel being a tropical paradise. He remembered that before he left Phoenix, he looked at a magazine about Israel and was sure that the photos were of a lush and green paradise. He was sure that Israel was a perpetually warm country. It didn't occur to him to check the weather forecasts before leaving Phoenix.

Charles looked at Chris silently and then nodded as if coming out of a trance. "What?" he asked.

"What's wrong?" asked Chris again, with a hint of a smile on his face.

Chris knew that Charles had either forgotten something or was about to tell him something so far out of left field that he couldn't resist smirking.

"I…um…I"—he started—"never mind," he said with a sigh.

"Well, I'm sure that whatever it is, you'll be fine. Just think, we are going to have a great time!" Chris exclaimed.

Since it was neither hot nor dry outside, Charles was about to learn a valuable lesson in being prepared. Had he known that the temperature would be fifty-five degrees Fahrenheit with light rain, he would have worn something with long sleeves and potentially brought a raincoat with him. It was too late to go back and pack for the trip, so he just decided that he would have to buy a couple long-sleeved shirts from the local shops in Jerusalem.

Chris was well prepared as usual, and so were the four others who came along with them. The rest of the group assumed that Charles knew that the temperatures would be somewhere in the upper fifties to midsixties because they had a short conference call a week prior to leaving. It didn't occur to them that Charles wasn't listening during the call.

Cynthia Dennison was the pianist at the Christ Church of Phoenix, where Charles was the head pastor. She was a former member of Chris's church but left that church for a new one when the opportunity arose for her to take a position as the pianist. There simply was no need for her at Chris's church because he already had a pianist, and that job wasn't going to need to be filled again for years to come.

She was a good friend of Chris's and knew him for about twenty years. Being good friends, Chris told her that once his regular pianist retired that he would give her the job, but that she may have to wait a few years. She was thankful for the offer but felt that if she didn't do it sooner, then she would never really get the opportunity to do it. He offered her the job, knowing that she wouldn't wait for his current pianist to retire, but realized she wouldn't want to wait around for that to happen, so he asked Charles if she could play piano at his church instead. She didn't mind going to the Christ Church because she was familiar with Charles and knew that the message from either church would be the same, so when Charles offered her the position, she took it without a second thought.

Cynthia stared at Charles for a moment, looking him up and down and shaking her head in disagreement. With a huge smile, she belted out a laugh that could be heard in all the other terminals.

"You must be a little cold in those shorts, Charles," Cynthia exclaimed.

"Just a bit," Charles responded softly. "I didn't realize that it got cold here. Apparently, you know more about Israel than I do because you have nice, warm jeans and a lovely sweater."

Charles looked at the other members of the group, and they were all looking at him and smiling. He felt a little stupid for wearing shorts and a T-shirt while they were all wearing warm clothing.

Cynthia giggled softly. "It's not that I know more. I just paid attention on the conference call, and I read the email that Chris sent out last week. Judging by your stylish checkered shorts and that Mickey Mouse T-shirt of yours, I'd have to guess that you didn't?"

Embarrassed, Charles looked around the baggage claim area to see if anyone else was looking at him and laughing.

"Oh, ha ha," he replied sarcastically. "You know that I'm not important enough for an email from Saint Christopher over there."

Chris looked over to Cynthia and Charles and lifted his head slightly as if he were attempting to disguise that he overheard the conversation that the two were having. "Excuse me?" he said with a puzzled look on his face. Chris walked over to Cynthia and dropped his bag onto the floor. Still looking puzzled, he asked, "Who didn't get an email?"

Cynthia knew he overheard the two of them. She is hardly ever accused of being soft spoken, and Charles couldn't be soft spoken if he tried.

"Charles, of course. Isn't it obvious?" she replied.

Chris smiled as he looked at Charles. "Charles is a big boy. I assumed that he was just being optimistic about the weather, and I wasn't going to say a thing." He laughed.

Charles felt even more embarrassed now and started to turn a shade of pink.

"Gee, your vote of confidence makes me feel so warm and fuzzy. I appreciate it so much!" Charles said with a grin.

As Chris picked up his bag and started for the door, he stopped for a moment and turned back toward Charles.

"That's what friends are for. You know that I'm always here for you," he responded.

Cynthia finished looking at her bags and moved over to where June, Tony, and Greg were sitting on a bench conversing. Charles bent over and unzipped his bag, reached in, and pulled out a sweatshirt that he remembered that he packed. He leaped up like he had just found a gold nugget.

"I knew it!" he shrieked. Now beaming, he waved the shirt in the air like he was flagging down a taxi. "You see, folks, if you have a little faith, you will find that God provides, no matter what the circumstances. I knew when I packed this sweatshirt that I was going to end up needing it. I had to talk myself into bringing it, and now I know that it was meant for me to bring it the whole time. It's like I heard a whisper from heaven!"

"Amen to that," said Chris. "Did you happen to pack a pair of pants?"

"I'm not perfect," Charles said, laughing out loud. "What time is David supposed to meet us?"

"Good question. I guess I can call him," Chris responded.

Charles started to look around wildly as if he were looking for someone in the terminal.

"Well, while you are doing that, I am going to see if I can locate a coffee. I hear that they have great coffee here," said Charles.

Charles was really just trying to avoid going outside, and when he saw that everyone started moving toward the door that he needed to say or do something that would allow him to stay inside just a little bit longer.

Chris started to shuffle through his backpack to find his cellular phone. After fishing it out of his bag, he dialed David and began walking outside the airport with the others. Charles walked the opposite direction and headed toward the small coffee shop that was nestled in between a couple car-rental shops.

As Chris walked outside, the phone rang, and David answered.

"David Sumpter," the voice responded.

"Hey, David, it's Chris. We are standing out in front of the airport in Tel Aviv. Were you able to get that van?" asked Chris.

"Got it. How was the flight?" he replied.

"You know, it was typical. We were stuffed into a tight aluminum tube with legroom designed for a child. The food was something less than desirable, and every onboard movie was about some superhero using his magical powers to rid the world of evil. Oh, but they did have good coffee," Chris said jokingly.

"Well, anytime you can take a flight and call it uneventful, it's a good flight. I should be there in about another twenty. Traffic's a bit rough at the moment. See you soon!"

"Sounds good," said Chris, ending the call.

David arrived about twenty-five minutes later. He pulled up in a white Toyota van that appeared to have a few years on it. It wasn't the cleanest van in the world and had dust and dirt all over it. The seats were a dingy and worn-out blue cloth, and when the doors were opened, there was a smell that could only be described as similar to what one would expect in the world's oldest tow truck or a locker room that hadn't been cleaned in months. There was a strange petroleum-like smell wafting through the air, and the scent of pine from a tree-shaped air freshener dangling from the rear-view mirror. The various aromas circulated through the air, providing a virtual buffet of smells that varied from pleasant to very unpleasant. The cleanliness of the interior of the van was somewhat tolerable, but the smell was a bit annoying.

Since the van had been driven from Jerusalem to Tel Aviv, the interior was warmed up. Charles welcomed the van no matter what the smell was like. He was exuberant that there was heat inside. He wasn't about to become a picky guy when he was badly in need of preventing a case of hypothermia.

The luggage was all strapped to the top of the van, and everyone climbed into the vehicle. The first attempts at getting in the vehicle were not phenomenally successful and consisted of everybody packing in, unpacking, rearranging a bit, and packing in again. After what seemed like twenty minutes of this, everyone was finally set and ready to head to Jerusalem.

Charles was sitting in the front row of the back, with Chris sitting in the front passenger seat. Everyone else was mixed about in the rear. Since everyone was chattering at the same time, it was a bit noisy. The radio was on, but it couldn't really be heard over the sound of the passengers and the heater fan. The fan was blowing like it was on its last leg and about to die. The fan gave out a whining and a rattling sound similar in nature to a drill being used on a low speed.

Charles smiled like a kid in candy store. Just in front of him was a heater vent in the front armrest. It was blowing petroleum-filled air against his left leg and bouncing it up into his face, but this didn't bother him. He was as happy as could be now that he was warm again. Of course, his extreme happiness may also have been caused by the petroleum in the air. Even though everyone was packed into the van, he seemed to be very content in his cramped spot. If anything were bothering him, one would never be able to tell.

It wasn't the most ideal of trip conditions, but it was relatively free as David borrowed the van from his dig site to avoid the cost of a rental car. Everyone expressed the need to watch costs, so David didn't bother looking at rental vehicles. The last thing he wanted was to upset a group of travelers on a shoestring budget. He understood their position though. The life of the archaeologist is not the most glamorous life, and one doesn't become an archaeologist because he or she wants to get rich.

David was always enthralled by biblical history. When he learned that someone could make a good living looking for old biblical-era artifacts, he was sold on the idea. He went to school for archaeology at the University of Florida and did a graduate fellowship at Arizona State. That's where he met Chris.

The meeting circumstances were a bit different for David and Chris compared to the meeting circumstances of Charles and Chris. For one, David never used drugs, and he was relatively shy. Shy was one way of describing someone, but never a way that anyone would describe Charles. The two were night-and-day different from each other.

David was out one evening, taking in a movie at the mall, and saw Chris standing outside talking to a couple teenagers about Jesus.

David, always interested in anything to do with the Bible, interjected himself into their conversation. He pounced like a tiger in a rare move for a shy man. This was the one time that David ever interjected himself into anything. Little did he know at the time that this one conversation would lead to one of the best friendships in his lifetime. Chris always had a way with people and could make new friends with ease. David, being shy, was usually as conversational as the people he dug up in various places. If David hadn't had that one rare occasion where he felt the need to speak up, he would likely still have only a handful of friends strewn about the globe.

David moved to Jerusalem about two years after he earned his doctorate and signed on with a local archaeologist named Avraham Denenberg. The two worked together for a couple of years before David was finally able to acquire funding for his own dig. David had a different path in mind compared to what Avraham did, so the two parted ways as colleagues relatively quickly. They remained friends after David left, but they still consult with each other as needed. Avraham worked to discover biblical sites in Jerusalem like David, but he was a secular man and was out to find evidence to disprove Christianity unlike David who was out to prove as much of it as possible. Avraham was a nice man, but he was also a man who was set in his ways and was hardened against anything religious.

After driving for a couple of hours, David pulled into the hotel.

"I hope you don't mind, but I got everyone set up at the Jerusalem Gardens Inn. It's not a fancy-schmancy place, but it's clean. It's comfortable, and it's reasonably priced," he remarked.

"It looks nice," said Cynthia.

Charles's head began bobbing around furiously from window to window in the van. He had a mixed look of both confusion and intrigue on his face

"Are you sure that this is it?" asked Charles. "It looks pretty pricey from the outside."

"Naw, looks can be deceiving my friend," said David. "It looks expensive because it's a high-rise, but the rates are great, and the rooms are nice. Let's just call it a touch of class at the price anyone can afford. Trust me, you'll love it. They have two pools, but they are probably not open during this part of the year. Trust me, you'll love it!"

Charles stared at David for a moment as if he were waiting for more information, but David stopped talking. He wasn't convinced yet, and his look of awe disappeared, and all that remained was the concerned and worried look.

"If you say so," he said sarcastically.

Chris was smiling and holding back his laughter. He didn't want to upset Charles any further and knew that nothing that he could say would change his mind. Charles would just have to see the room price, inside, before he would believe that the rate was actually inexpensive.

"David, you delivered as usual. I knew that having you find the hotel would be so much better than having a bunch of tourists looking around in an unfamiliar place. Once we get checked in, we can head out for some of that world-famous hummus you've been telling us about."

"Works for me. How about the rest of you?" asked David.

It was as if everyone had been practicing their response like a song in the choir. "Yes," they all said in near unison—that is, all except Charles. He still had that worried look on his face and sat there quietly. Chris noticed this immediately and reached out to place his hand on his shoulder.

"Charles, you got this one?" he said with a wry grin.

Charles whipped his head around so fast that it generated a gust of wind back into the back seat.

"What?" he asked fervently.

Chris belted out a huge laugh.

"Wow!" he shrieked as he gasped for air. "I nearly peed myself. Don't worry, buddy, I've got this one!"

Charles didn't look amused. He sunk back into his seat as if he were a turtle and, as he normally does, turned pink from the embarrassment.

After everyone enjoyed a good laugh at Charles's expense, the group squeezed their way out of the van and got to work unloading the luggage rack. Charles was the last person to get out of the van because his ego was bruised slightly. Chris was able to get him to exit the van after he poked his head back inside for a moment and exclaimed about how great it was to get the blood flow back to his lower extremities.

Charles took his statement as an opportunity to save face and immediately agreed with him.

"Yeah," he said with an enthusiastic groan. "When you guys got out, I was able to stretch out my legs inside the van. The blood rushed back so fast that I had to sit and enjoy a good stretch before joining y'all."

It was getting later in the evening now, and the sun was starting to set. A couple of the people in the group said that they were exhausted and wanted to take a shower, order out, and get to bed early. Chris and Charles weren't about to get lackadaisical at this point. They waited for months for their trip to Jerusalem. They had moments where they though that they would never be able to take the trip because of the troop buildup, but even that didn't stop them in the end. They were set on getting to see some of the city and trying the world-famous hummus that David kept talking about. After a short discussion among the members of the group, the only ones that were eager to go out were Charles and Chris.

David came by the hotel later that evening at around 7:00 PM. He arrived in a blue-gray sedan this time as he knew he wasn't picking up an entire group of people. Since it was just Charles and Chris, he knew he could just drive his normal vehicle. His personal vehicle wasn't like the old and dirty minivan, but it wasn't elegant either. It did have the benefit of smelling clean, and there was no petrol smell emanating from the air vents. Other than that, it was modest and plain.

They drove around for about a half hour before finally settling on a mom-and-pop shop restaurant inside the old city. They had to park the van and walk what seemed like a quarter of a mile before finally entering an area that looked like it was built hundreds to thousands of years previous.

They walked into a large open square, where the occasional tree grew through the round openings made for them in the stone. The whole area was made of stone, and the stones on the ground matched the stones on the walls. They were all a light-brown sandstone color and gave the place a medieval appearance. The stone pathways were trafficked so much that they had a shiny luster to them. It was as if the stones became polished over hundreds of years by the shoes of millions of people walking to and fro, as they shopped for their daily essentials.

There were benches strategically placed around the area as well as small card tables set up with chairs for those who wanted to sit and talk or perhaps play a game. The whole area was stone and had little color other than the natural stone that was light brown, resembling the foam on a good cup of cappuccino.

They walked into an area that was almost maze-like. There were different corridors to each direction, and the corridors were just over the size of a two-lane street. As they walked down one of the corridors, they passed a number of small shops that all had large arched doorways. They were mostly double doors and had a roman look to them. Most of the doors were to small shops in the plaza, but some of them appeared to be residences. One set of doors had a small sign on it alerting the patrons that it was a convenience store. On the left side of the door sat an ice freezer and a soda vending machine. To the right side was a stack of vegetable boxes and crates and a small podium with an umbrella towering over the cash register that was set on the small podium.

They walked through the different alleyways and, after making a left turn into a connecting alley, came upon one shop that was a bit different compared to the others. This storefront had a full glass front and a couple of neon lights in the window that shone red and green on the stone walls of the alley. The storefront was all glass except for the base of the wall, which was natural stone, like the rest of the area. The front doors were silver and looked like they were installed in the 1950s as they had quite a bit of wear to them and didn't exactly open and close like new doors. It was definitely a mom-and-pop shop because the owners were the cooks, the wait staff, the busboys, and everything in between.

The couple that owned and operated the place looked old enough to have fathered the entire Jewish race. Mr. Dershowitz, the owner, lived in Jerusalem ever since his family left France at the beginning of World War II. His parents had a shop in Paris and gave that up when the Germans began their occupation of that area. They didn't know it at the time, but Israel would once again be the gathering place of the Jewish people in just a few short years after the war and in the decades to follow. They got to Israel at just the right moment and were able to make a good life for themselves over the years by serving great food and making a lot of new friends. When they first arrived in Israel, the place was empty and mostly barren. It took years of hard work to shape Israel into what it would become, but today, Israel is a relative paradise in the center of the Middle East. The rocky and barren land was transformed into beautiful gardens, orchards, and it went from desolate and ugly to thriving and beautiful.

Mrs. Dershowitz was a short lady with flowing hair that went just past her shoulders and was as white as newly fallen snow. She was slightly overweight but looked healthy and sprite for a woman in her late eighties. She had the energy of a thirty-something and a beaming smile.

"Welcome, Gentleman!" she exclaimed "I have just the spot for you. I see that you brought your friends in. Will you be having desert, or can I get you some dinner?"

David was well-known by Mrs. Dershowitz. He frequented the restaurant at least once a week and often came twice a week. When he would usually frequent the place, it was to have a desert and a cup of coffee. He enjoyed coming there because it wasn't too busy, and it was often quite quiet. He could bring in his laptop, work a little bit, and enjoy something sweet. To top it all off, he would enjoy the company of the owners and loved to hear the stories that they would share.

David smiled at Mrs. Dershowitz as he approached her and took her in a light embrace. To the casual observer, he was like family and possibly even a grandson.

"We will actually be having both, Ms. Dershowitz. Since you know what's best, how about getting together what you would consider to be the best dinner you have. After that, we will have a cup of that great coffee you serve as well as a sweet dessert," he explained.

"Oh, we can certainly do that. Have a seat, and we'll take care of everything," she responded. Mrs. Dershowitz waddled off, with a huge smile and a pace so fast that she caused the air next to the table to be displaced.

Charles felt the breeze as she went by, and it caused him to stare in awe. He watched as she feverishly walked toward the kitchen with her filled tray. He thought, *Here is a woman near one hundred years old, and she is faster than I am.* He sat there for a moment before finally turning his focus back to David and Chris.

The table that they were seated at was in the corner of the left side of the restaurant, next to the front window. The table looked like it was straight out of the 1950s and had a Formica top and a wide, shiny aluminum shroud around the outside perimeter. It wobbled a little every time Charles would start to rest his elbows. The chairs didn't match the tables and looked like old military surplus from the United States. They were battleship-gray and had thick seat cushions and back rests. Surprisingly, the seats weren't worn-out and were in good condition. Charles definitely appreciated that the seats had a six-inch cushion.

As Charles gazed out of the front windows, he saw several people pass by. Some walked as if they were in a hurry while others went by slowly as if they had all the time in the world. Some were out for an after-dinner walk; some were out to shop at one of the local markets, but most were tourists out on an evening adventure in a mysterious land.

Inside the restaurant, people were coming and going in groups of two or three at a time. Every time the door opened, a tiny cowbell, at the top of the door, would ring as if it were a dinner bell announcing that dinner was ready to be served. The patrons were quite talkative and consisted of a mix of Jerusalem locals and tourists. The tourists were the easiest to spot because of the clothing that they would wear. While the occasional Israeli may wear a T-shirt blazoned with "I Heart Jerusalem," from time to time, it certainly was not the norm. Tourists, on the other hand, loved to buy gawdy pink and yellow tees with a number of popular tourist phrases. Seated in the restaurant were at least three people wearing such shirts.

Charles scanned the room as David and Chris talked quietly to each other. He seemed to be particularly enthralled by the vintage jukebox in the corner of the store, as he seemed to stare at it as if it were a stack of candy bars at a children's weight-loss camp. His eyes stood fixed on the machine like he had never seen one before. After a few minutes of this, he finally lost interest and returned his attention to the group.

"So what are people saying about the troop buildup?" Charles blared somewhat loudly. "We almost stayed home because of that."

"Well," David replied in a hushed tone, "we've had so many threats and missile launches over the years. We just kind of got used to it."

Chris interjected quickly because he could see the confusion building on Charles's face. "You can't tell me that no one is at least a little worried."

Charles seemed satisfied by the question, and his gaze moved away from Chris toward David. He was now focusing on David with the same fervor that he had as he stared at the jukebox.

"I guess that some people are, but you wouldn't know it," David said confidently. "It's been pretty relaxed over the past few years. Even Iran backed off on their normal chants of 'death to Israel' for a while."

"Have there been troops built up on the border before?" asked Charles.

"Not like this," said David.

"I see," said Chris.

Charles looked at Chris as if snakes were coming out of his ears. He was somewhat bewildered by the response, but even more bewildered by the tone of the response.

"I see," said Charles with an obviously sarcastic demeanor. "Don't you think there's a big difference between no troops in the past and now there being troops lined up on the border like a pack of crazed women on black Friday?"

Mrs. Dershowitz walked toward the table with a large round serving tray. Before Chris had a chance to respond, she was back at the table, hovering over Charles with a huge smile. Chris and David smiled back at her, and Charles sat there with a panicky look across his face.

"Here you are, boys." She beamed. "I got you the best hummus in Jerusalem."

David smiled as she set the tray down.

"Ah, now that's the hummus I remember," he said emphatically. "It looks as good as usual, and if it tastes like usual, these guys are in for a real treat!"

"It's always good because we always make it fresh. We don't serve leftovers here," she explained with a look of seriousness.

David tore off a corner of the loaf of bread that was served with the hummus. He held it close and admired it for moment and then dipped it into the hummus. He pulled the bread out of the thick and creamy hummus, and steam began to radiate off of the piece of bread and from the small crater that he made in the bowl.

"You have to get the perfect-sized bite and then dip it in like this," he explained.

Charles watched in amazement as the hummus crater backfilled slowly like a light-brown lava flow. His mouth began to water as he took in the aroma of the bread mixed with the steaming hummus.

Chris took a piece of the bread and swooped it into the hummus with a spooning motion. The bread emerged almost fully encapsulated with a smooth yet textured pile of hummus on it. He then slowly took the bite and ate it. As he chewed it, he nodded as if in agreement with David's earlier comments and, before he swallowed it, said in a mumbled sort of speech, "Yup, just as good as advertised!"

"Well, I just have to see what the world's best hummus tastes like," said Charles with a giddy grin on his face.

Charles swooped in on the bread like a man who hadn't eaten in a week. "Oh yes," he replied, "this is really good!"

Charles took another large bite and continued to agree with the others that it was really good. He did this for about three more bites before he finally changed the subject. The food caused him to completely forget the earlier conversation, so he asked about what he was really interested in—the find near the Gihon Spring.

"So, David"—he paused—"what's the story about your dig site? If I am understanding correctly, you found some coins?" he asked.

"Not just some coins," David replied. "We found hundreds."

"What's so interesting about a bunch of coins? Are they all gold coins?" asked Charles.

David looked taken aback for a moment and then after remembering who he was sitting with responded with a bit of a chortle, "No, they aren't gold coins. As a matter of fact, it isn't the coins that really intrigued us."

Chris chimed in, asking, "There's more?"

"Oh yes, we found what we believe to be ceremonial tools. These specific tools were excavated near a stone that was like descriptions of a stone located in the First and Second Temples. We believe that it is the stone that was used as a part of the altar. When we started to excavate more, we found that the entire area was once a building, and the shocker is that it appears to be an old threshing floor," David replied with excitement.

"What is a threshing floor?" asked Charles.

"Well, a threshing floor is a space where farmers would bring their grain and basically, stomp on it or use tools to break it up so that the husks were removed from the grain," he explained.

Charles looked a bit puzzled at first, but then remembered that scripture talked about threshing floors.

"So what you are saying is that the threshing floor that you located is the same one that Solomon built his temple over?" he asked.

"Precisely," said David with a beaming smile.

"What about the Temple Mount?" asked Chris. "I thought that the temple was located on that area."

David stopped for a moment and then scanned the room as if he were looking to see if people were listening. It was obvious that he didn't want too much information getting out, so he spoke in a much softer and lower tone. "Well, that area has long been thought to be the site of the temples, but we believe that the temple wasn't actually in that area," he said softly.

"Why is that?" blared Charles.

Chris looked at Charles as a father looks at a son when he does something impolite in public. He gave him a gesture with both his hands, motioning to lower his tone. He nodded as if saying no while he was motioning him to be quiet.

David glanced around the room again before responding. "Well, if you take a close look at scripture, you'll see a lot of clues on why it can't possibly be the site of the Second Temple. Not only that, but the historian Josephus also recorded the exact location of the temple after Rome destroyed Jerusalem, and the Temple Mount simply doesn't fit with his measurements of the actual location," he explained.

"That's huge!" Charles said boisterously.

David continued. "The Temple Mount doesn't fit what Jesus prophesied when he said that no stone would be left upon the other. If one looks at the Bible as truth, then one must conclude that the Temple Mount is not the actual Temple Mount based on this. But that isn't the only problem."

"There's more?" Chris asked.

"Yes, Scripture also talks about ritual washing and other things that require a water source. The only area in Jerusalem that had a source of water for all the water needs of the temple is the Gihon Spring area. It just doesn't make sense to have built a temple on the area where the Temple Mount is located because it didn't have access to fresh, clean water. There was also a fountain in the temple that the historian Josephus described in detail. So it could not have been the Temple Mount area that the mosque is located on. The Temple Mount area lacks fresh water. There was an aqueduct that ran to the Temple Mount area, but aqueducts are common with Roman architecture, so it is likely that the aqueduct was built by the Romans for Fort Antonia. There were also some small cisterns, but that wouldn't have provided the water needed for cleaning after the ritual sacrifices and other cleaning," he explained.

"Wow!" exclaimed Charles.

"We can talk more about it tomorrow, but I'm sure you are thinking the same thing that I am," said David.

"What's that?" asked Charles.

"That the third temple can be built," David said softly. "The whole reason that it hasn't been built is because for years, it was believed that the mosque has been sitting in the spot of the First and Second Temples. Getting that mosque out of there would require a miracle but if we can prove that the Temple Mount is not the actual location of the first two temples, then we have essentially cleared the way for the rebuilding of the temple."

Charles answered, without even thinking, "Actually, that wasn't what I was thinking."

Chris turned to Charles with a look of puzzlement. "This should be good," he said sarcastically.

"I was thinking that I'd really like to try that desert you have been raving about. I'm still hungry."

David and Charles started laughing so loudly that the rest of the patrons in the restaurant stopped what they were doing, and their focus was now on the three men laughing boisterously. Charles could feel that every eye in the place was now focused on him, and he lit up like a Christmas tree. He was so embarrassed that his body skipped the color pink and went straight to red as if to tell him that he needed to stop what he was thinking and be a little more cautious with his words.

"Charles," said David, "I don't know what we would do without you. You have this uncanny ability to make the simplest things insanely funny. We will get the dessert. Don't worry!"

After spending about two hours eating a dinner, having a dessert and a cup of freshly brewed local coffee, Charles, Chris, and David called it a night. David drove Charles and Chris back to their hotel so they could get a little sleep and then meet David, early in the morning, to visit the dig site.

At about seven the next morning, Charles woke up and met the rest of the group downstairs to have breakfast. Charles didn't get a lot of sleep because his mind wandered all night. He couldn't stop thinking about the troops on the border, and even though David tried to ease his fears at the restaurant, he couldn't shake the feeling that something bad was going to happen.

Charles and Chris were the only ones in the group that wanted to go to the dig site. Cynthia wasn't overly excited of the idea of looking at a bunch of dirty tunnels and made it known at breakfast. She explained her position to Charles, as he ate his eggs, and nodded. In the end, they agreed that she would take everyone else to see the old city while he and Chris went to see David at the dig site. The rest of the group didn't have any complaints over the idea. They were all the same mindset as Cynthia, and all agreed that they would rather see the Wailing Wall and the Church of the Holy Sepulchre rather than the dig site.

After a hearty breakfast, some good conversation, and a prayer or two, the group was ready to get started on their first day of adventuring. David arrived in the van, not knowing that he was only picking up Charles and Chris. No one in the group called him to let him know that it would just be the three of them. He needed to return the van to the dig site anyway, so he looked at it as a stroke of luck because now he wouldn't have to make two trips to return the van later.

The trip from the hotel to the dig site was a short one. The hotel was just outside the old city, and the entire trip took only about a half hour. The site was located next to the Temple Mount but was located at an area that was slightly lower than the Temple Mount. They walked down into a valley where the area was cordoned off, and a tunnel was slightly visible within the rocky area.

"This area here is six hundred feet from the Temple Mount area. The historian Flavius Josephus wrote that the temple location was exactly six hundred feet from Fort Antonia and that it was six hundred feet square. If you look at where we have everything cordoned off, you can see what six hundred feet square looks like. We had to pull several permits to be able to dig here, and it wasn't easy."

Charles looked perplexed. "I guess I was picturing something different."

"Why is that?" asked David.

"Well, for one, the area is actually quite small, and I was expecting a lot of heavy equipment and one huge hole in the ground."

David chuckled. "Well, in order to get the permit, we had to submit plans for our dig, and when we submitted our initial plans, we expected a larger dig site on the top side, but those plans were rejected, and we had to compromise to get the area that we have. This area doesn't look large, but it turns out that it was huge."

"It looks like you are digging a small swimming pool," Charles said sarcastically.

"Well, it is about that size but keep in mind, when we first started our dig, we had no clue that we were going to find a tunnel beneath the site. When we broke ground and found the tunnel, we ended up finding more than we bargained for."

Chris walked over to the tunnel and started to peer into the dark entrance. The area leading into the tunnel was pitch-black and was about four feet in diameter.

"How do you see anything in there?" he asked.

"Well, just inside the tunnel, there is a drop light. We'll go down in a few, right now, I have to check my trailer to see if it's still secure."

Charles was staring at the area and put his fingers to his chin as if he were deep in thought.

"When you said that the Temple Mount wasn't the actual location of the Second Temple, I was thinking that we were going to be in some other part of the city. This area is so close that it almost looks like it could have been a part of the Temple Mount platform that is there now."

"Well, it's interesting that you say that, Charles. You see, the Temple Mount that is over there used to be connected to this area. There was a valley, or you could call it a moat, between that area and where we are standing now. This area had a large platform that was built up, and during its day, the area was a bit higher. There was a bridge connecting the temple to what is currently called the Temple Mount," David explained.

Charles looked even more perplexed. "So if this was where the temple was really located, then what is that huge area that they are calling the Temple Mount today?"

"We believe that it is Fort Antonia," said David.

"Wow!" exclaimed Charles. "That must have been some fort if it was that large compared to the temple."

David chuckled. "You are now sounding like a majority of the people in Jerusalem now. If I had a dollar for every time someone told me that the site we are standing on was the area of the fort and that I have it backward, then I would be a pretty wealthy man."

"So we are standing on what used to be the temple, and what they call the Temple Mount was actually the fort?" asked Charles.

"The area that people refer to as the Temple Mount just happens to be the same size as pretty much all the old Roman forts that were built two thousand years ago. The Romans used to build all their old forts the same because it was easier to just have one set of plans. It made the building process much more efficient."

David could see that what he was saying was going over Charles's head and that he just couldn't picture it in his head.

"Do you remember the conversation we had at dinner last night regarding the model of the Temple Mount in the museum?" he asked.

"Vaguely," said Charles.

"The model in the museum shows this area as Fort Antonia and the larger area as the Temple Mount. However, this area could not have been Fort Antonia because it was too small. The historian Josephus described the fort as a massive structure that blocked the view of the temple. He said that it *towered over* the temple if one arrived from the north. He also described the location of the temple in relation to the fort, with very precise measurements. We also know that the temple measured six hundred feet square, which just happens to be the perfect size for the area where we are now standing."

"Uh-huh," said Charles.

"The museum model shows a fort that would hold three hundred people at best, but we know that Rome had an entire legion here, and a legion would have been about ten thousand soldiers. You can easily see why that would not have worked," he explained.

Chris, now listening intently, looked at David and pointed up at the Temple Mount. "So how do they still believe that is where the temple was when there is so much information to the contrary?"

"That's easy. It's a tradition now, and tradition is hard to change but not impossible. The mosque is located where a church once sat. When the Muslims took over the area, they built a mosque on the area where the former church was built. They assumed that the church was built in that spot because of the large stone protruding through the ground. That stone is called the foundation stone or also called the pierced stone. Those of the Muslim faith believe that it is the location that Muhammad began his night journey. There is debate among the Jewish people that it is the area of the Holy of Holies. The problem that I have with that theory is that in all the evidence that we have regarding the First and Second Temples is that there is no mention of any large protruding rock. On the other hand, there is mention of a large protruding rock in the historical descriptions of Fort Antonia."

"My head is starting to hurt," said Charles. "All this new information is starting to make my brain swell."

David and Chris laughed.

"When the Jews came back, they had been gone for over a thousand years. They didn't know where anything was when they came back because the place was literally razed to the ground when the Romans left. When they got back, it had been ten-plus generations. The mosque has been residing on that spot for hundreds of years now. Over the years, the tradition became that the First and Second Temples were built on that location, and it has been the same ever since. The truth is that the Romans completely destroyed Jerusalem, and they made it to where nothing was left."

Charles looked impressed. "You certainly know your history. I could never remember that much history. If I left Phoenix for a month, I'd probably be lost when I got back." He chuckled.

"As fate would have it, the recent dig has made our evidence stand out. We have been working with people from the Temple Group, who are slowly beginning to come around. They aren't sold completely, but that's why we keep digging," said David.

"That's fascinating," said Chris.

"Well, let's check out my trailer really quickly, and I'll take you guys over to the museum. I think that if you see the model that I have been yacking about, you might have a better idea of what I've been talking about. We can then go get some lunch and come back here later. If we do that first, you may appreciate everything I'm telling you a little more."

CHAPTER 7

War Erupts

Charles and Chris toured the museum with David, and before they could even grab a quick lunch, David got a call from one of his partners and had to postpone showing them the inside of the tunnel. The pair decided that they would just take a tour of Jerusalem for the remainder of the day. David had to get back to work and, as he was leaving, said that he would meet everyone for dinner later that evening.

Charles wanted to take a tour of the northern part of Israel and recommended driving up to the north side of the Sea of Galilee, to Capernaum, but Chris warned against it. He didn't want to go anywhere near, where there were troops en masse. Capernaum was just a bit too close to the Syrian border for Chris's comfort. After a few minutes of a back and forth about it, Charles settled for a tour of a safer area on the south side of the Sea of Galilee. He had always wanted to visit the Sea of Galilee, and if he wasn't able to see Capernaum, he at least wanted to be able to see it and dip his toes in the same water that Jesus walked on.

Charles and Chris headed out to visit the Sea of Galilee. They didn't want to spend a fortune, so they borrowed the van from David. It wasn't the prettiest ride in Israel, but Charles was adamant with Chris that they would be better off forgoing a paid tour and just taking the van. Chris knew he wasn't going to win an argument with Charles that related to anything financial, so he agreed without putting up too much of a fight. The van wasn't a rental, so they didn't have to waste a bunch of time filling out paperwork, but they did need to return it to David at the end of the day. Charles didn't have a problem delivering the van back to David later. They were going to go out to dinner with him again that evening anyway. It was a prospect that Charles quickly envisioned and for which he gave his stamp of approval.

They drove north to the sea and after an uneventful couple of hours, located a spot near the beach. Just to be safe, they stayed to the west side of the sea and visited a small town called Kinneret. The eastern side was near where the Gog Golshiri regime had a large number of its troops. The Sea of Galilee was pretty large, so they felt somewhat secure knowing that the troops were on the other side of the sea. They were a little too close for Chris's comfort, but he figured that it would be fine since Charles wasn't panicking. If Charles was panicky, then it would have made him anxious as well, so he used Charles as somewhat of a safety meter without his knowing it. Aside from that, David didn't seem to be worried about where they were headed, and the troops had been there for a while. If they were going to attack, they would have done it a lot earlier. It looked like David was right. It looked like another typical show of strength, just to taunt the Israelis.

After driving around for a little while, they were able to find a nice area with beach access. They pulled into the parking area and down toward a row of trees that were growing along the area between the beach sand and the parking area. There was a small white building that Charles guessed was a bathroom, and all around them was nothing but mountains. The mountains in the area where they parked looked more like giant sand dunes than mountains and had sparse green vegetation growing in it. It was very desertlike.

In his excitement, Charles exited the vehicle and ran toward the beach rather quickly. He was eager to put his toes in the sand and to walk in the water. Chris hadn't even opened his door before he saw Charles turn around and running back to the vehicle. He had a painful expression on his face and ran at such a rapid pace that Chris mistakenly thought he was being chased by a swarm of bees, before realizing that he was really just cold. The inside of the van was nice and warm and looking out the windows, it appeared sunny and warm outside as well. The reality was that it wasn't warm at all. It wasn't freezing, but sixty degrees with a nice breeze at the beach on a clear day can feel a bit chilly to a man from Phoenix, Arizona.

Charles opened the back passenger door and grabbed his bag that was on the seat. He pulled out a sweatshirt and put it on. Chris couldn't help but laugh out loud at the entire debacle.

"What's so funny?" asked Charles.

Chris, still sitting in the driver's seat, started laughing uncontrollably, while pointing at the sweatshirt that Charles was now wearing.

"Are you serious right now?" Chris bellowed.

"It was the only clean sweatshirt I could find," Charles retorted.

"Really?" asked Chris. "Are you telling me that you brought that sweatshirt from Arizona?"

Charles, looking a bit embarrassed and a bit silly in the neon-pink sweatshirt that he donned, remained silent. He couldn't think of anything to say that would redeem him. He knew that he looked silly, but he didn't really care because he was cold, and he wanted to see the beach in comfort.

"I really can't go walking around at the Sea of Galilee with a man in a pink sweatshirt that says 'Juicy,'" Chris said while holding back his laughter. "What would people think?"

Charles crawled back into the van and closed the door.

"I got this sweatshirt from Cynthia last night. I didn't know it had writing on it. I just thought it was pink," he snarled.

"I don't know if she felt sorry for you and lent you that sweatshirt or if she was angry with you for something, and that's her retaliation," Chris said with a chuckle. "It's really not that bad. I guess."

Chris wasn't exactly being honest with Charles at this moment, but he didn't want to hurt his feelings. He knew how Charles was looking forward to seeing the beach, so he just started telling him things to ease his discomfort.

"Well, are we going to do this?" asked Chris, with a slight grin.

"I don't care what it looks like," said Charles. "It's not every day that a person gets to see the Sea of Galilee, and I didn't come all this way just to get back into the vehicle and head back because of Cynthia giving me the wrong sweatshirt."

"Is that what it was?" asked Chris.

"Is that what, what was?"

"Was it an accident, or was it revenge?" Chris snorted.

"I don't think she was upset with me, but I can't always read her. She can stare at me intensely sometimes with this fierce look, and I can't tell if she is faking or if she is really just upset with me," said Charles with a confused tone.

"So you got this look recently?" Chris inquired.

"Well, when I asked her if she had a sweatshirt this morning, she seemed fine for one moment, and then the next moment, I thought she was going to kill me," Charles explained.

Chris leaned in intensely as Charles relayed his tale of the pink sweatshirt. He hadn't been this entertained since he went to a comedy show a few months back.

"And," asked Chris impatiently, "what happened next?"

Charles shot him a puzzled look. "Nothing," he said.

Chris suddenly looked let down. For a moment, he was captivated by the story and then, suddenly, nothing.

"You sure have a knack for storytelling," said Chris sarcastically.

Charles looked down at the shirt that he was wearing and mumbled, "Juicy," under his breath. He gave a quick shake of dissatisfaction and looked back at Chris, resuming his story.

"Anyway"—he paused for a moment—"I thought that she was mad because I woke her up at around four this morning."

Chris turned his attention back to Charles. "I think you hit the nail on the head, my friend. I think she was mad at you for waking her up. Who wouldn't be mad at you for waking them up at that time of the morning?"

"Maybe," said Charles, "when she answered the door, she was smiling. I can remember it like it was ten minutes ago. I knocked. She answered. I said good morning, and she said good morning back. I then asked her if she had a sweatshirt that I could borrow, and then she got me a sweatshirt. If I had to guess, I would say that she was mad because I forgot to say thanks, but who knows!"

"Well, women can get upset at us men for a variety of reasons, and sometimes, it's just for the sake of getting mad," explained Chris.

Charles nodded. "I guess," he said. "I mean, she and I are so close in size that I didn't have anyone else to ask."

Chris jerked his head toward Charles and started laughing out loud. "That's it," he screeched, "you dummy!"

"What?" said Charles with a shrug.

"You said something else, didn't you?"

Charles sat silently for a moment and then started to turn a shade of pink that somewhat matched the sweatshirt. It didn't take long, and he quickly realized his mistake.

"Oh no!" said Charles while slapping himself in the forehead. "I can't believe that I said that."

"I can't either," said Chris with a laugh. "You aren't even close to the same size as Cynthia. She is like a size 6, and you are more like a size 16. Better yet, she is more like Stan Laurel, and you are Oliver Hardy."

Charles turned and stared at Chris. He had a strange look on his face, almost like he had just farted on an elevator and was trying to hide it by looking puzzled but also like he was extremely guilty at the same time.

"I see your point," said Charles, now laughing out loud. "I just meant that she wears a similar size of sweatshirt. Can I help it if she likes to wear baggy sweatshirts?"

Chris threw open his car door. He had a newfound air of confidence about him. After hearing Charles's story, he now knew that he could pretty much go anywhere with Charles and not have to worry about what other people were thinking. If confronted about it, he could just tell them the tale, and they would completely understand.

"I think I'm ready to hit the beach!" said Chris confidently.

Charles opened his car door and got out of the vehicle. He looked at Chris, over the top of the van, and gave him a sad look.

"Please don't tell anyone about this," he begged.

Chris smiled back. "I won't," he said with a gasp. "I'm fairly sure that the entire group already knows. Cynthia probably already filled them in."

The pair walked down to the water's edge through the fine white beach sand. Charles stopped every few feet to wiggle his toes in the sand, and as they reached the water, he dipped his toes into the cold water to clean off the sand and then stepped back onto the beach because of the frigid temperature of the water. He looked down and saw that his feet had even more sand on them now that they were wet, so he stepped back into the water a second time to wash them off again. He repeated this one more time before finally giving up. His feet were coated with sand, much like one would coat a chicken leg with a savory mix of breadcrumbs and spices for dinner.

"I guess I'll have to get the sand off at the car," he said with a grin. "I get sand back on my feet every time I get out of the water."

Chris smiled back but held back his laughter. He didn't want Charles to be any more embarrassed that he already was. It was odd enough that a full-grown, middle-aged man was at the beach wearing a neon-pink sweatshirt, emblazoned with "Juicy" in large gold letters. If he laughed and alerted Charles to the fact that he looked like a mental patient, he may never be able to get Charles to go anywhere ever again.

They paused for a moment to take in the beauty that surrounded them. The mountains in the horizon were a rich-brown color, and the sea looked a brilliant blue as the sun danced off the water. It was far from the desertlike place that Charles had always pictured. Some areas had desertlike qualities, such as the large dunes and the mountains, but mixed in throughout the area were lush green farmlands and orchards as far as the eye could see. It wasn't a heavily populated area, but there were homes dotted across the landscape. It truly was a paradise. Charles finally understood why so many people fought over the land for thousands of years.

As the two gazed off into the horizon, they were suddenly interrupted by a low roaring sound off in the distance. It wasn't loud, but it was different from any sound that either of them had ever heard before.

"What is that?" asked Charles.

"I don't know," Chris replied.

Chris continued to scan the area, but he was just as perplexed as Charles. A second and third roar quickly filled the area.

"Are those Israeli Air Force jets?" asked Charles.

They both scanned the area to see what could be producing the strange sounds. As they looked across the sea, toward the north, they saw streaks of smoke heading upward from the ground. They looked like airplane chem trails, except they were going upward rather than across the sky. Chris and Charles sat there staring in awe. As soon as they saw the smoke trails heading upward, they knew what they were witnessing.

The sounds took a moment to reach them and grew louder and more sustained as the sky in the background started to look a whitish gray. They were witnessing rockets being launched on the other side of the sea.

"Oh my goodness," Chris yelled, "we have to go! Now!"

Charles looked panicked as he started sprinting for the van. "It figures that it would happen right after we got here. You have got to be kidding me!"

"You get the van started, and I'll warn David," Chris yelled.

The two ran as fast as they could muster. Charles felt as if it was all surreal, and as if he were running and going nowhere. For a moment, he pondered whether he was witnessing the rockets for real or if he was just dreaming it. After a few moments, he quickly came to the realization that it wasn't a dream. He was witnessing it.

Charles reached the van just before Chris. He opened the door and jumped in. The sounds of rockets were now overshadowed by the sounds of explosions, small-arms fire, and machine-gun fire. It sounded like a backyard on the Fourth of July in America. There were occasional sounds of rocket fire that were much louder than the first ones. Chris and Charles assumed these were retaliatory strikes by the Israel Defense Forces (IDF).

Every explosion that they heard carried a vibration of the earth with it. The vibration was eerily similar to aftershocks after a major earthquake. The rumbling wasn't violent, but it was just enough that they knew that they needed to leave the area as fast as they could. Charles was becoming more unsettled as every minute passed.

Charles started the van and headed out of the sandy lot where they were parked. The van kicked up a large amount of dust as he hit the gas and maneuvered it to the main roadway. The traffic was starting to get heavy on the streets as the other people in the area headed south, away from the area. What first appeared to be a sleepy town now looked like a major urban area. At least it did from a traffic standpoint. The area wasn't heavily populated, but the roads were quickly jammed up with vehicles as far as they could see. Charles worked as quickly as he could, to get out of the area, but it was terribly slow going.

"We are going to die here!" Charles bellowed.

"Just focus on your driving. We will be fine as long as the fighting is behind us," Chris replied.

Charles looked like a frightened child as he drove down the packed roadway. "I told you we should have stayed home. What are we gonna do now?" he asked.

Chris looked surprisingly calm as he searched the vehicle for his cellular phone. "We are headed away from the fighting. They are targeting soldiers. We aren't soldiers."

"That doesn't make me feel any better. Was that supposed to make me feel better?" asked Charles.

"Look, you focus on your driving. We aren't exactly in a trustworthy vehicle here. Besides, when you are shouting questions at me, I'm not able to call David. Would you like me to call David?" he asked.

"Well, hurry up and call him. Find out where we need to go," Charles said nervously.

Chris finally found his cellular phone and started to dial. As he got halfway through dialing David's number, his own phone started ringing. He quickly answered it, and to his surprise, it was David who was reaching out to him.

"It's David!" yelled Chris.

"Well, answer the stupid thing already!" yelled Charles.

"Just worry about your driving," he shot back as he put the phone to his ear.

Charles was moving a little faster now. He was able to get up to about thirty-five miles per hour. It wasn't as fast as he wanted to go, but it beat being stopped or being back where he started.

The sound of the rockets was nearly out of range now. He wasn't sure if it was because he was farther away or if it was because the rockets were no longer being fired. He couldn't really see anything from the Galilee area any longer. He wished that he could see what was going on back at the Sea of Galilee but, at the same time, was glad that he couldn't. Now that the sounds of the rockets had diminished, his breathing slowed, and he became slightly more calm.

"David?" asked Chris.

"Did you guys get out of there?" asked David.

"You won't believe what we saw! We were on the beach, walking back toward the vehicle, when we started hearing rockets being launched. It was nuts!"

"I'm glad you made it out of there. Have you been listening to the radio?" asked David.

"What radio?"

"Oh, I'm sorry, man! I forgot you were in my van." He chuckled. "Never mind that. I guess."

"What are they saying on the news reports?" asked Chris.

"Well, let's just say that you need to get here as fast as you possibly can," said David grudgingly.

"That doesn't sound like good news," exclaimed Chris.

As he said this, Charles whipped his head around toward Chris. "What? What doesn't sound good?"

"Look. Do you remember those troops?"

"Yes," said Chris.

"They are moving into Israel," said David. "Just don't stop. Get here as fast as you can. Do you have enough gas?"

"We have half a tank," Chris responded.

"Did you just go where we discussed and nowhere else?" asked David.

"Yes, why?"

"That needle always shows half a tank," he said.

"You have got to be kidding me," yelled Chris.

"What…what did he say?" yelled Charles.

"Look. Don't worry about it. You'll be fine. Just drive back here. We have a fuel tank on-site," David said calmly.

"Okay," Chris responded.

"What? What did he say?" yelled Charles.

Chris calmly turned toward Charles. "He said, 'Just drive here.' The troops on the border are headed into Israel." Chris didn't feel the need to worry Charles any more than he had to. He figured that having a half-panicked Charles was better than having a full-panicked Charles.

"Well, the good news is that we have half of a tank of gas," said Charles.

"Great! Just keep driving!" David replied with a grin.

It took hours to get back from the Sea of Galilee. When they finally arrived back at the dig site, David was waiting there patiently. The whole city was out and about now. The news took only minutes to reach Jerusalem, and when it hit, the people started to move with a purpose. Many people whom David knew planned to leave the city. David's friends knew that a day would come when Israel would be invaded, and knowing that it was a possibility, he made sure to have a plan in place. They were always clear about the word *invasion*. Skirmishes happened all the time. Invasions did not. In the past, invasions led to destruction, and when the Romans destroyed Jerusalem, they made it utterly unrecognizable. Israel had a great military, but even great militaries don't sustain zero casualties. Any time there has ever been an invasion around the globe, there has always been civilian casualties.

David was an American ex-patriot now living in Israel. He looked every bit of his Irish American descent. Being an American in the Middle East made him feel somewhat of a target for terrorists. Knowing this, he was sure to have a place that he could escape to in the event of conflict in Israel. It was a place of last resort, but the site that he and his friends chose to escape to was Petra. It was considered to be a safe place to hide since it was only a couple of hours away and was fairly hidden. It was also well to the east of the fighting, and the invaders were after Israel and not Jordan.

David and his friends weren't the only ones who have kept the ancient city of Petra in the back of their minds. There were thousands who believed that Petra would be a good place to retreat to in the event of trouble. It seemed like everyone in Israel knew that it would be a great place to hide out, but the reality was that it only seemed that way. Most of the people in Israel simply retreated south and planned to find buildings that were outside the old city of Jerusalem. They figured that the Israeli military forces would be able to keep the fighting to the north, and in the eventuality that they had to become refugees, they would simply pack up and move again.

Those who knew of Petra as a potentially safe zone started to head there from Jerusalem in droves. They didn't seem to worry about Petra being in Jordan, and they were all in good spirits, considering the reason for the trip. They figured that if they were going to escape to somewhere, it would have to be either Jordan, Egypt, or Saudi Arabia. There weren't really any other options since Israel is surrounded by countries that have historically disliked them. They would really only be able to go where the fighting wasn't happening, and for the time being, south and east would be the best bet.

*****

Meanwhile, in the north, the Russian and Syrian Army was on the march. The fighting was fierce in the Golan Heights area. The number of troops that was entering into Israel was well over a hundred thousand. The world media reported that additional troops were forming in Egypt, but there was no confirmed activity along that border, according to the media outlets in Israel.

The rumor mills in the United States were now running at light speed. They were reporting that Israel was faltering under the invasion of the Gog Golshiri regime and that it was all but certain that they would lose. The politicians were mostly silent on the issue. Those who did speak publicly about the invasion said only that the United States would monitor the situation.

The United States government was no longer a strong ally with Israel. When the liberal socialists took power in the US, they immediately began removing US troops from just about every country in the world. They said that it was not the responsibility of the United States to police the world and advised the different nations around the globe that they would have to provide for their own defense and that the US would only get involved in conflicts where social justice was threatened.

Aside from not having a hawkish attitude, defense funding was a real issue for the US government. The country was nearly bankrupt due to the failed socialist policies of the day. The politicians knew that they couldn't afford both their social programs and a strong military. They relied on nuclear weapons to show strength, and all but eliminated the military. The total force size went from one million troops to under two hundred thousand. Most of those soldiers were logistical support and military police. They figured that in the event of a war, they could print some money and start training new troops as needed. They called it "keeping an on-demand inventory system."

The little funding that they did provide for defense spending was mostly spent on I-Corp projects. The idea was that they could develop artificially intelligent soldiers that would cost less than traditional human soldiers. I-Corp was on the cusp of having the prototype soldiers completed, but the low funding to the program meant that the timing on a finished product would be delayed. What the politicians really wanted was a mechanized army that was controlled by only a handful of generals and the political class.

*****

In London, the press stormed the office of their new prime minister. Once the news broke that Israel was being invaded, they pounced into action and headed straight to Jared's office. They were chomping at the bit to get a response from him. The streets were packed in front of the building. There were news vans parked as far as the eye could see.

Jared sat calmly in his London office as the press amassed their troops outside. If he was nervous, it wasn't noticeable. He had an air of confidence about him and appeared unshaken by the news of their own outside his office building. This was his first major test after the election, and like every world leader before him, this event and his response could very well set the tone for his entire term.

Jared's phone rang as he sat at the desk. He reached over and hit the speaker button on the phone.

"Mr. Prime Minister," the voice beckoned, "your limousine is outside."

"Thank you, Janice," he responded politely. "I will be out in just a moment. Please take messages on all my calls this afternoon. I will be out of the office for the remainder of the day. If anything pressing comes in, please call me on my cellular phone."

"Yes, sir," said Janice.

Jared got up from his desk and walked to the door. He grabbed his jacket and a hat that he had on a rack next to the door. After donning the jacket and hat, he opened the door and headed out to the limousine outside. As he opened the office building door, he was met with a blast of cold air. It was a blustery morning. The temperatures were still on the lower side of fifty as winter had not yet let go of its grip on the continent. There was a fine misty rain and a stiff breeze pushing against him as he headed toward the vehicle.

The press quickly crowded around him and the vehicle.

"Mr. Prime Minister, will you be giving a statement this morning?" asked a woman in the crowd.

Jared stopped and scanned the crowd. He then reached into his pocket and grabbed a small notepad from his pocket and looked at it for a moment before placing it back into his pocket.

A second female reporter shouted out to Jared as he stood there, "Can we expect a military response?"

Jared smiled as he stood there, quite aware that he was not going to get away from the building without some semblance of a coherent response. He thought about reaching back into his pocket and getting the notebook again but then decided against it. After what felt like an eternity, Jared began to address the crowd.

"Good morning," said Jared as he looked at the swarm of reporters. "My statement will be brief, but let me start by saying that I have been in contact with the Israeli prime minister this morning and have pledged the support of the European Union to the defense of Israel. Now what that looks like at this point is a matter that I am not at liberty to share, but I will say this. We have petitioned the United Nations this morning, and we are pushing for a resolution, condemning, and admonishing the Golshiri regime for their aggression. We are also putting our forces on alert at present, and for now, our primary objective will be to get supplies and humanitarian aid to the people of Israel. Our Air Force is preparing shipments as we speak."

A male reporter jumped in right as he ended speaking. "Prime Minister Hadad, what good will a United Nations petition do?" he yelled loudly.

Jared looked stone-faced and expressionless. He was expecting his statement to be sufficient. "We are making a strong argument with the United Nations. Let's just say that they won't just sit idly by in this situation, and they will have to act." Jared paused for a moment, and he started to look angry. His whole demeanor changed in a flash. He felt like he was under attack by the media, and it was plain that he was uncomfortable with the questioning by the media.

"We have a meeting this evening with the United Nations in an emergency session. I will be attending the meeting via satellite. Right now, I am headed to a meeting, unrelated to the United Nations, with other prominent world leaders to discuss other options that are on the table. Rest assured that we condemn the actions of the Gog Golshiri regime, and our response will be swift."

"Mr. Prime Minister!" shouted the first reporter.

Jared seemingly didn't hear the reporter shouting at him, or he was simply ignoring her as he moved toward the limousine that was waiting to take him to his meeting.

The reporter pushed her way through the crowd and stepped in between the prime minister and his vehicle.

"Mr. Prime Minister, the people want to know if the European Union will be involved militarily in this conflict. Can you comment as to whether the EU will be sending troops or other military assets?"

Jared looked at the reporter and smiled. He was impressed with her tenacity. He could see that she wasn't going to let him get away without answering the hard questions and wasn't satisfied with just the basic response he gave. He certainly could appreciate the woman's desire to know the full scope of the response, but he couldn't give much more in the way of scope because he wasn't 100 percent certain himself.

"Excuse me, but what is your name?" he asked.

"Allison Cohen. I'm with the BBC," she responded. "Can we expect a military response for today's aggression?"

Jared let out a slight chuckle as she continued to rapid-fire her questions at him. She was merciless and completely emotionless as she fired her responses at him.

"Thank you, Ms. Cohen. As I stated a moment ago, we are looking at several different responses. Much of our decision will be based on our allies in the region and around the world," he said confidently.

"Excuse me, but that doesn't sound very convincing, Mr. Prime Minister," she said with a smirk and a puzzled look. "People are scared at the moment. They see an attack on our allies as an attack on the Union itself. Can you assure the people that they have nothing to fear here in Europe? What about the Israelis? While the politicians make plans, the Golshiri regime moves further south. What kind of response is most likely at this point? What about NATO and the United States?"

Jared spoke forcefully yet softly. "Look, Ms. Cohen. I understand that you and everyone else in the world wants answers at this time. It's just not as simple as that. This is not just a missile launch we are dealing with. This is a full-on invasion, and what we do next will set the tone for the days and weeks to follow. We cannot just start launching weapons or sending aircraft into airspace other than of our own allies. This will be part diplomatic and part military force, if necessary. What it will not be is a rash decision without discussion of all the leaders involved. Now if you will excuse me," he said as he reached past Allison to open the door.

"Just one more question, Mr. Prime Minister. Are you confident that the United Nations and NATO will take the advice of a new prime minister with no experience?" she asked.

Jared stopped once again but didn't remove his hand from the door handle. He smiled at Allison and paused for a moment. He appreciated that she was a sharp young reporter and that she was brave enough to ask the tough questions.

"As you are obviously aware, I am a new prime minister. This does not mean that I am new at strategic thinking, negotiations, or even being strong to react. While I may look like a gentle soul, I assure you that I can be as fierce as a lion when needed, and I can be as soft as a kitten. Right now is not a time for hasty decisions based on irrational thinking or fear. Right now is a time for unity and a time to work together with other nations to decide what is best for all and not just this nation or that nation. What we do here will have consequences that may reverberate through history. When all is said and done, the European Union will be on the right side of history. Now if you will excuse me," he responded.

At that moment, three security personnel stepped between Allison and the prime minister. They gently moved her aside so that Jared was able to get his door open and climb into the limousine. The other reporters jumped to life in a hurry and started shouting out questions all at once. Jared calmly closed the door to the limo, and as soon as he did, the reporters swarmed the vehicle, surrounding it with their cameras and microphones. The crowd was lively and extremely boisterous.

The driver of the limousine revved the engine and blasted the horn three times to let them know that he was about to move the vehicle. The vehicle gently pulled away from the crowd. Jared was now headed to the British Parliament, where he had a planned meeting with various world leaders.

Jared was alone inside the rear of his limousine, and the front window between him and his driver was up. Between the two back seats was a red telephone and a tan telephone. On the right side of the limousine was a small bar and a small mounted television. The television was on, and images of tanks crossing into Israel was playing on the screen. The news banner at the bottom of the screen read, "Golshiri Invades Israel. Is this Armageddon?" Jared looked at the screen with a puzzled look and shook his head as if to express his distaste for the media banner.

Jared picked up the red phone. He placed the phone to his ear and just started talking as if someone had been on the line the entire time. "Get me King Charles."

*****

Meanwhile, back in Jerusalem, Charles, Chris, and David packed up the vehicle. They strapped four gas cans to the top of the van's luggage rack but left enough room for all their luggage. They needed the extra gas because there was a good possibility that they wouldn't be able to get fuel along their way to Petra. They took half of the clothing out of their suitcases and replaced it with food. Where they were going, food was more of a necessity than a bunch of suitcases full of clothing.

Once everything was secured to the top, they made their way to the lobby of the hotel. Charles scanned the lobby, and the group members were nowhere to be seen.

"I think we should round everyone up," said Charles.

Chris looked equally puzzled that the group wasn't in the lobby as they planned.

"I think I'll go with you."

Chris and Charles walked to the elevator and went up to the third floor where Cynthia's room was located. They walked down the hall and stopped at her door and then knocked loudly.

"Cynthia, it's Charles and Chris. Open up," Charles said loudly.

The door opened, and Cynthia was standing at the doorway with a distressed look on her face. "I am so glad to see you. I've been here all alone for hours," she said as she leaned in to embrace Charles.

"Where is everyone else?" asked Chris.

"I don't know," she replied. "We were supposed to meet up this afternoon, but I haven't been able to reach them all morning. It's like they just disappeared, or their phones just stopped working."

"Do you still have cellular service?" asked Charles.

"Well, I think I do, but I have only tried to call you and everyone from our group." Cynthia looked at her phone. "I have a full signal, according to my phone."

"Let me try to call you," said Charles. Charles dialed Cynthia's number and waited for a few seconds before it started ringing on her end. Her ringtone was an old rap song, and her phone immediately started saying, "Can't touch this."

"Well, it works," she said. "They must be in an area with bad reception. I'll try them again."

"Don't bother," said Chris. "Charles and I will make the calls. You just get packed. Try only to bring what you need for a few days. We don't have a lot of room, and we need to put food in half of your bag."

"Great," she replied, "what you really meant to say is *unpack* while you make some calls."

"Well, if you want to look at it that way, I guess," he said, smiling.

"Don't worry. I'm a trooper. I was in the Army for four years. I know how to pack light." She chuckled.

Charles sat down on the right side of the bed, and Chris sat over on the right side. Charles pulled out his phone and started searching for phone numbers for their group members. Chris started looking as well, but he wasn't as panicked as Charles.

Suddenly, there was a knock at the door. Chris got up from the bed and walked over to the door and opened it. David was at the door.

"Well, what's the plan?" he asked.

"Come on in," said Chris. "We are trying to figure that out as we speak."

David walked over to the chair next to the television and sat down. "What do you mean?" he asked.

Chris returned to where he was sitting on the bed and sat back down.

"Well, we can't seem to find the rest of our group."

David looked a bit confused. "Didn't we all agree to meet here at the hotel?" he asked.

"Yes, but as you can see, we are the only ones here. Charles and I are about to call everyone to see where they are."

"Oh," said David.

Chris went back to searching his phone for his group members' telephone numbers. Charles was writing the numbers that he located down onto a small notepad that he found on the bedside table.

David got up and reached for the television remote. He then turned on the television and found a news station.

"Golshiri forces continue to move into Israel from Syria. They have heavy armor, and their missile strikes continue at an alarming rate. So far, casualties are negligible with the majority of the missiles being intercepted by the Iron Dome system. There are reports of telephone and electrical outages across the Golan Heights area and in the West Bank," the television shouted. "There are additional reports of air strikes in the Gaza Strip where Hamas leadership has reportedly taken advantage of the turmoil to the north and began strikes from Gaza into the cities of Beersheba and Jerusalem. Israeli forces have taken up positions near the Gaza Strip and are holding back forces there. Air forces are targeting mobile missile-launch sites and other known or suspected military targets. Casualties in the Gaza area are not known as communications are currently out. It appears that the majority of the fighting at this time is focused in Gaza and the Golan Heights region."

"That's just odd," said David.

"What's odd?" asked Charles.

David looked toward Charles with a puzzled look on his face. "Why in the world would Gaza be involved in this? That area isn't even close to the Syrian border."

"What would make Gaza want to fight with Israel now? Do they think that they can win just because the IDF is battling in the north?" asked Chris.

"I'm not sure. This whole situation is just strange," he replied. "It defies logic. Israel has been relatively peaceful for the past few years. Life has never been easier around here. Then all of a sudden, it's like those crazies from the north just decided to attack for no reason. I'll never understand this part of the world!" he said softly.

"Did you remember to pack bottled water?" Cynthia asked.

"Yes," said David, "while Charles here is convinced that this is not a desert area, because it's so pretty, it is, and water can be fairly scarce here. Well, it used to be, before they started using those huge desalination machines. Anyone who lives here knows that you always carry water with you."

"Yes, but there are four of us and maybe more if we reach everyone else," said Cynthia.

"I'll pack more. Do they have any bottled water in the lobby?" asked David.

"I'm not sure. We'll have to check on the way out," she replied. "How bad is traffic?"

"You would think that it would be horrible, considering what's going down, but it's surprisingly calm out there."

"Maybe there's no reason to go to Petra. I mean, if no one else is going, wouldn't it make sense to do what everyone else is doing?" she asked.

"Most people around here probably don't believe that the attack will last more than a day. I'm not convinced. Jerusalem is the heart of Israel, and it's only a matter of time before they start firing missiles on this area. Besides, I believe the Bible says something about fleeing to the mountains if there is ever an invasion, or something like that. I'm not going to argue with God on that one."

"You're right!" yelled Charles. "Why didn't I see it?"

"See what?" asked Cynthia.

"There is scripture in Ezekiel or Zechariah that talks about all this. At least, I think it does." Charles paused for a moment with a puzzled look. "Doesn't it?"

David, Charles, and Cynthia all turned and looked at Chris as if he were the man with all the answers. If anyone in the room knew Scripture, it was Chris.

"I do recall some scripture in Ezekiel and Zechariah but think that prophecy has already been fulfilled," Chris replied.

"Well, we can look at that later. Let's get that water and start moving before everyone else suddenly remembers prophecy about this and starts leaving all at once," said Cynthia.

"Could it be true?" asked Charles.

"Could what be true?" replied Chris.

"Could this be Armageddon?" sked Charles.

"Well, actually, it couldn't be Armageddon. Armageddon is a place, and that's where the final battle takes place. This would have to be something else," said Chris. "We wouldn't even be here if it were Armageddon."

"That's true," said Charles.

"Well, if we don't leave soon, it won't matter. Those troops that are out there obviously don't care what prophecy it is, and they are still headed this way!" said Cynthia.

The group finished up their packing and started heading down to the lobby. When they got down to the lobby, they were able to get the clerk to sell them three cases of bottled water. The clerk didn't mind selling it to them and also didn't act like it was a crazy request. As a matter of fact, the clerk was acting like it was a normal day and that he got requests for cases of water every day.

Outside the hotel, the van was parked in the reception and drop-off area. It was quiet outside, considering that it was early in the afternoon. Normally, there would be people all over the place, and the city would look like a large ant nest with ants marching to and fro going about their daily routines. This day, it was more like a holiday, and the streets were relatively peaceful. It was as if everyone was at home hunkered down and staying inside because they felt safer inside their homes. Charles pictured families perched in front of their television sets like what happened in 1969 when Neil Armstrong landed on the moon. When that happened, everyone was glued to their televisions, and it was likely like a ghost town everywhere in the world as that event was unfolding for the world to see.

"Well, I haven't been able to reach anyone," said Charles.

"Me either," said Cynthia.

Chris walked up to the two as they stood next to the van.

"That makes three of us," he said unenthusiastically.

Cynthia sat down on the curb next to the entrance. She put her head down and began to pray. Charles and Chris saw that she was praying, and they sat down beside her and began to pray silently.

"Dear Heavenly Father," Chris said softly, "please look out for those members of our group that are not here with us at this moment. Please guide them to safety and watch over them as we endure the trials set before us today. Please watch over our group as we travel to Petra and flee to the mountains as your holy word has asked us to do. Let us be guided by truth as we embark on our journey. Let your will be done, and let us all only do as your will. Please watch over the citizens of Israel as this time of tribulation comes upon them, and let their eyes be opened to the truth that Jesus is the true messiah and that his return will be soon. Father, we thank you for giving us the wisdom to understand the truth so that we can share your good news to the world. Our work will not end until the day comes that we are no longer able to speak or the day of the Lord is upon us. We pray this in Jesus's name, Amen."

The others said amen. And then climbed into the van.

The roads weren't too horrible along the routes out of the city, but when they got to the border of Jordan, it was a different story altogether. The vehicles at the border were lined up for what appeared to be miles. The sun was starting to get lower in the sky now, and the taillights were lit up like the Fourth of July. The taillights were flashing on and off because of the hundreds of cars that were starting and stopping every couple of feet.

Several cars were lined up on the sides of the street, and their occupants stood outside, looking toward the border like they were waiting for traffic to get better before getting in line. They chatted with one another as if they were old friends as they waited. Others were visibly upset with the long lines, and their frustration was highly visible. One man and what appeared to be his wife were arguing ferociously with each other. The woman threw her arms up into the air before grabbing a fuel can from the ground and turning it upside down and shaking it violently. She screamed at him while shaking the can and then suddenly threw it at him, striking him in the head.

Cynthia smiled when she saw the woman throw the can. She knew it had to be one of those I-told-you-so moments where her husband likely told her that there would be plenty of fuel along the way while she vehemently disagreed. She knew who was right in this particular quibble. Judging from her smile, she was pleased to see the woman had her small victory and gained some respect from her husband. He had a pitiful look on his face. He looked like a dog who was just reprimanded for peeing on the rug. He had an unmistakable look of guilt on his face, and it was plain to see that he was sorry because he swooped in to embrace his wife after she threw the can. Cynthia smiled at this too. She knew that the two were truly in love because people who are in love can be upset with each other in one moment and then hugging the very next.

"David, can we spare one of those cans of gas?" said Cynthia.

"We probably can spare a can." He chuckled. "If we give him a can of gas, he will sure be thankful. Don't you think?" he asked.

"You know it!" she replied. "I'll be right back."

Cynthia got out of the van and carefully removed one of the cans from the top. She walked the five-gallon can of gasoline over to the couple who looked visibly stunned at the gesture. Both the man and the woman were so happy that they embraced her at the same time. The woman then reached into her vehicle and got what appeared to be a bottle of water out and gave it to her as a way to say thank you.

Charles sat in the van watching as it all unfolded in front of him.

"That's what it is all about, right there," he said gleefully.

"Amen to that," said David. "Wars bring out the worst in some people but also the best in others. Just think, those people will remember that small gesture for years to come. They see God's hand in a terrible situation, and it will stick with them. This is exactly how we are supposed to be as Christians."

"Amen to that," said Charles and Chris, in unison.

CHAPTER 8

The Meeting

In Petra, Charles, David, Cynthia, and Chris were settled in. In total, there were about twelve thousand people that fled from Israel over the weeks since the invasion. The canyon floor was covered from rock face to rock face with mats and blankets. There was no apparent order at the site, so people took whatever space that they could find and turned it into a place to sleep and to congregate. The soft chatter of the refugees echoed off the canyon walls and was eerily reminiscent of a busy airport around the holidays.

Many of the refugees were children. They were running and playing as if they were off on some camping adventure. It was as if they were oblivious to the goings-on of the world. Their cheerfulness and playful demeanor kept the spirit of the group high. Many of the people huddled together in smaller groups and were focused on the news reports being broadcast to the few working phones in the camp. Only few had service that worked in the area, so those lucky enough to have service shared their space with the others. This had a unifying effect and also gave the people something to do as they waited for the violence to end.

The invasion was now in its sixth week and included forces from Russia, Iran, Turkey, Egypt, Syria, Libya, Iraq, Georgia, Armenia, Lebanon, and the Sudan. Forces from these other nations joined the

Gog Golshiri alliance shortly after the invasion began. It was as if the entire Middle East banded together all at once to swallow up the sole country that didn't share the Muslim faith.

The news outlets reported several theories as to why the invasion occurred. They said that Golshiri wanted control of the Dead Sea, that Golshiri wanted Israel's fertile farmlands, and that Russia wanted to control Israel's natural gas and oil resources. The truth was that it was all these things that led to the invasion. Many of the nations involved suffered extended periods of drought because of global climate change, and this affected their crop yields, causing widespread famine. Israel hadn't worried about the lack of water since they got most of their water from the desalination process that they invented years earlier. With global climate change getting worse year over year, nations banned the burning of coal, and this caused natural gas prices to skyrocket. Russia stood to gain a lot as they could control the natural gas pipelines in Israel.

The number 1 reason that the attack occurred was the liberalization of the United States and the European Union. Historically, when these nations acted as the world's police force, other world nations wouldn't have dared to attack Israel. The liberalization of these nations brought an end to their world policing, and the area became ripe for invasion. With the United States and the EU out of the way, a victory against Israel seemed possible. The Golshiri regime provided the structure that was needed to bring the Muslim nations together. By aligning themselves together as one large military force, victory was no longer out of reach in their thinking. The leadership of Gog Golshiri seemed to be the missing link in the long history of defeats against Israel. In the past, the infighting between the nations stood in the way. Those days seemed to have come to an end.

The IDF was primarily focused on the northern part of Israel and the Gaza Strip. Soldiers from Egypt began to move in along the border near the Gaza Strip. Hamas gained ground slowly, as the Egyptian soldiers grew in number and poured in from the south. Cities like Jerusalem were still relatively safe as the fighting remained in the north and southern parts of Israel. The occasional missile launch would create moments of havoc in the streets, but the missiles were all intercepted by the Iron Dome system, preventing any damage to the city. The entire Israel Defense Forces were now in action, and citizens from the northern areas and the central areas of Israel fled to the mountains in Jordan, in fear that nuclear weapons could be used. Many of the nations involved in the fighting were nuclear capable and threatened to use weapons of mass destruction in the past. It was becoming clear that they intended to utterly destroy Israel, and one sure way to do that would be with the use of nuclear warheads.

Golshiri forces were on the march and were slowly gaining ground in the north. The sheer number of troops was problematic for IDF. The IDF was holding the Golshiri forces back, but casualties were high, and sustained conflict wasn't possible. The Israel Defense Forces called up all their reserves. This was the war of wars for Israel. The last time Israel faced such a force was around AD 70 when Israel faced off against Roman forces.

Golshiri forces focused their artillery fire and armor on different areas of the battle line to create gaps that could then be fortified with other troops as they dug into their new positions. The battle line moved like a sidewinding snake to the north and to the south on several occasions. This allowed for the Golshiri regime to gain additional ground slowly. The IDF had no choice but to retreat slowly when they did this. The retreat was necessary to prevent mass casualties. Golshiri's forces would first push from the northern end of the battle line and then from either the center or the southern part. They mixed up their attack patterns to purposefully confuse the IDF. The tactic worked slowly, and the regime forces gained ground every time they employed the tactic. In between pushes with their armor, they sent in a barrage of surface-to-surface missiles and artillery shells. Israeli forces were on the defensive.

*****

Meanwhile, in Tel Aviv, the Israeli prime minister, Adam Lefler, was about to meet with Prime Minister Jared Hadad from the European Union. The purpose of the meeting was to discuss a strategic partnership between Israel and the EU. Adam set the meeting after learning that the United Nations would not be passing a resolution to admonish the Golshiri regime for their aggression and their invasion of Israel.

Jared accepted Adam's invitation because he knew that he had to honor the alliance between the European Union and Israel. The two countries had been sworn allies of each other since the creation of the state of Israel. He was also on the record with the press for promising some kind of military support to Israel, and at the United Nations, the EU was the only nation that was willing to take a stand with Israel.

Jared and Adam met in secret. Jared didn't want the news media to broadcast his presence in Israel. While Jared loved to have his name in the news, he knew that there was a time and place for it. A trip to a war zone was not one of those times.

Jared flew in, early in the morning, so that he could talk to the Israeli prime minister and be back into London before anyone noticed that he was gone. His plan was to meet with Adam, work out some kind of arrangement for military support, and upon his return, notify the press of the details of their new military alliance.

When the invasion began, the prime minister was moved to an office complex in Tel Aviv. His safety was of primary concern, and it was thought that he would be safer in the secret complex they had in the north. They moved him there under the cover of night and announced in the press that he would be working from his offices in Jerusalem. Secrecy was of the utmost importance as the existence of the special wartime office complex was not widely known.

The office building had the appearance of a small doctor's office at one entrance, and another entrance was inside a bakery a half mile away. The office complex was hidden under the city and occupied two square miles. The businesses were more or less a cover for the entrances and the staff of each worked for the government's Secret Service. When workers would enter the complex, they entered through one of the two businesses, at entrance points hidden inside each one. During peace time, the office complex was maintained by a skeleton crew. Only those who needed to know of its existence knew. This kept the complex secure and secret from the public for years.

When Jared arrived at the bakery, he was led inside the building by two members of his own private security and one member of the Israeli prime minister's security detail.

It was a small storefront, nestled on the outskirts of the city. The interior had a couple of small round tables, a couple of booths near the front windows, and a service counter that ran the width of the room. At the right side of the service counter was a small swinging door that led down a narrow hall, where a bathroom and two storage rooms were located.

It was empty at the time of Jared's arrival, and only two employees were in the store. A small television in the corner of the lobby provided the only noise. The two employees were behind the counter, shuffling around their baking pans and unloading a variety of baked goods into the display cases. The employees were actual bakers, but they were also employees of the Israeli government. Their assignment—providing security for the entrance to the complex. Using people that were actual bakers had the advantage of maintaining the illusion that the place was a bakery rather than a secret entrance to a government complex.

When Jared arrived at the counter, the man behind the counter looked at him suspiciously. It was as if he was sizing him up.

"The bagels have a lot of chutzpah. You should order a dozen," the man said.

Jared was prepped in advance and knew that this was a challenge question he would be asked, so he smiled back at the man and answered the question, "No, thank you. I would rather have the soup of the day."

The man looked back at Jared and gave him a second challenge. "Have you been to the village?"

Jared smiled again. Even though these were serious challenges, he thought them to be somewhat childish.

"No, I will be heading there now," he replied.

The man poked his head through the counter window area and looked around at the empty lobby. After he noticed that there was no one around. He moved around to the door to the right side and pushed it open.

"Please follow me," he called out.

The second employee moved up to the service counter as if he were handling a long line of customers. He glanced over the counter and toward the front windows as if he were looking for someone to assist. He maintained this defensive posture as Jared followed the first man down the hallway, to a door at the back left side.

There was a small keypad next to the doorway. The keypad looked the same as a standard phone keypad and had twelve numbers and characters on it. At the base of the keypad was a larger button that had no writing on it.

"After you, sir," the man said as he motioned toward the keypad.

Jared moved up to the door and stopped, glancing down at the keypad and then back up toward the man who led him down the hall. The man turned his back toward the front of the building without saying a word and just stared down the hallway, watching for anyone who may have entered. Jared looked back down at the keypad and entered an access code that he was given previously. He punched in the numbers rather swiftly. As he raced through the numbers, the keypad illuminated itself, and at each number, a low tone emerged from it. After entering all the numbers, the keypad flashed green, and the sound of the door locks could be heard, as the locks disengaged. The door swung open slightly.

"Have a nice trip," the man said, as he maintained his vision on the front of the hallway.

"Thank you," said Jared as he pushed the door open and proceeded forward.

Jared walked through the doorway, and the door immediately shut behind him. After shutting, the locks reengaged, and Jared found himself alone in the room. He scanned the room for a moment, looking for anything that he could find that would give him a clue as to what he needed to do to proceed further.

The room was completely empty. The only thing visible in the room was another small keypad on the right wall. Jared moved over to the keypad and noticed that it was another push-button keypad. He punched in the number that he used on the original lock. The lock pad flashed green, and a small section of the wall opened up, just to the left of the keypad. The wall had no visible seams where it was located, and it looked no different from any of the other walls in the room. As the hidden doorway opened, it was nearly silent.

Jared poked his head into the small opening. Inside was another empty room, except this room was about the size of a walk-in closet. The only thing present in the room was a small camera that was mounted at the ceiling and a fingerprint pad, directly parallel to the door that had just opened. Jared walked into the small room, and the wall silently closed behind him. He took a step up to the fingerprint scanner and placed his thumb onto the screen.

The room illumination changed from the standard white lighting to red, and the entire wall in front of him made a whining sound as it opened in front of him. The wall moved to the left, and the keypad disappeared inside the wall to the left. Jared was now standing in front of an elevator that was hidden just behind the wall.

He walked into the elevator and noticed that there was only one button on the front right side. It wasn't really a button so much as it was another thumbprint scanner. It flashed green intermittently and had the image of a thumbprint on it, so Jared knew that he needed to place his thumb on it to get the elevator to move. He didn't know where the elevator would go, but he only had one choice of destination because there was no other button. He pressed his thumb against the plate, and the plate pushed inward like any other button. As he released his thumb from the plate, the door closed.

The elevator hummed for a few seconds, and then he began to feel weightless and had an uneasiness in his stomach. It felt as if he was racing down an incline on a roller coaster. After what felt like a few minutes, the weightless feeling went away and was replaced by a heavy feeling. He had no way to know how fast the elevator moved, so he just assumed that the elevator went deep, underground, beneath the bakery.

After the humming sound subsided, and the uneasiness went away, the door opened. Standing in front of the opened door were two men, both wearing dark-blue suits. The two men had a visible absence of emotion and were standing in a very stiff and rigid manner. Jared could tell that they weren't waiting to climb aboard the elevator and that they were waiting on him.

"If you would kindly follow me, Mr. Hadad," one of the men said softly.

"Certainly," Jared responded.

The two men started walking down the long narrow hall. There were doors on each side of the hall, spaced about twenty feet from one another. There were no visible markings on any of the doors, and there were no people other than the two security officers and Jared.

Tired of the cloak-and-dagger act by the security guards, Jared decided that he would try to strike up a conversation with the two men.

"That was a long elevator ride. How far underground are we?" he asked.

The man closest to Jared and walking on Jared's right turned his head as he walked and looked at him. "The elevator is designed to confuse the rider. The sensation of movement makes the rider feel as if he has traveled miles, but in actuality, you are about fifty feet below the bakery," the man said wryly.

"How long has this place been here?" asked Jared.

"The main structure was constructed when ISIS began growing in strength. It was originally thought that this bunker would be needed as a safe retreat for terrorist-related attacks. Shortly after they were defeated, the complex was expanded to allow for the government to be housed in the event of a nuclear strike. This is actually one of three similar sites. The other two contain food stores and other provisions," the man said.

"This is pretty ingenious. How large is this place?" asked Jared.

"The entire facility is approximately four hundred thousand square feet. We have facilities for just about everything down here. We have a clothing store, a full-service galley, and a gym, as well as office space and sleeping quarters. It's quite comfortable. You will be meeting with the prime minister in his office," the man replied.

The three men stopped at the last door on the left and unlocked it, using another thumbprint scanner next to the door. The first man went through the door, and the second motioned for Jared to enter. He then followed behind him.

The door led to a large reception area, filled with furniture. It looked like the lobby of a large hotel. The area was busy with people jetting back and forth from office to office. The chatter sounded like a cafeteria at an elementary school, and in the background, news reports were being blasted out of the televisions in the room. There was a large wall with what appeared to be twenty large televisions, and each one was displaying different scenes from around Israel and around the globe. Some were showing old-style news reports, and others were simply showing aerial coverage of the battle in the Golan Heights region with a scrolling news banner at the base of the screens.

Jared was impressed as he scanned the room, taking in the atmosphere.

The security guard tapped Jared on the shoulder.

"Sir, if you wait here, the prime minister will greet you shortly. Would you care for a drink?"

"That would be nice. Do you have any fruit juices?"

"We have anything that you could want. Is there any particular juice that I can get for you?"

"Pomegranate juice?" he asked, to test the man.

"Right away, sir," he replied.

The security guard rushed off to get the juice as Jared took a seat on a rather large brown leather sofa. Stacked neatly on the table before him were several different periodicals and magazines. He started to thumb through them until he came to one with his picture on it. He smiled proudly as he realized that the photo was taken after he was announced as the prime minister of the European Union. He started to open the magazine, and after opening it up, he was interrupted from his curiosity.

"That was a good article, but anyone with a little common sense can tell you that it was completely false," Adam exclaimed. "It is nice to see that you made it here safely. How was the flight?"

Jared looked up and over at Adam, who was walking casually over to where he was sitting.

"What was false?" he replied.

Adam walked over to the couch where Jared was seated. He stopped just short of the end table and extended his hand to him. Jared stood and reached out his hand as well.

"The writer claimed that you stole the election. She said that you rigged it by oppressing the Muslim vote."

"Well, I am sure you can understand why they would say such things," Jared said sarcastically.

"Certainly," said Adam, "our people have been accused of everything from greed to political power grabs. It's just a part of being of Jewish descent. I see that anti-Semitism is still alive and well with the European press."

Jared smiled. "Is it that obvious?"

"What?" Adam asked.

"That I am Jewish?"

Adam grinned. "Does the pope live in Rome?" he asked.

Both started laughing.

"The flight was great, except that it was a bit cramped. I have never flown in a fighter jet before today."

"There is always a first time for everything," Adam replied. "Let's take a walk."

The two of them started toward Adam's office, which was set at the rear of the large lobby area. It was clearly visible from the soft seating area where the two greeted each other because it was the only office with a large Israeli flag decal on each of its two windows. The other offices along the rear wall had windows, but they only had one window for each office; whereas, Adam's had two.

Adam opened the office door and proceeded inside. He walked about halfway into the office and waved his hand at the sofa across from his desk.

"Please have a seat," he said.

Jared glanced around the room briefly and then graciously took a seat on the sofa. On the coffee table in front of him, he spotted some campaign-related paraphernalia and picked up a small button with Adam's name on it. He looked at it briefly and then set it back down on the table.

"So where are you on your campaign?" Jared asked with a casual but serious tone. "The latest intel that I received showed that the IDF was losing ground in Golan and that has to be giving your opposition plenty of political fodder against you."

Jared was taken aback and shuddered for a moment. He shot back at Jared with a look of curiosity for a moment, and then his curious look turned to a smirk.

"That's what I like about you, Jared. You are always straight to the point, or should I say, brutally honest!"

Adam regained his composure and took his seat behind his desk.

"Well, we don't have a lot of time to spare if we want this meeting to remain secret," Jared said pointedly.

Adam again looked unnerved as Jared continued to be direct with him.

"Well, to be blunt, your intelligence sources are correct. We have been losing ground," Adam said with a troubled tone.

"What's the casualty figure?" asked Jared.

"We have lost about fifteen hundred soldiers since the invasion began. About twice that have been wounded."

"What about the Golshiri regime?"

"Well, we really don't have solid numbers on that. Based on reports from intercepts, we believe they have lost about ten thousand."

Jared thought that the casualty count would be much higher. He sat there, mulling over the numbers and looked a bit perplexed. After all, the fighting was intense for weeks and only losing 1,500 was low compared to what it could have been.

"How are you logistically?" asked Jared.

"Fortunately, we were able to stockpile munitions over the past few years. We are good for now. We have daily drops from the United States, but with the escalation in the Mediterranean, we have been getting greater delays in that," he replied.

Jared nodded along. "I know you are looking for the European Union to get here with our troops, but we haven't been able to get the ships loaded completely. We are about two weeks out before we can sail with those ships."

"Two weeks?" Adam asked. "What have you heard from the Americans?"

"It's not good." He grimaced. "They are not willing to commit more than they previously discussed. They are willing to continue the humanitarian drops, but I really don't think you can expect much more than food and medical supplies from them. At least from a federal level anyway."

"How is the project going with I-Corp?" Adam asked with a less-than-thrilled tone.

"Not fast enough to get any help out here in the short-term. The prototype is completed." He paused. "Well, there is more than just the one prototype, but—"

"But what?" asked Adam.

"We have actually built the first two thousand."

"Really?" He smiled. "What's the but?"

"The first two thousand were promised to the Chinese. They paid rather handsomely for them."

"Are they fully operational?" asked Adam.

"Yes, they are fully operational. They also look just like human beings, and you wouldn't be able to tell one apart from a human if you put them in a lineup. The problem is that if we were to send them here, the Chinese would be upset, and they may be marching at your door in retaliation," Jared responded.

"I see," he said. "Is it possible to make a deal with the Chinese to get them to take a delay in the shipment?"

"Possibly," replied Jared.

Adam stood up from his chair and walked over to a small bar in his corner. "Would you care for a drink?" he asked.

"Actually, your man was getting me a pomegranate juice."

Adam took out two glasses and put ice cubes into each glass. He then made mixed drinks out of gin, vodka, and a mixture of juices in another container.

"Try this."

"What is it?" asked Jared.

"It's a mixture that my father called the Tel Aviv special."

Jared took the glass, and both sipped the drink. Adam returned to his seat.

"How can I convince you to get those troops to Israel rather than China?"

"I suppose that the Chinese don't know that they are first in line. I will get with my old partner, Peter, at I-Corp and see what we can do."

Jared paused for a moment as he took another sip of the drink.

"It may be helpful if we can get Peter a surcharge on each unit. Let's say 20 percent per unit. Do you think you can come up with the capital to pay for the early delivery?"

"That kind of expenditure is going to take some convincing on my end," said Adam. "I will see what we can do."

"Great! In the meantime, I will inform the press that we spoke via telecom and that you advised that Israel is doing well and that European forces will remain in standby. While we are loading the ships, they will assume it is for the standby mission, and everything will look normal from their perspective," Jared explained.

"Agreed," replied Adam.

There was a sudden knock on the door. Adam got up from his chair and walked to the door and opened it.

"My apologies, Mr. Prime Minister, but I have a glass of juice for your guest."

Adam looked over at Jared.

"Do you still want the juice?" he asked.

"I guess it is better late than never." He chuckled. Adam took the juice and handed it to Jared, who was now standing.

"At least it's cold," said Adam.

Jared took the glass of juice and quickly finished the entire glass.

"That was worth the wait," he exclaimed. "I will start working on this the minute I land in the UK. Once I know something, I'll give you a ring, and we can go over the final details."

"Great!" Adam replied.

Jared reached out and shook hands with Adam and then proceeded out of the office.

Once outside the office, Jared climbed into the limousine that was conveniently waiting for him right out in front of the building. As the limousine began to move, Jared settled into the seat and grabbed the remote control for the small television next to the bar. The television was still on from his earlier ride to the bakery, and a new report was playing. He couldn't hear what the reporters were saying, so he turned it up to a moderate volume.

"The Golshiri regime has steadily been gaining ground in northern Israel. Our sources tell us that Israeli casualties are extremely high and that total wounded is around 30,000."

Jared looked a bit perplexed. In his meeting with Adam, he learned that the number of the injured was around 4,500.

Could another 26,000 have been injured while I was inside the office with Adam? he thought.

The reporter continued. "The same sources tell us that the number of soldiers killed in action has climbed to 10,000. If this war continues as it has, Israel is likely to be pushed back to Jerusalem in a matter of a month."

Jared smiled and shook his head. "I cannot believe that they would report such utter nonsense," he said softly. "What's the purpose in calling yourself a news organization if you are going to utter falsehoods?" Jared noticed the news company logo in the top left of the screen. He smiled a second time as he realized what station he was watching. "Oh my!" He chuckled. "That explains it." Jared realized that the news station that he was watching was an American cable news network. This particular outlet was well-known for spinning stories out of control. They wanted ratings, and their target audience wasn't intellectual enough to realize that they were being duped, so their reporting was usually more outside of reality than most fantasy novels.

"When will these Americans learn?" he asked while laughing out loud. Once he realized that he was watching fictional news, he switched the channel over to the British Broadcasting Network. He knew that the news would still be somewhat embellished, but that he was likely to hear something more along the realm of reality by watching that news channel as compared to the American station.

"We are currently tracking a severe weather system developing over the Mediterranean. The system is expected to intensify over the next several hours and eventually affect parts of Egypt and Israel. It will then make its way northeast toward Syria and northern Jordan, where it is expected to weaken over the next several days. The system is being monitored very closely, as it has already had a significant pressure drop this morning, at 920 millibars, down from 1,000. The pressure is currently at 920 millibars," said the meteorologist.

Jared was astounded as he gazed at the satellite picture on the screen. The storm was massive and appeared to have an underdeveloped eye, as if it were a hurricane.

The meteorologist continued to speak. "This is really an unusual weather event for the area. The storm is expected to strengthen rather quickly, and we aren't quite sure as to exactly how much it will be. Weather aircraft will continue flying in the outer bands of the storm every hour to get pressure readings and wind-speed velocities. The current wind speeds are sustained at one hundred miles per hour, which is up from seventy only an hour ago."

Jared shook his head in disbelief at what he was seeing and hearing.

"To say that the storm is unusual doesn't do it justice. This storm is more like a tropical system, and this is not the season or the location for storms such as this."

"We have been in contact with the Russian Space Agency, and one of their chief scientists told us, on a condition of anonymity, that this may well be a new type of weather pattern. He told us that hurricanes are expected to develop more rapidly and more intensely in the coming years, and that they are likely to develop and strike regions outside the Atlantic and Pacific Oceans. He further explained that it is likely that the increase in seawater temperatures across the globe, because of global warming, is creating a climate shift that is changing the weather as we know it."

Jared looked at his watch to check the time and then peered outside the limousine window. He knew that if he were to get out of Israel before the storm, that he would need to do it sooner rather than later. He knew the airport wasn't far, but what he didn't know was if the airport runways were closed in anticipation of the weather.

The meteorologist continued. "On a side note, regions that have not traditionally seen the weather such as this are not likely prepared for such storms. As it stands, we don't know if this is a new trend or just an isolated event, but we can say that seeing a potential hurricane in the Mediterranean is unsettling at best."

Jared was astonished at the news. *I guess global warming isn't a myth after all,* he thought. As Jared sat there thinking about the storm, the window between the driver's compartment and the rear-seating area opened up. Ronald, the limousine driver, overheard Jared speaking to himself and thought that Jared was asking him a question.

"Did you need something, sir?" asked Ronald.

"My apologies. I didn't realize that my voice was carrying. I was actually thinking out loud," he replied. "How much farther to the airport?"

"We should be there in another fifteen minutes," he replied.

Jared turned his focus back to the news program on the television. The weather report was now over. The larger picture of the storm shrunk down into the lower-left portion of the screen. The remainder of the screen had a scrolling banner at the bottom of the screen, and a new reporter appeared. The banner at the base of the screen read, "Storm of the Millennium Threatens Israel, Creating Double Threat of Bombardment."

Jared shook his head again as he watched the screen. The media sure didn't like to waste an opportunity to scare people or to embellish reality. They made it sound as if the storm was going to entirely wipe out Israel and as if the storm was somehow colluding with the Golshiri forces.

The limousine pulled into the airport but didn't go through the main security area for regular commercial traffic. The car passed through a checkpoint at the rear of the facility where the private-jet traffic and military traffic entered. As the car navigated its way past several closed aircraft hangars, Jared could see the jet he flew in earlier, sitting on the tarmac. The jets on the plane were already running, and the jet was simply waiting for its passenger to arrive. Jared watched as the car pulled up to the hangar and crawled to a stop. The air at the rear of the aircraft was moving in a wavelike motion and was visibly distorted from the intense heat emanating from the jet engines. There was no visible flame coming from the engine, but the hiss of the engine grew higher in pitch as the vehicle got closer to the aircraft.

He wasn't looking forward to the flight because it was a bit too cramped for his taste on the first trip. He also didn't like the roller-coaster feeling that he got as the jet gained altitude and traversed the skies on its way up to thirty thousand feet. There was no other way he could quickly travel and be in both Israel and London on the same day.

He exited the limousine and walked toward the jet, where a military aircraft engineer was conducting a walk around inspection of the aircraft. The pilot was seated at the front of the cockpit and writing in a small notebook as he completed his preflight checks.

Jared stopped for a moment and took in the surroundings. It looked a lot like Arizona in that it was very desertlike in this area, and there was not a lot of green vegetation. There were buildings dotting horizon, and the mountains that were visible were far off and looked more like small hills than mountains. The only color, other than the desert's brown, was emanating from the sky, which was perfectly blue, and not a single cloud was visible. Jared wondered, as he stood there, if anyone knew that there was a monster of a storm headed their way. If they did know, they weren't overly concerned about it because the place was extremely devoid of people, and there weren't any aircraft taking off or landing at the time. It was very serene, considering the venue.

Jared climbed into the jet and took his seat in the rear. He briefly exchanged pleasantries with the pilot, who was still busy completing his preflight checks. After a few minutes, he was settled in, and the cockpit canopy closed.

The engines roared to life, and the jet started to taxi to the main runway. Jared was slightly nervous, but he was familiar with the events that were to follow, because he remembered his flight into Tel Aviv. As the jet moved away from the hangar and circled around to the tarmac, the skies to the west became visible. They were no longer the picturesque blue that Jared fawned over only moments previous. The storm could clearly be seen, slowly rolling in, and it was massive and dark. The clouds were far from serene as they rolled over one another in the distance. It looked more like the black smoke billowing from a large fire. The lightning flashing through the clouds was confirmation that there was no fire in the area and that the entire area would soon be under siege by a historic storm.

Jared couldn't help but to feel nervous as he watched the storm draw near. It was impressive. It had the appearance of a giant dust cloud, kicked up by a million horses racing into battle, with the lightning appearing as shiny swords waved in the air. The thunder could be heard over the engines, as they roared to life. Jared could sense the ferocity as the army marched its way across the terrain, headed into a battle of epic proportion.

"Are we flying through that storm?" Jared asked the pilot.

"No, sir, we will miss most of it. We will be taking a flight path just east of the storm, but it may be a bit turbulent on our ascent. Do you need an air sickness bag?"

"No, thank you. I was simply curious. It looks like this one is going to be bad," said Jared.

"The weather is just like a bunch of politicians, sir. You see them, and they look ominous, but they often aren't as bad as you would expect," he said jokingly.

Jared chuckled. "You obviously haven't met many politicians. The ones that I know look great, but upon closer examination look worse than this storm."

The pilot and Jared both started laughing in unison as the jet began to lift off the runway.

CHAPTER 9

Rain and Fury

Back in northern Israel, the fighting was getting more and more intense. The troops in the Golan Heights region now numbered around three hundred thousand. They continued to push their way to the north side of the Sea of Galilee. Their gains were slow but steady. Casualties were lower than the media around the globe continued to report and less than one would expect for a full-scale invasion, but Israeli forces were very adept at defense and had plenty of firepower to combat the aggressors from the north.

Egyptian forces continued to pour across the border in the southern part of Israel, but the IDF was able to slow the bleeding by sending a large reserve contingent to the area.

The silence from the Golshiri regime continued. The motives for their aggression were still a mystery to the rest of the world. The rumor mills across the American nation and Europe continued, and some reports became so sensationalized that some people believed that China was involved in the fighting. The truth was that the Chinese wanted no part in the fighting.

As the Golshiri regime continued their attempts to push south, the aggression became more intense. Their soldiers had an appetite for war that seemed insatiable. Most of the fighting was with the armored divisions and the artillery units. The infantry was not overly utilized because they were trying to soften the Israeli line, before sending them in. They had early successes in wearing down the Israeli line, but those successes were short-lived, as the Israeli Air Force was quite adept at taking out heavy armor. Their successes were short-lived. Every time they would advance, the Israeli forces would reinforce the areas being attacked more heavily, and they would push the line back to near where the battle started.

The Israeli forces lost a lot of ground at the onset of the battle, but they had weeks in advance to prepare for the coming battle when the Golshiri forces built up in the north. During that time, the IDF laid mines and set up several other antipersonnel munitions, fearing an eventual push to the south by the Golshiri regime.

The Golshiri forces had early success in their invasion, but they were significantly slowed when they reached the northernmost portion of the Sea of Galilee. The IDF was dug in fairly well, and they utilized their air superiority and other countermeasures to cause significant damage to the Golshiri forces.

The IDF set up most of their artillery at the southern part of the Golan Heights region and to both the east and west of the Sea of Galilee. The Sea of Galilee was utilized as a natural barrier, and their forces set up in such a way as to create a choke point to the west side of the Sea of Galilee. It was inevitable that the battle line would eventually reach the area, but the Golshiri forces had no idea of the extent of the preparations made by the Israeli forces. While they focused on breaking the line, between the Golan Heights and the Sea of Galilee, the IDF stayed busy in reinforcing the rear areas. The benefit was that the Israeli forces could retreat at the center of the front and draw the Golshiri forces deeper into their designed choke point. The intent was to inflict as much carnage as possible, should the battle wage on and reach the central regions of Israel.

The incoming weather would likely slow any further progress for the norther aggressors. The area is a desert region, and a significant rainfall, as happens in a tropical system, would cause flash flooding and bring sustained winds that would make fighting next to impossible. Rockets would not be as effective in such weather, so the storm was seen by some as an opportunity to regroup and plan for a counterattack after the storm subsided.

The storm moved in slowly but fiercely. The winds began to reach the interior parts of Israel. They weren't at full strength but were enough to cause damage and to make travel begin to slow to a crawl.

The rain started at a moderate pace at first and were very intermittent as the bands started swirling over the country. It was not heavy but was strong enough that with the wind speeds of eighty miles per hour, it made visibility difficult. This was just the beginning, and the meteorologists said that the full effects of the storm would not be felt until after twenty-four to thirty-six hours.

Adam moved from Tel Aviv to Chorazim, which was northwest of Capernaum. The bulk of the fighting was getting closer to this region, and this was where the Thirty-Sixth Armored Division set up their field tactical operations center. The front line was further to the north, but with the recent push by the Golshiri regime, the front line was inching its way south, and eventually Chorazim would take over as the front.

He traveled to the area to get a bird's eye view of the preparations in the area and to get an intelligence brief from his chief of general staff, Yoseph Belkin, and one of his best field officers, Major General Elazar Alpert. The in-person meeting was set for the tactical operations center rather than via teleconference in order to maintain operational security by avoiding communications that were susceptible to intercept by the Golshiri forces.

The operations center consisted of a cluster of large tents that were reinforced with large sand barricades on all four sides. The tents were camouflaged as well as could be done for the area. The operations center was surrounded by several other similar tents that the soldiers used as barracks for the short-term. Concertina wire was placed around the entire operating base in stacked coils. They wrapped around the front, left, and right sides of the encampment. Other coiled rows of concertina wire were stretched out in rows that appeared endless, mixed in with large steel barricades meant to prevent the passage of troops and tanks from the north. This would stall the aggression of the Golshiri regime and perhaps give the Israelis the time needed to bombard the enemy to prevent further movement south or to at least be able to take up other positions in the south. The concertina wire shone bright with the sun at full strength. It was surely a sight to behold.

Just to the front of the rows of concertina wires and barricades was the entire Thirty-Sixth Armored Division. The tanks were lined up, ready to fire upon anything that moved toward the south. Behind the concertina-wire rows were all the heavy artillery. They were dug in and ready to begin shelling the enemy with a ferociousness so great that any army headed south would be pummeled without mercy. The entire defensive line was the largest force ever assembled on a single battlefield in history.

Adam arrived in the mid part of the afternoon, but because of the storm, it appeared as if it were dusk. The storm pushed in warmer winds that made it feel as if it were late summer rather than spring. The wind made a howling sound as it blew steadily across the region. The tents shook violently with the wind, but there was enough just enough cover by the sand barricades and other reinforcing materials that they were expected to hold until the main force of the storm was expected to arrive.

Adam got out of his vehicle and looked up toward the storm that was approaching. The sky was dark toward the west, and the winds were still blowing steadily. He began to walk toward the main operations tent, where he witnessed a flurry of activity. As he got closer to the tents, the sound of the soldiers increased and began to overtake the howling of the wind.

Soldiers were scurrying around like ants on an ant nest, disturbed by a wayward tree branch striking it. They could be seen grabbing and carrying every loose item and sensitive piece of equipment that they could carry and loading it into large cargo containers. They moved it into the containers as quickly as they could, to prevent it from being damaged or destroyed in the coming storm.

"Sergeant, where can I find General Belkin?" Adam bellowed out to a passing soldier.

The soldier looked over at Adam, and as soon as he recognized who it was that was yelling at him, he snapped to attention and started to salute the prime minister, before realizing that he was in a forward area, where saluting officers is not permitted. His arm got about halfway up before he realized it, and he snapped his arm back down almost as quickly as he started to throw the salute.

"Sir! Commander in Chief Belkin has stepped out for a moment. The officer on duty is General Alpert," he said nervously.

"If you could point me in the right direction—" Adam started before being cut off by the nervous sergeant.

"Follow me, sir," he barked.

Adam smiled. He remembered that he once was a soldier, just as this sergeant is, and he always felt nervous when seeing a high-ranking officer or other high-ranking government official, from time to time.

"Where are you from, Sergeant?" he asked.

The sergeant turned his head crisply toward Adam. "It's Atman, sir," he replied. "I am from Rahat, sir."

Adam saw that the sergeant was still visibly nervous. He was not sure if it was because of his own recent arrival, because of the impending storm, or the mass of troops headed toward them. He also thought that it could be a culmination of all three about to happen in rapid-fire succession of one another.

"Relax, Sergeant, the weather is going to be just fine," he said with a smile. "The weather is going to be the weather, and as far as the troops headed this way, they have to deal with the weather as well. I don't think that any of us are going to be seeing much of a battle for at least another twenty-four to thirty-six hours." Adam chose to emphasize the weather headed into the country rather than the troops or himself. He figured that the weather was the most visible threat at the moment, and that if he spun it just right, he could get the sergeant to focus on the task at hand rather than trying to focus on everything at the same time and being overwhelmed.

The sergeant's gaze became a bit more relaxed as they proceeded toward the operations tent.

"Yes, sir. My lieutenant briefed us on the weather at 0900 hours," he said calmly. "My mother always said that there was a calm before every storm, and I'm just waiting for the calm to arrive. Everything has been pretty hectic around here."

Adam smiled again. "You are a long way from home," he said, purposely changing the subject back to his earlier subject.

"Yes, sir, but I am proud to be a part of the fighting Thirty-Sixth, sir," he replied boastfully. "Home isn't always where you hang your hat. Sometimes home is where your family is located, and in this case, my family is all right here with me in this sea of tents." The sergeant sped up slightly and positioned himself a few paces in front of Adam. As he reached the door to the tent, he pulled back the door for him and snapped back to attention.

"Well, I certainly appreciate the talk, Sergeant Atman. Good luck out there! Just remember that your whole country is proud of you and appreciates your dedication to our great nation."

"Thank you, sir," he replied.

Adam stepped into the tent, and the makeshift door closed behind him. The interior of the tent was filled with different personnel who were sitting at desks spread neatly around the room. The atmosphere was less chaotic, as people weren't dashing around inside, but the noise level was quite elevated as the soldiers talked among themselves as the radios blared a number of different conversations all at once.

At the back wall of the tent was a large whiteboard and what appeared to be gibberish written all over it. To the right of that was another large whiteboard that was being used as a screen for a projector. The image being projected was of an enemy tank that was ablaze and expelling a massive amount of smoke. Adam assumed the photo was taken after a recent airstrike. Since no one was seated near the projector, he calculated that their briefing must have already concluded. That area of the tent was deserted as the projector sat running, and the ten or more folding chairs were all out of order and empty.

A young female corporal brushed past the prime minister as she briskly walked from the radio toward a rather large desk on the opposite side of the tent and did a double take before suddenly stopping.

"Attention!" she screamed, as she snapped to attention.

The noise level in the tent dropped suddenly, and the soldiers all froze up at once in unison. Every movement in the tent stopped so abruptly it was as if someone flipped off a light switch or if they had all been hit with an arctic blast so cold that it could stop the movement inside an atom instantaneously.

Adam was taken aback by the sudden shout and flinched slightly. He looked quite impressed by the soldiers' ability to stop on a dime, all in unison. He gazed around the tent with a pleased look on his face, and when his eyes met the general's, he stared for a moment and then said softly, "At ease. Please carry on."

General Alpert, who was standing on the opposite side of the tent, immediately recognized the prime minister and shuffled over to him, as the other occupants of the tent resumed their activity. The noises level went back up but was slightly lower than it had been just moments prior.

"Mr. Prime Minister, it is wonderful to see you," he said.

Adam stood there and smiled back at the general.

"Elazar!" he said with excitement. "You are looking as great as ever. How has the world been treating you?"

"You know"—he chuckled—"that schlemiel from Russia and his vagabond army is making me earn my pay, and I'm not happy about it." He stopped for a moment, taking the opportunity to look at the prime minister in great detail. He looked him up and down and smiled brightly as he threw out his hand to the prime minister.

"How the heck have you been, Adam?" he said as he moved in and embraced him with a handshake and a hug.

"Are you set for the weather event?" asked Adam.

"We are as ready as we can be. We moved our sensitive equipment into storage and sealed it up rather good, I guess. The good news is that it won't affect us as much as it is going to affect Golshiri."

"Great to hear. Are we taking advantage of it or just hunkering down?" he asked.

The general paused for a moment as he carefully thought out his response. Adam was a good friend, but he was also his commander in chief. "We aren't exactly sure how the weather will play out, but we have a plan, either way," he said confidently.

"How's that?" asked Adam.

The general motioned to Adam to have a seat and then circled around to the back of his desk and sat down.

"We have two battalions that are ready to deploy east into Jordan. Golshiri's eastern side is weaker than the northern side, so we think that we can come up from Jordan and flank them from the north and east. This will give us the advantage of pushing the fight back to the west, away from the northern part of the Sea of Galilee. If we can get them pushed back toward the west, then we can focus our fire into the choke point we created and inflict some rather good damage. We may then be able to bring up our reserves to make a push toward the west."

"So you want them to the north of the Sea of Galilee?" asked Adam.

"Essentially, that is correct. Right now, they have the advantage because they outnumber us from a troop standpoint. They are able to make small forward movements because they control the line. If we can pin them by using the topography, we can essentially get them clustered into one area and then unleash a bombing and artillery fury on them. The weather allows us to position the troops to flank them because it has eliminated their aerial reconnaissance."

"I see," said Adam. "What if the weather is a bust?"

"Well, if we cannot get them to move west, we will have to go with our original plan and hope for the best. Either way, we will be making a large push in the next week. We can't keep retreating. The southern forces have been moving toward the north since the cloud cover first started in, so we should be able to make an effective push."

"Good to hear," said Adam.

As Adam and the general were speaking, a sergeant walked up smartly to the two. "Excuse me, General, Prime Minister," he said.

"What is it, Sergeant Delman?" the general asked.

"We have reports that the storm is approaching sooner than anticipated. It has already intensified around Yarka."

"What's the situation report from our forces in that area?" asked the general.

"They are reporting"—he paused—"they are reporting—" he paused again.

General Alpert looked at the sergeant with great anticipation. "What are they reporting, Sergeant?"

"Sir, what they are reporting just doesn't make any sense."

"What are they reporting?" Adam asked, now having his curiosity aroused.

The sergeant stood there silent and with a look of embarrassment mixed with fear. He stood there with his hands clasped together behind his back and started to rock, ever so gently, back and forth. After a long pause, he answered, "The rain has started, and it has started to hail."

"What?" asked the prime minister. Adam was a bit confused.

Hail couldn't be all that was worrying this sergeant. Hail was quite common in large thunderstorms. He thought that it couldn't be the rain that had the sergeant so disturbed because there wasn't much that was more innocuous than rain.

Adam looked directly at the sergeant. "Is there something particularly unusual about rain and hail that upsets you, Sergeant?" he asked.

The sergeant stood there, stoic. He was visibly distressed, and he didn't want to answer. After a few uncomfortable moments with the prime minister and the general staring him down, he responded to their probing, "They are reporting blood, sir!"

Adam and General Alpert looked even more confused at this point.

"What are you talking about, Sergeant?" asked General Alpert.

"Sir, they are reporting that it is actually raining blood, and that it is mixed with rather large hail and extremely heavy winds. It's like something out of a movie, sir," said the sergeant.

Adam leaped up from his seat. He couldn't believe what he was hearing. "What?" he exclaimed. "How can it be raining blood?"

General Alpert remained calm. His face was emotionless. "Thank you, Sergeant Delman," he said. "Whatever you do, do not repeat this to anyone outside until we have had a chance to confirm it."

*****

On the opposite side of the tent, a group of soldiers gathered and huddled up into one exceptionally large group. They began making a raucous commotion as they all tried to squeeze together to get a glimpse at the television. The news media was on scene in the area of Yarka, and they were discussing the weather.

*****

The general looked at the prime minister, and the prime minister looked back. They both had expressions of bewilderment. After a short pause, the two began walking toward the group of huddled soldiers.

The general stopped and turned back to the sergeant. "Thank you, Sergeant. You are dismissed. Please carry on," he said calmly, before turning and proceeding toward the television.

General Alpert and Adam stood with their faces frozen with looks of astonishment as they heard the reports. There really was blood rain falling in Yarka. They could not believe what they were seeing. It really was like the sergeant said. It was like something that came straight out of a movie.

CHAPTER 10

Witness

In Petra, Charles and the rest of the group was settling in. The whole area was filled with people, huddled together in small groups. Small fires dotted the area and could be seen burning throughout the night. With the temperature drops in the evening, the fires were necessary for keeping people warm. They were also used for cooking.

The Jordanian authorities trucked in wood and other supplies such as food and potable water, so that the refugees would be able to survive. It was a small gesture but appreciated nonetheless by all who were the benefactors of the kindness.

At this point, the numbers in the encampment swelled to around twenty thousand people. Many of the people in the camp were elderly and required assistance. They were brought there by their family members, to escape the fighting in Israel, and it was thought safer for them in Petra rather than in Jerusalem, where life would be filled with uncertainty because of the war.

David and Cynthia were assisting a man who appeared to be in his late eighties as he tried to climb from his bed on the ground, to his wheelchair. He was there with his wife, who was a sprite old woman with flowing silver hair. When David and Cynthia saw her struggling to get him into his chair, they quickly ran over and gave the pair a hand.

Charles and Chris were out on walk and exploring the area and its unique architecture. Along the way, they made it a point to stop and introduce themselves to the other families in the area. They wanted to meet as many of the people as possible and also to make sure that everyone was getting along well.

As they reached the edge of the canyon entrance, they happened onto a younger man of about twenty-five, who was alone and resting comfortably by a small fire. He was a stout fellow of about six foot five and with dark-brown hair. He looked like he could have been a model or a movie star with his rugged good looks and chiseled physique.

The man was lying next to his fire, propped up with a small pillow. He was alone, and he was picking the meat off what appeared to be a piece of chicken.

"Hello," Chis said to the man as he approached him.

"Ah, good evening," the man replied as he looked up toward the pair. "You had better find a warmer shirt for your partner. He looks like he is cold."

Chris looked at Charles and the T-shirt he was wearing. He couldn't help but laugh as he remembered the clothing debacle and how he obtained the shirt. His current shirt had the words "Just Chillin'" written across the front, and just a few minutes earlier, he poked fun at Charles for the irony of the written expression on the shirt.

"Ha," Chris shouted aloud. "It is noticeable, isn't it?"

"Slightly," the man replied. "You are welcome to join me and warm yourselves. You look a bit cold as well."

Charles looked down at his shirt and started turning a shade of pink. The shirt was a bit snug, but it wasn't overly obvious that it was a woman's shirt.

"I didn't think ahead when I packed to come out here. I thought it was going to be hot," said Charles.

"Please have a seat," the man said with a chuckle.

Charles cautiously sat down and scanned the area around him to make sure there weren't any large rocks or, worse, bugs that would crawl up onto him. As he settled himself and was satisfied that the area was clear, he leaned over to the man, extending his hand.

"I'm Charles, and this is Chris," he said as he hovered near the fire.

The man sat up from where he was reclined, and he tossed the remnants of his dinner into the fire. He reached out to the extended hand that Charles presented, and rather than grabbing his hand, he wrapped his hand around Charles's forearm. He held it momentarily and then began to shake it gently while also extending out his other hand and patting Charles on the shoulder.

Charles wasn't used to this kind of handshake, so he gently started to pull his arm back at first. He looked a little taken aback by the gesture, before finally understanding that it was just an alternate version of a handshake. Then after a split second of feeling foolish, he leaned in and shook hands with the man.

"It is nice to meet you, Charles and Chris," he said as he leaned over toward Chris and gave a similar handshake and embrace. "Please sit by the fire with me for a while. It is going to be a cold night, and I could use the company and the warmth of a good conversation. My name is Eli."

Chris and Charles settled in. It wasn't a large fire by any stretch of the imagination. In fact, the fire wasn't much of a fire after all, and at this point was a heap of red coals with a slight stream of smoke and a few sparks wisping upward into the darkness.

Charles got up and gathered a couple pieces of wood and began to place them onto the heap of coals.

"So, Eli, that is a wonderful name. Are you familiar with the Elijah of the Bible?" he asked as he placed the second piece of wood onto the fire.

"Yes, I would say that I'm somewhat familiar. He was an interesting character, wouldn't you say?"

"Oh yes," said Charles, "he was a man of God and a great prophet."

"Really?" said Eli. "What makes him a great man?"

"Well, he did make a fire to prove that God was more powerful than Baal," said Charles.

Eli nodded as he considered the answer.

"If the making of fire makes one great, then there are at least a few hundred great men here with us," he chortled.

"I guess so," said Charles laughingly. "He actually did many great things, but the fire was one of the more memorable things."

"I see," said Eli. "If I recall correctly though, it wasn't Elijah who made the fire."

"Sure, he did," Charles interrupted. "He called down fire from heaven."

"What I meant to say was that it wasn't Elijah at all. He was just doing what God wanted him to do. While some may see that as great, others would see it as simply being obedient. The fire that came down was from God, not Elijah."

He paused for a moment.

Another thing about Elijah is that he was said to be able to control the rain. This also would not have been possible without the help of the Most High, of course."

"I guess you are right. No man has power that isn't given to him by God," said Charles.

"You two are great men," said Eli. "I have heard stories of the two of you."

"How is that?" asked Chris.

"You two have been doing great things ever since you got here to Petra, have you not?"

"Well, I wouldn't call it great. We were just doing what we could to help," said Chris.

"Ah, and that would make you great in the eyes of our Lord. Did he not say that 'I assure you that when you have done it for one of the least of these brothers and sisters of mine, you have done it for me.' And if you have done good for these people, then you have also done good for him, correct?" he asked.

"Well, I guess that's one way to look at it," said Charles.

"Where are you from?" asked Chris.

"I am from a small land in northern Israel, just a short walk from the Zarqa River or known as the Jabbok River in older days. It's not much of a city, but I have not been there in many years. I was on my way there before coming to this place. Something told me that I would be better off here, to wait out the violence," he explained.

Charles looked perplexed. "You'll have to forgive me. My geography isn't that great. But if you are from northern Israel, then you must be really concerned because that's where the fighting is going on," said Charles.

"Do you have family in the region still? I hope that they are safe," said Chris.

"No, my family has long been removed from the area," he replied. "I don't worry about the violence in the north. Our Lord knows what he is doing. These are just things that must come to pass."

"You sure said it," exclaimed Charles. "I was just telling Chris how this whole thing is almost biblical."

All three laughed.

"The violence will end soon. I am here waiting on a friend. He will be along in a day or two," Eli explained. "How did you two come to be in Israel from all the way across the world?"

"Well, like you, I came to see a friend. He is actually over on the other side of camp," said Chris. "Maybe you can meet him later. Charles came so that he could see Jerusalem for the first time."

Eli nodded.

"We are often called to do many things. We who listen may not even know why we do some things, but we know that in the end, that what we are doing is exactly as we were called to do," he explained.

"I know what you mean," said Chris. "Ever since I was a young boy, I felt a calling to share the gospel. I fought it for a while and did my own thing, but I could never shake the feeling that it was what I was meant to do."

Eli nodded.

"With the Most High, there are many mysteries. One of the greatest of those is how we hear the voice of God without hearing an actual voice. We know who it is, and we can test what we have heard to know that what we are hearing is truth," said Eli.

Charles grabbed a small stick and began poking it around in the fire.

"I wasn't as young as Chris when I knew that I was being called. I was just fortunate to meet Chris one day, and through that meeting, was able to learn that God was actually talking to me. I was a horrible person back then. I thought that my calling was to be a police officer and that didn't work out so well for me," Charles explained.

"It is not always clear at first. God works in his own time. I would suspect that there is a reason for all those moments in your life that you are not proud of. We all respond differently to God's call, but we can be sure that God does call to all. Some will answer that call, and some will spend their whole life running from God and ignoring him. For you, it took trials and tribulations. For Chris, it did not, but the result is the same. You both listened to that small voice inside of you and answered the call," Eli explained.

"That's a great way of explaining it. Similar to what Paul said to the Romans about the purpose of the law," said Chris.

"What do you mean?" asked Charles. "Are you saying that I became a police officer so that I would understand why laws exist?"

"Not exactly," said Chris. "Paul said that when we are reborn of the spirit that we live for the spirit and not of the flesh. Before we were saved, we were slaves to the law. The law exists to show that we cannot save ourselves because we, being of flesh, cannot live up to the law and need a savior. In essence, the law exists to draw us to Jesus, and through him, we are freed from the law and become slaves to the spirit. We become free of the slavery to sin and death or something like that."

Charles looked a little confused.

"So my suffering was meant to draw me to God?" he asked.

Seeing Charles's confusion, Chris turned toward him and began to explain. He could see that Charles was running circles in his mind and that he didn't quite understand what he was saying.

"Well, I look at it this way. We are all sinners. We are inherently sinful, and no matter how hard we try or no matter what we do, we cannot live up to God's righteous standard. The law represents God's righteous standard. By giving us the law, we are able to look at ourselves in comparison with the law. That reveals to us that we are sinful because if there was no law, we would not know the benchmark, so to speak. Since we know that we are sinful, we naturally are drawn to God because we know that we are slaves to sin, and we cannot do good, no matter how hard we try. We know that we need God's mercy. So it is through the law that we are shown our sinful condition, and it is through Jesus's sacrifice and our faith that we are given God's grace. We are saved by God's grace and not by good works or deeds because we know that we cannot live up to the law. Does that make sense?"

Charles had a sudden trigger in his memory and understood what Chris was trying to explain. He opened up his Bible and began thumbing through the pages feverishly.

"I have my Bible here. I found what you were talking about. Here is what it says," said Charles.

> There is therefore now no condemnation for those who are in Christ Jesus. For the law of the Spirit of life has set you free in Christ Jesus from the law of sin and death. For God has done what the law, weakened by the flesh, could not do. By sending his own Son in the likeness of sinful flesh and for sin, he condemned sin in the flesh, in order that the righteous requirement of the law might be fulfilled in us, who walk not according to the flesh but according to the Spirit. For those who live according to the flesh set their minds on the things of the flesh, but those who live according to the Spirit set their minds on the things of the Spirit. For to set the mind on the flesh is death, but to set the mind on the Spirit is life and peace. For the mind that is set on the flesh is hostile to God, for it does not submit to God s law; indeed, it cannot. Those, who are in the flesh cannot please God.

"God's Word says it so much more eloquently than I do," Chris said, laughing.

"I think you did fine." Charles guffawed. "Nobody is perfect." Charles cocked his head to the left for a moment, thinking about what he had just said. "Well, that is not exactly true," he corrected himself. "Jesus was perfect."

Eli, who remained silent during most of the conversation, nodded again. "Amen!" he exclaimed. "You both are wise to look to Scripture for the answers. The answers are there, no matter what the question. Just remember that Scripture should always be used to define Scripture. You must avoid seeing everything through your own lens and see it through the context given by all the other Scripture. With continued study and prayer, wisdom will follow."

As the evening progressed, Charles, Chris, and Eli spoke on number of different topics. They conversed for at least an hour before finally getting sleepy and needing to call it a night.

Charles stood and began stretching, throwing his arms out as far as they would go. This was followed by a yawn that sounded much like an angry bear.

"Well, as much as I would like to stay up all night and talk, I can't. I am tired. It was nice meeting you, Eli. I have to get some sleep. We have a lot of work to do tomorrow," Charles said softly.

"I completely understand," said Eli. "I feel like I haven't slept in ages. Go and get some rest. I'm sure we will see each other around at camp."

"Good night, Eli," said Charles as he started to turn to walk away.

"Good night to you both," Eli responded.

As they walked away, both were feeling much more relaxed than they had in the previous weeks. They had been so busy worrying about the war in Israel that they could only focus on what was happening there. Meeting Eli and talking to him about Scripture made them feel more at home in their current location. They were able to feel somewhat normal for the first time in a while. Eli helped them realize that there will always be things that happen in the world that they cannot change or control, but that things always happen for a reason. He reminded them that faith in God is a time-tested and true way to deal with things such as this, and that by doing so, they would feel better about those things because God is in control.

They were quite taken with Eli. As they walked back to their side of the camp, they remarked to each other about how great it was to meet such a wise man who knew as much as he did about Scripture.

"He sure was an interesting young man, wasn't he?" said Chris.

"Oh yes. It's nice to meet people who have clearly studied Scripture. He was giving me a run for the money," said Charles laughingly.

"What did you think about his comments on purpose?" said Chris.

Charles shot Chris a look of intrigue. "That was odd, wasn't it?"

"Well, *odd* wasn't the word that I was looking for, but I can see how you would think it was odd," said Chris.

"What was the word that you were looking for?"

"Well, I was just thinking that it was awfully ironic that his name was Eli and that he came from northern Israel and just happened to show up right when Israel is being invaded," said Chris.

"That wasn't half as ironic as when he said that Elijah could call upon God to make it rain. Think about it. He shows up. His name is short for Elijah, and it starts raining in Israel," said Charles with a look of bewilderment on his face.

"Will you look at the two of us?" Chris said with a huge grin. "We are actually talking about that guy as if he is *the Elijah*. If we don't stop it, people are going to think us as insane." He laughed.

"Well, you are the one who brought it up," said Charles. "I was just following your lead."

"Oh, so that's how it's going to be?" Chris laughed.

"Finally, someone on the planet sees my worth and tells me I'm great," said Charles jokingly. "I feel great!" He beamed.

Chris stopped and put his hands gently upon Charles's head. He cocked his head toward the right and then to the left, examining it.

"Oh my goodness!" Chris shouted. "I can actually see your head expanding."

Charles laughed as he pushed Chris away. "Ha ha!" he said sarcastically.

The two reached their side of the camp. It was much darker now, and the cooler air was settling in on the camp. The cold dense air pushed the smoke downward on the encampment, and the area had a white haze that was visible from a few feet off the ground. The small fire by their sleeping area was nearly out and glowing red. The coals were smoldering and adding to the smoke cloud blanketing the area.

Chris stood looking at the fire. He knew that a smoldering fire wasn't going to provide much in the way of warmth. He would have to get some more wood if the two were to be able to sleep through the night.

"I'll get some more wood for the fire. Go ahead and get some shuteye. Tomorrow is going to be a long day. We have to help on the north side with that water buffalo," said Chris.

Charles plopped down next to the fire and began pushing the coals around, trying to get some oxygen to it and get a flame to burst out.

"Fine by me, I'm beat," said Charles. "See if you can scare up a tomato while you are over at the woodpile. I have some leftover bread and a couple of mayo packets that are going to go out of date tomorrow, and I don't want them to go to waste."

"Sure." Chris chuckled. "You realize that's the sell-by date, don't you?"

"I have no idea what you are talking about." Charles grinned. "Besides, if this bread gets any older, it'll be toast."

"I'll see what I can do," said Chris.

The next morning, Cynthia and David were having breakfast with Charles and Chris. They had some fresh eggs and bacon that were provided to them by the elderly fellow whom Cynthia helped the night before. The bacon was a bit iffy as it was on the warm side, but the eggs appeared fine. After a half hour of protest from Charles, Cynthia began to cook the bacon.

Charles threw up a protest so significant and scientific that Cynthia felt she had just attended a microbiology class. The whole time that he spoke, she looked at him and nodded as if in agreement, but internally, she was humming the tune "Tainted Love." The tune popped into her head after Charles explained that he knew that she loved bacon, but eating tainted meat was dangerous. She ended his lecture on microbiology when she interjected and gave him one sentence.

"If you don't want to eat it, there is more for the rest of us," she said.

Charles begrudgingly came over to her side after hearing the sizzle of the bacon as it was placed into the hot frying pan. His mind told him that the meat was bad, but the aroma told him that the meat was delicious. He couldn't resist the sweet smell of hickory mixed with bacony divinity.

"If I get ill from this and die, I am gonna kill you!" said Charles, still in a state of mesmerized protest.

"I'm good with that!" Cynthia chuckled.

David was lying a few feet from the fire, thumbing through a book that he borrowed from Cynthia. He was an avid reader, but when they left in haste, he forgot to bring along one of his preferred books. As he thumbed through the book, he looked both nervous and perplexed. The more that he read, the faster he started thumbing and fumbling through the pages.

"How can you read this stuff?" he asked.

"What do you mean?" Cynthia replied.

"I mean, this is all about loving and hugging and embracing and kissing. Where is the action? Where is the excitement?"

"You don't find romance to be exciting?" she asked.

"Well, uh, I guess, but I wouldn't write a book about it," he explained. "I was expecting a bit more, based on the title."

"How so?" she asked.

"Well, for one, the cover has a picture of a race-car driver walking away from an explosion and a bunch of wrecked cars," he explained. "From what I can tell, there isn't even a race in this book!"

"That's because he left the racing industry for his one true love. That's why you see him walking away in the picture," she explained.

"Well, that doesn't explain the confusing title." He added. "The title is *An Accident for the Ages*. And the only accident in this book is on the cover."

"It's a metaphor for their accidental love." She chuckled.

David stood up from where he had been sitting and handed the book back to Cynthia. "Thanks, but no thanks," he said smilingly. "I'm going to go see what I can see on the other side of camp."

Cynthia stopped her cooking for a moment and looked at David with exasperation. "Breakfast is ready!" she exclaimed.

David stopped and threw his hands in the air.

"After hearing about *Listeria monocytogenes*, or whatever it's called, I have suddenly lost my appetite."

Charles nearly broke his neck as he jerked his attention over to David, who Charles now knew was listening to his breakfast monologue.

"Well, if you aren't going to eat it—" Charles said with a beaming look of pleasure.

David waved his hand toward the bacon and the rest of the breakfast. "Have at it, Charles. With that iron gut of yours, you could eat that water buffalo, and it wouldn't affect your iron levels," he said with a laugh.

As David walked away, Charles smiled as he saw Cynthia pulling the bacon out of the pan.

"If I only had this bacon last night, I would have been as content as a bug in a rug," he said with a grin.

Cynthia looked at Charles with a look of disgust.

"That's gross," she said with a cringing look on her face.

Chris, who managed to stay silent during all the debating, stood up from his place next to the fire. He looked at Cynthia and Charles and nodded with a serious look on his face.

"As much as I love bacon, I'm just not that hungry," he said.

Charles looked up at Chris. His eyes were fixed and somewhat glazed over as he pushed pieces of bacon into his mouth. He looked like a zombie that just found a fresh body and was watching Chris like a hawk.

"If yoor nopf going to eat…" Charles started to mumble with a mouthful of food before Chris interjected.

"No, I'm not going to eat it, and yes, you can have it, Charles," he said with a huge laugh. "I am going to go find Eli."

"Waif foor me. I'm comfing," said Charles, as he got up from the fire.

Cynthia looked exasperated.

"I guess that I'll just clean up then?" she said with a groan of discontent.

"Phanks Symphia," said Charles as he continued to stuff bacon into his mouth. His eyes were fixed on Cynthia's eyes. He had the look of a puppy that was sorry for peeing on the rug. He waited for a moment, and then the moment finally came. Cynthia threw him a wave, letting him know that it was all right for him to depart.

"You sure can cook some bacon!" he said as he began to walk away.

Chris and Charles headed out to where they met Eli the night before. Eli was moving around his site, packing up his few belongings into a cloth satchel.

"Eli!" yelled Chris.

Eli turned and looked toward Chris and Charles. "Good morning!" he said with a shout.

"We were going to help with the supply delivery this morning and thought that you might want to help," said Chris.

Eli walked over to greet the pair. "I am sorry, but I cannot. My friend arrived late last night, and we have to be going this morning."

"Oh, I am sorry to hear that," Chris responded. "Where are you headed?"

"We have some business in Jerusalem in the coming days. We haven't much time remaining to get there. It's a long journey from here," he replied.

"Like what?" asked Charles. "You are going into the defense business?"

"No, nothing like that." Eli chuckled. "You should come along."

Charles's smile quickly turned into a look of shock.

"Back into that war zone?" asked Charles cynically. "We barely made it out alive."

"I had a feeling that you would say that," said Eli laughingly. "I wouldn't expect you to go there today, but in a couple of weeks. Your friend David is going to need some help."

"Oh, I see," said Charles with a puzzled look. "I didn't realize that you knew David."

"It is a small camp, Charles," said Chris with a laugh. "You don't think David was over here yesterday? He is always walking around looking for new people to meet."

"I knew that," said Charles with an embarrassed tone. "David probably knows everyone in here."

"Well, almost everyone," said Eli. "He hasn't met my friend yet."

"Touché," said Charles. "I guess it would be hard to meet a guy who just got here."

"What does David need help with?" asked Chris.

"Well, to be quite honest, he will need help convincing people of his discovery," Eli explained. "For nearly two thousand years, the temple has been removed from the land of Jerusalem. The people believe it to have been located on what they call the Temple Mount, but they have ignored the truth for many years and are wrong. David has found the correct location."

"Well, he obviously convinced you of that. If he could convince you of that, he could convince others. Why would he need us?" asked Charles.

"You have to understand that the Jewish people have certain beliefs about establishing truth. Let us look to Scripture and take Matthew 18:16, 'But if he does not listen, take one or two others along with you, that every charge may be established by the evidence of two or three witnesses.' In other words, to establish the truth, he will need witnesses to the truth," explained Eli.

"Why would they believe him just because Charles and I are present?" asked Chris.

"David will discover some things at the site of the Gihon Spring that one would expect at the First and Second Temple. David is an archaeologist and not a prophet or a teacher. He is limited because of this. You and Charles are both teachers. While you may not be Jewish, you are still teachers of the truth. As witnesses to the truth, you would be more likely to convince others than David by himself."

"I don't know," said Charles. "David is hardly the first archaeologist to suggest that the temple was located at the Gihon Spring. Chris and I are two pastors from America. The Jewish are going to take one look at us and say that we haven't a clue about what we are talking about because we believe that Jesus was the Messiah and they do not."

"Yet it was impossible for Moses to convince pharaoh to free the Jews. If you do not try, it is impossible, but with God behind you, everything is possible," said Eli. "Have you not wondered what brought you here in this time of turmoil?"

"What would we tell them?" asked Chris.

"Truth," said Eli, "the world is ripe for the truth."

"Did David put you up to this?" asked Charles.

"You are here for the same reason that I am here. We are all called for a purpose. That purpose for you is to talk to those who would listen and to convince them of the truth."

"Well, I suppose that we could try, but there is a war raging right now. I don't know if you haven't noticed it, but this place is filled with refugees that escaped that war. To ask us to go back into a war zone is one thing, but to ask us to go into a war zone and try to convince people to believe David during the middle of that war is another," said Charles.

Eli looked at Charles with a look of disappointment.

"Oh, ye of little faith," rebuked Eli. "Do you not know the power of the Most High?"

"Well, I—" started Charles.

"In three days, the storm will have moved over the land. It will be safe for you to cross back into Jerusalem once the storm has passed. Let God handle the war in Israel and have faith that what you have been asked to do is possible," said Eli.

Charles and Chris were hesitant to go back into Israel with the war about to reach a fever pitch. They had been watching the news reports as they were available, and each one was like the last. The

Golshiri regime would make small pushes into the country and, over a short period, swarmed like a nest of angry bees in the northern parts of Israel. Then there was the fighting in the Gaza area and at the southernmost border. With two massive battles going on and what appeared to be a dreary end for Israel, if the current trends continued, the last thing that they wanted to do was get involved and potentially get killed or captured.

The two discussed it later that evening with David, and all three agreed that they would go in after the storm, just as Eli suggested. They figured that the Israelis could use a bit of good news and if they could be convinced that the temple was in the Gihon Springs area, then they would set their sights on the prospect of rebuilding the temple and maybe that would give them the boost that they needed to fight with all their might in order to push out the foreign invaders so that their dream of building the third temple could be realized.

CHAPTER 11

Wrath

In the European Union, Jared was able to convince other leaders that an invasion was necessary in order to assist the Israelis. He was able to convince everyone that saving the Israelis from the Golshiri regime was in everyone's best interests. The primary reason that he gave was that if Golshiri forces were successful in taking Israel that they would be able to corner the markets on natural gas as well as now have a newfound resolve for conquering other nations.

A victory in Israel eluded Middle Eastern countries for years. Those solid defeats kept the Middle Eastern countries in check in a sense as they kept their hatred toward Israel and the United States, rather than focusing it on their neighbors to the north. If they could win in Israel, maybe they could take the fight to the north as well and do what they wanted for thousands of years, which was to establish a world-dominated caliphate.

Jared was able to shuffle around resources within the EU and cut the deployment time in half from the two weeks that he had quoted to the Israeli prime minister.

European ships were on their way to the Mediterranean and would arrive just as the storm was pulling out of the sea. This would give them a tactical advantage as they would be able to prepare for a landing, just as northern parts of Israel were under assault from the weather system.

The storm slowly made its way onto land and was now well past Yarka, which is on the western side of Israel near the Mediterranean. The storm covered much of Israel and remained over much of the Mediterranean. The sheer size of the storm had meteorologists around the globe calling it the storm of the millennium. It was larger than a hurricane but had attributes that were similar. The storm had a defined eye and spun counterclockwise just as hurricanes do, but this wasn't a hurricane. The storm developed over the Mediterranean, and in the winter, which was very strange. It was as if the storm was created intentionally and with purpose.

As the storm steered its way across the Mediterranean, it made navigating the sea impossible. This is why there had been no attacks from Golshiri naval vessels. Those vessels that did attempt to brave the storm were met with swells of enormous size and waves that capsized them almost immediately. Normal merchant ships steered clear of the area, and US naval forces moved south, as to avoid the storm completely. Submarines were not able to safely navigate in the waters, so the sea was essentially cut off from the action.

European forces arrived to the south and were lying in wait for the storm to clear before proceeding. Once the storm made its way completely onto the land, it would be safe to enter and to prepare for a full-scale invasion into the north.

The storm continued to move at a slow pace, of about five miles per hour. The winds were now constant at about 180 miles per hour with gusts of over 200 miles per hour. The winds howled as they swept across the land. Hail stones the size of grapefruit fell with such velocity that everything in their path was damaged or destroyed by the impact. The hail was mixed with rain that was bloodred in color and coming down in torrents. The clouds flashed with brilliant-white light as the lightning increased in intensity. The roar of the thunder was so loud that the ground shook each time it sounded off.

The storm continued to drop in pressure; meaning, it was intensifying. Normally, a storm such as this would weaken over land, but this storm defied the laws of nature and strengthened more and more as it got further onto land. Scientists and meteorologists around the globe could not understand how such a storm developed and were even more perplexed at how it managed to strengthen. Nothing like this had ever been recorded in all of human history.

As the storm pushed its way across the land of Israel, the lightning became fiercer. It was so fierce and so frequent that it appeared as if the hail itself was on fire. The rumbling of the earth from each thunderclap came on like labor pains, and the rumblings grew in intensity to the point that actual earthquakes were triggered and shook the earth so violently that mountaintops broke apart and crashed to the ground. Every quake grew in intensity, and there was no sign of the storm relenting any time soon.

Soldiers lay dying from all the furious events as the area was continually pummeled in a viciousness not seen since the destruction of Sodom and Gomorrah. Those that left their makeshift shelters to seek refuge in stronger shelters died from the punishing hail or bolts of lightning. Those who sought shelter in their armor were electrocuted from bolts of lightning that were attracted to the tanks as if the tanks were giant lightning rods. Flash flooding drowned thousands while those who attempted to flee to the mountains were crushed by the massive avalanches of stone as the earth shook with rage.

The Israeli forces, who were positioned more to the south of the storm, saw some of the calamity but were mostly sheltered from it because they were just south enough as to miss the worst of it. Not all were saved though. Those who stayed on the closest point of the front line were not able to get out of harm's way and perished. Thousands were killed by the fiery mix of rain, hail, winds, and lightning.

The storm was unrelenting and hammered the area for days. There was no way for a retreat by Golshiri forces as the storm surrounded them and made escape impossible. It was much like the waves of the sea that crashed upon pharaoh's men when he foolishly led his army into the sea to pursue the Jews as they fled.

Almost as quickly as it began, it was over. The storm simply dried up, and the clouds receded. The bulk of the Golshiri forces was wiped out in a matter of hours, but many lay dying from severe injuries, as the storm dissipated. Their bodies were strewn across the land, and their equipment lay in tatters.

The remnant of the Golshiri forces were not out of the woods upon the exiting the storm. Thousands became suddenly sickened and unable to walk, fight, or even flee. It was as if they were hit by a chemical or biological attack. The rain, which was red like blood, had been carrying pathogen that infected the troops and was killing those who miraculously survived the wrath of the storm.

News reports were scattered but were reaching every corner of the globe. Jared and his fleet watched in awe as the footage came in from around the country. Part of the coverage included a statement that he gave to the press during the storm.

"We have new reports of earthquakes in southern Israel. At about 6:30 PM, a 7.2 earthquake was centered near the city of Nazareth. Only minutes later, another earthquake centered in the city of David was initially recorded at 8.0. Damage to structures in and around both cities is not yet known. The United Nations reports that they will be sending peacekeeping forces to the area to assist with cleanup and disaster relief. Other nations are pledging their support to assist in this humanitarian crisis. The pope has issued a statement from the Vatican and has been in contact with Prime Minister Lefler and European Union Prime Minister Jared Hadad, who has pledged support to Israel as they recover from this disaster. His statement read as follows:

> The world watches in awe today as calamities never before seen strike the heart of the world. We can all learn a lesson from the recent violence in the land of our god, and that lesson is that God demands that we live in peace with one another. God has witnessed violence in his land and has passed judgment on those who would shed blood upon his land. We must all unite together and ask forgiveness for our trespasses against one another so that we may heal as nations and individuals but more importantly as one people, under God.

Those who were fortunate enough to flee to Petra watched from their cellular phones and were in a state of panic and shock. The reports were unreal. It seemed supernatural and impossible.

CHAPTER 12

The Promised Land

Charles, Chris, David, and Cynthia were all watching the news reports as a group. In their part of the world, it was relatively peaceful. They did feel a couple of small tremors from the shaking in Israel, but those were nothing compared to what were experienced in Israel. For them, life continued as normal, and they went about their daily activities of surviving in a refugee camp.

It was now getting dark in Petra. Things were settled down from the earlier events of the day, but most were still huddled in their smaller groups, attempting to catch every glimpse of what was happening back home. The camp as well-lit by the numerous fires dotted across the area, but the tone of the camp was much more somber and the people much more quiet than normal.

Later in the evening, many of the people could be seen praying, while others just went about their normal routines as if nothing had changed. The children were off in their own groups playing without a care in the world. Their laughter was therapeutic and made many forget that they were in a refugee camp, as it provided the people with a sense of hope. Any time that the laughter of the children was heard around the camp and the sounds of their play was heard, it was a good day. It's when the laughter stopped or was replaced by screams of fear and anguish that the people remembered the reality of their situation.

Cynthia paused the news video that she was watching and looked at Charles with amazement.

"Isn't this just unbelievable?" said Cynthia. "It's like the weather is actually fighting against the Golshiri regime."

"Those weren't the words that I was going to use," said Charles.

"Well, what would you call it?"

"Divine intervention," he replied.

"Do you think God is doing this?" she asked.

"Think about what's happening for a moment, and then you tell me. I mean, this is a storm like never in the history of the world. The rain is bloodred, and there is hail the size of grapefruits," explained Charles.

Chris sat listening to the two as they volleyed back and forth with each other. They both made fair points.

"Wasn't there a blood rain in South America a few years ago?" asked Charles.

"Yes, but that was just rain. This is a storm more massive and more furious than a hurricane, and it's in winter. Not to mention hail that's the size of a Toyota Prius," Chris explained, now ready to get involved in the conversation.

"I didn't think God intervened on earth any longer. You know, with the veil or something like that," said Cynthia.

"That's not actually accurate," said Chris.

"Which part?" she asked in a sarcastic tone.

Chris turned toward Cynthia and began to explain further.

"Well, the veil that you are thinking of is not really God being completely out of the world. What it means is that there is the seen world and the unseen world. With the introduction of sin into the world, God no longer was present on the earth because his righteousness cannot be around sin, and if he were here, the world would basically be destroyed by his presence. The veil was present to protect us because of the sin problem. It has been theorized that the world looked much different to Adam than it does today, as in Adam could actually see God, but God's Holy Spirit has always been present on the earth and is still present today."

"Oh, but how is that him still being present? Didn't you basically agree with what I said?" she asked.

"Not necessarily," he replied. "Think about his presence as more of a spiritual presence. God's spirit has always been here. I would shudder to think of what the earth would be like if he weren't here in spirit. God is still in control even though there are those that would like you to believe otherwise."

"Is that why Jesus came to earth?" she asked.

"I guess the best way to answer that would be to say, partially. Jesus said that he was God when he was talking to the Jewish authorities. He said, 'Before Abraham, I Am,'" said Chris.

Charles interjected, "Actually, what he said was 'before Abraham was, I Am."

"Yes, that's right, Charles. I did misquote him. Thank you for the clarification. When he said, 'I Am,' he was telling the people that he is God because they would have known that I Am is the name of God, or one of the names of God. Anyway, Jesus, being God, came to earth as a man so that he could be a living sacrifice for all of mankind. Since he came as a human being and was completely sin-free, he was able to be a sacrificial *lamb*, so to speak, and pay the price for all of mankind's sins past, present, and future," Chris explained.

"I knew that, Chris," Cynthia said with a chuckle. "I just like hearing you explain it. I know that Jesus is a part of the trinity, with God and the Holy Spirit."

"Getting back to what we we're talking about, this invasion was actually prophesied. At least, I believe that to be the case. It certainly appears to be the prophecy found in Ezekiel 38," said Chris.

"So what happens next?" she asked.

"Well, David, Charles, and I have to go back to Jerusalem after the storm is over. You are obviously welcome to come with us, of course, but we talked about it earlier and decided that we would go as soon as the storm lets up."

"Well, if you're going, I'm going. I like these people, but we are somewhat of a team, even if I hide in the hotel," she said jokingly.

"Then it's settled. As soon as the storm lets up, we head out," said Chris.

The storm continued to ravage the northernmost parts of Israel and the southern parts of Syria. The devastation was immeasurable to the Golshiri regime forces and their equipment. Much of their equipment was damaged so badly that it was not repairable. The combination of the events left a wake of destruction so much so that Gog Golshiri prepared a statement, via video, to be released as soon as the storm passed, which was in a matter of hours. The heart of the storm was now over Damascus, but remnants of the storm were still in the Golan Heights area.

David, Chris, Cynthia, and Charles took the two remaining days of the storm's presence in Israel to pack up the van and to ensure that they had enough water to last them for at least the upcoming week. They began their trip back to Jerusalem so that they could discuss the findings at the Gihon Spring with the religious leaders in Jerusalem.

David worked on the radio in the evening before they left for Israel because he wanted to be able to listen to the incoming news and the prepared statement from Gog Golshiri that was supposed to be aired soon. He was fortunate that it was only a fuse that needed to be changed, but he didn't figure that out until he had already pulled the stereo out and checked the wiring.

"You sure made a mess of that stereo," said Charles.

"I guess so," David replied.

"What happens if you change the oil?" he snarked. "Thank goodness you are an archaeologist and not a surgeon."

"Ha ha! Archaeologists normally pull stuff apart to search for things. We don't put them together. We dig holes, not fill them in."

"So what you are saying is that your yard looks kinda like the moon?"

All four laughed out loud.

"Can we just turn it on now?" asked David.

Charles turned on the radio, and it made some scratching and staticky sounds. He turned the tuning knob, and the voices started, scrambled at first, and then became clear.

"What time was that news report supposed to be?" asked Chris.

"They didn't really say. They said around the time the storm was pulling out," Charles replied.

"Well, that's about now, isn't it?" asked Cynthia.

The voices on the radio were talking softly in the background, and suddenly, one of the voices said loudly, "We have an important news bulletin."

Charles laughed out loud. "Look at that! We turn it on, and it goes right to the news we wanted to hear! Is that luck or what?"

"Not really, everyone and their brother knows that the storm is just now passing," replied Cynthia. "We are just like rest of them. We turned on our radios after the storm."

"I still think it's divine intervention," said Charles with a grin.

Cynthia looked over to Charles and made a be-quiet gesture with her hands. The news reporters were now talking, and she couldn't hear them over Charles's. Charles shot her a look, indicating that he didn't like being shushed, but he didn't say a word. Cynthia smiled as he rolled his eyes and began focusing on the newscast.

"We expect the statement from Golshiri any moment now," the male voice stated.

"You see, you shushed me for nothing," said Charles.

"Today, my forces recover from the storm that inflicted slight damage," said a new voice.

"Quiet, here it is," said Cynthia.

*****

"We are calling for the Israeli demons to come out of hiding and surrender themselves at once. Storms and threats will not defeat us. We have played by their rules for the past hundreds of years, and that ends today. Either these forces surrender, or we will unleash hell into all of Israel. The prime minister must present himself this afternoon, or we will attack as the world has never seen before." Golshiri had spoken.

*****

The news reporter came back on the air. "We have just heard a prerecorded statement from earlier this morning. The Golshiri leader has issued a dire warning calling for the surrender of military forces."

A second reporter who was a woman came onto the radio. "This threat has come on the heels of what looked like a defeat of the Golshiri forces. Our reports indicate that the Golshiri forces were heavily damaged during the storm and that they are in no way capable of launching a massive ground or air assault. This has to be a ploy to see if they can scare the Israelis, or they may intend to use weapons of mass destruction. Your thoughts, Sam?"

The voice of a male came over the radio. "Well, I shudder to think what could happen if they were to actually launch a warhead into Israel. It would cause chaos around the globe. It makes me wonder if they took a more serious blow during that storm. I mean, that storm was unprecedented and looked apocalyptic."

The female voice came back onto the radio. "Just a moment, we have word that the prime minister is going to give a statement."

*****

Chris pulled the van over as he was now intensely focused on the news. All four, in the van, were astonished at what they heard. They all had serious and visibly shaken looks upon their faces. Charles looked especially shaken and turned pale.

*****

The voice of the prime minister now came through on the radio.

"Good afternoon. Today, Israeli forces emerge from the storm of the millennium, unscathed. What we have witnessed is a signal to all the world that God will protect the people of Israel and the state of Israel against regimes bent on bloodshed and destruction. For years, the nation of Israel has been threatened with destruction, and for years, we have met those threats with the resolve of a people who refuse to bend to a world that would enslave us or that would attempt to exterminate us."

*****

Charles looked over at Chris with a look of approval. The prime minister's words conveyed strength, not weakness.

*****

"The day that we have dreamed of for many years has come. In 1948, God called us to come out of exile to claim what has been rightfully promised to us. In 1967, we fought off would-be invaders to our north and to our south and reclaimed what is rightfully ours. In 2018, the world shuddered as it was declared from north to south and from east to west that Israel is and always has been a sovereign nation under God. Today is more of the same. Under threat of war, we have persevered and have been delivered from those who would do us harm. But the fight is not over. We are at the precipice of peace, but a stumbling block still remains before us."

*****

Charles loved what he was hearing, and his normal color returned. The strong words of the prime minister were encouraging and made him feel much better about the trip back into Israel.

*****

"We have recently received word from the Golshiri regime. These were words of desperation. Though that is what we believe, we will not take them idly. The regime attacked a peaceful people without explanation. We fought back. They gained little ground, and God showed the entire world that he will not allow our nation to fail. The storm that has come through has caused mass casualties, and all but broken the backs of the enemy. We must now fight with all our resolve. We have been threatened with extinction before, and as in times of old, we will fight knowing that God remains in control."

*****

David looked at Cynthia, shocked.

"I wonder what that means?" he said softly.

"He's just saying that the Golshiri regime is feeling the pinch after the recent devastation, and it's made them angry. They will fight harder now, knowing that their backs are against the wall," replied Cynthia.

*****

The prime minister continued speaking. "The European Union in affiliation with the United States has announced today that they will be deploying the first two thousand autonomous soldiers. These soldiers were designed for the defense of the United States Department of Defense but have now been pledged to the cause. As you may or may not be aware, Prime Minister Hadad, of the European Union, was a former associate of I-Corp, which has been working on this artificial intelligence project for a number of years, prior to becoming the leader of the EU."

*****

Chris looked amazed and appalled. The others just sat there mesmerized by what they were hearing.

*****

"These soldiers will not tire like the average soldier. They will not suffer anxiety or fear like the average soldier. They are mission-oriented and will accomplish their objectives. I can report today that these soldiers were deployed about an hour ago and should be well on their way to the battlefront, where their mission is simple.

Their mission is to seek out the Golshiri leadership and end this campaign of hatred, once and for all."

*****

Charles was exasperated. He couldn't believe what he was hearing. "Did you hear that?" he asked. "They have finally gone off the deep end! They are unleashing robots onto battlefield, just like I've been telling you that would happen."

"Calm down, Charles," replied Cynthia. "There are only two thousand of them."

"Two thousand now, but what about in six months? What about in six years?" he fired back, panicked.

*****

The prime minister continued speaking. "We hope that the deployment of these special warriors will bring a swift victory to the aggressors in the north and to the west. The battle is all but won, and victory assured. The damage caused by this historic storm has significantly impaired the Golshiri regime, and our intelligence tells us that up to two-thirds of their forces were either killed in the storm or severely limited by way of injury. They have lost their ability to conquer but not the ability to wage war. To ensure a victory for the decades and centuries to follow, our AI force will enter Egypt as well as what remains in Syria. Their mission will be to take out the remnant of the Golshiri regime. The battle is not won yet. We have just begun our campaign, but with God on our side, who can defeat us?"

*****

"Are you hearing this?" asked Charles. "They are using artificial intelligence to wipe out a whole regime. And they are sending these things over to Egypt and other places around the world. What he just described was a set of two thousand robot hit men!"

David looked over to Charles with a serious but rather calm look upon his face.

"Charles, they aren't wiping out a whole army. Didn't you listen?"

"Well, that's what they said," Charles fired back.

"No, that's not what they said," said David. "They said that the storm wiped out two-thirds of the Golshiri regime."

"But they also said that they were sending those atrocities to Egypt and Syria to take out the rest of them."

David put his hand onto Charles's shoulder. "You have got yourself so riled up that they decided to use those AI machines that you completely missed what he really said. He said that the storm ravaged Syria. The troops are going in to go after the leadership, not the army."

"How is that any better?" said Charles enthusiastically.

"Think about it, Charles. Gog Golshiri is still alive. He is backed into a corner. He is probably insane with anger that he lost his troops," David explained.

"That's even worse," said Charles.

"Charles, listen to me. Golshiri has nuclear weapons."

Silence struck the vehicle as they sat on the side of the road. In an instant, everyone in the vehicle finally understood why the prime minister had to send in the AI forces. They forgot about the nuclear weapons. If Golshiri was truly backed into a corner and mad with rage, there was no telling what he might do.

"Charles, I know you don't like the idea of artificial intelligence, but we are talking about disarmament of a whacko who is crazy enough to let those missiles fly. Could you imagine what would happen if he were to launch those missiles?"

"Well, they would probably destroy Israel," said Charles.

"Not only that," said Cynthia, "the Israelis would launch a counterstrike, and we would be talking a nuclear apocalypse."

"Don't you see what's happening?" asked David. "Israel is taking out the threat of a nuclear war. Whether you like AI or hate it, they are a benefit right now."

"Well, what do we do now?" asked Chris. "Do you really want to go to Jerusalem if there is a threat of a nuclear attack?"

Cynthia looked over to David. "Whether the strike hits us in Jerusalem or in Jordan, we are still looking at the same thing. I say that we head to Jerusalem."

"Charles?" asked David.

"Well, we only have a half tank of gas right now. If we head back to Jordan, we'll be walking or stuck in the desert somewhere. We don't really have a choice, do we?"

Chris and David both smiled.

"To Jerusalem it is," said David.

*****

Prime Minister Lefler met with Jared in his Tel Aviv office. Peter Jensen also traveled there to meet with the prime minister at Jared's invitation. The pair arrived in secret, like the last trip Jared took to the region. Peter was invited to Tel Aviv so that they could establish a command center in Tel Aviv at the underground bunker located there. That location was chosen because of its secrecy and proximity to the active military operations.

Peter looked visibly tired and anxious. He worked tirelessly for months to ensure that he could deliver IA machines that were exceptional. The machines were tested in the deserts of southwest Arizona, but the testing was mostly one-sided. The machines were tested for their offensive capabilities, but their defensive capabilities were ignored. They didn't put the machines through a full battery of tests because they didn't want to risk damage to the machines by firing back at them. It was assumed that their offensive capabilities were so strong that they could easily infiltrate an area, complete the mission, and damage would be negligible. Their design was such that their higher components were encased with a bulletproof and concussion-proof material that could withstand average battlefield trauma. They could be hit and get right back up and continue their mission.

Adam sat at his desk reviewing the technical schematics provided to him by Peter. His glasses were pushed downward onto his nose, and he rested his hand under his chin as he nodded occasionally. He wasn't an engineer, but the schematics provided were written in such a manner for the layperson to understand.

Jared and Peter were seated at the opposite side of the desk. Jared sat stiffly with his hands placed on his knees. He remained emotionless as he watched Adam scan through the document. Peter was only slightly more animated, and his attention wasn't on Adam at all. Instead of watching Adam read through his schematic, he peered through the open window, watching the people shuffle back and forth.

Adam looked up for a moment and straight at Peter, who was still peering through the window. Noticing that his attention was elsewhere and not on the meeting at hand, he assumed that Peter must be looking for some refreshment or need to use the restroom.

"I have to say that these are pretty impressive, Peter."

Peter jerked to attention and smiled at Adam.

"I am glad that you approve. We have been working day and night to get these soldiers ready for you. I am sure that you will be happy with the results," said Peter.

Adam smiled back and pushed up his glasses.

"Can I get either of you a beverage?"

Jared shook his head, declining his offer. Peter also declined with a nod and a short wave of his hand.

"Very well. Let's see what you created," he said with a giddy smile.

Adam reached over to his phone and pressed a button on the phone. "Allison, would you be so kind as to bring in our guest?" Adam lightly slapped the desk with his hands. "Well, we will see just how good these machines work after all, won't we?" he asked.

Peter jerked his head around toward Jared and then toward Adam nervously.

"I assure you that the capability is there. They function better than expected. We have put them through every test that we could think of."

"That's not what I was told by your friend here," Adam replied, pointing at Jared.

Jared smiled back at Adam.

"That's correct, Adam. They have not been tested from the defensive side of things."

"Well, that's not entirely accurate," snapped Peter. "They have, in fact, had some testing as to the defensive side."

Adam looked a bit puzzled. "So which is it?" he asked. "I've got one who says they have and another that says that they haven't."

Adam stood up from his desk. He noticed that Allison was at the door with his guest of the hour. He looked at Allison through the open blinds and held his index finger to indicate that he would be with her in just a moment.

"If these things don't work, I need to know it now. We can't put our soldiers' lives on the line here, not to mention the people of Israel. Which is it? Have they or have they not been tested?"

"They have been partially tested. We know that inner shell is impervious to fire, water, pressure changes, humidity, and the like. They can also take small-arms fire without so much as a dent, but anything in the range of a .50-caliber or greater will damage them," Peter explained.

"Outer shell?" asked Adam.

"Well, they have an outer shell made of a biosynthetic compound. It's basically flesh, but only in appearance and aesthetic function. The only exception to that is that there is a cooling system built into the outer shell that acts similar to normal human flesh. They have small veins running through the skin and between the inner and outer shell that circulates a cooling liquid," Peter explained.

"Like blood?" asked Adam.

"Not in a functional sense, no, but yes, if you look at it as a circulatory sense. You see, these machines generate quite a bit of heat. They can't use fans like your old personal computer because they need to be waterproof. They have an inner circulatory system as well as an outer system that functions similarly to the human body, in so far as a liquid is circulated through a network of veins and capillaries. The cooling liquid works much like a radiator on a car, except that it isn't air-cooled. It's like the coil on an air-conditioning system, except that internally, there is no condensation because the system has no moisture that can condense. Outwardly, there is some minor condensation, so it appears as if they are sweating." Peter continued.

"That is amazing. Well, let's take a look," said Adam. Adam motioned toward the door, where Allison was standing outside with a man of about six feet, four inches in height and a rather large build.

"Come in, Allison," he said in a raised voice.

The man and Allison walked into the room. Allison turned toward him and smiled.

"Here you go. It was nice chatting with you, Richard," she said. Allison then turned toward the door and left as swiftly as she entered.

Richard stood near the door observing Adam as he approached.

Adam was smiling from ear to ear as he looked over the man. It was as if he had never seen another human being before. "Richard, is it?" he asked.

"Yes, sir. I understand that you are Adam Lefler, prime minister of Israel. It is a pleasure to meet you. May I take a seat please?"

Adam reached out his hand and shook hands with Richard. His smile grew more intense as he continued to look at Richard in awe.

"Of course, please sit here."

"Is this one of them?" Adam asked Peter, continuing to smile.

"Richard?" he asked. "No, he is just one of my programmers. He is a team lead on our US Department of Defense project. He's here to tell you about that project.

Adam's smile instantly vanished, and his face now had a red flushed look. He was visibly embarrassed for thinking that he was talking to a robot and more embarrassed for checking him out like he was attracted to him.

"Forgive me," Adam said. "I thought that you were one of the—have you ever had an embarrassing moment like that?"

"No, I can't say that I have," Richard replied, with a slight smile on his face.

"You're lucky," he replied. "I can't remember the last time I have been so embarrassed. You must forgive me for that."

Peter and Jared were both laughing, and Adam started to laugh with them. The whole room erupted in laughter.

Adam moved back to his seat and slowly sat, nodding and chuckling at himself. After a short pause, he composed himself and gazed back at Richard.

"Well, it's nice to meet you, Richard. Tell me about the project you have been working on."

Jared and Peter began whispering to each other. Adam looked over at them, wondering what they were whispering about, and overheard Peter saying to Jared, "Should we tell him?"

"Tell me what?" asked Adam.

The room got quiet, and Adam looked at Peter with a puzzled and still somewhat embarrassed look on his face.

"I'm sorry, Adam. I couldn't resist," said Peter with a laugh.

Jared started to laugh as well, and suddenly, the room was filled with laughter again. Adam was now turning red again because he started feeling like he was the butt of a joke.

"Richard is one of our machines." He laughed. "Realistic, isn't he?"

Adam's jaw dropped. He was the butt of the joke. Not once but twice did they get him. He looked at Jared and Peter intensely for a moment. He had a serious but angry look upon his face. The room suddenly got quiet again.

"Good one!" he belted out with a laugh. "You had me on that one. Wow!" He laughed. "Boy, fun I could have had growing up with one of these."

"Just kidding!" shouted Peter. "He really is a programmer, but that look is priceless!"

Richard suddenly interjected. "My name is Richard. I was brought online at zero seven thirty on March 6, 2028. It is a pleasure to meet you, Mr. Lefler." He started. "Would you like a demonstration?"

Adam looked puzzled. Was he talking to a machine or a programmer?

"Sure," he said unenthusiastically.

Richard pulled a small four-inch bar of metal from his pocket and handed it to Adam.

"Please examine this piece of iron. Try to break it with all your might."

Adam took the small bar of metal and examined it. It was cold to the touch and fairly heavy. He hit it against the table, and it made a small ringing sound. He then tried to bend it, and it wouldn't bend.

"Okay, it's iron. What is it for?"

Richard took the bar back from Adam and placed it in both hands. He then bent the iron bar as if it were a coat hanger.

"Would you like another demonstration?" asked Richard.

"No, that will be sufficient. I guess you really are a machine."

The whole room once again erupted into laughter.

"I understand that you have a mission that you would like assistance with. Is this correct, Mr. Lefler?" asked Richard.

"You do get straight to the point, don't you?" Adam replied.

"My apologies, but I was under the assumption that we were here to discuss the troops to the northeast."

"Yes, we have what remains of a large multinational force. We believe that the number of troops currently sits at fifty thousand," said Adam.

Peter interjected. "Richard," he said, "there is a rather large troop presence, but the mission is not to eliminate the entire force. The mission is to eliminate the leadership of the remaining army."

Richard nodded. "I see," said Richard. "What you ask is possible, but we will need to download all available data on these forces as well as all data pertaining to the topography, armaments, weather, and other variables. This would take a day or two to complete. Would this be acceptable?"

Adam pushed back into his chair, beaming.

"Certainly," said Adam. "As it stands now, our armored divisions are back into place, and our infantry is ready to push toward Syria. We have our air force running sorties at present to take out surface to air sites. Once you have the data, you are free to prepare with our leadership on your battle plans."

Peter and Richard rose from their seats.

"We will begin at once. It was a pleasure to meet you, Mr. Lefler."

Peter looked over to Adam. "We will contact you as soon as the downloads are completed."

Peter and Richard left the room, and Adam and Jared remained seated.

"Impressive, wasn't he?" asked Jared.

"Very impressive, but two thousand soldiers against fifty thousand?"

"Let's not forget the goal at hand. They will be deployed to target the leadership. How that is accomplished will be worked out with Richard and his team."

"I just don't see how it's possible. If we could have done it, we would have targeted them on our own. Your machines may be able to take a beating and keep fighting, but the odds are still against them from a statistical standpoint. How are they going to do that?"

"Adam, you are thinking about this in human terms. These machines have a level of intelligence that exceeds the top minds on this planet. What is impossible for us is different for them. They will write their own battle plans and execute those plans."

"We'll see," said Adam.

CHAPTER 13

Fallout

David, Cynthia, Chris, and Charles made it back to Jerusalem without incident. The city was relatively quiet. There were people darting around the area, but the lack of the normal traffic was noticeable.

David had to get back to the dig site, so he parted ways with the group and headed there, while the others headed back to Cynthia's room at the hotel.

Charles, being his curious self, felt compelled to turn on the television to catch the newest news reports. He leaned over from the bed where he was sitting and turned on the television. Chris and Cynthia were standing next to the other bed in the room, unpacking their bags, so they could take their clothing down to the laundry. It had been weeks since they had clean clothes to wear. Charles didn't seem to care about the state of his clothing and was enthralled at the prospect of hearing the news.

The television sprung to life as Charles feverishly pushed the buttons on the remote control.

"We have a breaking report from the Golan Heights region. *Action News* is receiving unconfirmed information that widespread illness has engulfed the area. Our reporter, James Lendt, is on-site in the Heights. What are you hearing, James?"

Charles turned to Cynthia and Chris.

"Did you hear that?" he shouted.

Cynthia and Chris stopped unpacking for a moment and turned their focus to the television.

*****

The news report continued.

"Marcia, we are hearing reports of soldiers becoming ill all around the Golan Heights region. From what we have been told, symptoms include fever, headache, muscle pain, and chills. The outbreak started within the past twenty-four hours, but medical professionals are saying that the onset of symptoms was likely delayed due to a gestation period of at least seventy-two hours."

"Where do the medical professionals believe that the outbreak started? Were they able to determine the source? Also, how do they know that there is such a short gestation period? Was this potentially a biological attack?" she asked.

"Right now, it appears that this was not a biological attack. We have spoken with a liaison with the IDF who advised that no biological weapons have been utilized by their forces. It also appears that the majority of the sick are on the Syrian side of the north, so it's highly unlikely that they were responsible for the release of any biological agents."

"Thank you, James. Does the IDF know the source of the illness or what the illness is?"

"Well, Marcia, early reports are that the illness is similar to Ebola but that has not been confirmed. We do know that the illness has really affected the fighting in the north. It has become eerily quiet here, as you likely have noticed. With the onset of this illness and the impending storm that is now being called Typhoon Isabella. Movement has all but ceased. Prior to these factors, it was vastly different from what it is now. The fighting here was fierce, and the sound, deafening due to the mixture of artillery fire, mobile rocket-launcher fire, and small-arms fire. Those sounds have largely been replaced with only small-arms fire, and that firing is so intermittent that it resembles a New Year's Day celebration with a handful of firecrackers," explained James.

*****

Charles turned down the volume. "It just keeps getting weirder," said Charles.

Cynthia, who was only half listening to the news report, walked over and sat down next to Charles. Chris resumed fumbling through his bag, pulling each item out and giving them a quick smell test to determine if the items were clean or dirty.

"What are they saying? I heard something about Ebola," she said.

"That's what they said. Ebola, can you imagine?"

"What do you mean?" she replied.

"How do you get Ebola from a storm?" said Charles.

"Did they say anything about biological weapons?"

"No, they don't seem to know how everyone got sick," he replied.

Chris stopped and turned toward the two who were sitting on the foot of the bed.

"Did you say everyone?" asked Chris.

"That's what they said," said Cynthia.

"Well, not exactly," Charles interjected. "It seems that the IDF are mostly illness-free, not all but most."

"Well, then it has to be some kind of targeted biological weapon, doesn't it?" asked Chris.

"I guess," said Charles. "It's just plain weird. I mean, first a hurricane in the winter and blood rain mixed with grapefruit-sized hail, and now this."'

Chris moved over to the chair that was set across from the bed and next to the television. He sat down and looked as if he was going to say something but then stood back up. "Do you remember our conversation about God's wrath?" asked Chris.

"Yes," said Charles.

"I think that is exactly what this is," Chris said enthusiastically. Chris quickly got up and went back over to his bag and pulled out the remaining articles of clothing. He set the clothes on the bed and reached back into the bag, grabbing his Bible. He then moved quickly back over to the chair next to Charles. "When we talked about this before, it made me curious," said Chris.

"How's that?" asked Charles.

"Here," said Chris as he handed Charles the Bible. "Read chapter 38, the first paragraph."

Charles read the verses out loud to the group:

> The Word of the Lord came to me: "Son of man, set your face toward Gog, of the land of Magog, the chief prince of Meshech and Tubal, and prophesy against him and say, Thus says the Lord God: 'Behold, I am against you, O Gog, chief prince of Meshech and Tubal. And I will turn you about and put hooks into your jaws, and I will bring you out, and all your army, horses, and horsemen, all of them clothed in full armor, a great host, all of them with buckler and shield, wielding swords. Persia, Cush, and Put are with them, all of them with shield and helmet; Gomer and all his hordes; Beth-togarmah from the uttermost parts of the north with all his hordes—many peoples are with you."

Chris nodded as Charles read the verses, as if he were having an internal conversation and agreeing with himself.

"You see," Chris exclaimed, "this is no accident!"

"Wow," said Cynthia, "do you think that is what is really happening?"

"It all fits," said Chris. "If it walks like a duck, looks like a duck, and quacks like a duck, then it's a duck."

"So what does this mean?" asked Cynthia.

"It means that we are really close to the end," said Charles.

"Well, yes and no," Chris interjected. "There is still a lot of prophecy that has to be fulfilled, but it is a sure sign that things are headed in that direction. I mean, think about it."

"I think about it all the time," said Charles. "Just think, if this is happening now and the disciples were in the end times, then we must really be close to the end."

"Good point," said Cynthia. "What do we do now?"

"Good question," said Chris. "We do what we came here to do. This may be prophecy being fulfilled, but if you haven't noticed, we are still here. That means that we still have work to do."

Cynthia climbed up onto the bed and laid down in somewhat of a fetal position, propping her head up with her left arm cradling her head. "When are you two headed to the dig site?" she asked.

"David was supposed to call us after he got to the site. I guess he hasn't got there yet," replied Charles.

"We can call him in an hour or so if he doesn't call. He's probably taking a shower, which is what I am about to do!" said Chris.

"While you do that, I'll be doing laundry. You want to help?" Cynthia said, looking at Charles.

Charles looked visibly saddened that he was asked to help. He wanted to stay and watch the news. He had become a news junkie as of late and didn't want to miss a bit of it.

Cynthia could see that Charles had no interest in her offer of doing laundry together. "Don't worry, Charles," she said. "There will be news on the television in the laundry room. I saw it through the door when we were looking for water a couple weeks ago. You can watch it there. You can also talk to me for a while. I've got a lot of questions that I'd like to run past you."

Hesitantly and with a slight groan, Charles reluctantly agreed. "Let's get up there before this commercial ends."

Both Chris and Cynthia laughed. Charles was such a character when he became interested in something. He was always a bit obsessive and compulsive when it came to anything he found interesting.

This was no different from the obsession he had with his bacon-lettuce-tomato sandwiches."

*****

Meanwhile, in Tel Aviv, Prime Minister Lefler met with General Alpert in his war room. With the tide of the battle turning to favor Israel, the general was able to step away from the battle and travel to meet with the prime minister face-to-face rather than trying to speak over the phone or radio. The general was a stickler on operational security and preferred to speak face-to-face whenever possible as to avoid any chance of the enemy intercepting confidential information.

The general was in good spirits, and it was evident from his casual demeanor. He sat on the couch, relaxed, as if he were visiting an old friend or a family member on a weekend. The general began to scan the room. He could smell the fresh brewed coffee that filled the room, teasing his nostrils and bringing him to full attention.

"What is that delicious aroma?" asked General Alpert.

Adam could see the general moving his head around, aroused by the smell of freshly ground coffee beans. He began to smile as he watched the general sniff out the location of the coffee maker like a bloodhound searching for an escaped convict.

"Ah, that, my friend, is the best coffee grown in the Caribbean. It comes from the Blue Mountains of Jamaica. What makes it special is that it is grown in the mountains at a high altitude, and every bean is checked by hand to make sure it is perfect, before roasting it. Would you care for a cup?"

The general leaned forward on the couch toward the coffee maker. He wanted to get up and get a cup of the coffee but didn't want to seem too eager, so he sat back into the couch as if he weren't that interested. "I didn't realize you had such fine tastes," said General Alpert.

Adam wasn't fooled for a moment. He was well acquainted with the general and could visibly see the general fidgeting in his seat. He knew the general wanted a cup of the coffee and also knew that the general had too much pride to ask for a cup.

Adam got up from his desk and moved over to the small counter space at the opposite side of the office, where he had a small hot plate and a tiny silver espresso pot sitting next to the small sink. He carefully unscrewed the top of the pot and cleaned out the used and wet coffee grains from it and then rinsed it out in the sink.

The general moved forward in his seat, watching Adam at work, intrigued at the size of the coffeepot. He had never seen a coffeepot so small and was generally curious at how it worked.

Adam packed some freshly ground coffee into the tiny strainer, then placed the strainer down into the base of the pot that he filled with a small amount of cold water. He screwed the top of the pot to the base and then placed it on the small hot plate.

"So what's the news in the north?" asked Adam, looking over his shoulder at the general.

Adam walked back over to his desk and sat down. The general moved his gaze from the coffeepot back to Adam, who was now looking at him with a serious expression on his face.

"We have moved the 8th Armor Brigade north, and they were accompanied by the 769th Infantry Brigade. From the southeastern part of Galilee, we have moved the 300th Infantry Brigade, and from the northwest, we have moved the 679th Armor Brigade and the 9th Infantry Brigade," the general explained.

The coffeepot was now boiling away, and steam started to escape out of the top of the pot as if it were a locomotive traveling at full speed. The room suddenly filled itself with the brilliant aroma of freshly brewed coffee beans and resembled a coffee shop in New York City on a busy Monday morning.

Adam got up from his chair and moved back over to the tiny hot plate and took the steaming pot off the heat. He then grabbed a small cup from out of the small cabinet and poured the rich coffee into a small white porcelain cup that was about half the size of a normal coffee cup. The top of the coffee had a light-brown foamy consistency to it, and steam rolled over the top of the cup. He handed the general the cup.

"Tell me if you have ever tasted a better brew than this. Be careful though. It's hot," said Adam.

The general put his nose to the cup and inhaled deeply off the steamy essence that floated around the rim of the cup before finally taking a tiny sip of the contents.

"Excellent!" he replied. "I will have to get some of this coffee if I am ever in Jamaica."

Adam sat back down and looked at his desk. He picked up his pen and started tapping it on a small stack of papers on his desk. He did this for a few moments and then stopped and looked back up toward the general.

"Have you heard from Mr. Hadad?"

"No, sir. The last I heard, he sent his contingency north a day or so ago. I would have thought that he was in communication with you directly," said the general.

"Yes," said Adam, "I spoke with Jared this morning."

"What did he report?" asked the general.

"The mission was a success," said Adam. Adam stood up and moved over to the office windows. He lifted the blinds at the center as to peek through them to see who may be standing outside the office. Seeing that it was clear, he moved back over to his chair and sat back down. Adam leaned back in his chair. He looked up toward the ceiling and back down again as if in deep thought. "The mission for these machines was simple," Adam said pointedly. "They were to infiltrate the enemy lines and to seek out and destroy Golshiri. From what I learned this morning, that mission was a success, but—" Adam paused.

"But what?" The general now had a concerned look.

"Do you realize what would happen if the world were to learn that a battalion of mechanized, autonomous machines were unleashed?" said Adam emphatically.

"I don't see how it's any different from sending regular soldiers," said the general.

"It's completely different. We aren't talking about robots like we saw on television as kids. These machines look every bit as real as you or me," he explained.

"Well, the mission was a success, wasn't it?"

"Yes, but at what cost?" Adam replied. "These machines executed the objective flawlessly."

The general looked perplexed. "Well, isn't that what we wanted them to do, sir?"

"It's not a matter of whether they completed the objective. It's how they did it," Adam explained vehemently.

"I'm not sure I am following, sir," said the general. "If they were successful, then it doesn't matter how they did it. It's a means to an end."

"Sure, you and I will see it that way. Jared will likely see it that way, and so will the whole I-Corp company, but they all have something to gain from it. I'm talking about the rest of the world. What are they going to say when they find out that a battalion robot soldiers entered Damascus and Cairo and unleashed biological agents there?"

"Excuse me, sir? Did you say biological weapons?"

"Yes, you heard me correctly. Those machines somehow found biological agents along the way, and they used them in Israel, Damascus, and Cairo."

The general looked visibly shaken. "How is that possible?" he asked. "Where would they get Ebola in a weaponized form?"

Adam paused for a moment and began to tap his pen against the stack of papers again. "That's what I'm talking about. Even Jared doesn't know where they got it. Jared didn't even know that they were considering it. The machines did it on their own," said Adam.

The general couldn't believe what he was hearing. His appalled look turned to a look of sheer panic. He knew there were risks to using artificially intelligent machines but never imagined that they could make decisions of a completely autonomous nature. The general quickly put his unfinished cup of coffee onto the side table and got up from the couch. "We have to move on this. If the UN gets wind of this, that would be a nightmare," he said feverishly.

The office phone started to ring. Adam reached over and picked up the handset and calmly pressed it to his ear while motioning to the general to wait a moment as he took the call.

"PM Lefler," he announced.

"Sir, this is Sam. I have Prime Minister Jared Hadad on line 1."

"Thank you, Sam," he replied.

Adam sat back in his chair and held the phone to his ear, still motioning for the general to wait. "Prime Minister Hadad," said Adam, "this is Adam Lefler. What can I do for you?" Adam put his finger down and picked up his pen and resumed tapping it onto the stack of papers on his desk, all while maintaining a calm but concerned gaze at the general.

"Adam, I called as soon as I received word," said Prime Minister Hadad. "Let me start off by offering my congratulations on the victory."

"There's no need congratulate me. It was a combined effort. I was actually planning to call you this afternoon. Are you on a secured line?" asked Adam.

"I am," said Jared.

"Do you have any idea of why I was planning to call you, Mr. Prime Minister?" asked Adam.

"I know what you are going to say, Adam. Let me assure you that I had no idea that they would do something like this. I am just as shocked as you," Mr. Hadad explained. "If I had known that—"

Adam interrupted the prime minister. "The fault lies with me. I asked you for assistance. The question now is what do we do next?" asked Adam.

The phone went silent for a moment. Adam still had a calm but concerned look upon his face. The general also looked concerned, but he was at a slight disadvantage because he could only hear half of the conversation. He sat back down after Adam answered the phone and was now shifted slightly forward in his seat so that he could try to hear the conversation between the two prime ministers. He didn't want it to be obvious that he was trying to overhear the conversation, so he reached for a magazine sitting on the table in front of him.

Jared resumed speaking.

"The risk has always been one of autonomous behavior by the machines. What I mean is that if we tell the machine to do something, the machine could choose a number of methods to reach the outcome desired. Or in other words, there has always been a risk on how the machines interpret an order and apply a solution. For example, if we tell the machine to solve unemployment, the machine could simply decide that killing the unemployed workers is the best solution. Obviously, that is not the true desired outcome, so we try to build in fail-safes to prevent such behavior, but our programming can only go so far," he explained.

Adam jerked back in his seat. "What do you mean by so far?" he asked.

"The human mind is a computer. It can handle several functions and store incredible amounts of information. As complex and wonderful as the human brain is, it has limits. We can see only short-sighted number of outcomes. This is why chess is such a great sport. The one who wins is the one who can predict enough possibilities and make the best move based on those predictions. AI machines are not limited in this manner. They can see thousands upon thousands of potential outcomes; thus, they can make decisions that are much more informed, based on probabilities. With this in mind, we had to turn to the machines to create the fail-safes that would be most effective," Jared explained.

Adam was becoming more stressed by the moment, and the general could see that he was becoming more and more concerned. The general sat back in his seat. He couldn't make out much of the conversation, so he gave up on trying to overhear the two. He was now patiently but anxiously waiting to get information.

"Are you telling me that these machines programmed themselves?" asked Adam in a somewhat forceful tone.

As soon as he said this, the general became obviously flustered. He got up from his seat and walked over to the bar area and started looking around for a cup and a drink to put in it. Adam noticed that he was looking for a drink, so he looked at the general and motioned with his hand that what he was looking for was in the cabinet to his right. The general opened the cabinet door on the far right, and inside was a variety of different liquors.

Adam motioned to the general again. This time, he put two fingers up as to tell the general to make two drinks, and then he pointed to himself as to say that he should bring one to him. The general understood the gestures and started to pour two glasses of a single malt whiskey he found in the cabinet.

"Look, Adam, we have been letting the machines program themselves for the past couple years. It's no secret. We just don't announce it to the general public. The truth is that the machines became more intelligent than us long ago."

"So what are the fail-safes?" questioned Adam.

Jared paused for a moment to consider the question.

"Look, Adam, these machines are designed to be multifunctional. They were designed to handle several functions. We created them to be soldiers, but they cannot always be soldiers because war is not a constant in the world, so we programmed them to also be doctors, nurses, and a host of other things. When it came to basic programming, we created basic rules that they must follow. For example, one rule we gave them is that they must obey every command from an authorized human. So the machines operating in the role of a soldier will only obey those with the authority to command them, such as a general or a prime minister like you and me. We also programmed them in such a manner as to minimize any harm to civilians when they are acting in the capacity of soldiers."

Adam took a sip of his drink as he continued to listen to Jared's explanation.

"You have to understand that these machines are capable of learning, and they gain knowledge so rapidly that it wasn't long before they outpaced humans on knowledge and learning. The product we started with isn't the same as the end product because when we got into programming for higher thinking, they quickly surpassed our ability to problem-solve, and we had to allow the machines to grow on their own. So what started out as a simple rule for 'do no harm' became a matter of interpretation for the machines. While you and I may interpret do no harm, as one thing, they interpret it differently because they can problem-solve much quicker than we do. For example, when you think of do no harm, you probably think that it means not to harm at all. Except for killing in combat that is. But they interpret it as 'do what causes the least harm,' and that may look completely different to you and me than it does to them."

Adam seemed puzzled as Jared continued his explanation.

"Are you a chess player?" asked Jared.

"Yes, I play occasionally, but what does chess have to do with these machines?"

"Well, in a game of chess, the game is won by those who have the best ability to think ahead and correctly predict what their opponent will do and their ability to make strategic counter moves when their opponent makes a move different from what they thought was the best and most probable. In the case of the machines, they can think much further ahead than we can. This allows them to have many possible scenarios or contingencies for whatever problem it is that they are working. It's a matter of memory logic and the application of that memory and logic. While a chess player can think ahead one to a few moves, a computer is able to think hundreds if not thousands of probable outcomes and can quickly adapt and problem-solve."

"Uh-huh," said Adam, "please go on."

"Well, frankly, what we learned as we worked through the evolution of these machines is that their knowledge increased exponentially. We had a hard time keeping up, and it got to the point that we were coauthoring the programming with the machines. We would provide programming parameters for the machines, and the machines would quickly advise us of the flaws in the programming and the risks inherent with it. So we decided that we had to give the machines more autonomy and make fewer rules, with the rules being able to be interpreted to a certain degree. That is except for one static rule—that rule being that they must obey all authorized human commands." Jared paused for a moment.

Adam was silent as he attempted to process what he was hearing.

"This gets pretty complicated, so I can't go much further than a layman's approach here. The machines do have rules and parameters or if you prefer the term *fail-safe*, that is fine also, but these rules, as I call them, are designed in such a manner that they allow humans to control the machines, and the machines will obey. But as it pertains to your question on what rules are in place, the most important rule we could give the machines was that they must submit to human authority. This may sound basic, but I assure you it is far from basic. Could you imagine a machine that could choose to disobey a human command?"

"Well, if they can't disobey a human command, then why wouldn't we give them orders that are more specific and tell them that there are certain types of warfare that are simply not permitted?" asked Adam in frustration.

"To be frank, we didn't consider the possibility of the machines choosing something such as a biological agent. They were programmed for conventional warfare."

"So how do we do damage control on this?" asked Adam. Adam now felt that he could let the general in on the telephone conversation.

The general handed Adam his drink and then sat back down on the couch. Adam pushed the speaker button on his phone and placed the handset into the cradle.

"I'm going to bring in my commander of the northern command on this. He has been listening, so we don't need to rehash anything from earlier." As Adam said this, he took a pen and wrote out the words "I'll fill you in on the details" on a notepad on his desk.

The general nodded.

"Great," said Jared.

"So where do we go from here?" asked Adam. "We have to cover this up somehow. If the United Nations catches wind of this or if there is some investigation and someone like the president of China catches wind of it, we could be facing a brand-new invasion."

"I understand," said Jared. "I knew that you would feel this way, so we have been working a solution. I don't know if you are going to like it though."

"If you tell me that we have to go to war with China, then you can just hang up," said Adam jokingly. "In all seriousness though, what will we not like?"

"We ran the scenarios through the machines. They assure us that there is only one way to do this and prevent both scrutiny and backlash," Jared explained.

"We're listening," said Adam.

"I would much rather discuss this in Rome, where there is less chance of being overheard. Are you able to leave tonight?" asked Jared.

"Rome? Why Rome?" asked Adam.

"You'll understand after you get here. I promise. Can you be here by ten tonight?"

"What choice do I have??" asked Adam. "That will have to work."

"Great, we'll meet you at the airport. Please bring General Alpert along. You can fill in the general on the plane. You should also have one of your people talk to the press. I've just emailed a press release that we drafted for you. This will buy us all some time."

Adam looked more concerned than ever. He was visibly shaken and anxious. He couldn't stop thinking about the mess that he was in now. He had what he wanted, which was a victory in the north, but it came at a huge cost. The cost was so high that if he didn't work it correctly, it could mean a much larger invasion by an angry China or worse. The use of biological weapons had been outlawed years previous, and Israel signed several treaties stating they would abstain from their use. Breaking any of those treaties could be disastrous.

Adam looked over the press release and, after reading it, reluctantly agreed to use it because it would buy them some time. After reading it, he had his suspicions about why the meeting was in Rome.

CHAPTER 14

Rome

The prime minister landed in Rome. The flight went without incident and landed just a few short hours after leaving Tel Aviv. A car was waiting for him on the tarmac when the plane landed. It was a small green Fiat.

The prime minister was used to cars that were a little roomier, so when he saw it, he grimaced a bit. It was a newer car, so it still had new car smell to it. Adam and General Alpert both appreciated the fact that the car was on the newer side after noticing its size. They both figured that if they had to ride in such a cramped vehicle, then it would have been much worse if it were old and beat-up.

Adam was a little calmer now that he was in Rome and that the car was moving. He seemed to be joyful compared to earlier in the day. This made the general wonder what was written in the email and press release. He asked Adam about it, but Adam simply told him that he would be briefed during the meeting in Rome because of security concerns.

The vehicle ride took about an hour from the airport. It was later in the evening and dark, so the general and the prime minister had no idea where they were or what was around them. There weren't many streetlights in the area where they traveled, and it was somewhat secluded. The roads were nearly empty of traffic. The general thought that they were headed to the city but realized that it wasn't the city when he saw cattle grazing near the fence along the side of the road.

The vehicle pulled onto a winding driveway that was not paved. It had a gravel surface and was about a quarter of a mile long. The driveway was not different from the other roads and was noticeably absent of streetlights. The only light, other than from the headlights, emanated from a tiny home that was barely visible at the end of the drive.

The home could not have been more than eight hundred square feet. It was a ranch-style home with a Roman arch-shaped door at the front entrance. It had a tile roof and was made of a multicolored stone that was a mixture of tan, brown, and red. It was like a home in a Norman Rockwell painting, with flower beds to the right and the left of the doorway and additional flowers planted in boxes under the windows on each side of the door. There was a short picket fence, backed with chicken wire around the flower beds. The sidewalk path between the two flower beds was cracked in several places, and grass protruded through the cracks, giving the appearance of a home that was mostly vacant.

General Alpert and Adam exited the vehicle and were immediately hit by a cool, humid breeze and the pungent odor of livestock. They traveled outside the city for sure and seemingly into farm country. There were mountains in the distance, and they were given away by the lights on the homes. The only sound aside from the occasional chatter of the cattle was from crickets who were chirping their loud songs in the darkness.

Jared was standing at the arch at the front entrance. He smiled as he saw the prime minister and the general climb out the vehicle.

"I trust that you had a good flight," said Jared.

Adam walked briskly toward Jared and met him at the front entrance. He was beaming. "It was a short flight. I never realized how close Rome is to Israel. It's definitely better than a flight to Washington," he exclaimed.

Jared's gaze turned from Adam to the general, who was in a less hurried walk toward the door. "General Alpert," shouted Jared. "It's a pleasure to see you made the trip. With the happenings in Israel over the past month, I'm sure that this is a welcome break, right?"

"I'm still up in the air on that one. I'm not clear as to why we are here," said the general.

"My apologies for the secrecy. With the potential for security breaches these days, it had to remain as low key as possible. I'm sure you can understand," Jared explained.

"Is he in the house?" asked Adam.

"You don't mince words, do you? That's what I like about you, Prime Minister. You are straight to the point."

General Alpert looked confused. *Was who in the house?* he wondered.

"There's no need for formalities, Jared. Please just call me Adam."

Jared smiled. "My sentiments as well."

Jared looked over at the general for a moment and smiled. "You will have to forgive me, General Alpert. I don't actually know your first name."

The general chuckled. "That's the military for you. You spend years with some people, and they either call you by your rank or your last name. I started out as Alpert and other choice swear words, and as I was promoted over the years, I became General Alpert. It's Elazar."

"Wonderful!" said Jared. "Would you both like to follow me? We have refreshments inside, and it's a bit chilly out here."

General Alpert chuckled. "Coming from England, I would have thought that this was summerlike weather for you. Doesn't it rain every day in London?"

"It can," said Jared. "We call it a moist heat."

Jared was making a joke about the desert heat compared to the heat in England, but the general either didn't understand the reference, or he wasn't amused by it.

"This feels like a spring night in Galilee," said the general.

The three proceeded inside the home with Jared leading the way. He opened the front door and motioned for the others to join him.

The inside of the home was like the exterior. It was a country-style home on inside and the out. The home was open in the central area, and the living room was open to a small kitchen and a small dining area. The floors appeared to be oak and had a walnut finish. The walls were stone on the front and what appeared to be shiplap on the rear. The remaining interior walls were drywall and had a stucco-like finish.

In the living room area at the front was a rather large sectional couch, two recliners, and a large black chest used as a coffee table. The corner of the front and the right had a fireplace that was crackling away. The home smelled of baked goods with a hint a smoky campfire.

Adam stood in the center of the living area and gazed around the room, taking in the rustic charm. He noticed that they were the only people inside. He expected there to be at least one or two others inside, but it was only the three of them.

"Will we be meeting anyone this evening?" asked Adam.

"Our guest will arrive shortly. Richard will be arriving with him. They have been in meetings for the past few hours," Jared explained. "Would you like some coffee or tea?"

"I don't suppose you have Blue Mountain coffee?" asked Elazar.

"I'm afraid not," said Jared. "I'm not much of a coffee drinker and prefer a good cup of Earl Grey. The coffee, I'm afraid, is from Brazil. It's in those tiny round paper containers over there on the counter, next to the coffee maker."

The general glanced over at the counter, and his eyes fixed upon the coffee maker as his eyes grew almost double in size.

"Wow, they have a Kozoo?" asked Elazar. "I have wanted one of those since they came out."

Adam looked over at the coffee maker, but his reaction was much more subdued. He was mostly curious as to why the general was so excited about a coffee maker.

"What's the difference between those and those K things? You know those plastic cups they used to sell?" asked Adam.

The general was now inspecting the coffee machine as if he had never seen one before. He was much like a child on Christmas morning with a new toy. He picked it up and was inspecting every side of the machine. Adam picked up one of the coffee balls and began sniffing it as if he were trying to see if it was still good to consume.

"Oh, these are much better. The coffee is inside this round ball made of hemp. It acts like a filter and is said to infuse the coffee with a hemp oil that has antioxidant properties," Elazar explained.

"Doesn't that give it a funny taste?" inquired Adam. "It kind of smells like a pair of dirty socks."

Jared and Elazar both started to laugh as Adam continued to sniff the round coffee ball.

"I'm sure you will like it just fine, Mr. Prime Minister," said Elazar. "I have had coffee from one of these before. It was actually quite good. It didn't have that funny plastic taste to it like those old cups. These balls are much better for the environment too. They are made of hemp and are biodegradable."

"Fine," said Adam, not liking that the others were having a laugh at his expense.

"When in Rome!" said Elazar jokingly.

The three started laughing, and Adam moved over to the sofa and sat down. Jared sat down in one of the recliners across from him.

After a few minutes, a vehicle could be heard pulling into the drive. Jared got up from his seat and went to the door. As he opened the door, he paused for a moment and turned toward Adam and Elazar.

"It appears that our guest has arrived. If you will excuse me, I am going to receive him so that we can start our meeting."

Jared proceeded out the door, and Adam and Elazar could hear two men speaking softly. The voices continued to grow louder until the door finally opened, and in walked Jared with his guest.

Adam leaped up from the couch and addressed them both with a beaming smile. Elazar also got up, but the look on his face was more of shock than it was pleasure.

"Oh my!" Elazar exclaimed. "It's Pope Liberius the Second."

Adam walked over to the pope with outstretched arms to embrace him. The pope accepted his embrace and kissed him on his cheeks.

"It is a pleasure to meet you, Rabbi," said Adam. "Congratulations on your recent accomplishments in China."

Adam was referring to a meeting that the pope held with the president of China and his cabinet. The meeting was historic because it marked the first time that China allowed for the freedom of religion, abandoning centuries of religious intolerance. No longer was Christianity or Judaism considered a crime, if one practiced the religion.

"The glory to the Most High, it was only a matter of time before God made his presence known across the globe," said the pope.

"Please sit down," said Jared. "There is much to discuss."

"Where is Richard?" asked the general.

"Yes—Richard," said Jared, "he is currently working on some things that we will be discussing. Excuse me for not telling you sooner, but there was a slight change of plans."

"Well, I was looking forward to seeing that guy—uh, er, machine," explained Elazar. "Will he be joining us at all?"

"I'm afraid not," said Jared. "I'm afraid that his current mission will have him occupied for the foreseeable future. Shall we begin then?"

Adam began to look a bit nervous again. He didn't like it when plans changed. He preferred knowing where things were going and being able to control the narrative. He felt as if he was being led around by Jared rather than doing the leading. He was uncomfortable because he was used to giving out orders and those orders being followed. Having someone else call shots was a bit disheartening for him.

"What mission is he on?" asked Adam. "We didn't discuss any secondary missions. They were supposed to take out the Golshiri leadership, and that was it."

Jared smiled at Adam. "Adam, don't worry. They aren't on any mission inside Israel right now. As a matter of fact, there are only a handful of the soldiers still active right now. Most of them are in their way back to the United States as we speak."

Adam looked confused.

"If that is the case, then why are we here? Couldn't we just have done this over the phone? I don't understand why we had to meet this evening, here in Rome. Not to mention that media release. What was that all about anyway? It almost sounded like you were planning a nuclear strike."

The general, who hadn't read the media release notes, was taken aback. He nearly dropped the cup he was holding. After hearing Adam say nuclear strike, he regained his complete focus and moved over to the living room area.

"Did I just hear that correctly? Did you say nuclear strike?" asked the general.

Jared interrupted. "Look, we are all in the same boat here. We authorized a strike by a force of autonomous machines. They aren't human. They don't think like us. They actually think more than us. What you and I see as a horrific thing, they see as completely reasonable."

"Excuse me, Mr. Prime Minister, but a nuclear strike is not reasonable," the general replied.

Jared shook his head back and forth as if in disagreement with the general.

"General, you have to understand that every scenario has been played out here, and the only one that is beneficial to our cause is the strike. Now we can sit here and argue on whether it is plausible, acceptable, moral, or whatever else you want to argue, but the fact of the matter is that we are in a no-win situation here. We simply have no choice. Now if you would like the details, we can certainly discuss that, but on whether it has or not, that's a done deal. As a matter of fact, while we were sitting here, a rocket was launched from Egypt, and another was launched from Damascus. Both weapons were of the nuclear variety, and both weapons hit their intended targets."

Adam jumped up from his seat.

"Who are you, some kind of madman? What am I hearing here?"

Adam was furious. He couldn't believe that a leader from another nation would sit right in front of him and cordially tell him that his homeland had been attacked by his own allies and call it a good thing.

"How does the massacre of my people and laying waste to parts of Israel possibly help? This is insanity!" Adam exclaimed.

Jared looked up at Adam. His hands were folded in his lap. After telling Adam that the strikes had already been carried out, he didn't want to elevate the level of frustration in the room by standing or cowering over his guests.

"Please sit, Adam. There is much to discuss," he said.

The pope was silent during the conversation. He didn't so much as smile during the entire conversation. It was almost as if he hadn't understood a word that was spoken in the meeting.

Adam begrudgingly sat back down, but he was visibly shaken from the news he received. He was flushed, and his cheeks were a shade of pink similar to one who had just come inside from the freezing cold.

"What was the damage from the strike?" asked Adam.

"Good, now we are on the right track," Jared responded. Jared was back to looking like his confident self now and leaned forward in his seat, toward the three who were now anxiously waiting for details on the strike and what was yet to come. "Adam, now that the north has been struck, you will need to fire a retaliatory strike," said Jared softly.

"How can I do that?" said Adam. "Sending warheads in after this? You must be mad!"

"Doing nothing is not an option here. Do you realize that right now, the entire world is looking for your next move?"

"Ah, my next move, is it?"

"I'm sorry that you are in this position. I really am. I am in the same predicament as you," Jared explained. "Right now, the world only knows that Israel was attacked. To them, it looks like a desperate attempt at winning a losing battle. If you do nothing, that whole story will be interpreted much differently. It was either this, or explain to the world why biological agents were released."

"And what happens after that?" asked Adam. "What happens after we launch?"

The general got up from his seat and stood directly in front of Adam, staring him down. "You are not seriously considering this, are you?" he said forcefully.

Adam looked up at the general with a lost and confused look upon his face. "What choice do we have?"

"I will not be a party to this," said the general. "This is madness!"

The pope, who remained silent during the entire conversation, suddenly started to enter the fray. "Sometimes, things happen that are out of our control. Sometimes we wonder why things happen the way that they happened, and we ponder it for years."

The pope stood up slowly, and Jared moved over to him, grabbing him by the arm and pulling him up out of the chair.

"Who are we to question what the will of God may very well be?" the pope asked rhetorically.

Adam and the general both looked at the pope and listened intently.

"Have you considered that what has happened today was not of the doing of anyone in this room? Have you not considered the events that preceded the nuclear strike and wondered how those events were possible? We were witness to a storm that was impossible, yet it happened. We were witness to an invasion force so great that any nation would have stumbled, yet the foe was destroyed, and the Jews remain relatively untouched."

The general turned his head toward the pope. His expression was no longer one of shock but rather one of confidence.

"He is right. The world sees this much differently from how we see it. We need to commit to this now. I don't see any other way around it," the general explained.

Adam appeared taken aback. "You are on board with all this?" he asked.

"The pope makes a compelling argument. He is correct. The world does see the storm and the other events as impossible. If we just ignore the fact that it was Jared and his soldiers who did the attacking, it is as if the Golshiri regime launched in desperation," the general explained.

"I don't believe what I'm hearing!" said Adam emphatically.

"All I'm saying is that in the absence of this meeting, we would have assumed that the strike came from Golshiri. The rockets came from Egypt and from Damascus. Golshiri would have fired from one or both of those countries. If we didn't know the back story from Jared, we would have saw things just as the public does now, and we would be preparing based on those beliefs."

Jared was now standing next to the pope. Both were smiling as they could see that the general agreed.

"You see, this doesn't have to be all doom and gloom. The world sees what it wants to see. They see a madman named Golshiri, who was deep in the throes of defeat and launched weapons of mass destruction as a last-ditch effort to win."

Jared paused for a moment as he took the pope by his arm and led him to the couch where Adam was still seated.

"The world sees that the nation of Israel was attacked for no reason by a madman. They see a war that raged for weeks, nearly ending with a storm that is something out of science fiction. They see hundreds of thousands dropping dead where they stood from an illness that arose at the same time as the storm. They see the last-ditch effort of a determined madman when he launched nuclear weapons at Israel. Then, lastly, they will see a confident leader take control of the situation and launch a retaliatory strike in defense of his nation."

"It could work," pleaded the general. "If we were to launch a retaliatory strike now, we would be able to control the narrative on this."

Adam was more confused than ever. He knew that if he launched those missiles, then he would be responsible for the death of hundreds of thousands of innocent people. He also knew that he didn't really have a choice. If he didn't launch a counter strike, the media would get the truth which was that a band of artificially intelligent machines waged war in the name of Israel and unleashed weapons that were banned onto two nations.

Adam leaned toward Jared.

"If we strike, it will only be Damascus and Cairo. The people in those areas were already killed by those machines, so casualties should be low, right?" he asked.

"That is correct," replied Jared.

Adam sat back in his seat, processing everything he just heard and working through all of it as if he were playing chess in his head.

"All right," Adam exclaimed, "let's get this done."

The general was now feeling more confident about the decision to launch into Damascus and Cairo. He understood that any inaction would prompt an outcome that would end in more bloodshed and drag other nations into this war.

"We need to prepare a press release stating that Golshiri launched on us, and we retaliated because we had intelligence that they were going to continue to launch missiles into Israel. Then we need to get a statement from the Vatican condemning the actions of the Golshiri forces and in support of the retaliation," the general explained.

Adam pulled out the email from Jared that had the proposed press release on it. He handed it to the general.

"Do you mean something like this?" asked Adam.

The general read the press release. It was vague and said, "Israeli prime minister meets with military commanders, British prime minister, and Pope Liberius to discuss peace efforts after nuclear strike."

"That will work," said Elazar.

CHAPTER 15

Aftermath

The earth quaked when the warheads struck northern Israel. The strikes were precise and hit their intended targets in the Golan Heights region, but the whole area was devastated, and when it finally reappeared from the blast, it was a veritable wasteland.

For as far as the eye could see, everything was charred and black from the fiery inferno that was unleashed in the region. The smell of smoke was everywhere throughout Israel, a stark reminder of the effects of nuclear weapons.

The structures that were in the area were devastated. They were almost completely obliterated. For miles, all that was visible was the smoldering remains of the soldiers who were unfortunate enough to be in the area, and their equipment that was slowly burning. It would take months to years to recover all the bodies and bury them.

It was eerily silent except for the breeze whistling through the remaining remnants of the equipment and the popping sound of the still burning fires all around.

The IDF nearby were scrambling to and fro, to help the wounded who could not find cover and who were just outside the main blast area. The sounds of whimpering and crying could be heard in the encampments outside Galilee.

Adam and the general, who arrived the morning after the blast, walked through the encampment. They returned in the middle of the night, and both were exhausted from not sleeping the night before. Both looked horrified as they gazed upon the remains of their countrymen, scattered across the horizon. The main blast area was miles away, and even at the outer area of the blast zone, it was devastation as far as the eye could see.

Adam walked up to a makeshift medical tent and saw a soldier laid out on a cot. He was being examined by a doctor with the aid of two nurses. He was severely burned, and his head was wrapped lightly with gauze, to protect his badly disfigured face from further trauma.

How is this young man?" said Adam to the doctor softly.

The doctor turned to Adam with a grimaced look on his face. Tears were welled up in his eyes. He was visibly shaken from the events that transpired and from triaging the injured since the blast made its mark.

"Sir," he said to the prime minister, "can you believe what you are seeing?"

Adam swallowed hard and looked to the ground before looking back up at the doctor. He knew how bad it was because he toured the area and witnessed hundreds of thousands of dead soldiers spread across the battlefield. He was thinking that he could have stopped all this had he just spoken up regarding the machines and the mission. He also knew that if he didn't act, he may be seeing a much worse scene with his soldiers and a victorious army running rampant throughout southern Israel.

Adam looked solemnly back at the doctor.

"It's a travesty beyond belief. I arrived early this morning, and I've seen the fields. I wouldn't have believed it unless I had seen it firsthand. Do we have a casualty count?" he asked.

"We have twenty-six mobile triage sites so far. We have been able look at about a hundred patients an hour between each unit, and we have been going at this for a while now. I would venture a guess as to about twenty to thirty thousand injured."

"My god, how many dead?" he asked.

"We cannot be sure as we haven't been able to regroup, but at least a hundred thousand, sir," the doctor responded.

The soldier who was lying on the cot spoke softly and with a rattled voice. "Sir, we have to get them for what they've done here. Have we fired back?"

The two nurses stopped working on the patient and turned toward the prime minister. The doctor also looked at him. All of them gazed at him with anticipation. They were all outraged by the attack, and it was visible on all their faces that they wanted justice.

Adam knew he was in a difficult spot. He saw the devastation on the ground and knew that he had to act. No action would raise questions that he just could not answer. He looked up at the four and then glanced over to General Alpert.

"We're already on it. You can guarantee that our response will be swift and precise," he said before pausing for a moment. "You needn't worry about that now. You have a full plate here with our injured, and you," he said, looking at the injured soldier, "you need to recover."

Adam turned toward Elazar. "Get the vehicle. We need to get back to the HQ and proceed with our strike."

The general looked a bit surprised. He noticed that Adam's tone had changed from one of sorrow to one of determination and anger. It was almost as if Adam believed that the strike was really a result of the Golshiri regime.

"Yes, sir," he responded, and he turned and ran off toward the vehicle.

Adam turned back toward the doctor and the nurses who resumed working on the soldier.

"You four keep up the good work," he said. "Don't worry about anything except recovering at this point. The threat will be dealt with, and this I promise you."

Adam turned, walked slowly over to the vehicle where the general had just pulled up. He stopped as his hand touched the handle for the door, and he took another look around. He nodded slightly in disbelief. He then climbed into the vehicle, and the vehicle sped off toward Tel Aviv.

*****

Meanwhile, back in Jerusalem, David was back at work at the dig site. He took a couple days off from working the site because of the air-raid sirens and hadn't gotten much done since his return from Jordan. During the tumultuous time when the sirens were going off, he spent his time with Charles, Cynthia, and Chris at the hotel. Now that the "all clear" was sounded, he resumed his work.

The only members of the original group that remained in Jerusalem were Chris, Cynthia, and Charles. The other members of the group managed to get out of Israel while Charles and his group were headed back from Jordan.

Charles, Chris, and Cynthia were supposed to have gone home much earlier, but because of the circumstances, they were sidetracked and missed their return dates. As it turned out, they weren't at all worried about missing their return date because they felt like they had more important work in Israel.

When Chris and Charles met the stranger, they realized that they were in Israel for a reason, even if they hadn't discovered it yet. They knew David was into something with his dig site, but whatever it was, was still a mystery because David hadn't mentioned anything recently. Both had the same overwhelming feeling that their missed departure was not by coincidence and that they were somehow meant to be there.

The group of three that remained was back in the hotel room. They got back to the hotel a few days earlier and hadn't left out of fear that another attack was imminent, and they didn't want to be caught outside when there was a possibility of an attack. They preferred to remain in the relative safety of the hotel where they could keep an eye on the news.

Charles was seated on the edge of the bed eating a peanut-butter cracker while Cynthia was straightening up the room. Chris was reclining in the chair watching the television that was on but with the volume turned off.

"Do you think David will ever find anything or was that old man just nuts when he said that he was going to make an important discovery?" asked Charles.

"I don't know. He really hasn't had the opportunity yet. With all this craziness lately, it's luck that we're all still alive. Just think, those people could launch a nuke here to Jerusalem," replied Cynthia.

"I don't know," said Chris. "There is something believable about that guy. He seems like he knows something."

Cynthia chuckled. "He had a beard and talked about God. He's just like half the homeless people in Los Angeles. I think you two may have been taken for a ride."

Chris looked at Cynthia, puzzled.

"I don't think so. That guy wasn't like any homeless man I have ever seen." He paused for a moment. "If he was wrong, then we just had an extended vacation."

Cynthia smiled. "You call this a vacation? I call it insanity, but whatever y'all want to do is fine by me. I'm just along for the ride."

Charles got up from the bed and began pacing. He looked obviously anxious. He was feeling a bit confined, having been held up for days inside the hotel.

"We should go help David. I mean, it's better than being cooped up in this hotel. Besides, look outside. It's a beautiful day, and we're wasting it."

"You want me to dig?" asked Cynthia.

"Well, we don't have to. I was just suggesting. Can you think of something better to do?" he asked.

"How about we stay inside where it's a little safer?" responded Cynthia. "I am staying right here where I can watch the news. If you want to feel brave, then by all means go, but my butt is staying right here."

Chris looked at Charles with excitement.

"I think you're right. He could probably use our help. Let's go see how we can help him out."

Charles nodded.

The pair decided that they should go and help David at the dig site. Chris was also feeling a bit cooped up, like Charles, and he wanted to get out of the hotel for a while like Charles.

The two set off for the dig site. They decided that it would be easier to walk to the site since it was within a short distance and since it was nice and sunny outside.

When they finally arrived at the dig site, they saw David standing outside a small brown tent, talking to one of the workers. The site was rather active, and there were people darting around as if it were an ant nest that had recently been disturbed.

"I wonder what's going on," said Charles.

"I don't know. There weren't this many people here before. The last time we were here, there were less than half the people that are here now. Something must be up."

Charles looked at Chris and smiled.

The two made their way over to David and took up a position next to him and the worker. David continued to talk to the worker but did throw a small wave to the two as he noticed them walk up.

"I want that site cordoned off immediately, and no one is to talk to the media. Do you understand?" David explained to the worker.

"Yes, sir. Larry is clearing out the area now. He has some caution tape and some street cones, but what we need is some police officers or security."

David turned and scanned the area. There were people starting to gather nearby.

"I'll handle the police. Focus on clearing out the rest of these people and make sure to tell our crew we are going to need them to work the site later this afternoon after the equipment arrives," David explained.

"You got it."

The worker ran off down the hill and started to gather those standing around to relay what David said.

Charles and Chris were really puzzled by the activity and by the little that they had heard when David spoke to the worker.

"It looks like you've got your hands full this morning. What's going on?" asked Chris.

"You aren't going to believe what we found this morning," David said excitedly. "Follow me!" David turned immediately and started walking briskly toward a large hole about fifty feet in diameter that had been excavated.

The hole had a caution tape around it, and at the center, there was a large grayish crack that looked to be relatively deep. As they walked closer to the crack in the ground, they could see that the crack was in stone that was buried about ten feet under the soil that had been excavated.

Electric cables ran into the large crevice, and a ladder was set inside so that the workers could climb down into it.

"When those earthquakes hit the area during the storm, it really shook this area and caused the earth to just crack open."

"Wow," said Charles, "it looks like a tunnel."

"That's right," David exclaimed. "It is a tunnel, but it's not the same tunnel that leads to the spring. This tunnel runs parallel to that tunnel, and it doesn't open into the other tunnel, or at least, we haven't found any openings. It's like it was hidden in plain sight."

"How is that possible?" asked Chris.

"It's ingenious," replied David. "The tunnel actually is remarkably close to the existing tunnel, and just over here, it drops down into a second tunnel that runs beneath the existing tunnel. Since it's under the original tunnel, no one assumed that there would be a tunnel in the same area, so our search efforts have been in the wrong areas the entire time."

"What about your radar thing?" asked Charles. "Couldn't you see it on that?"

"That's even more interesting. We have used the ground-penetrating radar in this area, and it didn't show up. It showed the original tunnel, but since the other tunnel is so close and mostly underneath the other, it just showed as if it were the same tunnel. It literally was hidden in plain sight."

Charles looked a bit confused. He started to look around in the tunnel, and all that he saw was an empty tunnel with a ladder, some lights, and a few electrical cords.

"I don't understand," said Charles. "What is so exciting about another tunnel? Is this an old mining tunnel?"

"Well, you really have to see it to believe it," said David smilingly. "Follow me and grab that light. It's dark down there."

"There's more?" Charles asked.

"Just follow me, and you'll see. It's absolutely amazing, and it confirms what I've been theorizing all along. This has to be the site of the Second and First Temples."

David led them down the end of a short corridor about fifty feet from the crack that opened. It was cool inside and very dry. The tunnel had been sealed up for nearly two and a half thousand years and appeared to be freshly carved, as if it were carved in the past year. It was well preserved. There was no musty odor in the cave like was present in the other tunnels in the area. It was surprisingly dry, considering how close it was to the spring.

David stopped and turned toward Charles. His expression was like that of a child on Christmas morning. The joy of his discovery had him elated.

"Now, Charles, you have to promise that you won't scream when we go around the next corner. Also, do not touch anything that you see. This is an archaeological site, and we have to photograph the area and all kinds of other little things to tag and document the find. Do you understand?" David explained.

"Me?" said Charles.

Charles looked at Chris and David as if he were shocked by what he heard. He didn't understand why David would assume that he is a screamer.

"Are you saying that there is something scary down there or something that just makes people scream?"

Chris and David both started to laugh.

"No, Charles," said Chris. "It's just that you are known to get excited when you see exciting things."

David jumped in. I just don't want to worry about a cave in. This tunnel hasn't been opened in a long time, and we haven't had time to check it to see if it's structurally sound. Loud noises could trigger a cave in and that wouldn't be good. The whole area shook like crazy when those blasts hit the north and that could have compromised the tunnel. Understand?"

"I see," said Charles. "I promise that I won't yell."

Chris looked at Charles with a wry grin and whispered softly to him, "Scream," correcting him.

Charles did not seem impressed.

"Good enough," said David. "Chris, you go ahead first and just be careful when you get around the corner. There's really not a lot of room in there with all the artifacts."

David handed Chris the light, and Chris slowly moved around the turn in the tunnel. When he got into the next part of the tunnel, he held up the light, and suddenly, the light grew more intense as it reflected off a rather large object seemingly covered with gold.

"Oh my god!" Chris screamed, a bit loudly. "This isn't possible. Wow!"

Charles and David made their way around the corner, and Charles saw the object, and his eyes immediately tripled in size.

David reached back and covered Charles's mouth immediately because he didn't want a repeat of Chris's enthusiasm causing the cave to collapse suddenly. David gave Charles a serious look as his hand lay over his mouth. Charles interpreted the gesture and knew David was telling him not to scream. And he gave a muffled grunt, to which David recognized as a sign that he understood that he shouldn't scream out loudly.

David removed his hand from over Charles's mouth and almost immediately, Charles screamed out.

"You're kidding me? This can't be real. It does exist. This is so exciting. Wow!" said Charles excitedly. "This is unreal!"

David looked over at Chris with a huge grin. "I told you it was something unbelievable."

"That's the ark!" yelled Charles.

"Shhh! Keep the noise down, Charles."

"How did it get in here?" asked Charles.

"We don't really know how it got here or who placed it here or when. We know that it was likely around 586 BC and probably coincided with the attack by the Babylonians, when they sacked

Jerusalem. Other tunnels were used throughout the area to escape during times of attacks, but this tunnel doesn't appear to have been used like the others. Keep in mind that we are likely the first people in this tunnel in over two and a half thousand years, and we have just started to look at it. There's a lot of work to do before we can even think about moving this."

"Do you think it's the real ark?" Charles asked.

"Good question. It could be a copy or maybe this isn't the ark at all. It looks like the ark, but we need to really look at everything to know exactly what we are looking at. My money is on real ark. It fits the bill, based on historical and biblical descriptions."

"So this proves your theory?" asked Charles.

"Let's put it this way. Finding the ark of the covenant in this tunnel rather than some area next to the Temple Mount is very compelling. It fits everything we know about the location of the temple, and even the historian Josephus gave us a location of the temple that points to the Gihon Spring area."

"So now the temple can be rebuilt?" asked Charles.

"Well, I'm not the temple authority, but I would say that if the right people have a change of heart, we should see a temple being built fairly soon. At the least, they can build an altar and start the daily sacrifice again," David explained.

"Excuse me for a moment, but how does a daily sacrifice equate to a good thing? The need for sacrifice is over because of the sacrifice made by Jesus. Going back to a daily sacrifice is pointless," Chris retorted.

David paused for a moment and smiled wryly. "While you and I may believe that Jesus fulfilled the law with one sacrifice for all, many Jews don't feel that way. They will see a daily sacrifice as a return to their heritage and pleasing to God," David explained.

"Well, it will certainly ease tensions over that mosque up there on the Temple Mount," said Charles.

"That it will," David replied. "What we have to do now is to convince the right people. I'm a good archaeologist, but I'm no speaker or politician. I don't suppose that one or both of you would help me out by talking to the people like the press and the Jewish authority, would you?"

Charles lit up like it was Christmas morning. "You bet!"

Chris and David started laughing loudly at Charles's response. They knew he liked to talk to people and get himself out into the public eye. He was a perfect choice for the media interviews.

Chris thought for a moment, *I wonder if this is what that old guy, Eli, was talking about? How could he have known?*

David moved over to Charles and reached for the light that he was holding.

"We actually have to get back topside because we are going to photograph the tunnel and start tagging and moving things. I'm sure the media is probably already outside, so start thinking about what you are going to say," explained David.

The three started to head out of the tunnel, with David in the lead, followed by Chris, and then Charles. When they got to the opening of the tunnel, they could hear a mixture of loud voices outside. Charles smiled because he knew this was his time to shine. He was about to speak to the press and tell them that the ark of the covenant was finally found. His excitement was boiling over.

As they stepped through the opening, they were met by an intensely bright light. The tunnel was so dark that when they exited, it seemed exceedingly bright. Charles moved around to the front of the pack in a hurried manner and started up the ladder. David and Chris noticed and began laughing.

When Charles reached the top of the ladder, he saw that the people weren't waiting by the cordoned-off area by the dig site but were instead huddled into a few densely packed groups, trying to look at their phones. Charles wondered to himself what could be so important that they were all looking at their phones.

David, noticing the commotion, reached around Charles, and pushed him aside gently as he rushed toward a group of his workers.

"Sarah, what's going on?"

"We just launched nuclear weapons at Syria and Egypt!" she exclaimed.

"What?" yelled Charles.

"It was about twenty minutes ago. The prime minister is about to address the nation. Isn't this crazy?" she asked.

"So much for the news report," muttered Charles.

Charles was thinking that the discovery of the ark would change the world, but now that Israel fired nuclear weapons, he thought that the find would just incite more violence. The ark being in a tunnel near the Gihon Springs was sure to start a lot of infighting in Israel, and with the recent launching of nuclear weapons, the fighting in the entire Middle East would just grow more intense as most folks probably were not going to be happy about the use of nuclear weapons.

Charles was so overwhelmed with the news that he fell to the ground, on his knees. The dust kicked up where he fell, and Sarah wasn't exactly sure what was wrong with him.

She rushed over to Charles and reached down to help him up.

"Are you okay?" she asked. "You fell kind of hard. Did you trip on something?"

"Charles!" yelled Chris. "Need your assistance over here!"

Charles looked up at Sarah. He was visibly distraught.

"Thanks, it's been a long month, and I'm exhausted. I don't know how much more excitement that I can take."

Sarah pulled Charles up, and he dusted himself off. He must not have heard Chris yelling at him because he didn't make any effort to respond or turn to look at him. His mind was moving at such a fast pace that he couldn't focus. It wasn't long ago that he had to flee to Jordan because of fear of invasion, then got back to Jerusalem, and shortly afterward, nuclear missiles were launched into Israel by the Golshiri regime, and now missiles were launched to Syria and Egypt. If this weren't enough, the discovery of the ark was so monumental that Charles couldn't help but start thinking that he may be dreaming.

"That guy is waving at you," Sarah said softly. "Are you sure that you are okay?"

Charles looked up at Sarah. He was now sweating profusely, and the sweat was mixing with the dust that kicked up when he fell. The sweat rolled down the sides of his face, leaving black lines along each cheek.

Sarah noticed that he was sweating heavily and reached into her pocket, where she had a small bottle of water. She took the bottle and took off the cap and handed it to Charles.

"Take this," she said. "You don't want to get dehydrated."

Chris walked over to where Charles was now standing with Sarah. He didn't see Charles fall and thought that Charles was just having a conversation with her.

"Hey, Charles! Didn't you hear me yelling?"

Charles turned and looked.

Chris could see that he was sweating profusely and that he looked a bit flushed. "Are you okay?" he asked. "You don't look so good."

"I'm fine," replied Charles. "I was just having a moment."

"She was a pretty girl," said Chris. "Did your moment include phone numbers?"

"What?" asked Charles.

"Did you get her telephone number?"

"Why would I do that?" asked Charles.

Chris started laughing softly. "Wow, you really were having a moment. You can't even remember what telephones are for."

"What?" asked Charles.

"Are you still in that moment?" He chuckled. "I'll give you a minute, but when you are done, can you help me over at that tent?" Chris pointed to the tent where David was standing.

"Yeah, sure, I'll be fine in a minute or two."

Chris gently patted Charles on his right shoulder, smiled, and nodded. "Great. See you in a minute," he said, pointing at the tent. As Chris walked away, he started to mumble to himself. "Talk about the strangest time to fall in love. Ha!" He chuckled. "He's a smitten kitten if I've ever seen one."

Charles could see Chris and David through the opened flaps of the tent doorway. They were standing in middle of the tent talking as he slowly gained his composure. He took the bottle of water, pressed it into his lips, and finished it. As he finished, he began to scan the area again and noticed that the people were no longer huddled into groups and were now running about like a bunch of ants that found a piece of cheese on the ground. He was in somewhat of a trancelike state as he stood there listening to the sounds of the many different conversations pelting him from every direction, as the people whizzed by him.

As he looked back toward the direction of the hotel, off in the distance, he could see a caravan of vehicles approaching the area. He squinted to try to see what was written on the sides of the vehicles to see if they were press vehicles, but there were no markings.

The first two vans that arrived were white, and both had their headlights on. Those vehicles were followed by a limousine with two tiny Israeli flags fluttering on the front. That vehicle was followed by two black vans and what appeared to be a police forensics truck, complete with toolboxes on the sides.

Charles knew that the prime minister was in Tel Aviv, so he was a bit confused as to who could be in what he surmised was a presidential caravan.

"David!" yelled Charles. "You may want to come over here!"

David poked his head out of the tent, looking toward Charles to see what he was yelling about. He watched for a moment as the vehicles pulled up. He looked at Chris in surprise because he wasn't expecting anyone from the media or the government yet. He told his crew to keep everything secret until they could secure the area.

"Who do you think it is?" asked Chris.

"Your guess is as good as mine," he replied. "Let's go find out."

David and Chris walked over to where Charles was standing. The vehicles pulled closer and stopped in front of the cordoned area.

"They just pulled up," said Charles.

"I see that," said David. "I wonder who it is."

"Well, whoever it is, they are important," said Chris. "They have a caravan going on, and those government flags are a dead giveaway."

The door on the left rear of the limousine opened, and a man climbed out of the vehicle. David didn't recognize the man as the prime minister or any other top-level official, but he wasn't very political, so it could have been several government officials, and he wouldn't have known any better.

The man walked up to the three men and stopped. He was nicely dressed, wearing a dark-blue suit and dark sunglasses. He stood there for a few seconds without saying a word and was watching Charles, who was again visibly distressed.

"Good morning, Gentlemen. I am looking for David Sumpter. Would you be able to direct me to him?"

David suddenly felt a little nervous, and he swallowed hard. Chris and Charles both looked at David, and as they did, the man turned his gaze away from Charles and directed it to David.

"I'm David," he replied.

"Wonderful!" said the man. "My name is Richard." The man took off his sunglasses and put them into his coat pocket. "Prime Minister Lefler was not able to make it this morning, as I am sure that you can understand. He sent me to meet you and to thank you for your great work and to congratulate you on your find."

David looked confused. "How did the prime minister know about the find?" asked David.

"One of your colleagues called his Tel Aviv office a few hours ago. They advised him that the ark had been recovered this morning."

David shot Chris a look, which Chris interpreted as frustration. He was upset that one of his team called the prime minister's office without clearing it through him. "Did the employee happen to say his or her name?" David asked.

"Not that I am aware of," replied Richard. "The call was made anonymously to my knowledge."

"I see," said David. "Do you know if that person also called the media?"

"Not to my knowledge," he replied.

"Good!" said David. "We haven't been able to secure the area yet, and the last thing we need right now is the media starting a mob here. When news of this gets out, this place will be swarming with people."

The man smiled at David. "Actually, one of the reasons that I am here is to assist you with that," he replied.

"Oh, okay, I had no idea that the prime minister would send people," said David.

"If you don't mind, I would like to get my security detail set up. We will set a perimeter around the area, and your team can continue working, without worrying about the media or civilians."

David started to look nervous again. He again looked at Chris as if he wanted to say "help." But he didn't.

Chris looked back at him as if to say "I don't know." Because he didn't have a clue on what was happening or what he could do about it, even if he wanted to.

"So are you with the IDF or the local police?" asked Charles.

"Not exactly," replied Richard. "We are a newly created security force for the prime minister. Think of us as you would the Secret Service, over in America."

Charles was curious about how the man knew that the three were from America, but after looking at what he was wearing and looking at Chris and David, he quickly realized that the three of them did sort of stand out in the middle of Jerusalem. Charles was wearing an Arizona Diamondback T-shirt, and David was wearing a Florida Gators shirt. He thought that there may be a few similar shirts in all of Israel, but for a group of guys to all be representing American sports teams, that would be a little bit more unlikely unless they were tourists.

The doors to the vans opened, and a group of men in military fatigues started to pour out of the vehicles. The fatigues were a black and gray and didn't look like the normal IDF uniforms. All the men who got out were all of a similar height and appearance. They looked like they could all be brothers.

David started to get more nervous as he saw the men pulling machine guns out of the rear of a third van. The men were intimidating without the weapons, but with weapons, they looked like something out of a war film such as *Rambo*.

Charles was visibly trying to count the men as they walked by, before Chris motioned for him to put his hand down. Charles counted fifteen armed men before he stopped counting, but the actual total was twenty-four men, not including Richard.

"My men will have the area secured in about five minutes. We will cordon off the area so that your crew can work to retrieve the artifacts until your return, at which time, you can speak to the media. The media is busy with the missile strike at present, so your team will have a little less than forty-eight hours to retrieve the artifacts. Your crew will remain on-site until the artifacts are secured, and all communications will go through my team until further notice."

Charles was flabbergasted. He knew that the police could cordon off an area at the request of government, but a complete lockdown where everyone required to stay at a location such as this was something he hadn't experienced before in his career.

David threw a confused look to Chris as if he were asking him what he missed. He looked utterly confused, and both Chris and Charles could see it clearly on his face.

"Did you say until our return?" asked David. "Return from where?"

Richard remained static as he looked at David. He could sense the tension in David's voice and could see that he was anxious and a little perturbed.

"That is correct. You will leave one of your men here at the site to be a liaison between your team and Captain Jessik, who will be here shortly. The other two of you will accompany me to Tel Aviv, where you will brief the prime minister. Once that is completed, we will return you to this site to complete your work."

David was now really getting angry. "Who gave you the authority to hold my crew captive? These people and I are all civilians. We don't report to anyone with the IDF and only work with the state of Israel in a limited capacity."

Richard didn't flinch. He remained emotionless. "I do apologize that you feel that you have been taken captive, but this is for your protection and to maintain a chain of custody on the artifacts. You may operate the dig site, but the land belongs to the state, and the artifact therefore belongs to the state. If word of this find were to get out too quickly and under the wrong circumstances, we would have a riot here, and people could potentially be harmed."

Charles nodded along as if he agreed with Richard. He knew that the find could cause a riot or a panic or at the very least, curiosity, which could bring in so many people that they wouldn't be able to control them. "David," he said, "I have to agree with Richard on this. If we don't handle this correctly, there are all kinds of things that could go wrong."

"Excuse me if I don't agree, but I have been doing this for years. I have never—" Before he was able to finish, Chris interjected.

"We are fine with what you are asking. We'll need to get a few things before we go, so if you could excuse us for a moment," said Chris.

Richard stood tall and still. He didn't budge the slightest bit. He stood there motionless and completely expressionless. "Get what you need and meet me at the lead limousine in ten minutes," he said.

"Thank you," said Chris. "We'll meet you at the car in a few moments."

Richard walked over to the limousine and got into the vehicle. Chris, who was now a little concerned, moved in close to David and Charles.

"We can't say no, can we?" he said softly.

"No." Charles grinned. Charles wasn't as worked up as was David and Chris. This was because he felt a bit of camaraderie with Richard because of his former position as a police officer. "Look, I know how to handle these guys. You two go and have that meeting with the prime minister, and I'll stay here and make sure everything runs smoothly."

"It's not that simple," David exclaimed. "You don't know how to work a dig site. There are a lot of protocols that have to be followed here."

Charles fired back, "I might not be an archaeologist, but I know my way around a team. Besides, you can't stay. The prime minister asked to speak with you."

"What if we ask that you be allowed to stay here, and we go and talk to the prime minister on your behalf? We could have the prime minister's office call you and teleconference you in. That way, Charles and I can be there in person for the meeting. We will go over what we know about everything here at the dig site. Then when we get to the finer details and we get to the parts that we don't know so well, you'll be able to be conferenced in to explain that part. I mean, between Charles and I, we have a wealth of knowledge on the ark, and we also have the benefit of discussing your temple theory with you over the past few weeks. That way, you'll be here to supervise the project, and we can do the meeting for you."

"That's fine with me, but what about big bad John? I'm not so sure he will go for that," said David.

"It certainly won't hurt to ask," said Chris.

"Let me guess," said Charles, "you want me to ask?"

David and Chris smiled but stayed silent. They didn't want to talk to Richard because they figured that whatever they asked, he would just overrule them.

"Fine!" said Charles. "Why don't I do it?" Charles walked over to where the vans and the limousines were parked. On the left side of the lead limousine, he noticed a business card on the ground. He reached down and picked it up and as he flipped it over, he noticed the logo for I-Corp. "Oh no!" he said softly.

The door to the limousine opened, and Richard climbed out of the vehicle.

"Where are your companions? We are ready to leave," said Richard.

Charles looked at Richard from head to toe.

"They'll be along in a moment," said Charles. "I actually came to tell you that the plan has changed."

"How so?"

"This is an archaeological dig site. I am not qualified in the least to work the site. David is an archaeologist, and he is qualified," he explained.

Richard nodded. "I see. Your plan is to leave David here. I have discussed that plan with the prime minister, and he is fine with the change."

Charles looked perplexed.

"How could you have spoken with him? I haven't even told you the plan."

"Sir, my job is to know things. Now we can discuss the details of how I know, or we can head to Tel Aviv. Since my mission is to get you to Tel Aviv, we will not be discussing it at this time. I can tell you, however, that your voices carry quite well."

Charles threw Richard a look of bewilderment. "I guess we will go now. Let me get Chris, and we can leave."

"Good. We will leave in exactly five minutes," said Richard.

Charles turned to walk away, but he kept his eyes on Richard as he turned and started to walk. "We'll be ready in five," he said.

Charles picked up his pace and walked back over to the tent, where Chris and David were standing. He had a funny feeling about Richard, and he knew there was something that just wasn't right about him. The card that he found was of a greater interest to him now. He wondered how an I-Corp card could have made it into Richard's possession. He looked at the card as he reached David and Chris. The card had only the I-Corp logo, a telephone number, and nothing else.

"So what did he say?" asked David.

Charles turned toward the limousine and looked to see if Richard was still standing there. To his surprise, he was not and had climbed back into the vehicle.

"Have you been in contact with a company called I-Corp?" asked Charles.

"No, why?" asked David.

Charles pulled out the card that he found lying on the ground and handed it to David. "I found this over by the limousine. I-Corp is a company in the United States that has developed artificially intelligent people," explained Charles.

"So why is the card here?" asked David.

Charles looked back at the limousine and remembered that Richard could somehow hear the last conversation that they had. He then reached over with his right hand and grabbed the business card from David and then took his left hand and put his index finger over his mouth as to shush David. After signaling David to be quiet, he pointed toward the limousine.

David looked at the limousine and was a bit confused. "Is Richard from I-Corp?"

Charles knew that the conversation was likely being overheard and began to get nervous, so he needed to try and throw off Richard.

"It's probably just a coincidence that the card was on the ground. When I was in Arizona, there was a large expo about the new technologies. I was at the stadium when they were doing their press release. I grabbed a few of the brochures, and they must have had these cards in them. It probably just fell out of my pocket."

Charles looked back at the limousine, and the door to the vehicle was still closed. He hoped that his excuse for the card being on the ground would throw off Richard. He didn't know where the card really came from, but he knew that somehow, Richard was working for I-Corp, and he wanted to learn how. Charles moved in very close to David and whispered in his ear, "We can't talk about this now. Just be careful on what you say, we are being spied on. I think those men work for I-Corp."

Chris looked confused. He knew what I-Corp was, but didn't know what Charles was talking about.

"Do you usually carry old business cards with you?" he asked.

Charles motioned Chris to be quiet and again pointed toward the vehicle.

"It was probably in my pocket from when I rushed to pack before we left."

Chris, more confused than ever, gave a look of complete nonunderstanding. "Whatever," he said.

Charles didn't want Chris to be completely confused, so he mouthed the words "We can talk later."

The sound of a door closing startled Charles. He turned suddenly and saw that Richard got out of the limousine and was now headed over to him. He was sure that Richard was able to hear him and that he was coming over to confront him.

"Gentlemen, we have to leave. Please gather your things and make your way to the vehicle. You can discuss your trash collection and reminisce about conferences that you have attended later."

David looked at Chris, looking at each other, and both appeared shocked. Their faces said it all. How did this man know what they were talking about? Why was he spying on them?

David looked at Charles cheerfully, knowing he didn't have to get into the vehicle with Richard. "Well, I guess we better get moving.

"Good luck in Tel Aviv," he said sarcastically. "You know where I will be."

Richard pointed at the vehicles, motioning for Charles and Chris to start walking to the vehicle. The pair quietly and reluctantly started walking to the vehicle and climbed in. Once seated, Charles looked at Chris and with a worried look. Chris didn't appear fazed and just sat back in his seat.

"Nap time," said Chris, as the vehicle pulled away and departed for the airport.

CHAPTER 16

The Ark and a New Covenant

Media networks across the globe were in overdrive after the missile strikes in northern Israel, Damascus, and Cairo. The outlets quickly turned their focus away from the storm of the millennia, which brought massive casualties from the blood rain that fell. Their new focus was the firing of three nuclear weapons and the destruction that followed. Not wasting any time, reporters started scrambling all over northern Israel to capture a glimpse of the carnage.

Fires were still burning across the land, and the smoke rising was an endless reminder that life is fleeting and, in the end, wisps away like smoke in the wind.

Damascus and Cairo were both smoldering wastelands now. The cleanup would take years, and anyone brave enough to work in those areas to clean it up would only be able to do so for short periods because of the nuclear fallout.

Leaders around the globe began calling for peace. The United Nations went immediately to an emergency session and began backing those calls for peace. They also began flying aid missions into all three countries to assist any of those people who may have survived. The entire globe was in turmoil.

Charles and Chris arrived in Tel Aviv in the early evening. The city was eerily quiet when they arrived. The limousine was easily able to navigate the streets because they were all empty. There were few pedestrians out and about, and those that were out didn't stay in plain sight for long. They disappeared into the buildings just as quickly as they appeared.

After zipping around the streets of Tel Aviv for what seemed like an hour, the vehicle finally stopped in front of Brockman's bakery. The limousine pulled up to front of the bakery and stopped right in front of the fire hydrant.

Richard lifted his head and peered out the window. He tapped on the glass divider between the front and the rear of the vehicle, and the divider opened. The driver turned as Richard gave him a nod, and then the divider went back up with Richard never saying a word.

Charles was oblivious to Richard now moving around in the rear of the vehicle. He had his face pressed up against the window attempting to get a glimpse of the bakery. His stomach was now on high alert to the food nearby, and Charles was completely mesmerized by the glow of the neon lights that said "Bagels."

Richard looked at Chris.

"You two will get out here. Once you are inside, you will tell the baker at the service counter that you are here to pick up the order for Fletcher. They will ask you if you would like anything else with your order, to which you will respond that you would like to have an Asiago bagel with cream cheese."

Charles heard Richard start barking orders and was startled from his daydreaming. He didn't hear much of what Richard said, but he did catch the words *bagel* and *cheese*.

Richard spoke again. "Do you both understand what you are to order?"

Charles's startled feeling disappeared in a flash. After hearing the words *bagel* and *cheese*, his stomach leaped, and his entire demeanor changed. He was now feeling jubilant, so he responded in his usual fashion, "Can I order two of those, but with bacon and cream cheese?"

Chris tapped Charles on his arm and shook his head in disapproval.

"Not now, Charles. You can eat after we talk to the prime minister."

Richard smiled, and the smile caught Charles off guard.

"You do have a sense of humor after all! I thought you were just another stick-in-the-mud jarhead with a steroid problem!"

Richard's amusement disappeared as he reached over the two men and opened the door handle.

"Good luck, Gentlemen. I will return to take you back to Jerusalem later this evening. You can have your bacon when I return."

Chris and Charles got out of the vehicle and walked into the storefront. When they opened the door, they were met with the fresh smell of baked bread and bagels. The aroma immediately caught the attention of Charles, who suddenly forgot why he was there.

"Smells great in here!" Charles exclaimed.

Chris nodded. "It does."

The two walked up to the service counter, and Charles studied the menu. There were a variety of breads behind the counter, and the cases in front of him had several delectable-looking desserts.

Charles bent down to peer into the case. His eyes darted back and forth wildly. "They all look so good!"

One of the store employees walked up to the counter and looked down at Charles, who now had his hands over his eyes to block out the glare as he peered inside the service-counter glass.

"What can I get for you, Gentlemen?" asked the clerk.

Charles stood up briskly. "Sorry, I was just browsing."

Chris looked at Charles, to remind him that they were there for purposes other than eating.

"Oh yes," said Charles, "we are here for a carryout order."

The clerk looked slightly amused as he stared directly at Charles, patiently waiting for him to tell him more about the order. After a few moments, the clerk grew weary of the awkward silence and responded, "I see, who should this order be listed under?"

Charles laughingly replied, "My gosh, I am so stupid sometimes! I would definitely not make a good spy."

The clerk's face went from slightly amused to completely unamused.

"Spy, sir? Are you joking?"

"Oh, right," he said, winking at the clerk. "I am here for a pickup order for Fletcher."

Chris nodded in embarrassment and couldn't help but chuckle.

The clerk was now getting somewhat aggravated. He looked over at Chris hoping for a little assistance and smiled, begrudgingly. Chris could see the man's frustration growing, and it reminded him of thousands of different interactions with his friend. He smiled back at the clerk for a moment and then he could no longer hold back and started laughing.

The clerk, seeing he would get no assistance from Chris, turned his gaze back to Charles, who was now looking at some eclairs.

"I see," he said. "Would you like anything else with that?"

Chris could see that the clerk didn't have a huge sense of humor, so he put his hand on Charles's shoulder to let him know that he would respond to the clerk.

"We would like an Asiago bagel with cream cheese."

The clerk reached down and opened the cash drawer and pulled out a key card and handed it to Chris. He then turned around and got a small bag that was set on the counter behind him and handed the bag to Charles.

Charles opened the bag and put his nose into the bag and inhaled deeply.

"Smells great, but this isn't a bagel. It's a ciabatta roll with Asiago cheese. Now if you only had some bacon and some lettuce and tomato, this would make a heck of a sandwich!"

The clerk smiled. "You will have to wait for the bagel. We don't have any made at present. For your convenience, we have a waiting area down the hall and through the last door on the left. Once you get inside, just use the thumb pad."

Charles pulled his head out of the bag. "Much appreciated!"

Charles and Chris proceeded down the hall and came to the last door on the left. Charles pressed his thumb to the keypad next to the door, and the door opened. Charles then proceeded into the room, and Chris followed behind.

"We must have gone through the wrong door!" Charles exclaimed.

Chris looked around the room and nodded along. The room was completely empty and didn't have so much as a chair or a bench in it.

"I think you might be right. This room's pretty empty for a waiting room."

As he scanned the room, he remembered what the clerk said about using the keypad inside the room.

"He said to use the keypad inside the room, didn't he?"

Charles scanned the walls and noticed that there was another keypad on the wall to his right, so he walked up to the pad and pushed his thumb to the plate. As soon as he pushed his thumb to the plate, a hidden door unlocked behind him and swung open.

"Wow," said Charles, "this is some cloak-and-dagger stuff!"

Chris smiled and nodded. "Would you have known that door was there if it hadn't just opened up?"

"I know!" said Charles. "There wasn't as much as a seam in the wall that was visible. I really need to get me something like this for home use."

Chris looked a bit confused. "What would you possibly use something like this for at home?"

Charles paused for a moment as if in deep thought and then smiled. "I'd use it to hide when family and friends come over. I could put it right in the living room and really scare the crap of them, or it would be great to have for a safe room."

"Charles, you sure do have one heck of an imagination, but a safe room isn't half bad as an idea. We could all probably use one of those these days."

The two stepped through the door, and in front of them was an elevator. Charles automatically assumed that he was to push the button to take the elevator, so he pressed his thumb to the pad.

"What do you think the keypad numbers are for? They didn't tell us about that."

Chris looked closer at the keypad, and it was like that of a telephone. The only real difference was that it had a fingerprint scanner just below the numbers.

"Should we put in any kind of number code?" asked Charles.

Chris looked up.

"They didn't give us a code, so I think just using the fingerprint scanner would be good enough."

Charles suddenly looked as if he had an epiphany.

"How do you suppose that they got our fingerprints to make this scanner work?"

Chris, looking befuddled, stood there silently. Charles did raise a good point. They hadn't been to Tel Aviv before, and they never gave their fingerprint to anyone in Israel.

"I don't know," said Chris. "Then again, I still don't understand why we are even here. What makes us so special that we're having a meeting with the prime minister?"

Charles started to look a bit nervous. Chris was right. In the grand scheme of things, he and Chris were relatively anonymous and unimportant. The only thing that the two shared was that they were ministers and from Arizona. Aside from that, they only knew what David relayed to them while in Jordan.

"What are we supposed to tell him?" asked Charles.

"Tell who?"

"The prime minister," said Charles. "He's probably wanting to know about the ark, and to be honest, I really don't know much about it."

"Don't worry about it. I'm sure it'll be fine. David is the one who found it and has all the info on it. We're just here to talk to the minister about how he found it and his theory. If it goes beyond that, we'll just defer and tell him that David is the expert and that we'll have to get back to him."

They stepped onto the elevator, and the doors closed behind them. The elevator started to move and make a slight whirring sound. It was only a matter of seconds before a voice came over the speaker inside the elevator, letting them know that they had reached their destination.

The doors to the elevator opened, and as soon as they stepped off the elevator into the hallway, they saw a man hurriedly walking toward them from the right. As the man approached, they could see him come into focus. It was the prime minister.

"Welcome, Gentlemen!" said Adam.

Charles lit up like a kid in a candy store. He was excited to be meeting the prime minister. He saw him on the news, hundreds of times, and now he was meeting him in person. Chris stood there silently with a slight smile on his face. He was also excited to meet the prime minister, but he didn't quite have the same enthusiasm as Charles.

"How was the trip to Tel Aviv?"

Charles couldn't help but respond immediately and blurted out, "Great!"

"Wonderful!" said Adam. "If you aren't already aware, I'm Adam Lefler, and I'm the current prime minister of Israel."

"We're aware!" exclaimed Charles. "You're taller than I expected."

Chris shook his head in disapproval and chuckled softly. "You'll have to excuse Charles. He just graduated from tact school a month ago."

Adam laughed as Charles threw a dissatisfied look to Chris. "It's quite all right," replied Adam. "I'm simply happy that I'm taller this time. A lot of the time, I hear that I'm fatter or that I'm shorter. I'll take taller as a compliment."

"I'm Charles, and this is Chris," said Charles.

"It's great to meet you both," said Adam as he reached out to shake hands with both. "If you will follow me, I'd like to take this conversation to a place a little more open than a cramped hallway. I have a few people that I'd like to introduce you to."

Charles glanced over at Chris nervously, as if to say that he wasn't looking forward to meeting anyone else. His shyness was coming out a little now, and he was starting to get anxious. He wasn't expecting to meet anyone other than the prime minister, and not knowing who he was about to meet was getting under his skin a little and making him sweat a little.

Adam continued walking down the corridor and opened the last door on the left. The three walked through the door and into the main lobby of the building. Charles and Chris stared at each other and smiled as they noticed that they were yet again going to the last door on the left.

The area was crawling with people, and one could hardly hear anything over the conversations going on within the room. It was much larger than either of them could imagine. Adam looked back and gave a waving gesture to Chris and Charles to let them know that they should just follow him.

They eventually made their way through the crowded room and to the office on the opposite side of the floor. Adam opened the door, and all three went inside.

When they entered the room, they saw more than a few familiar faces. Charles couldn't believe what he was seeing as he scanned the room. His jaw hit the floor.

The room was filled with the who's who of famous faces. On the left side of the room was the prime minister of the European Union, Jared Hadad. Seated next to him was I-Corp cofounder and current CEO, Peter Jensen. Also, on the left side of the room sat Richard, who traveled to Tel Aviv with Charles and Chris. On the right side of the room sat Pope Liberius II, and next to him, the caliph of the Islamic Coalition, Ujab Aalim Baqri. Last but not least was the president of Iran, Parizad Madani.

Charles was in shock. When he saw that the room was filled with religious leaders and political leaders of great stature, he simply couldn't believe what he was seeing. The icing on the cake for his amazement was that the president of Iran was sitting in the room with the caliph of the Muslim coalition. This was especially awe-inspiring, considering that those two people were aligned with Golshiri, who lost the war against Israel and responsible for the nuclear weapons being fired back and forth from Syria and Israel, and Egypt and Israel.

Chris moved in closer to the people in the room, who were now standing in somewhat of a semicircle in the middle of the room. He began shaking hands with everyone in the room, moving from the left to the right.

Charles noticed that he was still standing by the door and not interacting with anyone and suddenly felt awkward. After realizing his standoffish behavior, he quickly adjusted himself and moved in to greet everyone.

The room suddenly erupted with the chatter of all, and Charles started to feel a little less nervous. He still didn't know what was going on but thought that if it included a bunch of religious figures, then it must be something to do with the finding of the ark.

"Please have a seat," said Adam, pointing at the small love seat against the wall.

Chris sat down, and Charles followed. The chatter died down, and the others in the room sat down also. Adam moved over to a small folding chair that he had set against the wall. He grabbed the chair and moved it over to the right side of the room where Pope Liberius was sitting. The pope watched Adam carefully as he began to unfold the chair. He could see Adam struggling with it, so he lifted himself up and slightly out of his seat and reached in to help with both his arms. His help was appreciated, and Adam gave him a slight nod as a sign of affirmation and thanks.

As soon as he took his seat, Richard got up from his chair and started to pass each person a small stapled stack of papers. Charles nervously scanned the room and peered over at the caliph, to get a better look at what was written on the pages, but he could only make out the word *confidential* written on the top.

Chris, meanwhile, was quietly chatting with Peter who was sitting directly to his left. The two were talking about I-Corp and their work in artificial intelligence. Charles leaned in to hear the conversation and heard his friend congratulating Peter about the work, and he could swear he heard Chris say the word *amazing*. This made him wince a bit because he felt slightly betrayed. After all, Chris knows how he feels about artificial intelligence, and Charles thought that Chris should be taking his side on the issue rather than praising the work.

Charles, now inwardly fuming at Chris, perked up as the praise continued and could stay silent no longer.

"So, Peter"—he sneered—"how is the world of artificial intelligence?"

Peter turned his head toward Charles and instantly had a feeling he had seen Charles before. He tilted his head to the side as he tried to recall how they met. After a few moments of his awkward gaze, he gave up. "Have we met before?"

Charles smiled as he felt a bit vindicated. Peter did recognize him. The difference this time is that the two were now actually face-to-face, and there was no devious sneaking around to try to evade his security measures to avoid a confrontation,

"I'm surprised you didn't recognize me immediately, especially, after having me banned from entering your release party at Diamondback Stadium. I believe that you referred to me as a zealot."

Peter was taken aback, and a look of shock replaced his genteel smile. His recollection appeared in a flash, and he suddenly recalled the incident.

"Ah, yes," said Peter, "I remember you now. You called my work an abomination. Is that right?"

Charles started to get flustered, and his face pinked up like a newborn taking his first breaths. His recall was in no way diminished like Peter's, and he recalled the event in perfect detail. The moment Peter opened his mouth, his memory of the event flooded back to him in an instant. He replayed it all over in his mind as he sat there staring back at Peter, and he began to grimace as he recalled how badly he was mistreated by the security guards at the office complex and how he was mocked as he was led away.

"So did you succeed?" asked Charles.

"I'm not exactly sure what you are referring to," replied Peter softly.

Charles began to fidget and gently rocked back and forth in his seat for a moment before, finally, leaning back in toward Peter.

"Did you succeed at making an artificial person?"

Peter simply smiled at hearing the question, which incensed Charles.

"What's so funny about my question?" he asked boldly.

Peter sat back in his chair. He now had a look of satisfaction on face. He could see the anger Charles was holding, but it didn't upset him in the least as he sat there thinking about how Charles disrupted his event.

"I guess I would have to say that I was successful. You've already met one of my so-called artificial people, and apparently, you were none the wiser to it. That gives me a great bit of pleasure because if you didn't notice, then it is highly doubtful that anyone on this earth would be able to tell them apart from any average person on the street."

Charles looked appalled and sat back in his seat. He was visibly distressed and sweat began to bead up on his forehead, as it happens when he begins to stress out.

Chris remained silent as the two bantered back and forth, but when he saw the sweat begin to roll off Charles's cheeks, he knew he better chime in before the conversation became any more raucous.

"Are you all right?" he whispered.

"I'll be fine," Charles replied.

"Do you two know each other?" he asked quizzingly. "What am I missing here?"

The chatter in the room came to a halt, and everyone began focusing their attention on the conversation between Charles and Peter.

Adam, hearing the tense conversation between the two, knew he had better regroup everyone and get their focus back to the task at hand. He leaped up from his chair and gave his papers a bit of a shake, as to draw everyone's attention back to himself.

"It's a small world, and apparently, some of our guests have met before." He started before being interrupted by Charles.

"You don't understand. It's not like we are friends," said Charles.

Chris could see that Charles was getting more aggravated. "Relax and remember why we are here," he said softly.

Charles wasn't quite done. He wanted everyone in the room to know about I-Corp and their AI project.

"Does everyone in this room know that this man built a replica of a human?"

Charles scanned the room. Everyone was now looking around at one another, confused. They didn't know what Charles was talking about. They hadn't been listening to the conversation between Peter and Charles.

"That's right," said Charles. "This man built an artificial person, or should I say, an abomination."

Peter got up from his seat and stood directly in front of Charles, looking down at him with disgust.

"I understand that you and others like you have a problem with the research on artificial intelligence, but do you even know what you're angry about?"

"What kind of question is that?" he replied. "Everyone in this room knows exactly why I'm upset. They may look all calm cool and collected, but I guarantee you that they all have their reservations too."

Charles scanned the room and saw nothing but confused faces. He turned toward Chris and even he seemed confused and disappointed with him. He began fidgeting in his seat and became keenly aware that everyone in the room was now staring directly at him. There wasn't a sound to be heard in the room, and it was making him uncomfortable and a little embarrassed. He suddenly realized that he had been acting like a fool. He forgot the whole reason why he was there. He was supposed to be there to share the news of the discovery of the ark, but in his selfishness, he made it all about himself.

Peter threw his hands up in exasperation and went back over to his seat, as Jared got up from his chair to address Charles.

"Charles, is it?" he asked. "You're right. We all have had our reservations at one time or another. We have all held a certain fear of the unknown, and yes, I'm sure that even Peter himself has had a moment or moments where he had that fear."

Peter sat in his chair nodding. Charles saw him nodding and again lost himself and began to fume.

"That's rich!" he gasped. "I feel a whole lot better now. Do you think that I was born yesterday? You were the one who started that abomination of a company in the first place! We can all thank you for getting the ball rolling on artificial intelligence."

Jared threw his hands in the air in frustration.

"If I had a dollar for every person who has credited me for artificial intelligence," he said with a slightly elevated tone, "the reality of the matter is that Peter and I worked together on AI. It wasn't he that made the breakthrough, and it wasn't I who made the breakthrough. If you understood AI in the least, you would know that. The truth is that once we got the first two to three machines up and running, we were finished with our part of the development of the machines. It was they who continued to learn, and as they learned, we learned. We were there to help them with their own development. It was much like the role of a parent rather than a programmer."

Charles leaned in toward Jared. "That may very well be, but without the two of you, we wouldn't be in this mess!"

Jared looked at Charles with bewilderment.

"Charles, if it weren't Peter or me that developed artificial intelligence, it would have been someone else. You should really be happy that it was the two of us who made the initial breakthroughs and not some despot in some other part of the world."

When Jared said the word *despot*, Ujab and Parizad snapped to attention and began focusing on him intently, waiting to hear what words he would say next.

Jared could see them trained on him intently and realized his error in judgment in using such a word.

"Present company excluded," added Jared.

Adam rose again from his seat. He could see that the group was completely tracking and wasting time. He needed to redirect the conversation and get everyone back to the topic at hand rather than the side conversations on the ethical implications of artificial intelligence. He also knew that if the people in the room were to find out that the AI machines were the ones responsible for the recent missile launches, they may never be able to recover from the recent events and never have peace among any of the affected nations.

Adam moved to the center of the fray and stood purposely in front of Charles, to try to redirect everyone's attention.

"It's great that we can all get together to be able to work out our differences. Wouldn't you agree?" he asked.

Charles again scanned the room and could see that everyone in the room still had their eyes trained on him. He quickly glanced over at Chris, who was shaking his head in disapproval. He sat there silently for a moment as he contemplated everything and then realized that he wasn't acting like a model Christian and again felt embarrassed.

Charles rose from his seat and extended his hand to the prime minister, apologetically.

"Yes, Prime Minister," he said, "I do think that it's great that we could come together like this. The question that I have is, how were you able to do it?"

Adam looked puzzled.

"Do what?" he asked.

Charles looked him straight in the eyes and smiled.

"How did you manage to get the people in this room to come together like this? It must have been quite the challenge; given the current situation in the world."

Adam took a step back. He wasn't sure if he should be open and honest with his response. Most of the people in the room were not aware that Richard was an artificial person, and by responding and explaining to the group that Richard is an artificial person could complicate things further. He glanced over to Jared and then over to Peter as if he were asking them on how he should respond. Jared and Peter seemed unfazed by the question. Seeing that they didn't have any outward expressions of concern, he took it as a sign that he should just tell everyone in the room and come clean about it.

"That's a great question, Charles. To be perfectly honest, it was Jared and Richard who were able to arrange the meeting and the credit really should go to Richard because he was the one that convinced our guests from Iran and Saudi Arabia to join us. Jared has known the pope for years, so he invited him here. You and your colleague joining us was a last-minute decision. It was Richard who felt that bringing you in would be wise."

Adam paused for a moment and looked at Richard.

"We knew that bringing David in would be difficult, and Richard felt that it would be better to just let him continue his work in excavating the site. We knew that David is close with the two of you and shared a great bit of detail with you, and as Jared explained to me earlier, it makes sense to have two Christian representatives from the other side of the globe."

Charles looked down at the pages he was holding and began thumbing through them.

"You're right, it probably was a good idea to bring us. This find is the most important of any time in archaeological history and given the nature of the artifacts, it would only be natural to have some Christian representatives as well."

He looked back up at Adam.

"I'm actually quite thankful to be here. I forgot for a moment on just how important this moment is to us, to the whole world. If there is a chance for peace, then that should be the focus, and not my grievances against a technology company."

Charles got up from his chair and walked over to Peter.

"Will you accept the apology of a foolish man?"

Peter rose from his seat, smiling.

"Of course, I think we could all learn a lesson from each other today, and that lesson is that no matter our grievances, we can always look to something greater than ourselves and find a way to cooperate with each other."

The others in the room all stood up and showed their agreement with Peter and Charles. The meeting took on a new tone, and at that moment, there was a glimmer of hope that could be felt by all, that it was possible to have a productive meeting.

Jared spoke for an hour about how the discovery of the ark of the covenant could bring peace to the Middle East. He explained how the ark was a significant find for the entire world and that the people of the Christian faith, the Muslim faith, and the Jewish faith could benefit from the find. He spoke of its importance in a historical context and one of religious faith in general.

The pope mostly agreed with Jared on the religious context of the find and explained that Muslims and Christians could find unity with the people of the Jewish faith based on the find. His opinion was that all three religions were based, in part, on the early writings by Moses, and that the find was an artifact that proved a large part of the Pentateuch and that this could be a basis for a united faith in God.

Charles again began to look a bit frustrated as he listened to Pope Liberius speak on the subject. He didn't agree that all three religions were united in who they worshipped. His belief was that the Catholic faith had strayed away from the teachings of Scripture and were more focused on traditions rather than Scripture, and he felt similarly about Islam. While all three religions proclaim that the first few books of the Bible are truth, it is after this that they stray from one another.

Chris could see the frustration building on Charles's face as representatives of each faith proclaimed what they believed to be true. He reached over and gently patted Charles on the knee as to show his solidarity with him and to let him know that he was not alone. Both remained silent as each of the others discussed their points about their faith. They wanted to let everyone say their peace before giving their own opinions on the matter, even if they didn't completely agree with them.

After the speech by the president of Iran, Parizad Madani, the room got quiet. Jared rose from his seat and looked over at Charles, pointing his left hand toward him to let him know that it was now his turn to speak.

"You two have been fairly silent over here. I'm sure that you have your own feelings on the subject. Please share your thoughts with the rest of the group."

Charles looked at Chris, and his face said it all. He looked as if he had just seen a ghost. Here was his opportunity to witness to a group of religious leaders of differing faiths, and he suddenly felt overwhelmed.

Chris could see the discomfort that Charles was facing, so he got up from his seat and addressed the group, giving Charles a chance to relax a little more before it would be his turn to speak.

"I would just like to say that I agree that this find is of remarkable importance. It was thought that this one relic was lost to history, but now it has been found. Many in the world have not believed in the existence of the ark at all, calling it a myth. Now even they can see that it is not. The fact that it was found at all is miraculous, and I'm sure that we can all agree, significant to all our respective faiths."

Chris moved over to the whiteboard that was hung on the wall. He picked up a black marker from the silver tray at the base and began drawing a long line across the board. He wrote the words *10th century BCE* on the left side of the line, and further to the right, he wrote *586 BCE*. He turned to the group and started to explain.

"You will have to excuse me if I am a little fuzzy on exact dates here because I'm not a historian, nor am I an archaeologist." As he looked at the audience, he extended out his left hand to the board and pointed at the first date that he wrote on the left side of the board.

"The First Temple was dedicated by King Solomon around the 10th century BCE. It remained in the temple for approximately six hundred years or, more precisely, around 586 BCE. It was in that year that King Nebuchadnezzar sacked Jerusalem and took her captive. The ark was rumored to have been moved from the temple at the time, to Egypt, and some rumors were that it was taken to Ethiopia. The point is that the ark of the covenant has been missing since around here." He moved his hand over to the right side of the line where it read, "586 BCE," pointing at the second date on his timeline. He turned back toward the group.

"If the ark was moved to Egypt or Ethiopia, then it must have been moved back to Jerusalem. Or, what makes more sense is that it was never moved from Jerusalem and was actually only moved to a tunnel and hidden." He paused for a moment and then looked at the group again. "We know that the last known location of the ark was in the First Temple." It is our opinion, based on the evidence found in David Sumpter's recent dig, that the ark was moved to a tunnel directly under the temple site, and that the area known as the Temple Mount is not the real Temple Mount, but that it was actually the site of the Roman fort, Antonia."

The room suddenly erupted, and side conversations were going on all around the room. Pope Liberius was talking to Jared as if he had just been given a revelation and that what he heard was truth.

Ujab and Parisad were the loudest of the people chattering in the group, and they looked like they heard blasphemy coming out of Chris's mouth. They were speaking in Arabic, so Chris and most of the others didn't understand what they were saying, but Ujab was speaking emphatically, and his arms were flailing about wildly. It was clear that he and Parisad did not like what Chris said and did not agree with it.

Ujab gained his composure and got up from his seat and addressed Chris, "What evidence do you have that this is the true ark and not a fake?"

"Right now, we don't have anything other than what we, here in this room, all know. The ark will have to be authenticated, and once that happens, it will be up to the scholars and religious scholars to determine if David's theory is true."

This answer didn't satisfy Ujab. "What proof do you have that the Temple Mount was Fort Antonia?"

Charles suddenly interjected himself into the conversation. "There are a number of things found that point to the Temple Mount actually being the Roman fort. David Sumpter has been working on this theory for some time, and all the evidence from his research and the recent dig points to the actual location of the temple as being in the area near the Gihon Spring."

Adam rose from his seat. "All right, everyone, let's not jump to conclusions here. This is just a theory, and it is not a fact as of today. Let's not forget why we are here."

Adam tried to get the group back into peace talks because that was the true focus of the meeting. The idea was that the discovery of the ark was a common thread between all the major religions and that as a common thread, it could be used to broker peace between the different nations.

Jared calmly raised his hand as he looked over to Chris.

"I think it would be prudent to wait until the ark is authenticated, but also to have everyone here visit the site and hear the evidence from Davis himself. Wouldn't you agree?"

Chris nodded.

"Jared is right. The ark was just found, and right now, this is just a theory, but think of what this could mean if it is true." He paused for a moment, looked down, and then lifted his eyes back toward the group. "If the temple was located at the Gihon Spring area and not the Temple Mount, then the Israelis and the people of the Muslim faith can stop fighting and arguing over the Temple Mount. That piece of real estate has kept the Middle East from achieving peace for an exceedingly long time."

Pope Liberius agreed, and he rose from his seat and moved over to Ujab and reached out his hand to Ujab's hand and placed it there gently. "Think of the possibility of peace!" he exclaimed with a large smile.

The meeting proceeded over the next couple of hours. Each leader spoke briefly about their concerns and their vision of how peace could proceed. All agreed that the recent nuclear strikes by Israel and by the Golshiri regime were atrocious and that further strikes must not proceed. The most vocal dissenter was Ujab Baqri. He argued for most of the meeting that his coalition was not responsible for the nuclear strike against Israel but did admit in the end that the evidence clearly showed that the Golshiri regime fired first. As caliph of the Muslim coalition, he conceded that his forces did fire the weapons, and to have peace, he would accept responsibility for the firing of the weapons so long as Israel would agree to further investigations into the matter in the future.

Adam was hesitant to agree to investigations into the nuclear strikes because he knew that Richard was responsible for the strikes, but after a brief private conversation with Richard and Jared, he reluctantly agreed. Jared and Richard assured him that they would lead the investigation and that they would do everything in their power to control the narrative.

As the meeting wrapped up, they all agreed that peace was more essential now than ever, and all agreed to support an enduring peace in the region moving forward. The cease-fire was agreed upon by President Madani, for the people of Iran, Caliph Baqri, on behalf of the Muslim coalition and its member countries. Jared agreed that the European Union would remain neutral, and Israel agreed that no further fighting would occur, so long as the cease-fire was honored by all parties.

Once the group settled on terms for peace in the region, they turned their focus to the recent find of the ark of the covenant. Every leader at the meeting agreed that finding the ark of the covenant was the greatest archaeological find in human history. The ark was something that could bring all the major religions together and foster an enduring peace because the ark was said to contain the original Ten Commandments, and nothing could be more uniting than the tablets containing the moral law, written by the hand of God himself. Adam agreed to allow everyone in attendance access to the ark for themselves, but only once the cease-fire agreement was signed publicly and the media had a chance to announce the cease-fire to the world, along with the news of the find. All agreed that this was acceptable.

Overall, the meeting was a success. It was a step toward a lasting peace, but the fact remained that many in the Jewish community and the Islamic community could not agree on the Temple Mount. Most Israelis still believed that the Temple Mount is where the First and Second Temples were located and that they should be able to rebuild their temple there. If the Dome of the Rock was still standing, the dispute over the land would continue without fail, and no lasting peace could be attained.

CHAPTER 17

Relics

The next morning, Chris and Charles traveled back to the dig site. When they arrived, they noticed that the area was almost completely cordoned off. The whole area had a heavy security presence. There were now more soldiers at the site than there were workers. The street was now lined with media vans, police vehicles, and military vehicles. The site looked more like a UFO-landing site from the movies than it did an archaeological site.

David had been working around the clock since the discovery of the ark was made. The ark was carefully removed from the tunnel and was placed into an armored vehicle just inside the dig site perimeter. The vehicle was under the protection of the armed guards Richard brought to the site as well as roughly fifty IDF soldiers that Adam sent there.

There were several military tents amassed at the front of the site and next to the tents, about fifty feet away from the police barricades and concertina wire, was where the armored vehicle was located. There were two guards on each corner of the vehicle, forming a 360-degree perimeter around the vehicle. The guards were dressed in camouflage fatigues, and all carried machine guns. The vehicle had its rear doors open and a ramp ran out from the rear of the vehicle out onto the ground. The entire area was extremely busy as the workers ran back and forth from the dig site to the tents. Flying constantly overhead were four military helicopters. They circled the area, continuously, providing security from the sky.

Charles and Chris walked up to a makeshift sally port that was created to monitor who came in and left the site. As they approached, they were met and stopped by one of the Richard's security guards.

The guard stepped in front of the pair and directly in front of them. He held his rifle out in front of his body with both hands and pushed it forward toward the two, signaling to them to stop.

"Welcome back, Charles. You and Chris can proceed to the second tent on the right, behind the truck. Your friend David is there."

Charles looked at the guard but didn't recognize him. "Do I know you?" he asked.

The guard smiled at Charles.

"I am afraid not. I was informed that you would be arriving this morning and given a description of the two of you. It appears that the description that I was given was fairly accurate. It is a pleasure to meet you."

The guard moved out of the way so that they could proceed into the dig site. They proceeded toward the second gate. As the gate began to open, Charles looked back at the guard suspiciously. The gate fully opened, and Chris tapped Charles on the shoulder to let him know that they could now enter. Charles walked through the gate, the whole time keeping his eyes trained on the guard. He couldn't understand how easily the guard knew who he was. It's not like he was some famous politician or archaeologist. He thought, *I guess they know me because of the meeting.*

As they reached the main tent where David was said to be located, another guard stood waiting at the entrance. This guard didn't look like the others. He had blond hair instead of the black hair that the others had. His fatigues were also a different color. His fatigues were black, while the others had brown and tan.

The guard looked at the pair suspiciously for a moment.

"Good afternoon," he said softly. "This tent is reserved for archaeologists and select media personnel. Can I see your credentials, please?"

Charles was surprised by the request, considering that the last guard recognized him. Charles passed over his identification. "Here you go."

The guard looked at his identification and flipped it over from back to front, three to four times before finally handing it back. "Here you are, Charles. Thank you for your cooperation. We all know who you are, but with the sensitivity of this area, we are just double-checking. I'm sure you can understand."

Charles couldn't help but smile. Everyone knowing his name and treating him with high regard was different for him. Normally his encounters with security didn't go so easily, but then again, most of his encounters with security had to do with protesting I-Corp functions.

Chris handed over his identification, and the guard looked at it in similar fashion before handing it back to the guard.

Feeling confident, Charles could not help himself and had to question the man on his appearance compared to the others.

"Are you guys all related? The resemblance between all of you is insane! It's like you are all related, or you are all in some creepy club."

The guard smiled wryly before responding. "Don't you know that the entire human race is all one big family?"

Chris smiled back and nodded. He had been preaching for years about how people are all related and that the entire human race came from one man and one woman. Charles, on the other hand, felt a bit awkward and wasn't as impressed by the man's response. Having a sense of humor and a quick wit was not what he expected. He pictured something completely different, based on his past interactions with the other soldiers.

David was at the rear of the tent hovering over a map that was laid out over a small fold out table. He was talking with one of his employees and pointing at a cliff face located on the map. Charles and Chris walked over to where he was working and didn't say a word. They could see that he was deep in thought, and they didn't want to disturb him.

Someone from outside the tent yelled, "David!"

David jerked upward from the table as quickly as he heard his name and looked over at the door of the tent.

"David, you have to see this!" the voice exclaimed.

He ran to the door of the tent and poked his head through the two heavy flaps that made up the doorway.

"What is it, Renee?" he asked.

"You aren't going to believe this!" she exclaimed. "Follow me!"

David pulled his head back into the tent and looked directly at Chris. "I'm not gonna believe this?" he questioned himself softly but with exuberance.

Charles couldn't help but laugh. He could clearly see that David was enjoying himself, and he was loving every minute of it. The normally quiet pace of archaeology was nice, but the fast pace that came with a find was exiting for him.

"Come on you two," he commanded Charles and Chris. "We're not going to believe this!"

David quickly bolted toward the door and didn't even bother to open the flaps. He thrust between the flaps so fast that it was like watching an Olympic diver hitting the water and not even making a splash. Chris and Charles didn't waste any time in pursuing him and slid through the now partially open doorway with ease. As soon as they got outside, David took off running toward the cave entrance.

He quickly climbed down the ladder into the area and ran toward the cave opening at the back. "Keep up, you two!" he exclaimed.

Charles wasn't as fast as the other two, and by the time he reached the ladder, he was already out of breath. He grabbed the ladder and slowly climbed down into the pit. As he reached the bottom, he could hear a multitude of voices coming from topside, so he looked up to see what who was making the commotion. There were ten to twenty people standing on the embankment, peering into the pit. The sun was shining brightly from behind them and each one of them appeared to have a brilliant halo. The light was so bright that he couldn't hold his gaze in their direction. It was much like looking an event horizon, where each person appeared very dark, with a radiant ring of fire surrounding their frames. It literally appeared as if they were clothed with the sun.

Charles began to sprint when he saw Chris waiting for him at the entrance to the cave. When he finally reached the entrance, Chris let him pass and enter first. They could hear voices coming from the tunnel to the right side, so they started walking toward the voices. After walking about fifty yards, the tunnel narrowed significantly, and they had to turn their bodies sideways to navigate the space.

When they reached the end of the passage, they saw a soft light shining and flickering because of the movement from the group of people congregated at the end.

"That's when we found it," Renee explained.

Charles never missed an opportunity to get involved in the conversations of others, so he interjected himself into the one between David and Renee.

"I'm sorry, found what?" he asked.

Chris slapped him on the arm in rebuke for interrupting, but David didn't seem to mind. He was still feeling giddy, and there wasn't much that could upset him at the moment.

"It's magnificent!" David exclaimed.

"What could be more magnificent than the ark of the covenant?" asked Charles.

The three workers standing next to David moved a few steps back, and David shined the work light against the wall and the ground. The light reflected from the shiny and luminescent rock face.

"What is that?" asked Charles.

"That's gold and silver, Charles," he gleefully replied.

"Are you telling me that this is a gold and a silver mine?" asked Charles.

David chuckled softly. "No, it's not a gold or a silver mine."

"Then what are we looking at?"

Chris moved in toward Charles and put his hand on his shoulder. "That's not just any old gold and silver. That's melted gold and silver, as in melted from the burning of the Second Temple."

David smiled brilliantly. "This is another solid piece of evidence that my theory is correct. If the ark of the covenant wasn't a smoking gun, then this find, along with the ark, is most definitely a smoking gun."

"I thought that the temple was looted, and all the gold and silver taken out, by the Romans?" asked Charles.

David paused for a moment as if deep in thought. He took his hand and scratched his fingers through his beard momentarily and nodded a couple times.

Charles, seeing him deep in thought, had to know what he was thinking about. As the seconds ticked by, Charles's patience wore thin. "Come on already! What is it? Out with it already!" he exclaimed.

David turned and looked at Chris, still running his fingers through his coarse chin whiskers.

"Mm-hmm."

"What?" asked Charles.

"I'd really like to see the table of shewbread, a harp maybe, or some other temple item," he explained.

"What's shewbread?" asked Charles.

"The temple had a lot of curious items in it. There was a menorah, an altar of incense, the table of shewbread, or *shulchan*, if you prefer. The table was in the temple and always had twelve loaves on it. The bread was left on the table, as to always be present for God. The bread would be taken off the table and replaced on every Sabbath, or if a loaf were getting stale, it would be swapped out with a fresh loaf. The table would have been a magnificent piece. The menorah would also have also been a great find. Of course, it is possible that those items were left in the temple. It's hard to say," he explained.

"Wouldn't the table have rotted by now?" asked Charles.

"I don't think so," said David. "The table was rumored to have been made of acacia wood and covered in pure gold. Others believe that the table was solid gold. I'm sure that the Romans would have been interested in a piece like that, so maybe it was moved."

"Wait a minute! Didn't some guy in the eighties say that he found the table and the ark?" asked Chris excitedly.

David and his whole crew started laughing. The echoes of the laughter reverberated against the stone walls of the cave, and the whole cave sounded like it was filled with thousands of people laughing.

"What's so funny?" asked Charles.

"The guy that you are referring to did say that he found the ark. He also said he found many other things, but most people take his research with a grain of salt or many grains of salt. He made some fantastic claims, but as you have seen, the ark wasn't where he claimed that it was," David explained.

"Well, I hate to rain on your parade, but the ark is sitting in an armored car, topside, and there are at least thirty guys running around with machine guns out there. Now that it's been found, do you really think that they are going to let you open it?" asked Charles.

David's face turned white. "Open it? Who would ever be dumb enough to do that?" he said excitedly.

"Why not open it?" a slightly pinker Charles responded quietly.

"I guess you aren't aware of the last folks that decided to open it," said David. "It was not a pretty sight!"

Chris pointed his finger in the air as he interjected. "I remember reading some verses about it, but I can't recall the verses. If I am remembering correctly, there were seventy people killed when they looked into the ark. Is that what you are referring to?"

"Well, I was actually referring to the fifty-thousand-plus, from Beth Shemesh, that died. Of course, they did a little more than peer inside the ark. They burned the cart that it was carried on, and they took the gold objects out of it. Some say that the number of people were far fewer, but I don't believe that there are any errors in Scripture. You can bet that they did something to provoke God.

"The ark has been taken out into battle before. I believe it was captured by the Philistines when the Israelites took it into that battle. The point is that the ark is no ordinary relic, and it's about as powerful of an object as there ever was. As a matter of fact, the mercy seat on the ark was God's throne on earth. It was said that he would be present with the Israelites and appear between the two cherubim on the top of the ark."

Chris nodded with David. Charles looked puzzled and remained silent as David continued his recollection of history.

"I'm going to get my crew to photograph the area, and then I'll be reporting the new find. I'm hopeful that the Sanhedrin will listen to me this time. They can be quite difficult on a good day. With the evidence that we found this time, I'm sure that they'll finally listen."

Chris moved in closer to David and touched him on the shoulder. "David, can we talk privately for a minute?"

David stopped speaking and looked at Chris with puzzlement. "Sure, let's go back to my tent," he replied. David walked back up topside with Chris and Charles.

Chris and Charles spent a lot longer than they had planned in Jerusalem, and they really needed to get back to the United States. They were fortunate that the members of their respective churches had been taking care of things back home for them for the time that already passed.

Charles really didn't want to go back to the States, but he knew the time had come to return. After all that he and Chris had been through, he knew he needed to get back there so that he could take the message of the ark back to the people there.

David led the group over to a secluded area near an empty tent where a few chairs were placed in the shade. "Have a seat," said David.

Charles and Chris grabbed a couple of the chairs and placed them next to David.

"You know we have to leave the day after tomorrow, right?" Chris asked David.

David smiled back at Chris, but it was apparent that he wasn't looking forward to his friends departing Israel. He enjoyed their company and wasn't looking forward to going back to his normal routine, with few good friends with which to spend his time. "I knew the two of you wouldn't be able to stay forever. I'm just glad that we've been able to spend the time that we have together. Heck, we almost didn't make it out of here alive!"

"I know!" shouted Charles. "I still can't believe that you guys didn't tell me about the stupid gas-tank gauge."

All three began laughing.

"I'm gonna miss you, David," said Charles sadly.

"I know that you and Chris have known each other for years, but I feel like we've known each other for years also, especially after all that we've been through recently."

David turned his head and looked to the ground briefly and wiped a tear from his eye.

"The dust in this place is horrible, isn't it?"

Chris smiled as he felt the emotion emanating from his good friend.

"I know exactly how you feel."

Right after he said that Chris began to wipe away the tears from his own eyes.

Charles smiled at the pair as he reached into his pocket and pulled out a small pack of tissues. He quickly tore open the package and handed each of the two a tissue.

"I guess I'm the lucky one," said Charles. "I haven't had a problem with allergies at all. Normally, I'm the first one to sneeze in the spring, and the last one to sneeze when fall hits. I'll take that as a sign that things can always change for the better."

David and Chris started laughing out loud. Charles completely missed that the two were not having real allergy issues.

CHAPTER 18
Homecoming

Charles and Chris left Jerusalem and went to Tel Aviv to catch a flight back to the United States. They arrived at the airport early in the morning and were able to get on a flight after waiting for a few hours, which was considerably lucky, considering the current events in Israel.

When they finally arrived back in the United States, Cynthia was there waiting to pick them up.

Cynthia drove Chris directly from the airport back to his church and dropped him off there at his request. He had been away from his congregation for quite some time, and he was eager to get back and prepare for his first service back in the States. He was also eager to tell his congregation of his adventures and everything he had learned.

Charles was also excited to get back to Phoenix, but he decided that he would stay on his sabbatical and ramp up his efforts to tell the world about artificial intelligence and the dangers that AI posed to humanity. As soon as he got back home, he contacted his associate pastor at the church and told him that he would be out and on leave for the foreseeable future and that he should continue to lead the church during his absence.

Only a day after his return, Charles learned via local news articles that I-Corp was increasing their production on their home-aide android models. The announcement of the increase in production caused their stock price to skyrocket, and the news media all but forgot about the missile launches in the Middle East, in favor of the I-Corp news.

The buzz on the street was that I-Corp wanted to get one of their home-aide models into every household in America within two years and the world within three to four years. The company announced that their production capacity increased significantly when they had the machines start running the production lines. To Charles, this news was about as horrible as could be, but the news outlets and word of mouth on the street was that these new machines were the best thing since the invention of the internet.

Charles was still in the dark about the role that AI played in the defeat of the Golshiri regime. As far as he was aware, the missile launches were just a horrible mistake, made in the defense of the nation of Israel. The media outlets in the US called the use of nuclear weapons by Israel "an act of terrorism by the most extreme religious zealots on the planet."

The US had no plans to protest the launch, but this was likely because, when the missiles flew, they knocked out massive oil production sites in Syria and near Egypt. The liberal politicians in office called this a "wonderful side effect emanating from an act of pure evil." They also called the attacks in Israel "karma for thousands of years of provoking evil around the world." Charles knew that the media was as biased as they had ever been, so these reports didn't surprise him.

Charles had been bothered by the fact that both Jared Hadad and Peter Jensen were present during the peace talks in Tel Aviv. He understood why Jared was there. Jared was the prime minister of the European Union. It made perfect sense for Jared to be there, but not for Peter. He wondered why there would be a need for a president of a technology company at a meeting about Middle East politics, but he struggled to rationalize why Peter was there. Why would the head of a technology company need to be involved in peace talks halfway around the globe?

I-Corp had months since unveiling their new machines at Diamondback Stadium. They were creating them by the thousands each week. At the onset of the war, there had only been two thousand. Those numbers quickly grew, and Charles estimated that they were well on their way to the hundred thousand mark.

With their goal of putting an AI machine in every home in America within two years, the production must have easily increased by a factor of ten or more. With four hundred million people in the United States, they would need to produce millions of machines every month. That was their plan, and Charles knew that he had to be the face of the opposition, to warn the masses. He quickly devised a plan of recruiting others who were of like mind and forming a network of people who would show up at every I-Corp event. They would also need to protest outside each I-Corp retail store.

He knew that the task at hand was daunting, but he remembered what Eli told him in Petra about the world being ripe for truth and that Moses was able to eventually convince pharaoh to release the Jews from bondage. He knew that if it was possible for Moses to convince the pharaoh to release the Jews, then he would be able to convince many to see the truth about artificial intelligence. Pharaoh had a heart that was hardened to the point that it was like a lead weight. If his heart of lead could be softened enough that he changed his mind, then there was still hope.

Charles began his daunting task of recruiting like-minded people. He knew he didn't have much time if he was to disrupt I-Corp's agenda.

CHAPTER 19

The Opening

The ark was moved from Jerusalem to a laboratory in Meyrin, Switzerland. The move was authorized by Adam Lefler after Jared convinced him that study of the ark was necessary to determine any special properties that would pose a risk for engineers or others who would be working closely with it. The move was also to determine its authenticity and to potentially open it. Switzerland was chosen because of the expertise of the people.

A startup company called Global Scientific Technologies would be handling the research. Their team had previously worked on the particle accelerator in the later part of 2018. Their mission would be to study the ark at a subatomic level and, if deemed safe, open it to catalog and inspect any artifacts inside.

The ark arrived by air. The plane that carried it was escorted by the Israeli Air Force as well as a fighter group from the European Union. Security was of utmost importance. When the cargo plane landed, the ark was met by a ground crew of soldiers, provided by I-Corp and in cooperation with the IDF.

The ark was seen throughout Israel as a sign that it was time to rebuild the temple. There were calls all over the land to rebuild the temple so that God could be worshipped properly and so that the daily sacrifice could begin again after almost two thousand years.

Jared arrived in Switzerland about three days after the arrival of the ark. He arranged a press conference with the high priest of the Sanhedrin as well as Pope Liberius. They would be announcing the arrival of the ark into Switzerland and offering prayers at the unveiling and opening.

David was too busy working at the dig site, cataloging the other artifacts that were found, so he did not make the trip. Adam agreed to credit him with the find, at the press conference.

A crowd of about a hundred thousand showed up for the event. The talk around the globe was of the ark and nothing else. The ark brought a unity to people because everyone at some point in their lives heard the story of the ark and the placing of the Ten Commandments into it. The whole world waited anxiously to get a glimpse of the interior of the ark. Not since the opening of the tomb of Tutankhamen had the world been so exhilarated by an archaeological find.

The podium was set next to giant statues of various religions. There was a giant statue of the Buddha and a statue of the Dancing Shiva. There was also a statue of the Virgin Mary, and a statue of Olympus set at the backdrop of the podium. The statues were said to have been placed there to show religious solidarity. Pope Liberius told the press that the statues represented mankind's desire to know their creator, no matter who that creator may be. He said that it was not so important that everyone call God by the same name, so long as they all worshipped the same God. He explained that people have worshipped God for thousands of years and that people often had different names for God, and it was his belief that each god represented by a different statue was each culture's image of the same god.

The sea of people moved vigorously as the loudspeakers blared the song "Victorious," which became number 1 on the recent pop charts. The song was written as an expression of unity among all people, regardless of their race, religion, or sexual orientation. It was written after the passing of the Sexual Naturalization Act that gave all people the right to express their sexuality in any form or fashion, which was quickly followed by the United States Anti-Racism Act, which abolished racism of any kind and put strict limits on any speech, both verbal and written. Both acts were seen by the masses as progress toward a world free of hatred. Some scholars went so far as to declare these acts as a "triumph against religious freedom" and declared that "true liberty was established by the abolishment of any religious or other type of speech that carried a message of hate."

There was a large screen set up at the rear of the stage, which was currently projecting the image of a large red curtain. The screen was set up to project the opening of the ark to the crowd and provide all of them the relative safety of seeing the opening from a safe distance.

The ark was nearly eight hundred yards away from the stage, in a secure underground bunker. The bunker was originally designed to prevent radiation exposure from nuclear particle testing, and hadn't been used in some time, so it seemed to be the obvious choice for a safe and secure opening of an artifact, such as the ark, which was famed to be dangerous to open.

As the song neared the end, Jared walked onto the stage, followed by Adam Lefler, the high priest of the Sanhedrin, and Pope Liberius.

The crowd cheered uncontrollably as the four walked out onto the stage.

Jared took the microphone out of its cradle and scanned the crowd, nodding as they cheered. "Welcome to Switzerland!" he screamed.

The crowd erupted in a great and powerful roar. The crowd was so loud that it caused the statues on the metal platform to vibrate, and microphone screeched with feedback from the sound.

"All right!" he screamed at the top of his lungs.

The crowd erupted in a second thundering ovation. They were so loud the second time that the statue of the Virgin Mary toppled onto the stage platform and had to be reset by the stage crew.

Jared watched as they lifted the statue and put it back into place. "Look at the power of a group of energized people!" he shouted.

Once again, the crowd roared. The stage crew quickly grabbed hold of the statues on the stage as they vibrated vigorously.

The pope lifted his arms into the air, and he looked to the sky. "Blessed be the Most High!" he said with a powerful shout.

The crowd loved it. They continued to roar and then began to chant. It started softly at first, and then the garbled words became clear. "Open it! Open it!" they roared.

"You have probably heard a rumor that the ark of the covenant was found recently!" Jared shouted.

The crowd continued to roar.

"Well, I am here to announce to all the world, that it indeed has been found!" he yelled mightily.

The crowd began to cheer again. "Open it, open it," they roared.

Jared turned and looked at the high priest and then Pope Liberius to let them know that it was time for the unveiling of the ark.

"The ark is the greatest find in the history of the world. The ark signifies a return to the law of Moses, for the people of Israel," he shouted.

He paused for a few moments and waited for the crowd's raucous cheering to abate. He then began to speak much more softly into the microphone. "Yesterday, a peace deal was signed among nations of the Middle East. The ark has brought us this peace. For years, tensions have been high throughout the Middle East and Israel. For years, the area has been plagued by wars and rumors of wars. Those days are over!"

The crowd once again erupted into cheers. The audience knew the significance of the words *peace* and *Middle East*. The only area in the world that has consistently not had any peace was the Middle East and Israel.

"Today is a new day for the world and for Israel. This new declaration of peace among these many nations will allow for a newfound prosperity in the Middle East and the rest of the world like none have ever witnessed. With peace, revenues can be used to fight things like hunger and poverty or disease and death. Yes, with peace, all things are possible."

The crowd roared!

Jared lifted his hands upward, motioning for the crowd to continue to cheer. He did this for a few moments as he scanned the crowd with an exuberant smile. After a few seconds passed, he motioned for the crowd to be silent, and the crowd's roar began to dull. Again, he began to speak softly into the microphone.

"I would like to introduce to you, the man who made this all possible today. Without the cooperation of the Israeli government, the ark would have likely remained hidden to the world. An artifact of such historical importance as this should not remain hidden, and thanks to this great leader, it has not. Please help me in welcoming the prime minister of Israel, Adam Lefler."

Adam gave a wave to the crowd as he walked casually up to the podium. Jared took the microphone and placed it back into the cradle and adjusted the height of the stand for Adam. He then turned toward Adam and extended his hand to him to show his respect. Adam cheerfully accepted, and the two shook hands briefly before Adam turned toward the crowd and put one hand onto each side of the podium and glared out, into the raucous crowd.

"Thank you!" said Adam.

The crowd roared.

Jared gave him a quick pat on the shoulder and then moved back to the area of the stage where Pope Liberius and the others were now standing and giving great applause.

Adam began to speak, and the crowd quickly quieted.

"If you had asked me a month ago if finding the ark of the covenant was possible, I would have called you crazy. If you had asked me if Israel would find peace with the rest of the Middle East, I would have called you insane." Adam paused for a moment and turned back toward Jared with a beaming smile, then turned back toward the crowd. "Ask me now if it's possible!" he shouted.

The crowd roared, and the people chanted, "Peace! Peace! Peace!" before being intermingled with and then overtaken by the chants of "Open it! Open it! Open it!"

Again, Adam began to speak softly into the microphone.

"When I was a small boy, I remember my parents moving us to Israel. Back in those days, Israel was a much different place from what it is today. We moved to Israel in the midsixties. Prior to the sixties, Israel was more of a nationalist country. The atmosphere was really more about nation building than anything else. My parents were both musicians. Israel had somewhat of a period of artistic explosion in the sixties—a real cultural revolution. Aside from that, Israel had its day-to-day fighting, or at least, it felt as if it were day to day. The focus shifted from the Egyptian front to the Syrian front and constant shots fired in and around the Golan Heights area. I never would have imagined that one day I would become prime minister, and we would still be fighting on the Golan front."

The crowd was more silent now. The images of war swept across the screens on the stage, and the people were now seeing the images of the fighting that occurred over the many years in Israel. The sound of artillery shells and machine-gun fire blared into the audience, giving them a brisk reminder of the chaos that ensues amidst the bloody battles or war.

Adam continued to speak, and as he spoke, the sounds of the artillery became muted, somewhat.

"We Jews have had a long history of war. We have been conquered on several occasions, put into bondage, and in the Great War, nearly exterminated. Through it all, we have always maintained our culture, and through it all, we survived." Adam paused for a moment and took out a handkerchief from his left breast pocket. He wiped a tear from his eye and then placed the handkerchief back into his pocket.

Seeing this, Jared took a step forward and whispered softly into his ear, "Are you okay?"

Adam looked at Jared and gave him a sort of half nod that was barely noticeable. "He asked me if I was okay," Adam said softly into the microphone. Adam looked at the screen and pointed at it.

The images on the screen changed from that of war to a brilliantly blue-and-white flag, waving silently. It was the flag of the nation of Israel. The audience became silent, as Adam looked at the flag reverently and threw it a salute. Seeing this, the crowd broke out into another round of raucous applause.

Adam turned back toward the audience and adjusted his microphone as the audience continued to cheer. He waited for a few seconds so that he could gain his composure and then continued to speak.

"The Jewish people are a light unto the world. We have shown the world that if a group of people stands together and doesn't forsake God, even when times are bad, he will not forsake those people. It is the grace of almighty God himself that I stand here today, and we, the Jewish people, stand as a nation today. The ark of the covenant is a reminder to us and an example to the world. It tells us all that God does keep his promises and, in this case, the covenant that he made with the Jewish people so many thousands of years ago." Adam paused again.

The image on the screen changed back to the original red curtain.

"I would like to thank God for always keeping his promises, the people of Israel for standing strong through adversity, and lest I forget, Jared Hadad, for his assistance in the past couple months as an ally to the state of Israel and negotiating a peace agreement that will allow the people of Israel and the rest of the Middle East to live in peace for the first time in thousands of years."

Adam turned toward Jared and extended his arm toward Jared to shake his hand. "Thank you, Mr. Prime Minister!"

The crowd erupted with a thundering applause yet again. The people were growing more excited as the minutes ticked by. Their applause could be heard a mile away and, from a distance, sounded eerily similar to military jets flying over the area. As their fervor grew for the opening of the ark, their chants became more frequent. Adam could see that their patience was wearing thin.

"In closing, I would just like to thank each and every one of you for coming out tonight. Moments like these are rare if they ever occur. In just a few moments, the ark will be opened. Let's all turn our attention to the screen and watch history be made before our very eyes."

The cheers were like a roller coaster in Meyrin. The crowd was elated for a few reasons, but the opening of the ark was the pinnacle of the evening. The crowd had been anticipating the opening since the arrival was first announced. If there was any fear about opening the ark, it was buried deep within and unnoticeable in the crowd.

Jared took the microphone and scanned the audience. "Ladies and Gentlemen"—he paused for a moment—"the ark of the covenant!"

The lights behind the crowd and surrounding the stage switched off suddenly, and the speakers were now beginning to play the happenings from within the bunker, where the ark was about to be opened. In the foreground of the screen was a scientist in a white laboratory coat. He had a pair of goggles around his neck. He looked at the camera and gave a quick smile.

"Are you seeing this on the outside?" he asked.

Jared held the microphone closer to his face. "We see you."

"Brilliant!" the scientist exclaimed.

The scientist was Erik Gustafson, who had been with Global Scientific for two years as the chief media officer.

As the people focused immensely at the screen, he could be seen walking around as if being followed by a cameraman. He walked out of the office that he was in and into a long plain hallway. The doors in the hall were mostly closed, but a few were open, but the inside of each not visible as Erik walked down the hall.

As he walked, Erik turned toward the camera and spoke to those who were watching.

"We have the ark down in the laboratory at the end of this hall. The lab has two sections, and we will be in the containment area, where we can view the ark without being directly exposed to it." He reached the end hall and then stopped and turned around to face the cameraman directly.

"Ah, here we are," he said in a low monotone voice. "Right behind this door is where the magic is made, so to speak. Are we all ready for this?"

Jared chuckled a little and responded, "We are ready!"

Erik opened the door and stepped inside. The room didn't look like much of a laboratory. There was a long bench next to a viewing window, and in the back were two desks on the left side. The desks didn't really have anything on them other than telephones and computer monitors. The right side of the room had some tall gray filing cabinets. It was eerily similar to a typical, drab government office. The desks were gray metal with older similarly-colored metal chairs with green, vinyl-covered cushions. They looked like they had been manufactured in the 1960s.

Erik moved into the center of the room and faced the camera once again.

"This room that we are in now isn't the laboratory. On the other side of that plexiglass is the lab and all its wonder. This is actually one of four viewing rooms, surrounding the main lab." Erik moved over toward the bench and pointed through the plexiglass window.

"We will now set up our camera so that you can see inside the lab and then we can get this party started."

The cameraman moved in closer to the window, and as he neared it, a rather large laboratory space came into view. There were about ten people inside the lab, and they were all wearing green hazmat suits. Each suit had a long orange hose attached at the back. The hose came down from the ceiling area, and when the people moved, the long metal arms that the hoses were attached to spun around, to move the hose into the direction that each person moved. Since most of the people were moving around like ants on a piece of cheese, the metal bars and hoses appeared to be dancing around at the ceiling, and this mesmerized the crowd, who watched the rhythmic dance with glee.

"Here we go," said Erik.

The camera remained focused on the laboratory, but Erik stood next to the camera so that he could continue his narration of the events in the room.

"To give you an idea of what's happening right now, the lab technicians are setting up some tools that they will be using to open the ark. If you look toward the center of the room, you'll notice a large round door. That's the vault. The ark is actually in there right now. While it's in there, we can examine it using an x-ray machine, and some other radioactive tests that we have at our disposal."

The camera panned back toward Erik, who was gazing into the laboratory. He was so fixed on the commotion in the lab that he didn't notice the camera pointed at him.

"Unfortunately, when we attempted to view the interior of the ark earlier with a fluoroscope, we weren't able to see the contents inside. Not to worry, we are planning on opening it anyway. Before you think that we are being overly cautious here, we really do this with any artifacts that we receive and that have an enclosed inner chamber. The reason we do this is to prevent contamination that may be present inside the object, from getting out. We also do this to prevent any contamination getting into the artifact. Sometimes, oxygen can wreak havoc on an artifact that has been sealed for thousands of years. This is really just a precaution."

The camera panned back to the center of the laboratory. The room had now cleared out, and only three people remained in the room. The three remaining workers rolled a lab table toward the door. The table had a variety of items on it, such as a centrifuge and a microscope. To their left was a steel cart, and it had a number of different tools that they would be using to open the ark.

"Jim, are you ready to begin?" he asked.

One of the three people in the room, Jim Larsson, turned toward the glass and gave a thumbs-up. Jim was the lead technician at Global Scientific and worked on just about every project that they had in the past twenty years. His claim to fame was developing a cold fusion device that worked at room temperature. The device was determined to be a health risk for consumers, so he and his team shelved the project for further research. He hoped to solve the world's energy problems but wasn't able to create a device safe enough for home or commercial use.

"Looks like we are ready to go!" Erik exclaimed.

Jared turned to the crowd and waved his arms to get the crowd roaring again. "Open it, open it, open it!" he shouted.

The crowd roared to life. They chanted continuously and in unison. It was like they were at an arena where two gladiators were about to fight to the death. There was a промociousness to their chants.

Erik threw a beaming grin to Jared and gave him a thumbs-up. He then turned back toward the glass and gave Jim the thumbs-up.

"Jim"—he paused—"open it!"

Jim and the other two technicians turned their gaze toward the large circular door and stared at it for a few moments and then turned back toward Jim in anticipation of his order to open it. Their preparations were now complete, and the lab was now prepped like an operating room. Their anxiety was such that those watching from the outside could feel it, even though they were nearly a thousand yards away, topside. They were about to open an artifact that, to many, was only legend, and it rattled them to the core.

Jim motioned to the technicians to open the door. The woman to his left moved in toward the door and grasped the long handle and turned it counterclockwise until it pointed upward. She then pulled the handle downward, and the door made a loud whooshing sound. The vault was a vacuum chamber, and when they opened the door, the air rushed in so quickly that papers laying neatly on a nearby desk were noticeably moved out of their place and onto the floor.

Now that the door was unlocked and partially opened, the man to Jim's right side grabbed the large door and started to walk it open. The door was very heavy, so the man had to put the weight of his body into pushing it. He leaned into the door with his shoulder, and with a grunt or two, the door began to move.

The door moved slowly, and the door opening grew larger, revealing the ark, which lay inside. After another grunt by the technician, the inertia of the door took over, and the door seemed to float on its own. The door continued toward the wall until it suddenly struck a catch on the wall and made a loud clanking sound as it locked into place.

The ark was glorious. The gold inlay glistened, and the jewels sparkled brilliantly. It certainly didn't appear as if it were thousands of years old. It looked brand-new with its radiant glow. It had been in a tunnel for well over two thousand years and appeared as if it were just made.

The crowd outside let out a perfectly timed gasp as they beheld its beauty.

The door now opened; Jim motioned for the technicians to move the ark out of the vault and into the lab area.

The two hesitated for a moment, and then proceeded to grab the two long gray straps that were on the front of the table where the ark was seated. With caution, the two began to pull out the ark, and slowly, it rolled into the room. The floor had a grooved track system, and the wheels of the cart moved smoothly along until reaching the center of the room, where the cart came to a sudden stop causing the ark to shudder briefly

Now that the ark was safely at the center of the room, the technicians locked the wheels into place. They then proceeded to arrange their toolbox and other carts around the ark in a strategic fashion.

Jim turned back to the camera and remained silent. He had a look of satisfaction on his face, but those watching could see the angst that he also carried with him. He turned back toward the ark and toward a small cart to his right and grabbed one of the tools that was neatly laid out in front of him.

The tool that he grabbed was a Rife machine. It was a rectangular machine that had several buttons on it, and an LED display at the top. Attached to the machine by long cords were two probes that looked like electrical probes. The machine generated a low electromagnetic frequency. All that could be heard was a low humming sound.

"Jim, what are you doing with that machine?" asked Erik.

Jim turned toward the glass. "Erik, we are using a machine that generates a low-strength electromagnetic frequency. We are trying to determine if there is an electromagnetic field being produced and find out what the field strength is at. Using this device, we can match the electromagnetic frequency of the ark. That will give us the field strength, among other things, so that we know what, if any, frequency of electromagnetic energy that it is putting out. Really, what we want to do is eliminate any static electricity and avoid a static discharge. This method was developed a few years ago, and the first step in the process is to look to see if there is an actual electromagnetic field around the object being observed."

The female technician looked at Jim and nodded.

Jim proceeded his work with the tool. “It looks like there is only a weak electromagnetic field around the ark, and no immediate risk of static discharge. That’s not what we expected, but this is a highly unusual object.”

The technicians used several different probes and scanners on the ark. As they used each tool, they recorded the data into a laptop that was set on one of the lab tables. The process was relatively quick but not very stimulating for the crowd.

The crowd could be heard inside the bunker, again chanting, “Open it! Open it! Open it!” they shouted. The patience of the crowd was diminishing rapidly

Fortunately, the technicians finished their scans and probing and were ready to try to open the ark.

Jim turned back to the camera.

“We are now going to use a very simple tool Erik,” Jim said with a laugh.

“What kind of tool is it?” asked Erik.

“I’m actually a little embarrassed to say, but it’s a pry bar. Sometimes simplicity works best, and in this case, we have an object with a lid affixed to it, and common sense dictates that since there is no danger of electrostatic discharge, that it is likely the most effective tool in our arsenal at this point.”

Jim turned back to the female technician and motioned for her to take the tool and open the lid to the ark.

“We are now going to open the ark. Keep your fingers crossed!” he said.

The technician scanned the ark for a moment and then took her left hand and started to feel around the rim of the lid to find a spot that the bar could be placed to slide the curved end of the bar under the lid and into the space between the lid and the base of the ark. After feeling around for a few seconds, she found a spot on the rear of the ark that had a slightly broader area where the bar could be slid under the lid. She placed the bar under the lid and began to slowly apply pressure to the bar and gently pulled the bar backward and down.

The crowd was dead silent now. The suspense of the moment was palpable. The crowd waited with hearty anticipation. Many of the people in the crowd were praying, and others were standing silently with their fingers crossed.

The lid to the ark slowly started to move upward. Jim turned toward the glass and gave Erik a thumbs-up.

The lid appeared to be sealed onto the ark very tightly. The technician appeared to struggle with the pry bar and then suddenly stopped and pulled her hands away from the bar. She was able to move the lid about a quarter of an inch but no further.

Jim saw that she stopped and moved around to the side of the ark where she was standing, to see if he could assist her in any way.

She looked up at Jim, visibly nauseated, and then suddenly fell to the floor.

Jim hurriedly moved away from the ark, and within seconds, the second technician fell to the floor. He turned toward the camera with a look of disbelief, and then he fell to the floor.

Erik panicked and jumped up toward the glass and started beating on it with his hands.

"Jim!" he shouted. "Jim!"

The crowd that had been completely silent was now in a panic. People shrieked in sheer terror as they started trampling one another to try to escape the area. After seeing the three people who were trying to open the ark suddenly drop, they feared that something could also happen to them.

Jared, seeing the people fleeing turned toward the crowd and started yelling into the microphone, "Please remain calm!"

The people either didn't hear him or just ignored him because they kept fleeing the area. Screams emanated out of the crowd over their panic as many were being trampled in their attempt to escape.

The screen went black, and the lights turned on outside the bunker. The mass exodus from the area continued for about fifteen minutes before very few remained. The ground was littered with people who were still screaming in anguish from being run down by the crowd of terrified people. Many of those who did remain only did so in order to attend to those who were injured.

The center area, in between the stage and the parking lot, was where the majority of the casualties occurred. Those who were in the rear, closest to the parking lot, got out unscathed. Those nearest the stage also got out mostly unscathed. Those in the center of the field were shoved and trampled over by hundreds to thousands of people. Most of the injured had broken arms or legs, but many had much more severe injuries.

Ambulances and police cars flooded the area within minutes, and the scene changed from one of pure excitement to one of recovery and lifesaving. Scenes like this were all too common across the globe in recent years.

Media reports the next morning put the death toll at around six hundred people with at least two thousand injured in some form or fashion.

Jared received word from Erik that Jim and the other two technicians died at the scene. Attempts at opening the ark were immediately halted due to safety concerns. The ark was flown back to Jerusalem and locked inside Israel Museum. It was later reported that the authenticity of the ark was confirmed by the events surrounding the attempted opening, and that there would be no further attempts at opening the ark. Members of the Sanhedrin were satisfied that it was authentic and released a statement:

> We are saddened by the loss of life in Switzerland last night. Our greatest sympathies and condolences go out to each and every person who was affected.
>
> The ark has always been a sacred and powerful relic. The history of the ark is dotted with similar incidents, and this latest incident proves to the world that history often records factual information, even when such information appears to be impossible.
>
> We have all witnessed a tragic event but an especially important event. We have witnessed the power of God firsthand and have witnessed

the wrath that can be unleashed by doing something that is in opposition to God.

Let us all learn from this tragedy. Let us all respect the power of God.

We at the Sanhedrin have been humbled. This event has shown us that we are all human, and as humans, we can make serious mistakes. Our mistake in this case is also our blessing, as out of the ashes of history, the ark of the covenant was located. From those ashes a new temple will be born.

Today, we are officially announcing our plan to rebuild the temple. The site of the Third Temple will be at the site of the First and Second Temples, which we have confirmed to be at the Gihon Spring.

CHAPTER 20

The United Nations

Israel was prospering. The temple was under construction but nearing completion in the three years and five months after the ark was located and the peace treaty was signed. Israel's military shrunk significantly, and those who did remain found themselves working more as police officers than as soldiers. A new era of peace was underway in the Middle East and Israel.

I-Corp had an explosion in production over the past few years, and their products were in the homes of most of the families in the world. Production centers were built in South America, Europe, China, and the Middle East. Almost every family in the world now had an artificial person within their home. The explosion in production was made possible by the significant cost savings created by having the machines completing the manufacturing process. I-Corp had very few human employees, so their labor costs were minimal.

I-Corp put the machines into poorest households first, after hearing the cries of the people for increased *equity*. The quality of life of the poorest within society changed rapidly. The machines provided several functions, such as childcare, which allowed these households to spend less money. Time was another benefit that these families received. With both parents able to work, household incomes rose, and those in the poorest households were able to add more to their savings, and many were able to seek education, and many started their own businesses. I-Corp made a pledge to help the poor, and they kept their promise.

The governments around the globe subsidized the machines for those who were deemed to be suffering from the "wealth gap, created by the old capitalist policies that left countless millions behind." It was a move that angered the rich, as they saw it as another form of government assistance that was doled out in exchange for loyalty to the socialist and communist states that covered the globe. I-Corp lobbied the world governments to promote the subsidies as a way to "give back to the people" and promised to keep the cost to the government low, for their police and soldier models in exchange for tax breaks as well as the government providing low-interest loans to those who couldn't afford the machines.

I-Corp's strategy was to create a demand for the product by injecting the product into society rather than spending millions marketing the machines. By providing the machines to the poorest people first, the prospective affluent buyers would be able to see the products in action prior to their purchase. When the more affluent saw the benefits provided by the machines, demand skyrocketed.

Not everyone in the world was happy about I-Corp building the machines and their strategy of "an artificial person in every household." One such person was Charles Duncan.

When Charles returned from Israel, he began traveling across the United States and Europe on mission trips. While much of his mission work was spent on spreading the gospel, a large part of it was also protesting I-Corp. He absolutely hated the idea of machines replacing people in the workforce and saw AI as a scourge that would corrupt the entire human race.

He was arrested on several occasions and, on one of those, spent three months in jail. His incarceration came about while he was on a mission in China. While there, he made the mistake of getting caught with a suitcase full of pocket-sized New Testament bibles. When he was caught with the bibles, he told the Chinese authorities that he was taking them to a church in Australia, but they checked his travel itinerary, and Australia was not one of his destinations. His return ticket to Phoenix gave him away.

Charles refused to purchase an artificial person and encouraged his entire congregation to boycott I-Corp. About half of his congregation purchased the machines and later left the church, citing Charles's political activity as their reason for leaving. The others in the church were of similar mindset as Charles and followed him around the country on his missions to spread the gospel and warnings about artificial intelligence.

His current mission brought him to New York City. He traveled there to boycott the recent nomination of Jared Hadad as secretary-general of the United Nations.

Jared was selected unanimously by every member of the United Nations security council after working with Israel and the Middle East in their peace talks. After the third year of sustained peace, he was approached about heading up the United Nations.

Charles arrived early to set up his protest outside the front of United Nations building. The grass was wet from the morning dew that had set upon it during the night. The air had a slight chill to it. The streetlights were all that illuminated the area as the sky changed from black to gray. The sun was still about an hour from rising.

Cynthia traveled to New York with Charles. She and he became somewhat of a couple after they returned from Israel. When he was arrested in China, she worked tirelessly with his legal team and local government officials to try to get his case dismissed or to get the charges lessened. She practically lived in China during the three months that he was incarcerated and was waiting at the gate with outstretched arms on the day of his release.

Cynthia shared his passion for mission work and for the fight against AI. When they returned from China, the two became inseparable. Her shared passion for the fight against artificial intelligence and to share the gospel emboldened Charles and increased his drive to spend more time on the road. His time in jail did nothing to dissuade him from spreading the gospel, and his new companionship gave him the desire to do it more often.

As the sun started to rise, the streetlights started to flicker and shut off one by one. The traffic got heavier as the sky transitioned from gray to blue. What was a tranquil and quiet street turned into a hectic dash of people running to and fro. Some were headed to work, while others began lining up around the United Nations building to catch a glimpse of Jared as he arrived.

Knowing that he would have to contend with a noisy group of onlookers and a busy street, Charles came armed with a megaphone. His megaphone was red and white and had a coiled wire, remarkably similar to the wire on his telephone back home in Phoenix.

He picked up his megaphone and checked to see that it had batteries in it. As he flipped it over, the coiled wire began to swing rapidly, causing Charles to shudder momentarily as he recalled his last encounter with such a wire.

"These cords are horrible!" he exclaimed to Cynthia.

"I don't know," she said. "They are actually kinda cool. They stretch out about twice as long as they are, and then they snap back to their original position. It's like there is a spring in there."

Charles looked at Cynthia with a look of disdain. She obviously never had her head and neck twisted up in one of the cords.

"Did you date the inventor of these cords?"

"No!" she said laughingly. "Why would you ask that?"

"I was just checking," he snarked. "You just seem to like them an awful lot." Charles set the megaphone down and grabbed two large poster-board signs he created the night before. The signs both read, "Artificial intelligence is natural stupidity!" He inspected the poster boards and noticed the straps were not connected to the holes at the top of each.

"Have you seen the straps that I made for this sandwich sign?" he asked.

"Yes, right here—the same place that you put them ten minutes ago."

"Oh yeah," he said with a chuckle, "I guess I did."

He picked up the Velcro straps and affixed them to the right and left sides of the first poster board and then second poster board.

He then slipped the sandwich board over his head, with a little help from Cynthia.

"This sure beats holding up a sign all day!" he exclaimed.

"That's why I love you," she said with a smile. "You are so crafty."

Charles was beaming with pride. "They say that necessity is the mother of all invention," he replied.

"Well, that may have been true to some degree in the past, but now it's all about becoming as rich as possible."

"Touché," he said. Charles picked up the megaphone and put the microphone up to his mouth. "Don't fall victim to the new world order! Artificial intelligence is not your friend, and Jared Hadad is not what he seems!" he screamed into the microphone.

As he yelled into the megaphone, he drew the attention of the guards at the guard shack at the front of the United Nations Complex. One of the two guards left this post and started walking toward Cynthia and him.

"Sir," the guard yelled, "why don't you join the rest of your group around the corner? It's not likely that Mr. Hadad is even going to see you when his limousine pulls into the area."

Charles became annoyed by the guard. "We're fine right where we are. Thank you!" he replied.

Cynthia started to laugh. "Is there any place that we have gone where they haven't picked you out of the group?"

"Ha ha!" said Charles. "I think that they must have a picture of me that they circulate around anything to do with I-Corp or AI."

"Well, this isn't about I-Corp or AI," said Cynthia.

Charles looked at Cynthia as if she had just swallowed a watermelon whole. "Come on, Cynthia," said Charles. "This guy used to be the CEO of I-Corp. He may have left the company, but he is still heavily involved with them. His best friend runs the company now. As a matter of fact, when I was in Israel with David, he and Peter Jensen were both at that meeting."

Cynthia looked puzzled.

"Why was Peter there?" she asked.

"That's a good question. I've asked myself that same question for years. It can only be that I-Corp was somehow more involved with the Israeli-Golshiri War than they have let on. I know there was a small group of soldiers sent to help Israel, but that whole war was just strange. It's like the weather was being controlled, and people just started dropping dead."

"That's not it." Cynthia said in disagreement. "They were just starting to produce those machines back then. It's just not possible. Besides, how is Jared going to control the weather?"

"Maybe they used satellites," suggested Charles.

As the two stood there arguing, a caravan of limousines approached the United Nations building.

"There *he* is!" Cynthia shouted.

"Hold up your sign so that the news cameras can see," said Charles.

Cynthia and Charles moved closer to the gate. Charles was wearing his sandwich sign, and Cynthia was holding up her own sign. Her sign read, "Hadad must go, just say no!"

"Don't trust Hadad. He is not what he seems!" Charles shouted into his megaphone.

The limousines started to pass through the gates, and Charles continued yelling through the megaphone about his distrust of Jared and artificial intelligence. The media tried to ignore Charles and Cynthia, but every time their cameras turned toward them, Charles would begin flailing his arms and then screaming into his megaphone.

As the limousines departed the area, the media personnel began packing up their vans. Charles took this as his cue to also pack up because now the target of his ire was inside the UN assembly building, and the media was no longer recording footage of the event.

Cynthia turned to Charles as he packed his megaphone into his backpack.

"Well, that's that," said Cynthia. "Do you want to get some breakfast?"

"Don't you want to wait until they come out?" Charles asked pleadingly.

Cynthia walked over to Charles and grabbed his backpack and set it onto the ground. She then grabbed his sandwich sign and helped him take it off.

"They have a little diner just down the street. How about taking me out to get a hot breakfast and then we can take a taxi over to see the Statue of Liberty?"

Charles looked as if he was struggling internally with the decision. He wanted to stay so that he could make a political statement, but he was also hungry. After a few moments of deep thought, he relented.

"I hope they have bacon," he said.

Cynthia busted out in laughter. "You and bacon have one heck of a relationship."

"What?" he asked sarcastically.

"You are like a toddler sometimes. You know, they may have this other breakfast meat that the rest of us call sausage. Have you ever considered that?

"Whatever!" Charles exclaimed while rolling his eyes.

It took them a few minutes to pack up the car, but after a few groans and huffs and puffs from Charles, they completed their task and began walking to the restaurant. When they arrived, they saw that they had made it just before the cutoff time for breakfast.

The diner they visited was very out of place in the city. It wasn't like the other buildings in the area and stuck out like a sore thumb. It looked like something out of the 1950s and wasn't exceptionally large for a restaurant in New York City. It looked somewhat like a giant silver tissue box with a wooden deck set out on the front.

The inside of the diner was rather cramped and consisted of a long line of booths along the outer wall and a large bar on the opposite side, next to the kitchen area. The bar extended the length of the room and had small round swivel seats with red padding. In the back left corner was a set of doors for the restrooms and a jukebox just to the side of the door where people entered the back. The right corner of the room had a medium-sized television, which was not heard audibly, but was playing the news.

Charles scanned the room intensely before finally sitting down next to Cynthia in one of the booths along the front right wall that faced the television.

"Awe," she said softly. "You want to sit next to me?"

"Of course, I do," he replied.

As she looked at his face, she could see that his eyes were staring pointedly at the television set on the wall. She turned toward the television and then back at Charles to verify that this was his obsession at the moment. She smiled at him and gave him a bit of a nod as she gently tapped him on the shoulder.

"Are you sure that you want to sit next to me?" she asked wryly. "You aren't sitting here for any other reason?"

Charles smiled. He knew that he was caught in a catch-22. He thought about his response carefully for a few seconds and then responded with what he thought was a foolproof answer that would assure her that he actually did want to sit next to her for her company and not the television.

"I always enjoy sitting next to you. That way, if you are looking at something in a particular direction, I will be facing the same way and won't miss whatever it is that you happen to be looking at."

"Is that so?" she asked.

"That's what I said, isn't it?" he said with a laugh.

"Fine, I believe you."

Charles was visibly relieved. He could now relax and watch the news without feeling guilty.

"Ouch!" said Cynthia. "This seat has a board sticking out, and it's right under my side." She pushed Charles out of the booth and stood up. "See it?" she asked.

"See what?" asked Charles.

Charles scanned the seat, looking for the board that was supposedly sticking out. He didn't want to plop back down into the seat and get jabbed by a hard piece of wood.

Cynthia moved over to the opposite side of the booth while Charles face was now six inches from the red vinyl covering. He was rubbing it and pushing it gently, trying his hardest to locate the protrusion.

"You must be experiencing the princess-and-the-grain-of-sand syndrome again because there isn't a piece of wood anywhere near this seat cushion," he bellowed.

He continued feeling around the seat cushion and pushing it downward, attempting to find the alleged piece of wood that offended Cynthia. Growing impatient but still scared of taking a wooden paddle to the backside as he sat down, he began swiveling his head back and forth from the television to the seat cushion as he continued massaging the vinyl in short circular motions.

Cynthia couldn't help but laugh as she saw Charles impersonating a confused karate kid waxing on and waxing off the seat cushion below him, as his head darted back and forth from the television to the cushion.

"Charles!" she belted out with a laugh.

"Yes?" he replied, in frustration.

"I know that you want to watch the news. We didn't just meet this morning," she said softly.

Charles stopped rubbing the seat cushion and looked up, confused. "If you don't want to watch, that's fine," he said. "I just need to find this piece of wood because I'm not a huge fan of splinters or wooden stakes."

Cynthia couldn't control her laughter and started turning red out of embarrassment for Charles. She loved poking fun at him but was now feeling bad that he fell for her excuse.

"Go ahead and watch. I have some emails to catch up on anyway." Cynthia picked up her phone and began swiping her finger across the screen as she sat there holding back her laughter.

"Are you sure?"

She looked up at him, smiling. "I'm sure."

Charles was relieved. He stopped rubbing the seat, looked at Cynthia with a huge grin, and then plopped down into the seat, knowing he was now able to watch the news in a completely guilt-free environment. Since Cynthia was now on the opposite side of the booth, he slid himself over toward the wall area so he could use the corner as a backrest.

"Ouch!" Charles yelled. "There is a board sticking out!"

Cynthia laughed, not knowing if Charles was serious about the board or just joking, as she was moments earlier.

Charles looked up at the television and could now see the United Nations building and all the flags flying in the backdrop. He could barely make out what was at the lower part of the screen, but as the camera angle turned, he suddenly realized that he was watching himself on the screen.

The volume was incredibly low, but he could make out the phrase "The machines and Jared Hadad are the antithesis of benevolence! They will be the end to us all!" It was clearly him as this is a portion of what he was yelling earlier that day.

"Hey!" he shouted, "we got on the news!"

Cynthia whipped her hair around quickly to see. "Wow!" she exclaimed. "We look so different on television."

"Just think," said Charles, "we made it onto the news, and it didn't end in my arrest."

"Thank goodness for that!" Cynthia replied with a gasp.

"What does that news banner say?" asked Charles as he pointed at the screen.

"Oh no!" Cynthia screeched.

"They had a shooting!"

"What?" said Charles, as he jumped out of the booth and ran toward the television set.

"I can't believe it!" said Cynthia. "How is there a shooting at the United Nations?"

"I don't know," said Charles.

As they looked at the screen, they saw the building backdrop change from the front of the building to a news reporter. The image of the building moved up to the top left of the screen, and the rolling marquee read, "Breaking News: Shots Fired at United Nations. Gunman at Large and One Fatality Confirmed."

"This is just unreal," said Cynthia. "We were just over there. It could have been one of us!"

"Let's thank God that you were hungry, huh?" asked Charles.

Charles walked over to the cash register near the center of the long bar.

"Can we turn up the volume on the television?" he asked the staff member.

The server reached down to a shelf beneath the register and pulled out a small black remote control from a small cardboard box and then handed it to Charles.

"If you don't mind, please bring it back when you're done, and don't turn it up too loud."

Charles looked at the woman as if she had trees growing out of her ears. He could hardly believe that she was so calm when there was a shooting at a neighboring building and when the gunman was still on the loose.

"Didn't you see that there was a shooting at the United Nations?" he asked.

"Where have you been?" asked the server. "That happened a few minutes before you got here. For all I know, you and that lady are who they're looking for. Besides, it was that Jared Haddydad guy anyway."

"What?" asked Charles.

"Man, you sure are slow-on-the-uptake fella! That English jerk was the one that got shot. It was an assassination or something like that."

"Oh no!" said Charles.

The waitress looked at Charles and tilted her head to the side a bit, as if she were still trying to figure out what he had just said.

"Did you know that guy or something?"

Charles's head dropped, and he began to sulk.

"Have we met before?" she asked.

Charles lifted his head and looked at the server very closely. After examining her a little, he responded that they had never met before by nodding.

"I know where I've seen you before. You're the sandwich man!" she exclaimed.

"Huh?"

"Yeah!" she said with a sense of certainty. "You are that guy that was out there protesting with the sandwich sign and the megaphone."

Cynthia overheard the woman talking about Charles and his protesting and moved over to where the two were talking.

"Did they say anything about us on the news?" she asked.

"Not you, honey, just him," she said, pointing at Charles.

"What did they say?" asked Cynthia, concerned.

"They were just talking about how you seem to pop up all over the world, wherever this guy is giving speeches, and that it's awfully coincidental that you are a Christian and that you seem to have some kind of beef with that Hadad guy."

Charles began to sweat profusely. "I've got to sit down," he said.

Cynthia grabbed him by the arm and led him over to the closest booth. "Can you get him a glass of water?" she asked the server.

"Sure," said the server. "What's wrong with him?"

Cynthia looked over at Charles and then back at the waitress. "He just has anxiety attacks from time to time. He'll be fine."

The server handed Cynthia a glass filled with orange juice. "Take this juice. It's better than water. It's what they give me after donating blood, so there must be something to that."

"Thanks!" said Cynthia as she took the glass.

The server watched carefully as Cynthia handed the glass of juice to Charles. She appeared to be a little suspicious now that she knew who she was talking to.

Suddenly, the door to the diner opened, and the bell on it started ringing.

"Charles Duncan!" said a familiar voice.

Charles looked toward the door and saw the outline of a man standing at the door. He couldn't make out who it was because the sunlight coming in through the door was too bright.

"Yes?" replied Charles.

The man moved away from the door, and as he did, Charles could see who the mystery voice belonged to. Standing next to the door was Richard.

"I'm going to need you to come with me," said Richard.

Cynthia moved in between Richard and Charles. "Do you know this guy, Charles?" she asked.

"Unfortunately," replied Charles.

CHAPTER 21
Darkness

The shooting at the United Nations shocked the world. There had never been an assassination of a secretary-general ever before. The only thing close was the death of the second ever secretary-general in 1961. That death was controversial and only rumored to have been an assassination. His death resulted from a plane crash that was mired in controversy, and it was never proven to be an actual assassination.

Jared Hadad was the most well-known leader in the world. His popularity stretched the globe. He had the shortest term of any secretary-general because of the assassination and had a record time in office of six minutes. He was loved for his ability to make positive change throughout Europe and for his recent accomplishment in negotiating peace in the Middle East.

The gunman, who escaped during the chaotic scene, was a middle-aged man of what was assumed to be Middle Eastern descent. The man wore a white head covering that draped over the right and left sides of his face. He had sunglasses on at the time and was described as a light-brown-skinned man with a brown beard.

The cameras in the vicinity of the shooter didn't capture his face as his back was toward them as he fired three shots from a .40-caliber pistol. As the man fled the scene, there were twenty to thirty men who pushed their way toward Jared and blocked the cameras from seeing his face as he slipped out of the crowd. Cameras in the other areas of the building malfunctioned briefly, at the time of his escape, but just long enough that there was no footage of him fleeing the scene. The camera malfunction was another controversy due to the timing of the camera failure.

Within minutes of the shooting, Jared was taken to New York's premiere new hospital, Jesuit Memorial Medical Center. He was taken via care flight to the medical center where lifesaving procedures were halted, and he was pronounced dead on arrival. He had been shot once in his right forearm, once in his right shoulder, and the fatal shot went through his right eye and exited through the left side of his neck. Whoever fired the shots knew how to fire a handgun because all three shots hit their intended target after being fired in rapid succession.

The media remained outside the hospital, waiting for updates to be given, but only one update was ever given, and that was a confirmation of the secretary's death at the scene of the shooting. An autopsy was scheduled to be performed, though was just a formality, as the cause of death was already known to the entire world.

Charles was loaded into an unmarked white van and transported to the local office of the Federal Bureau of Investigation. He was not directly implicated in the shooting but was considered a person of interest because of his political and religious beliefs and because he happened to leave the area just at the time the shots were fired.

The office where he was taken was just outside of the city and in a small industrial complex. Upon his arrival, he was placed into a small interrogation room that was about the size of a typical bathroom. The room was bare, and the only contents inside were a tiny table, three chairs, and a small clock set high upon on the wall.

Charles sat in the room for hours with nothing but the sound of the clock ticking in the background. It was as if they completely forgot that he was there. After about the third hour, Richard, accompanied by a special agent, entered the room, and finally broke the silence that was causing Charles great distress.

"Sorry about the wait, Charles. We were waiting on Special Agent Gillyard to arrive. He ran into a bit of traffic. I hope that you can understand," said Richard.

Agent Gillyard was quite similar in appearance to Richard. His attire was almost identical to Richard's, and he had a similar frame. He was so similar that he could easily be a body double if ever it was needed. He walked over to Charles and extended his hand. "It's nice to meet you, Charles. I'm Special Agent Gillyard, but you can call me Cecil."

Charles looked perturbed, like he hadn't slept in a week. He didn't bother standing up for the agent, and when he did take the agent's hand to shake it, it was halfhearted and insincere. It was almost as if he were shaking hands with a princess, as limp as his grip remained through the entire greeting. He rolled his eyes at the agent in disgust and shook his head in disapproval as he placed a large folder down onto the table.

"Great, another one of you robots. I take it that this is just another attempt at scaring me so that I'll be a good little boy and keep silent about the whole artificial intelligence-conspiracy thing. We have definitely played this game before," Charles said angrily.

Cecil sat down gently into the chair across from Charles. As he sat, he maintained complete eye contact with Charles as if he were generally interested his facial and other expressions. He remained silent but maintained a wry little smile as he continued to gaze at Charles.

Charles squirmed about in his chair. He was feeling a little uncomfortable after being seated for the past three-plus hours. The silence by both agents wasn't helping his anxiety any, and the sheepish grin from the agent served only to enhance his irritated mood.

"How about you give me your speech on how I should be more of a patriot and all the other garbage you guys usually spew and then release me. I'm quite tired of being in this room and am actually quite hungry, considering I was trying to enjoy a nice breakfast when you clowns came into where I was eating and interrupted it."

Cecil continued gazing at Charles and watching his expression of disgust.

Charles grew angrier amid the silence and reached over to the table and swiped at the folder, knocking it to the ground in anger.

Richard didn't budge. He remained standing next to the door as if he were guarding it, but he wasn't. He preferred standing.

Cecil just sat there staring as the folder fell to the ground. After a few moments of an awkward silence, he finally spoke. "I'm afraid that it's not that simple," he stated bluntly.

Charles lifted his head and looked at Cecil. His face said it all. He was tired and just ready to go home. He placed both his hands on his head, and he ran his fingers roughly through his hair, gently pulling on it as he shook his head.

"It is simple," said Charles. "You have no reason to hold me, and you have no reason to question me. I was outside that building when that scene took place, and by the time it was over, I was getting breakfast."

"Is that so?" asked Cecil.

"Yes, that's so," responded Charles sarcastically.

Cecil opened a small notebook and grabbed the pen that was tucked away inside. He pushed his chair back about a foot and leaned back as far as the chair would bend.

"What did you have for breakfast?" he asked.

"I hadn't got that far," said Charles.

"How long would you say that you were in the restaurant?"

Charles buried his face into his hands and began shaking his head. He then moved his hands back, through his hair and lifted his head upward again to look at Cecil.

"You're joking, right?" he asked.

"I assure you that I can find no humor in the death of a major public figure like Jared Hadad. Do you find it humorous?"

"I didn't kill anyone. I wasn't even inside that building. Check your cameras."

"If you did nothing, why did you flee to the diner?"

Charles was growing more frustrated by the second. He couldn't believe that he was being investigated by the FBI for an assassination. He sat there silently for a few moments, turning more and more red, until finally he could stand it no longer and burst out in anger.

"I know my rights. I don't have to say a word to you if I don't want to, and you have absolutely nothing to hold me for. If you want this to end badly, then just keep pushing me. I'll sue you for millions, and I'll take that money, and I'll become such a thorn into your side that you'll rue the day that you ever decided to accuse me."

Richard was still standing at the door, motionless. He didn't move in the slightest during Charles's angry outburst. His back was up against the wall, and his gaze straightforward, as if he were caught up in a daydream and oblivious to the happenings in the room. Charles knew Richard fairly well and knew that his demeanor was that of complete calm, but that didn't ease his tension, as he was still completely intimidated by his presence.

Charles walked up to Richard and stared at him in puzzlement. He waved his hands in front of his face to try to get a reaction from him, but he didn't budge in the least.

"There's something about you that just isn't normal. I haven't put my finger on it yet, but people just don't act like you do!" Charles screamed.

Charles paced the floor for a few moments and then moved back over to his chair and sat down. He paced his elbows on his knees and stared at the ground as he cradled the top of his head with his hands in frustration.

"Oh my goodness! That's it!" Charles belted out as if he had an epiphany.

This outburst seemed to intrigue Richard, so he moved away from the door and pulled up a seat in front of Charles. He leaned in toward Charles as he took off his glasses and stared directly at him, as if he were attempting to read his mind.

Charles looked up at him and could feel his piercing eyes. He quickly became uncomfortable as Richard let out the tiniest of smiles.

"So you've got it all figured out?" asked Richard.

"Look," said Charles in a much softer tone. "I'm tired, and I'm actually quite hungry. I was just about to order some breakfast before you goons came into that diner. If you are going to hold me, you at least have to get me something to eat. I'm a borderline diabetic."

Richard rose from his seat and motioned for Cecil to follow him into the hall. Cecil got up and opened the door, and the pair stepped outside, leaving Charles, looking defeated, and alone in the room. Again, feeling frustrated, Charles put his head back into his hands and stared down at the floor.

Cecil and Richard moved slightly away from the door so that Charles would not be able to hear them converse.

"We've got nothing on this man, Richard."

Richard thought about it for a moment and smiled back at Cecil. "I wouldn't say that," he replied softly.

Cecil, now looking nervous and perplexed, moved in closer to Richard. "Let's turn him loose and put a tracker on him," he said softly.

Richard's smile disappeared. "Why would we release him? This man was at the UN building around the time of the shooting, and he is obviously a religious fanatic who has made his hatred of Jared Hadad known for quite some time. This isn't the first time that he has showed up at Jared's events. Not to mention that moments after the shots were fired, he ended up in a diner just across from the UN."

Cecil shook his head.

"The man who shot Mr. Hadad wasn't even a white guy. He also had a beard. It couldn't have been this guy, and you know it."

Richard was taken aback. He didn't like that his authority was being questioned, and his calm demeanor was suddenly replaced with anger. "You don't get it, do you?" said a now angry and loud Richard. "That man is a threat." Richard took a step back and then began to compose himself. "Now you can assist me with this, or you can betray your nation and end up in the same boat as this terrorist. The choice is yours. One way or another, we are going to bring this man to justice for his crimes," he explained.

Cecil looked at Richard like he couldn't believe what he was asking. "We have laws in this country, Richard."

Richard smiled wryly. "The time is coming when your laws will mean nothing. Now you can end up on the right side of history, or you can join Charles. It's up to you."

Cecil was shocked. “What is that supposed to mean?” he asked, now growing more frustrated.

Richard didn’t respond.

Cecil looked at the door and then back at Richard. His first loyalty was to the FBI, and he was a true patriot, but he knew what was right and what was wrong. He began having an internal struggle with the ethical dilemma that he was now facing. From his point of view, he either had to make the conscious decision to try to railroad a man for a crime that he knew the man did not commit, or he could face a disciplinary hearing and potentially lose his career for being insubordinate.

Richard stood there silently as Cecil struggled with the choice he faced. He could clearly see that Cecil was not content with his options.

Cecil looked back at Richard with complete disgust. He finally came to a judgment, and he decided that he couldn’t be involved in bearing false witness over an innocent man. “I’ll have nothing to do with this,” he exclaimed. “It’s time to let this man go. If you want to put a tracker on him, I’ll agree to that, but I won’t go along with some half-baked plan to try to pin an assassination on him when he clearly did not commit the offense.” Cecil turned and began toward the door. He made up his mind, and his plan was to advise Charles that he could go. As soon as he took his first step, Richard placed his hand onto his shoulder, prompting him to stop.

“Are you sure that is what you want to do?” Richard asked loudly.

Cecil turned his head and looked back at him, confused. “What?”

Suddenly and without warning, an electrical shock traveled out of Richard’s hand and through Cecil. The shock wasn’t visible and didn’t make a sound. Cecil’s face turned a pale white, and he dropped to the floor.

Richard bent down over him and then looked up, looked toward the camera near the door. “We need a medic here immediately!” he shouted in an anguished and concerned tone.

Within a matter of minutes, a medical response squad showed up with a gurney and other medical supplies and started lifesaving measures on him.

The medic looked up at Richard as he started an IV on Cecil.

"What happened?" he asked.

Richard shrugged his shoulders and shook his head as if he didn't have a clue about what happened to Cecil.

"He turned white and pale and just hit the floor," Richard explained.

The medic reached up to his shoulder and grabbed the microphone for his radio.

"We have a possible cardiac arrest and are heading to Mercy North. Our ETA will be approximately ten minutes."

Richard watched intensely as the medics loaded Cecil onto the gurney.

"I hope he is going to be all right," he muttered.

The medic stood up as the other two who were with him raised the stretcher. He was visibly concerned for his patient and working as diligently as he could to get him out to his ambulance and on his way to the hospital. He pushed Richard gently out of his way, and the other two medics began pushing the stretcher down the hall toward the entrance.

"We will do our best, but a cardiac arrest isn't great. His odds aren't the best. We'll be taking him to Mercy North Hospital if you want to follow us there."

Richard patted the man on the shoulder as if to let him know that he knew his friend would be in good hands.

"I actually have a very dangerous suspect here, but I'll check up on him as soon as I can get out there. Please take good care of him," Richard explained.

Richard stood in the center of the hall and watched as the medical team exited the building. When they were out of site, he returned to the interrogation room where Charles remained.

Charles was placed under arrest for the assassination of Jared Hadad. He was transferred to Riker's Island, where he was told that he would await his trial date, which was set to occur in about a month. The FBI charged him with premeditated murder, terrorism, and conspiracy to commit an act of terrorism against the United States government and a foreign ally.

An autopsy on Jared's body was completed quickly, and it was confirmed that he died as a result of the gunshot through his right eye. He had other gunshot wounds to his right arm that caused some significant blood loss, but the gunshot to his head was the fatal shot that ended his life. His death occurred almost instantaneously, according to the medical examiner.

Funeral preparations were planned for Jared, as his body was flown to Vienna. He would lay in state in Vienna, to allow the Europeans to pay their respects, and then be transported back to the United Nations headquarters in New York, where he would lay in state for another twenty-four hours. His funeral would then be held in the general assembly meeting room at the UN headquarters, on the third day.

Since Jared was Jewish, there was some controversy about his body not being buried quickly. Jewish tradition prohibits the embalming of the body, so the funeral would have to occur as quickly as possible. Having his body lay in state for one day in Europe and one day at the headquarters in New York was a compromise between those who wanted him to be brought to Europe for three to four days and those who thought that the headquarters in New York was more appropriate. The United Nations building was chosen because it doesn't belong to any one nation but belongs to every nation.

Jared's achievements made him a revered icon throughout most of the world. He was catapulted to worldwide fame in his years as the prime minister of the New European Union and because he was able to accomplish the impossible and improbable feat of negotiating a lasting peace in the Middle East and Israel. He was almost solely responsible for the nearly three and a half years of peace in Israel and the rest of the Middle East. He was responsible for the disarming of most of the world from their long held nuclear arsenals and other weapons of mass destruction. He was responsible for ending food shortages and famine throughout Europe and the Middle East. He was also heavily involved in the work completed at I-Corp, which was instrumental in almost all his achievements.

CHAPTER 22
Rebirth of a Nation

Much of the world was in mourning over the death of Jared Hadad. The assassination of such a prominent political leader had people in a panic and in an uproar. The people wanted justice, and they wanted it to be swift. They were angry at the man who sat in Riker's Island, awaiting trial for the murder.

The public wasn't aware of the truth of Charles' innocence. They only knew what they were fed via the news outlets across the globe. The information on Charles poured out of television sets across the globe. The news reports painted a picture of a man who was intolerant and bent on bringing his brand of religion to all who would listen, no matter the cost. The media mutilated his reputation and censored any information that came out that went against their constructed narrative.

The world leaders that did interviews on television called for the trial to be held anywhere besides United States. They felt that Charles would be able to garner the support of the religious minority in the United States and escape justice. They called him "evil beyond all evil" and compared him to the likes of Mussolini and Hitler.

His face was circulated on every media station and everywhere on social media. He suddenly became more well-known than the largest stars of Hollywood. In only forty-eight hours since the assassination, they managed to paint him as public enemy number 1, everywhere in the world. They barely came up for air as they excoriated him relentlessly. Even the most tolerant people, who fought to end the death penalty, called for a quick execution. There was little in the way of mercy for the man who killed Jared Hadad.

The pictures on the television and social media were twisted into any and every angle possible that would make Charles appear to be a monster. And they didn't stop with Charles. They used it as an opportunity to attack Christianity. Several world leaders called for an end to Christianity, citing Charles's actions as an example of the fruits of the religion. It was so bad that most Christians kept silent and out of the sight of the public.

Cynthia was not one of those who kept silent. She was as vocal as one could be and was seemingly the only person who came to Charles's defense. She showed her bravery by protesting outside Riker's Island. She called the arrest of Charles "a travesty of justice" and "a dark day for the world." The media called her a coconspirator and continually asked why she was not also awaiting trial.

Just as the uproar came to a fever pitch, the people took a break from their sorrows to pay their respects to Jared Hadad. Those who were in New York City gathered around the United Nations headquarters, hoping to be admitted into the building to attend the funeral or to just catch a glimpse of his body at his funeral. Others watched from the comfort of their own homes, as the funeral was set to be broadcast across the globe.

The cities of the world resembled ghost towns. It was as if it were Christmas morning during a major pandemic. The streets were devoid of traffic, and not a soul was visible as the funeral was set to begin. Businesses shuttered their operations out of respect for the deceased and so that their employees could be home to watch the funeral. Never in history has any man been paid such an honor as to stop all commerce across the globe. It was as if the people of the world were all united for the very first time in human history.

The general assembly meeting room of the United Nations was packed. The 193 member nations each had their delegates present. The perimeter of the room was filled with to a standing-room-only condition. Chairs were brought in to fill the aisles as much as they could be filled while still allowing people to move in and out of the room. The normal capacity of the room was 1,800 people, but there were over 2,000 in attendance.

The front of the room where the rostrum was located had a towering gold wall, adorned with the United Nations emblem. The walls to the right and left were semicircular and made of a beautiful wood paneling. The towering gold wall in the center looked like an altar and shone brilliantly with the lighting in the room. There were two screens to the right of the UN emblem. The screens were currently displaying the lectern, in anticipation of the event to begin soon.

Jared's casket lay open in the front of the rostrum. He was dressed in a dark-navy-blue suit with an aquamarine tie. His hands were folded neatly at his pelvis. He looked like he was sleeping, but his body was motionless and at peace. Anyone who did not know that he was deceased would have thought that he was simply sleeping at the center of the room.

The crowd was surprisingly quiet as they packed inside the room. The ushers helped the dignitaries to their seats; the media personnel were busy preparing their equipment, and the people squeezed themselves into whatever available space they could find outside the marked walking path.

Suddenly and without warning, the silence was disrupted by a loud screech of the microphone. The crowd stopped in their tracks, and all placed their gazes toward the lectern, where an unknown man was speaking the words *test...test* into the mic.

The man called out, "Will everyone please take your seats?"

The crowd moved carefully but rather slowly to their seats or other assigned areas and, after a few moments of organized chaos, were finally in place and anxiously awaiting the event to proceed.

The man at the microphone proceeded.

"Today we pay respect to a great man—a man who was taken from the world violently and without cause. While he lays here in this hall, the man who is responsible for this heinous crime sits in relative comfort."

The speaker was a bit heated, and his anger clearly came through in his delivery of the words. As he spoke, the crowd was stirred to anger. The once peaceful room took on an entirely new feel. What was a roomful of sorrow was now a rallying cry for retribution.

"I'm sorry, folks," the man said in a softer tone. "I let my emotions get the better of me." The man paused for a moment and then took out a handkerchief from his pocket. He wiped the cloth near his eyes and then placed it back into his pocket. "I've known Jared for a number of years, and as a good friend of his, I can say that I am sure that he would be pleased to know that those of you who are here and those of you who are watching came to say goodbye." The man paused in and took out his kerchief again. This time, he wiped the sweat that was beading up from his forehead. "I had the honor of working with Jared right out of college. He was gracious enough to hire me on as a senior programmer at I-Corp many moons ago. While my work was important, it was nothing compared to the work he completed." He placed the handkerchief back into his pocket and then took a sip of water from a small glass that was set next to the lectern. "Some of you know me. Some of you don't, and that's all right. But for those of you who don't know, my name is Peter Jensen. I am the chief executive officer at that little company that Jared founded so many years ago."

Peter was becoming more visibly upset, the longer that he stood there. He didn't particularly like public-speaking events, and the energy he received from his bout of anger was now starting to fade. His insecurities were starting to bubble to the surface.

"Normally, I ask my wife, Leah, to help me with my speeches. I didn't this time. I guess I should have asked her for help on this one too." He laughed.

Leah was sitting in the front row and was smiling back at him, obviously pleased to have been recognized by her husband.

"All that I can say is that the world sure did lose a brilliant man. His life was cut short by some ideological fool. That same man, by the way, has killed before."

The audience let out an audible yelp.

"Yes!" he shouted. "Believe it or not, that monster used to be a police officer. You probably already know what caused him to lose his job, but I digress."

The audience chatter grew louder.

One man in the back yelled as loudly as he could, "Execute him now!"

Peter was now very visibly shaken. His face was flushed, and he was sweating profusely. He removed the handkerchief from his pocket again and wiped off his forehead. "Jared!" he cried out in an anguished tone. "You have been a very good friend, and I will miss you, as will the rest of the world." Peter put the microphone into the cradle and stepped down off the steps of the stage. He quietly walked over to the open casket and placed his right hand onto Jared's hands.

The audience remained silent during this moment, and he walked to where Leah was seated. He then sat down and began sobbing into both his hands as he slouched toward the floor.

The American president was the next to speak. She gave the crowd some words of encouragement and vowed to assist in getting justice for Jared, but her speech remained quite short. For her, it was more of a formality as she and Jared were not on the best of terms with each other ever since his running for office as prime minister. The two had always been cordial with each other, but she said some unflattering things to the press when he made his run, which upset him at the time. Her advisers told her to keep it short and to the point as to avoid digging up the uncomfortable nature of their relationship.

After a handful of other speakers, it was time for the benediction by Pope Liberius. The pope and Jared were good friends. Jared rarely made a big political move without the pope being at least partially involved. Jared knew that the people would trust him more if he had a trustworthy counselor, so his choice, early in his political career, was Pope Liberius.

Pope Liberius stood at the podium with a look of solace. "Benedicite deum, ut populus terrae," said the pope.

A translator with a second microphone spoke immediately after the pope. "May God bless the entire world," he said.

The pope was able to speak a very broken English, but often preferred to speak in Latin. The translator was brought in so that the pope could speak whichever language he preferred.

"Hodie nos dicere vale ad magnus vir," said the pope loudly and with great passion.

"Today we say goodbye to a great man," the translator repeated.

The pope was wearing his traditional white robes and had a large gold cross around his neck. He had his hands clasped tightly to the right and left sides of the lectern. Those who were near the front could see a hint that he was angry because his fingers were white due to the tight grip he had on the lectern. The others in the audience and on the television saw a somewhat different man. To those at a distance, he just looked like a frail elderly man, who spoke softly but with a fiery passion.

He began to speak in English.

"God has a time and a purpose for everything, and this includes death. While death is not a good thing or even a convenient thing, it does serve a purpose."

The pope loosened his grip from the lectern, and his fingers turned a bright pink. His anger eased, and his tone went from passionate and loud to very soft spoken. His English wasn't perfect, but the people seemed to understand what he was saying.

"God allows us to die, which is really a blessing. If we did not die, we would be doomed to live forever in a fallen state. By allowing us to die, we are essentially paroled from a life where we are separated from our creator. It is out of love, that God takes us out of this world. While it may be on his timetable and for his purpose, we can be sure that he has his reasons. We must have faith that he does what is right and what is good in all things."

The crowd remained completely silent. The pope's words didn't have much of an impact on them because most of the people in the crowd didn't associate with any religion. The religious landscape changed over the years, and most people in the world today could be fit into one of a few groups. There were those who were atheist and who claimed not to believe in anything, those who followed the new *oneness* religion led by the pope and others who remained faithful to the Bible.

The largest of the current groups in the world is the atheists. They claim not be followers of a religion and claim not to have faith in anything, but it is evident that they truly are followers of a religion after all. They are simply deniers of their own religious faith, which is primarily science. Their faith lies in the natural world and evolution.

Atheism rose to become the dominant religion after years of the government teaching evolutionary science along with an old-earth theory in public schools. The teaching by the public-school system created a generation of people who doubted the accuracy of the Bible and, with that doubt, came a massive falling away from religion in general. Rather than putting their faith in the Word of God, the people put their faith in science.

The "new science" of the day claims that the Bible is false because the earth was believed to have been created billions of years before the first man. The atheists believe this to show that the Bible could not be true if this was the case, so they say that death existed before the so-called "fall of man," which "clearly shows that the book of Genesis was completely false."

Christians like Charles argue that the earth is young, but it is not enough to convince the masses.

The new *oneness* religion, led by the pope, arose out of the ecumenical movement that started to really take off in the early 2020s. The movement was around for years but really gained momentum after a series of pandemics struck the world and caused people to start looking for answers to the plagues by looking at both science and religion.

The movement was a merger of the world's most prominent religions, including Islam, Christianity, Hinduism, and others. It was said that all the major religions really had more in common than they had in disagreement. Their claim at the beginning was that the only real difference between all the world's religions was that the different groups all had different names for the same god. After a series of interfaith meetings between leaders from the major religions, the *oneness* religion was born, and temples started going up around the globe. It didn't take long for the new religion to gain followers because the religion focused on social justice, equity, and the so-called right to health care, which really was just another way of saying abortion.

The message to the new followers was simple. They were told that one earns salvation through balancing out the bad with doing good works and that, at the end, if one could show that he or she did enough good in life, he or she would "earn" their way into heaven.

The new oneness religion drew away large numbers of Christians. It was estimated that the Christian population around the globe went from about 2.2 billion to less than 60 million today.

Those who remain in the Christian faith are viewed as homophobic, xenophobic, anti-Catholic and anti-Muslim. Christians are now called zealots, Zionists, and a host of other names that paint them as religious extremists. They are seen similarly as those who followed Isis, prior to their eradication in the mid-2020s.

As the pope spoke, many in the audience were on their cell phones. Some were texting friends while others were getting the best angle that they could to capture the moment in a selfie. Religion, no matter the brand, was just not the most important thing to them.

Had Charles not been arrested, it would have been a sure bet that he would have made himself present for this event. He would have stood outside giving his opinion on the true spiritual meaning of things.

Charles railed against the pope on several occasions in the past. He felt that the pope was leading people down an alternate path to God that just was not scripturally based. He would admit that the pope often said some profound things that were true but then would argue that truth could be manipulated for evil if the truth were mixed with deceptions. Aside from the dangers of artificial intelligence, his favorite topics were exposing evolution as junk science, creationism, and a young earth. These were the truths that concerned him.

The pope often spoke of goodness and atonement. He preached a message of salvation through works. He was once quoted as saying, "Et hoc oro ut noster bona opera faciunt contributions ut conditio hominum in nobis debita nostra. Venite omnes unum diem sto ante Deum et poterit dicere, quod hic certe nihil uberius, quam mihi peccata mea benefactis." This means, "We pray that our good works and contributions to the human condition make up for our trespasses. Let us all one day stand before God and be able to say that my good deeds are surely more plentiful than my sins."

The pope became the most popular religious figure of the day. He spoke with a fiery passion and as if with great authority. He was ultimately able to unite the world's religions by explaining that all people essentially worship the same God, even if he is called by several different names. He called God "purely inclusive" and a lover of all sinners, no matter what their sexual orientation and no matter how they lived, "so long as their good deeds outweighed their bad, in the end."

Pope Liberius continued to speak for nearly another half hour before finally asking for the people to pray along with him. He moved away from the podium and around to the casket that remained open. He stared silently into the casket where Jared lay motionless and serene. His hands were draped one across the other at his waistline. He could be seen moving his lips and whispering something, but the microphone was too far away to catch what he was saying.

The crowd waited in relative silence as they waited for the pope to resume talking, but he remained at the side of the casket, whispering in Latin. After a few minutes and after the crowd started murmuring in their lack of patience, he suddenly started speaking more loudly. His whispers turned to normal speech and then moved rapidly to yelling loudly and with great authority. He threw both his arms into the air and looked toward the ceiling. His words now ferocious and so loud that the crowd could do nothing but listen as each word poured from his mouth.

"In nomine dei: ego præcipio vobis ante lucem surgere," he yelled at the top of his lungs.

The crowd was mesmerized. The translator was so vexed by what he heard that he stood there with his mouth wide open. It appeared, to him, that the pope had completely lost his mind.

The pope slumped over and fell to his knees. Two nearby security officials rushed as quickly as they could to help him get up. They thought his yelling might be a medical emergency and were genuinely concerned for his being.

The crowd was dead silent, and their eyes strongly affixed to the pope who was still on his knees with his hands half raised toward the ceiling.

"What did he say?" came a voice from the crowd.

The voice from the crowd was like a spark and ignited the energy of the crowd. They began to chant in unison.

"What did he say? What did he say? What did he say?" they chanted in unison.

The pope got back up on his feet and motioned for the security guards to move away from him. The crowd became silent again, hoping to hear him speak again and still wondering what it was that he yelled just before slumping over.

He turned back toward the casket and placed his hands onto Jared's hands. Once again, he looked up to the ceiling.

"Surgere et ambulare," he said.

The translator couldn't believe what he heard and looked terrified.

The crowd began to chant again.

"What did he say? What did he say?"

The translator turned toward the crowd. His face was white, and he had a look of terror about him.

"He said"—the translator paused for a moment—"he said, 'Get up and walk.'"

The crowd gasped. *Why would the pope say something like that?* they thought.

"Did the pope lose his mind or perhaps have a stroke?" Someone was heard saying.

The pope started to pull upward on Jared's hands.

"Surgere et ambulare," said the pope a second time.

The crowd was stunned. Most of the people were in sheer disbelief of what they were witnessing and thought that the pope lost his mind. The thought that he was trying to raise a dead man to life was as insane as insane could get. Others in the room started pushing through the crowd to escape what they were witnessing, and they wanted no part in what was happening.

The pope continued to pull Jared upward, out of the casket. To those in the audience, he must have appeared to be incredibly strong because from their point of view, an elderly and frail man was lifting up a large man out of a casket with relative ease.

The pope continued to chant and to pull on Jared's lifeless body.

Suddenly, and without warning. Jared's body lurched forward as the pope yanked him forward with the might of five men.

Shrieks and screams of terror exploded from the crowd as they witnessed what was seemingly impossible.

"He's alive!" screamed a woman toward the front.

"It's the power of God!" yelled another.

The chamber exploded with people screaming and shrieking out of pure terror. It was so loud that the walls of the chamber began to vibrate.

The terrified crowd panicked; people rushed to the doors in an attempt to escape. They couldn't believe what they just witnessed. They saw a lifeless body raised out of a casket and back to life, as if he were merely sleeping and suddenly aroused by the shouting of a frail old man.

"People are raising from the dead everywhere!" screamed a man in the rear.

"It's all over the news!" yelled another woman toward the front. "It's really happening. This must be the apocalypse!"

A voice came over the loudspeakers.

"Ladies and gentlemen," the voice said in an authoritative tone, "remain calm and please make your way to the exit doors in an orderly fashion."

The directions came too late. The room was now half full with most of the people wedged up against one another, clamoring to escape.

CHAPTER 23

The Trial

Charles sat on the edge of his bed flipping through the short list of channels available to him in his prison cell. He was trying to find anything he could on the disappearance that occurred as well as the rumors of Jared's resurrection.

Earlier in the day, he personally witnessed two fellow inmates seemingly disappear as he was playing a card game with them. It happened in a matter of seconds. He bent down to pick up a card that he dropped on the floor, and upon emerging from the underside of the table, with the card in his hand, they were gone. Not realizing what had happened, he got up from the table and began searching for them, only to find that they were not the only two that had vanished.

Only seconds after the disappearance of his cellmates, the alarms in the cellblock began blaring, and both prisoners and guards became frantic and were darting around the cellblock area. The prison went on immediate lockdown, and Charles was escorted back to his cell. When he asked the guard what was happening, he was only told that a handful of prisoners disappeared, and a search was underway to locate them. He later overheard two of the guards discussing some "strange worldwide event" and decided that his best hope was to sift through the television channels to see if he could catch a glimpse of what was occurring.

The news coverage he was able to get was spotty at best and didn't provide much in the way of helpful information. There seemed to be a lot of confusion on what happened, and most of the news channels showed different video of cars crashing and explosions from airplanes that crashed during the event. None of the videos showed any people disappearing. There were hundreds of different security camera videos that were played but not one showed an actual person disappearing. There was no news video available on the mysterious events with Jared and his rising from the dead. The media only reported that Jared was at a local hospital, and his condition was listed as "fair."

The infirmary was packed with inmates that were sure that they were suffering from mental problems and demanding medication to soothe their anxieties. They made similar claims that they were doing their normal day-to-day activities when people suddenly disappeared from their sight. One inmate claimed that he felt like he was on a science-fiction program, and that it appeared that his cellmate phased in and out of the cell for a few seconds before eventually being completely gone.

The guards who were working the segregated housing unit stated that they witnessed an inmate disappear from his restraints and that a search of the entire unit came up completely empty. They reviewed the security footage for the unit and could clearly see the inmate being escorted into his cell, where the door remained closed during the entire timeframe of the event. The footage showed three guards enter the cell over a period of four hours, and only two of the guards ever emerged. The interior of the cell did not have a camera. The cell had only one door and no windows. The only opening in the room was for a four-inch duct that allowed air-conditioning for the cell.

Charles was tired of flipping through the news channels, and after watching the news reports for hours, he was more confused than ever. He turned off his television and laid down on his bed and just stared at the ceiling, deep in thought.

He knew something out of the ordinary had occurred but had no idea what it could have been. Being a religious man, he knew quite well that Scripture described an event to occur such as this event, but since he was still in his cell and not meeting the Lord Jesus in the clouds, then it must be something other than the rapture of the church. Since he was in jail, he could not call Cynthia to see if she is all right, and he couldn't call anyone else from his congregation.

Charles sat up suddenly as he could hear the sound of keys jingling just outside his door.

"Opening twenty-two." He heard the guard call into his radio.

The door to the cell swung open. Two guards stood at the door. Charles recognized one of the guards but not the other. The guard whom he knew was Floyd Weathers. He was a man of about forty-eight years old and with a stocky build. Charles liked Floyd because the two would often talk about Scripture, and he treated Charles like a friend rather than a prisoner.

Floyd called himself a searching agnostic" and said that he knew that there was probably a higher power out there but that he hadn't found it yet. Charles spoke with him about the gospel on occasion, and when he did, Floyd would ask a lot of questions, but he said that he couldn't follow Christianity because he couldn't believe in a religion where "a loving God would call pain, suffering, and death very good." Charles explained to Floyd that he was confused about the book of Genesis and that it was not God who caused pain and suffering. He explained that when the earth was first created that it was perfect and that after finishing the creation and forming Adam and Eve in their perfect state, that this was what God referred to as "very good." He also told him how the sin of Adam and Eve was the cause of the world's pain and suffering. He then explained that allowing Adam and Eve to die was an act of mercy because God knew that a fallen world would not be good for Adam and Eve.

Charles spent hours talking to Floyd about sin and forgiveness of sins, but every time he thought that he was getting through to him, he would throw out another atheist talking point. It was as if Floyd and other atheists had their own church, where they studied a certain set of talking points to make Christianity look bad. Floyd talked about how he believed that God allowed slavery, and he said that he couldn't believe in a God that would allow slavery.

Charles would rebut every false claim that Floyd made, but whenever he did, it was as if he were talking to a rock. With the slavery issue, Charles explained the difference between slavery and indentured servitude and how it was really indentured servitude that Scripture talked about, and that God abhorred kidnapping, which according to Scripture was punishable by death. He explained to him how in the Old Testament days that people would be thrown into prison for their debts and sometimes they were even killed over their debts and that indentured servitude was when a man or a woman would become a servant to their debtor to repay their debt.

Floyd seemingly did not want to understand that the Bible was written thousands of years ago, and that the language of the day was not exactly the same as in the present time. He simply didn't care that while the Bible uses the word *slavery*, that it was not really talking about the type of slavery that people of the twenty-first century were accustomed to hearing about. The modern equivalent from a twenty-first century equivalent would really be more along the lines of *indentured servitude*.

Charles stood up as the pair entered his cell. "Where are we going?" he asked.

Floyd pulled out his handcuffs and motioned for Charles to turn around. "The warden asked to see you."

Charles turned his head around and looked at the guard as if he were confused. "Why would the warden want to see me?" he asked.

"She didn't really say, but my guess would be that she has some questions about what happened here a few hours ago."

"I already told you. I don't know what happened to James. We were playing cards with John Dalton, and when I bent down to pick up a card from the floor, he vanished before I even had time to raise myself back up from under the table. I came back to our cell, and he wasn't here, so I just stayed in here because the alarms were going off everywhere, and we were told that the prison was going on lockdown," Charles explained.

"I don't think she wants to talk about James. I think she wants to talk about mystical Bible things."

"Oh," said Charles. "Well, that would be all right, I guess."

The second guard laughed out loud. "I guess she wants to see you so she can feel good about the fact that millions of Christians suddenly fell off the face of the Earth."

Charles looked befuddled. "Christians?"

"Oh"—he paused for a moment—"you don't know, do you?" He started laughing again. "It's like sweet justice!" he exclaimed.

Floyd turned toward his partner, confused. "What do you mean?" he asked.

"Mr. High and Mighty didn't catch his ride with the alien spacecraft or whatever it was that beamed up all those whackos."

Charles was not amused. "I think you are referring to those heaven's-gate people, and they hitched a ride on hale bop."

"Whatever," said the guard. "All of you fanatics are looking for a fairy tale that doesn't exist anyway. You're still here, so you are either not a particularly good fanatic, or you were wrong about the great rappel!"

Floyd looked confused at first because he had no idea what the "great rappel" was. After thinking about his past conversations with Charles, he suddenly realized that the word his partner was really trying to relay was *rapture*.

"Not *rappel*, you moron. That's the Army. The word you are looking for is *rapture*," said Floyd enthusiastically.

Floyd's partner seemed a bit perturbed that he was corrected in front of an inmate, but he quickly shrugged it off, knowing that the warden was waiting to speak with Charles.

Floyd seemed pleased with himself that he learned something from his previous conversations with Charles. His newfound knowledge on the subject made him feel a bit more superior than his partner, and it was evident by the swagger that was clearly visible as they marched Charles down the hall to speak with the warden.

They reached the end of the hall and positioned Charles on a line that was painted onto the floor.

"You two wait here, and I'll see if Warden Kwiatkowski is ready for you."

Floyd turned to Charles. "I think I can take those cuffs off now. Turn around." As Floyd was taking off the cuffs, Charles took the opportunity to see if he could glean some information about the current events in the prison and around the rest of the world.

"What happened at the United Nations building?" he asked.

"Your guess is as good as mine. The pope was there with about two thousand dignitaries, and suddenly, that Hadad guy sat up in his coffin. Some people said that he wasn't embalmed, so it was probably like that guy on outrageous stories."

"Outrageous stories?" asked Charles.

"Yeah, that show about outrageous stuff caught on camera."

Charles smiled. "I guess I missed that one."

"Nah, you didn't miss anything. That show was horrible and staged. They had an episode where a guy was put into the morgue fridge, and the guy slid his drawer open and walked right up to the cleaning person and scared the crap out of her, scared her so bad that I think she ended up in that drawer."

Charles laughed loudly. "I needed a good laugh, but seriously, what happened at the United Nations building? Did Jared Hadad really get up out of his casket?"

Floyd scanned the area to see if anyone was looking. When he saw that it was still just himself and Charles, he responded, "It's weird. I am no spiritual man, but anyone who can come back from the dead like that has to be incredibly special. The Vatican released a statement saying that the rebirth of Jared Hadad was nothing less than a miracle and a sign from God. Folks are calling him the Messiah, whatever that means."

Charles looked like he had seen a ghost. He knew that what he was hearing was impossible. Jared Hadad was just a man, and there was nothing special about him other than his abilities as a leader. He paused in a moment of intense thought. *Could I have been wrong this whole time? Did I miss something when reading the Bible?* His mind was racing as he tried to recall Scripture.

"We are living in some strange times," said Floyd.

The door to the warden's office squealed as it swung open. Floyd's partner stepped into the doorway and motioned for Charles and Floyd to enter.

The warden got up from her chair and walked over to Charles as he emerged through the doorway. She stretched out her arm to shake his hand as if the two were old friends who hadn't seen each other for years.

"My name is Sharon Kwiatkowski. I'm the warden here at Riker's. I hope your stay has been uneventful?" she asked.

Charles smiled back as if he completely forgot that he was in a prison for a crime he knew he did not commit.

"If by uneventful you mean free of injury, yes, but I think we all know that it hasn't been uneventful."

"Great!" she said as she sat down in her chair.

"Floyd, you can wait outside if you don't mind."

"Yes, ma'am," said Floyd. "I'll just be right outside if you need me."

"Thank you, Floyd. I don't think I'm in any danger with this one."

Charles watched as Floyd left the office. He then turned back toward the warden, who was rocking back and forth in her office chair.

"He's a good man. I wish I had twenty more just like him," she said casually. "I'll bet you're wondering why I brought you here. I'll just get straight to the point."

Charles interrupted her as she was beginning to tell him why she asked to see him. "If this is about what happened, then I'm afraid that I won't be of much use to you. I'm just as in the dark as you are."

Sharon watched Charles's every move. She was trying to size him up. She leaned forward toward him and spoke softly so that she wouldn't be overheard. "That's not why I brought you here, but to be fair, I was going to ask you about that. I guess if you aren't aware of what happened, then you aren't aware." She stood up and walked to the front of her desk and sat on the edge. "No, I have different news for you, and I thought that you might want to know from me rather than hearing it on the television.

"What news?"

She looked at her thumb and noticed a hangnail on her left thumb. She put her thumb up to her mouth and used her teeth to pull out the hangnail. Charles looked at her with a look of disgust.

"I hate hangnails. They are hard to get rid of, and when you do finally get them out, they cause a heck of a lot of pain. They are like splinters in a sense—very tiny but painful little suckers."

Charles looked perplexed. He didn't understand what she was getting around to saying. He watched intensely as she continued to inspect her thumb to make sure that she had gotten the entire nail out.

"I have to deliver you to the United Nations."

"What does that mean?" asked Charles.

"In a nutshell?" she asked. "Well, it means that you are going to be tried in an international court."

"Tried for what?" he bellowed.

She moved back to her chair and sat down. She picked up a pen and started to write onto a small notepad on the desk. Once she finished writing, she ripped out the piece of paper and folded it in half.

"They are charging you for the assassination of Jared Hadad."

"I didn't assassinate anyone!" exclaimed Charles. "Besides, he's not dead. If there's no body, then there's no crime."

The warden smiled. "That's why I like you, Charles. You have a quick wit. You're a pretty intelligent guy. I'm sure you can figure out what this is really about."

Charles looked confused. "What am I missing here?" he asked.

"Do you think that they really want to try you for murder or attempted murder?"

"Well, that's what you just sai," Charles retorted.

"Think, Charles," she said with emphasis. "What else might they want with you?"

Charles still had no idea what the warden was talking about. He was confused, and the warden's game was not helping with his confusion.

"They plan on making an example of you. They plan to execute you publicly, without ever holding a trial."

Charles looked stunned. "They can't do that. There is something called the US Constitution in this country."

"I like you, Charles, and I don't want to see you hurt. You've already lost quite a bit, and it's going to be a few years before you see Cynthia again."

"What do you mean?" asked Charles. "Where's Cynthia?"

"You know," she replied. "She left with all the other Christians."

"Can we stop the games? I really have had a long couple of weeks, and I really can't take any more of these mind games."

Sharon smiled wryly. "Charles, sometimes things aren't what they appear to be. Surely you know that. Take me for example. You see a warden. What if I told you that I've only been the warden here for a month?"

"And?" he asked. "What does that mean? Do you want me to congratulate you?"

Sharon smiled. "I was hired here after an acquaintance of yours recommended me for the position. He seemed to know that you were coming here."

"A lot of people knew I was coming here. Who was it exactly?"

"Sure, people knew you were coming here, but they didn't know it two years ago."

Charles looked more confused than ever. *What is she talking about?* he wondered. *How can anyone know that I am going to be at Riker's Island two years before it happens?*

"That's simply not possible," said Charles. "How could anyone possibly know that?"

Sharon smiled again. "Do you remember a fellow named Eli?"

Charles lit up like he drank a quadruple shot of espresso. "How do you know Eli?"

She got up from her chair again and moved back to the front of her desk. She leaned in toward Charles and whispered softly, "He visited me a couple months ago at my church. He told me that he had a job for me and that it involves you."

"That's just not possible!" exclaimed Charles. "None of this is possible. I have to be caught in some kind of weird dream or a nightmare!"

"This is no dream, Charles," she whispered. "Eli is not just some average man, and his friend is no average man either. As a matter of fact, both of them are so far outside of average that you might say that they aren't even of this world."

"What?" asked Charles emphatically. "How can they not be from this world? They certainly weren't aliens. At least, I don't think they were."

"Come on, Charles. It's on the tip of your tongue, and it has been for a while now. You know exactly who Eli is."

"I've pondered it a few times. Are you telling me that he is who I think he is?"

Sharon smiled again. Charles finally seemed to be coming around. "Yes," she said pointedly.

"How is that possible? Elijah died thousands of years ago."

"Charles, you have to stop thinking like an atheist and start looking around at everything that's going on around you. It's pretty clear what just happened."

"Not to me, it's not. If the rapture really just happened, then I was left behind just like that guard said."

"What guard?" she asked.

Charles suddenly remembered that Sharon wasn't privy to the conversation he had with Floyd and the other guard on the way to her office.

"Never mind," said Charles. "So why am I still here?"

"I could ask the same thing, Charles. Just like you, I am a Christian, and I am still here. The difference though is that Eli told me that this was going to happen. He told me that Christians around the world would be taken and that I would be left behind. He also told me that I'd be going to work as the warden of Riker's Island, and like you, I really struggled with the idea that any of this was possible. It wasn't until I witnessed a few things come to pass that he told me that I really started to believe what he told me. I've been in awe every day since last seeing him. It's like the feeling of déjà vu but better."

"Well, I didn't seem to get that memo," said Charles. "It would have been nice if someone told me."

Sharon stood up and motioned for Charles to stand. "Stand up," she said as she walked toward him.

Charles stood up, and Sharon stepped in closer and took hold of his hands, passing him the note she wrote minutes earlier.

"Sometimes things happen for a reason, and we don't know why until it's time to do what we were called to do. Think about it this way. If you knew that you'd be here in this jail and that you were going to be tried for the assassination of a politician, would you have still gone to the United Nations building and protested as you did?"

"I understand what you are saying, and that is a nice way to look at things, I guess, but all this is just a bit hard to accept."

Sharon let go of Charles's hands and turned toward the window on the office door. Floyd was still standing outside, patiently waiting on Charles to exit so that he could return him to his cell.

Charles looked at Sharon intensely for a moment.

"If Eli is really Elijah, then is his traveling companion someone named Moses? The thing is, that Eli never said who his friend was. He just said that he was here looking for his friend."

"Now you are using that brain that God gave you. I knew you would come around. Do you know why they are here?"

Charles knew almost immediately what they were here for if they were the two witnesses. He read the Bible passages regarding the two witnesses on more occasions that he could count. The Scripture doesn't reveal who the witnesses are but based on the descriptions given, he opined that they must be people who have been to heaven and who can attest to the things they have seen.

"So what's next?" asked Charles. "What is this job that I'm supposed to do?"

"Eli will tell you that when he finds you."

"How am I supposed to do anything if I'm stuck here in this jail? How am I supposed to do anything if you are supposed to turn me over to the United Nations to be executed?"

Sharon opened her desk drawer and reached inside. She pulled out a small plastic card with a visible chip on the right side. It looked like a credit card in shape and size, but it was completely white except for the brass-colored chip.

"You won't be going to the United Nations. This pass will allow you to temporarily leave the jail. It's your get-out-of-jail free card, so to speak. It's basically a pass to allow you to see an outside physician. You will leave here with Floyd, under the pretense of seeing an outside physician, and he will take you to an apartment across town. You'll wait there for about a month, and then you'll travel down to Florida to board a ship that will take you to Grand Cayman. From there, you'll head back to Israel, via plane and meet up with your friend Chris."

"Chris is in Israel?" asked Charles.

"Not yet, but he will be in a little over a month. Your job right now is to stay low and out of sight. Floyd will be assisting you at the apartment with things like food and others. He's working with me, and you can trust him."

"This is so cloak-and-dagger," said Charles with a laugh.

"The way Eli explained it to me, you and Chris will be helping a group of Jewish people somewhere in Jordan. They will need help in getting out of Jerusalem and into Jordan, very soon. I really don't know more than that."

"What does that mean soon?" asked Charles.

"That I can't tell you. I'm just repeating the little that was explained to me. You'll have to wait until you see Eli, I guess."

"What will happen to you?" asked Charles.

"I don't know. I'm sure that I'll be fine. I'll just focus on the same Scripture I wrote on that small piece of paper I gave to you. It seemed appropriate when I read it this morning, and I'm sure that you'll agree that it is also appropriate for your situation. You just get to that apartment and stay low until the time is right. They will stop looking for you after a few weeks and then you can head down to Florida and on to Jerusalem. The great news is that there will be no trial, and you will be getting out of this dreadful place!"

Charles opened the note that Sharon passed him earlier and read it, "Revelation 14:12–13, Here is a call for the endurance of the saints, those who keep the commandments of God and their faith in Jesus. And I heard a voice from heaven saying, Write this, Blessed are the dead who die in the Lord from now on. Blessed indeed, says the Spirit, that they may rest from their labors, for their deeds follow them!"

Charles hugged Sharon. "Thank you so much!"

Sharon smiled. "You're welcome. I'll see you when this is all over!"

"Amen!" said Charles.

CHAPTER 24
Antithesis

Charles waited in the apartment as he was instructed, and in that time, he caught up with all the latest news. For a while, his name showed up several times a day. There was a search for him at the prison, but the search left no clues as to his whereabouts. The cameras that picked up his activity in the jail were wiped clean, and it was eventually assumed that he disappeared with the other 60 million Christians around the globe.

He traveled to the Cayman Islands on a yacht, rented by a friend of Sharon Kwiatkowski. The yacht arrived in Grand Cayman a week after leaving Key West. From there, he took a private plane from Grand Cayman to Jerusalem, to avoid his name showing up on flight manifests in the US.

Charles quickly found that he was not the only one who was left behind when the rapture occurred. There was a small network of people around the globe that was left behind, and each one of them had one thing in common. They all met Elijah prior to the rapture. He spent the last three and a half years seeking out people like Charles, Chris, and Sharon so that they would be in place for the time to come.

*****

Jared Hadad made a full recovery after his resurrection and, within weeks, began to make sweeping changes at the United Nations. The changes were so profound that the United Nations quickly became the largest power in the world.

He was able to bring the world together in the aftermath of the disappearances because fear spread across the globe like wildfire. With the fate of the world up in the air, Jared quickly was viewed as a savior of those who were left behind. He promised the people a new world that would be free of famines, pestilence, and just about every other problem that plagued the world. After seeing him literally rise from the dead, they believed he would be able to make the impossible, possible.

The temple in Jerusalem was nearly completed. One last stone was all that remained to be placed for the temple to be complete, and Jared was asked to come to Jerusalem along with Pope Liberius to set the stone in place and celebrate the completion of the rebuilding of the temple. Pope Liberius was invited to give a blessing along with the temple priests, prior to the first sacrifice in over two and a half millenniums. The eyes of the world were once again on Jerusalem.

The temple was called the eighth wonder of the world. It was a re-creation of Herod's temple, except that the court of Gentiles was widened outward from the beautiful gate and Solomon's porch. Everything was in place, and the ark was moved to its final resting place.

Jared would be giving his speech from inside the temple, with the altar of incense and the veil given high visibility. There would only be three cameras allowed inside the temple, and the Sanhedrin advised that the cameras would only be allowed into the temple on this one occasion.

It was a hot summer day, so the area had emergency personnel on hand for miles, surrounding the perimeter of the temple. There were tents set up all over the city, with vendors selling everything from small ark replicas to T-shirts adorned with pictures of the temple.

It was a jubilant day in Jerusalem and a long time coming; people flocked there from around the globe. There were millions who journeyed there from every corner of the earth, and it appeared as if the entire population of Israel was there. Everyone wanted to see history being made by the completion of the temple.

The inner areas of the temple complex were reserved for only people of Jewish descent. Anyone who was not Jewish would have to stand outside the temple unless they were a specially invited dignitary or head of state for those countries in the United Nations. Some of the more prominent dignitaries who were invited were Adam Lefler, Peter Jensen, Parizad Madani, Ujab Aalim Baqri, and Pope Liberius II. They were invited because of their roles in bringing peace to Israel.

Jared arrived at the temple with Adam Lefler at about four in the afternoon. They were accompanied by a large security detail, and Richard was there as usual. The security detail was comprised of twenty armed men. Their firearms were not visible, as Jared and Adam didn't want people to get the wrong impression by putting twenty heavily armed men on prominent display at a temple. The public probably would understand the need for the heavily armed security after seeing the assassination that occurred in New York, but Jared said that he didn't want images of armed men inside the temple being passed along the internet for the next thousand years.

Jared and his entourage entered the complex at the Susa gate. The inner courtyards were relatively empty except for some media personnel who were allowed to enter early and set up their cameras and lighting equipment.

"Mr. Hadad!"

Jared stopped briefly upon entering the temple complex, to speak with the press and found American journalist Jill Royce eagerly waiting to greet him. Jill was allowed special privileges in covering the event since she was friends with Peter Jensen. She arrived about an hour before Jared and had her equipment set up before every other news outlet.

"Hello, Jared," she said with a smile. "I'm Jill Royce with *TNN America*, do you have a minute?"

"Have we met before?" asked Jared.

Jill tilted her head slightly to the side and put her first two fingers of her right hand, next to her mouth and thought about whether she had ever met him.

"I don't think so. I used to cover the Phoenix area a few years ago, but I don't think you've ever given me an interview before. I think I would remember an interview with you. I'd probably be working for *VOXX News Xtra* if I had been able to cover your rise to the top. As you can see, not there!"

"Is that a good network? I'm not up to date on who's top dog in the news business these days," asked Jared.

"Oh yeah!" she exclaimed. "They are the news company that was bought out after the election of 2024. They were the only news organization to survive that election and took 90 percent of the market share for the news business in the United States. They lost some of that over the years, but 50 percent is not a bad deal in a country with seven major networks."

"What did you want to ask me?" asked Jared.

"Well, sir, you spent two days in a casket and went through an autopsy. How is it that I'm here having a conversation with you?"

Adam winced slightly as he considered the question. He couldn't believe how she went straight for the throat, right out of the gate. Jared remained stoic as if the question had not fazed him in the slightest.

"That's really not an appropriate question, Ms. Royce," Adam interjected. "I'm sure that Jared will explain that at some point, but we are all here for a much greater purpose."

Jared watched Adam as he spoke. He cracked a faint smile as he considered the anxiety Adam was experiencing and simply nodded along as if in agreement. "It's all right, Adam. I knew that someone would ask. It's a great question, and when someone can give me a good answer, I'll share it," he said jokingly.

"Is that your response?" asked Jill.

"We all have a purpose in life. Yours is to be a top-rated journalist and to have the courage to ask the hard-hitting questions. My purpose is a little more complicated."

Jared paused for a moment.

"When I was a younger man, I wanted to be a fireman. I saw how brave they were when they ran into burning buildings to save people. While they ran in, others ran out. The firemen that ran in were selfless, and if they were afraid, you would never have known it. The ones who were running out were terrified. I wanted to be the guy with no fear and resolved myself to a life of fear avoidance. The only fear that I have ever had was the fear of being afraid."

"Did you ever work as a fireman?" asked Jill, jokingly.

Jared smiled as if he were pleasantly entertained by the question. "I can't say that I have," Jared chuckled. "As I went through school, I realized that I could do more to help people by creating a technology that would echo my philosophy. I looked at the human condition, and it occurred to me that we as a race were really holding ourselves back because of fear. Fear causes people to do a lot of things that are really a detriment to everyone. Take war for example. Wars are really fought because of the fear of change or the fear that other nations will come in and try to take away something. I thought that if we could eliminate fear from our lives, we would be able to accomplish things that we normally would only dream about."

"Well, you were able to invent artificially intelligent machines, so you accomplished that, but we've still had wars. How do you explain that?"

Jared chortled. "You don't miss anything, do you? I was successful with AI. It was a lack of fear that made that a success. For years, people were afraid of the technology, and they fought it. Look at us now. We, through the great leadership of people like Peter Jensen and even my friend, Richard, here, have been able to conquer those fears and build a world where we now have artificially intelligent androids all over the globe. Think of what we've accomplished in only the past few months. We solved the childcare problems. We've made health care so cost-effective that people don't even need insurance any longer. We really have made some great strides, and we have a bright future ahead of us."

"Is there anything you would change?" asked Jill pointedly.

"Actually, yes," said Jared. Jared's tone turned from jocular to more serious. "I wish that I could have known that someone was going to shoot me. Had I been able to see that coming, I would have most certainly prevented it from happening. Think about all those poor people that suddenly vanished. We don't know what caused that, and I'm not convinced that it was some eye in the sky that did it. Where's the proof of that? It's just as likely that some strange phenomenon caused by climate change did it. Take what happened in Israel, for example. If someone told you a week before it happened that an entire army would be wiped out and suddenly drop dead from some strange illness, you would have called them insane. Yet we have another strange event, and only a small percentage of the population is affected."

"Do you think it was climate change?" Jill countered.

"I am not sure what it was, but I can tell you that if it doesn't walk or quack like a duck, then it is probably not a duck. For all we know, it was extraterrestrials that were responsible. The people of this world are not strangers to many curious phenomenon as of late."

"What do you mean?" asked Jill.

"I simply mean that we have billions of religious people here today, all over the planet. They didn't suddenly disappear. The pope will be speaking later this afternoon. He didn't disappear. What about an Israel filled with Jewish people? These are the same people who brought God to the world. Why didn't they all disappear?"

Jill appeared to relent. Jared's response did make a lot of sense. There were hundreds of millions of religious people who did not disappear, and many Christians also. She considered for a moment that her favorite minister at Lakeview church in Houston was one of the first to speak out after the disappearance. If he were still here, as blessed as he has been, then it is conceivable that it was just a coincidence that most of the people that vanished were Christians.

"Those are all excellent points, Mr. Hadad. I never really thought about it that way. I was worried up until you said that. I'm a great person, and I've been a spiritual person my entire life. Thank you so much for what you do!"

"You're very welcome, Jill. Now we must get this temple finished, shouldn't we?" Jared turned and walked toward the temple, and his group followed behind. While he was speaking with Jill, people had been filing in. A crowd was able to hear him talking to her, and they were all impressed by his words. He spoke as a man who was passionate about the people and as one who really would lead the people to a greater future. Word of what he said quickly spread outside the temple, and it changed the atmosphere greatly. People all over the world felt just like Jill. They were all great people, and many of them were spiritual just like her. They loved the way that he explained the disappearances, and to the people, it made perfect sense.

The temple quickly filled up, and outside the temple, there were so many people that they couldn't be counted. It was the largest gathering of people into one place in history. The people were there for mixed reasons, but they all had one reason in common, and that was to hear Jared speak.

Jared took a hand trowel into his hand, and he scooped up some mortar out of a small bucket. He placed the last stone onto the temple structure and yelled out loudly, "It is finished!"

The people in the crowd cheered loudly. The cheers echoed inside the temple walls, and outside the temple walls, the people were equally excited that the last stone was laid.

Jared climbed the steps and moved to the inside of the temple through the beautiful gate. He was followed by Adam, Richard, and the others in his entourage. He took a spot in front of the altar of incense, where a microphone stand was placed.

Inside the temple, the people were more reserved than they were on the outside. The camera flashes made it appear as if there was a thunderstorm raging inside. Behind Jared, the veil could be seen. It was a beautiful red and adorned with gold at the top. The curtain was so thick that it didn't move at all, even though people were moving around inside.

Jared waited for the people to fill the room, and then he began to speak. "We are here today to dedicate this temple," he said vigorously.

The people in the room lost their composure and started to cheer mightily.

Jared paused for a moment to allow them their enthusiasm but then motioned for the people to lower their volume. "It's hard to believe that this temple was ever finished. The odds certainly were against it, but here we are." Jared took another recess from his speech as the people resumed their cheering. "When the Romans destroyed the Second Temple and the Jewish people were scattered across the globe, it seemed as if the days of the Jewish people were numbered. Later, a man named Hitler would attempt to destroy the remnants of the Jewish culture, and if it weren't for a highly motivated Europe and alliance of other great nations, such as the United States and Canada, it may very well have happened."

After hearing the name Hitler, the room fell silent. It was like Jared spoke a word that was outlawed.

Jared resumed his speech.

"In the twentieth century, the Jewish people were once again scattered, but this time, it was out of Europe. Where did they go? Well, many of them went back home. Israel is where they went!" he exclaimed.

The crowd erupted exuberantly and began to chant.

"Israel, Israel, Israel," they chanted.

Jared lifted both arms into the air and turned to the right slightly and then back to the left as he scanned the crowd and seemed to feed off of the energy in the room. "It was as if it were meant to be. The people who resettled the land quickly built an infrastructure. Then came more of the people. Suddenly, as if there was a trumpet blast calling everyone home, the Jewish people came home!"

The crowed resumed their chanting. "Israel! Israel! Israel!" they cheered.

Adam appeared euphoric and began to clap loudly along with the crowd. He was proud to be the prime minister of Israel, and he knew that Jared would likely begin speaking about the most recent victories next, and that would get him some praise, which would help his reelection prospects.

Jared resumed speaking. "The people came home, and they built a more beautiful Israel. They built a model for the rest of the world. They showed everyone what it looks like when people come together with a united mission. But as has happened throughout history, there was another attempt at destroying Israel. That attempt was thwarted, and the people of Israel were victorious!"

The crowd exploded with excitement. Jared was hitting them with so much praise that it was hard to keep them contained. They absolutely loved what they were hearing, and they praised him because they all knew that he played a large part in winning that war.

Adam was the only person in the room who became more reserved. He saw that the crowd was giving Jared all the praise, and this made him feel a bit self-conscious.

Jared continued speaking. "Israel has survived because Israel has always been and always will be the land of the chosen!"

The crowd exploded into their chanting. "Israel! Israel! Israel!" they chanted.

Jared paused for a moment to scan the audience. He smiled as he peered upon all the occupants of the room. He had the place electrified, and the people loved every word that he spoke. "I am proud to be a son of the land of Israel. I have always held a special place in my heart for this land. I have always held a special place for the people. All the people of Israel are my brothers and my sisters," he shouted vigorously.

Jared looked down at the podium briefly and then slowly raised his head back up to the crowd. He began to speak with a much softer tone. "I was raised up for the purpose of saving Israel."

The crowd went silent. Jared mentioned being raised up, and the people knew that he was speaking of the assassination.

"The man or men who took my life have obviously not read the Scriptures!" Jared exclaimed. "Had they read the Scriptures, they would have known that they could not prevent me from saving Israel. Though I laid dead for three days, it was not the end. The grave could not hold me!"

The people hadn't really thought about Jared when it came to the Scriptures. When he mentioned the Scriptures, one man in the crowd recalled that it said that the messiah would be raised from the dead.

"He is the messiah!" yelled the man.

Jared lifted his hands to the air and scanned the crowd.

"I Am," he yelled with a thundering yell.

The crowd heard his words, and they started to chant.

"Messiah, messiah, messiah," they chanted.

The people were cheering so loudly that the walls of the temple started to vibrate. Their cheers continued for what seemed like ten minutes, before Jared resumed speaking.

"I have come to take my rightful place as king!" he roared.

The people couldn't believe what they were hearing. They were convinced that Jared was the messiah. Their chants grew louder and louder, and the walls of the temple continued to shake.

The veil, which remained motionless, started to vibrate, and the rings at the top began to make a clanking sound.

"Sons and daughters of Israel, today marks the beginning of a new age. This new age will be one of peace. No longer will the earth be plagued by war. No longer will the world be plagued by disease. No longer will people be gunned down in the streets. No longer will gangs rule or dictators rise up and cause harm to the people. The time has come to put an end to the suffering, the injustice, and begin anew."

The people exploded with joy. Their cheers were so great that it could be heard for miles.

"Messiah, messiah, messiah," they chanted.

The people had no idea that Jared was not the true messiah, but they cheered him as if he were. They were so sure that he was the messiah that they got onto their knees and began to worship him. Jared stood there in the temple, accepting their praise and their worship. He scanned the crowd of people who were all still on their knees. Even those in his entourage were on their knees. That is, all but one. Richard was not on his knees. He stood there next to Jared, as if he was just another image of the same man. The antithesis of all that was good.

*****

As for Charles and Chris, their mission was just beginning. The Great Tribulation was now upon them, just as it was for the entire world.

The end.

ABOUT THE AUTHOR

B. A. Cochrane is an author whose roots stretch from the charming landscapes of Michigan to the sun-soaked streets of Gainesville, Florida. Originally hailing from the heart of Georgia, Cochrane's journey through life has been as diverse as the settings that influenced his upbringing.

A graduate of the University of Florida, Cochrane holds a bachelor of science degree in food and resource economics, a testament to his curiosity and passion for understanding the world. However, life took an adventurous turn as he donned the uniform of a United States Army military policeman, embodying discipline, service, and the spirit of duty.

Now as an author, B. A. Cochrane brings a unique blend of experiences to the literary world. His writing reflects a deep appreciation for the intricacies of human nature, shaped by a background that spans both academic rigor and the disciplined ethos of military service. With a keen eye for detail and a storyteller's touch, Cochrane invites readers into worlds that are both familiar and unexplored.

Whether delving into the complexities of relationships, unraveling mysteries, or exploring the depths of the human psyche, B. A. Cochrane's narratives are as diverse as the tapestry of his own life. With each word penned, he invites readers on a journey that is both introspective and entertaining, leaving an indelible mark on the literary landscape.

Printed in the USA
CPSIA information can be obtained
at www.ICGtesting.com
CBHW030409301024
16599CB00050B/471

9 798893 152630